PRETTY BLUE DEATH

To Nancy,

Hope you enjoy the book.

Dan Blair

DAN BLAIR

outskirts
press

Acknowledgments

Dedicated to my late mother, Mary Alice Blair; a real inspiration to me for this project. Little did I know as a child my mother was typing away in our upstairs spare room for years to make a little extra cash for family extras, selling short stories and poems to kid's magazines. Her unpublished novel and short stories were great reads and made me want to follow in her footsteps. Thanks mom.

My heartfelt thanks to my wife, Ronda, for her meticulous edits and putting up with my obsession, specifically, writing this book versus my many others.

Thanks to my tennis partner and fellow storyteller, Jim Bangel, for helping with his Vietnam anecdotes and the ending, and also to his better half, Louise, for editing help and encouragement.

Thanks to Mike Tafuri for his helpful suggestions.

Editing thanks to my daughters, Dana and Kelly; very appreciated even if the laughing at my misspellings was a bit over done.

A special thanks to my aunt Wilma Kentner who's input, edits and relentless encouragement to finish the book was a guiding motivation.

To all my friends who may see a part of themselves or at least a familiar name or two somewhere in my musings, it's merely coincidental I assure you. All of you are much more interesting and fun than any of my rogue's gallery of characters.

I hope you enjoy the ride with the Fords; top down and the wind in your hair!

Google Maps   Southern California

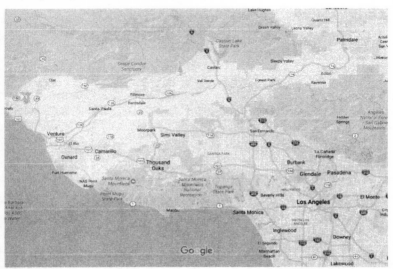

Southern California
California

The Poker Group

Mark & Daly Ford – The central couple living in San Fernando Valley and owning a security systems company in Santa Monica.

Mike & Dianne Gentry – Mike is a foods company executive and Dianne is a realtor.

Tommy & Pat Hemmings – Tommy is a foods company executive, and Pat is a teacher.

Jim & Louise Jensen –Jim is a food scientist and Louise is a gastroenterologist.

Chuck & Linda Kohler – Chuck is a retired nutritional aids company executive, and Linda is a zoo volunteer.

Ron and Janice Richmond – Ron is a retail grocery chain executive and Jan is a teen psychologist.

Michael & Mary Simon – Now divorced, Michael is a think tank consultant and Mary owns an import-export food specialty business.

Prologue

Her pearlescent blue eyes looked down at the pool's clear water. The flower petals rippled in the gentle waves dissipating from the earlier struggle.

A sense of peace and satisfaction settled over her.

The body of Tommy Hemmings was face down, half-floating at the surface. He would soon sink to the bottom as the air from his lungs was displaced by the chlorinated water; settling under his liquid blanket.

She knew what the coroner would find: asphyxiation by drowning. Her blue wild flowers, aconite, had done their job effectively. The residual neurotoxins would never be found in the typical autopsy of a drowning.

It was her mother's birthday, April third. It was hard for her to believe her mother had been gone for twenty-six years. She had waited far too long to assuage her pain, her loss. But 2014 was a good year to begin the healing.

What a nice present for mother.

She regretted she couldn't linger and watch Tommy sink to the depths of his pool, but she needed to move on. Mrs. Hemmings might happen onto the scene or some unsuspecting neighbor out for an early morning run could stop in for a coffee.

She approached the flowerbed at the edge of the pool's landscaping. Picking a few petals from the red carnations, white roses and blue violets, she then returned to the pool's edge. These little beauties provided just what she was looking for. She scattered them among the aconite already there; just enough to appear a gust had transported the flowers' remains to the pool. Not so much to garner suspicion. The petals floated to the water below.

Satisfied with the random appearance of the potpourri near Tommy's body, she exited across the concrete patio to a side-entry gate. Unlatching it, she stepped onto the path leading to the street and her waiting car parked around the corner.

About a half block away, she heard a distant scream coming from where she'd been.

The edges of her mouth turned up in a cold half smile. "There, there Mrs. Hemmings. He really wasn't much of a prize."

Part I

"…how does your garden grow?"

———◈———

Chapter One

M ark burst through the garage door into the foyer out of breath. "Wow. Great run," he huffed.

His wife, Daly, sat at the kitchen counter. Her cup of coffee in hand, newspaper on the counter, she was intently scrutinizing a crossword puzzle. Taking in Daly's dark brown hair and delicate facial features over full lips always surprised Mark a bit. She'd done nothing as far as make-up or primping, yet looked put together in every way. Only five foot four, she was proportioned nicely with an athletic build. Her form-fitting sweats indicated her anticipation of a work out a bit later. Mark's eyes lingered on her curvaceous parts with an impish smile. Leaning on their kitchen island, he continued to pant.

"That's nice," she said looking up briefly at his red face and sweat-soaked t-shirt. "Are you going to make it?" she asked returning her attention to the puzzle.

Mark's T-shirt was soaked in a large V down the front of his six foot two frame. His sweat pants were equally wet with a V leading to his butt crack. Short brown hair lay in dripping ringlets on his forehead. Above his red face, a dimpled chin and hazel eyes made for a handsome man. Not male model worthy, just manly and out of breath.

"Maybe. At least I'll die with a healthy glow," he replied moving to her side of the island. Looking over her shoulder, he asked "Anything I can help you with while I'm a little nasty? You know, there are many forms of exercise we could do together if the spirit moved us." As his hands made their way around her waist with hopes of higher ground, the phone rang.

"Great," he said disappointedly, abandoning his amorous notions to see who felt compelled to interrupt the great morning he was having.

"Hello, Ford residence," he answered using a mock receptionist's voice as he mugged stupid faces at Daly. She watched him out of the corner of her eye in mild amusement.

His face turned serious as he listened. "What?...No... How long ago?" He began to pace with his brow furrowed, listening intently to the caller. "All right. I'll be over as quick as I can," he said as he hung up the phone and turned to Daly.

He met her questioning eyes, "That was Mike. He said he just got a call from Tommy's wife, Pat. She found Tommy in their pool just a few hours ago. Looks like he drowned. She's out of her mind."

"Oh my god, that's awful!" Daly blurted as she rose from her chair, "How could that happen? Tommy swims all the time." A cloud came over Daly's face, "It wasn't...it wasn't on purpose...was it?"

"I don't know. The police are still there. I guess the

coroner arrived, so maybe they'll know more by the time I get there," he said over his shoulder. "I'm going to shower and head to Pat's. I'll call you when I can." He disappeared down the hall.

Mark got to Tommy and Pat's house around ten o'clock.

The pandemonium was in full swing with Life Squad, Fire Department and police cruisers filling the driveway and spilling into the street. Mark parked down the street and briskly walked up the sidewalk to the front door, which was standing open.

Inside a police sergeant was sitting with Tommy's wife in their living room trying to console her. She was crying. By the look of her puffy eyes and stained cheeks, she'd been doing it for a while.

Mark entered the room.

Pat met his eyes and let out a sorrowful sob, "Mark. Tommy's gone. I can't believe it. What am I going to do?" Her voice cracked and she stood up.

He hugged her tightly for a moment. All he could come up with was, "Pat. I'm so sorry," and the words seemed useless. He'd wished he'd said nothing at all.

Other friends and local family members were making their way into the room. Given the distraction, he gently broke away from her embrace.

Trying to catch the sergeant's attention Mark stepped forward touching his shoulder, "Sergeant, can I have a moment with you."

"Sure," he said rising from the couch, "Let's talk in the yard."

The sergeant had a distinct Irish accent. He wore a tweed jacket and a matching Irish wool driving cap. The cap had a small stiff brim in front, completing the appearance he'd just come from the golf courses of the UK or from the end of some rainbow where he guarded the pot of gold. He was of average build, maybe five foot ten inches, and had bright green eyes that probably twinkled under more pleasant circumstances.

They made their way to the pool area.

The coroner was working over Tommy's body, now lying beside the pool and rolled onto his back. Tommy's jet-black hair was wet and ringed his pale, blue face. His lips were purple and his mouth was gaping: the sleep of the dead in Technicolor.

Mark didn't notice any blood or marks from a struggle that might indicate Tommy's drowning was anything but an accident. The sight was too much to handle but Mark pressed on.

"Sergeant, I'm Mark Ford, a good friend of Tommy and Pat."

"Master Ford, I be sergeant McClarey and I'll be handlin this case for now."

Mark went on, "I can't believe Tommy could just drown like that without something happening. He swam every day, and usually for an hour or more."

"Well, the coroner should 'ave a cause o' death once he completes the medicals back at the morgue," the Sergeant offered. "Dat should confirm if anything here other than a might unfortunate drownin."

"Like what?"

"Oh, I've seen it'all, but it usually is what it looks like."

Mark asked a few more questions. Nothing really shed any light on what had caused Tommy's demise. No signs of struggle in or around the pool. No bruising or cuts on the body. No suicide note, or any indication from Pat that Tommy was anything but happy and well adjusted.

No reason why Mark had just lost one of his best friends, and Pat her mate of over twenty years.

What a shitty day this had become, and it wasn't even lunchtime.

Chapter Two

Clouds filled the sky as the drizzle incessantly fell on those attending the graveside service of Tommy. It was a Sunday, three days since Tommy's drowning. Pat, his wife, was holding together pretty well considering her lifelong partner had been snatched from her. Just as they were beginning to plan how they'd spend the rest of their life together, all plans were now reduced to nothing. And her life was taking a drastic and uncharted detour.

Mark held Daly's arm. She'd occasionally wipe away a tear with her free arm. She kept repeating to no one in particular, "I just can't imagine what Pat's going through."

Mark's thoughts went back to when he and Daly had met Tommy and Pat through a neighborhood poker group. The group had been playing together for over ten years. Mark joined at the suggestion of Pat shortly after he and Daly had married and moved into the Sagewood Community development in the San Fernando Valley, northwest of L.A. Seven couples had made up the poker group. Some of the spouses chose not to play, but instead spent the poker evenings socializing after they enjoyed dinner as a group. Since the initiation of the group, one couple had divorced, Michael and Mary Simon. Usually both still attended as they had remained on good terms, or at least as good as you could when divorced.

All of the poker group attended Tommy's graveside service. All looked as shocked and unbelieving as Mark and Daly.

Jim Jensen and his wife Louise approached them nodding hello, and taking their place next to them. Jim was a scientist for a large food conglomerate and his wife Louise was a doctor who specialized in gastroenterology and loved gardening and travel as her passions. Jim was typically upbeat and irreverent, making it strange to see him quiet and reserved in this setting.

Behind Jim and Louise, stood Mike and Dianne Gentry. Mike was an executive for a food manufacturer conglomerate. His wife, Dianne, was one of the most successful realtors in the Valley.

In the distance, Mark saw Michael Simon, a think tank executive for Consumer Packaged Goods companies. His ex-wife Mary, who ran an import-export company specializing in exotic foods, coffee and chocolates, was at his side.

Next to Pat Hemmings, Chuck and Linda Kohler stood, with Linda holding Pat's arm. Chuck was a retired executive for a nutritional aids company. His wife Linda actively volunteered for numerous city zoo projects.

The last couple from the poker group stood on the other side of the Kohlers, Ron and Janice Richmond. Ron was a VP for a national grocery retailer. His wife Janice worked as a psychologist for disturbed teens through a community organization in the Valley.

Many family members and friends attended the funeral. The service was performed by Dale Mullins, the pastor from the Hemmings' home church in San Fernando. Pastor Mullins and his wife, Karen, stood by Pat, supporting her in the reception line at the end of the service. Pat was surrounded with a sea of condolences. All those attending were in disbelief at how unfair it was to lose someone as vibrant and young as Tommy to such a senseless accident.

She nodded, hugged and went through the motions in what appeared a numb state of "being there." Her eyes were glassy and wet. Between hugs she stared into space like she wanted it all to end.

Mark caught Pat's eye as the graveside service came to an end. He and Daly walked towards her as they re-turned to their cars parked along the cinder path of the cemetery's through road. Picking up their pace to catch up with Pat and her son, who was her escort, Mark and Daly pulled up to her side.

"Pat, if there's anything you need, just ask," Mark offered.

"Absolutely anything," Daly added.

"Mark, you and Daly are the first ones I'll call if some-thing comes up. Don't worry yourselves for now. I'm just spending time with the boys and family the next couple of days," Pat said as she looked at her oldest son, John, on her arm.

Pat continued on to her waiting car as Mark and Daly fell back to join the group still lingering in the cemetery.

Jim Jensen sauntered towards Mark and Daly, extended his hand and then pulled it away just as Mark was about to shake it. "Too slow. How are you doing anyway?" he grinned as he slapped Mark's shoulder, obviously pleased with his schoolyard greeting. Jim's six-foot plus height was diminished by his poor posture as his shoulders perpetually slumped forward. His dark, curly hair outlined an impish face with bright green eyes that always sparkled mischievously beneath his shaggy eyebrows. His ears were large and comical, making it hard to ever take him seriously, even when he wasn't in a joking mood.

"Well as can be expected with the lowlifes I tend to hang with these days," Mark offered as he brushed past Jim to give Louise a hug. "Guess you've decided to keep him on as a charity case Louise. Or is it he won't move out when you ask him to?"

"You know how it is, Mark. Jim's too hard to pawn off on anyone who knows him, and strangers seem to sense he's got issues," Louise said wryly as she returned Mark's hug. "Glad to see you've still got the sense to keep this lovely by your side," Louise said as she moved on to hug Daly. Louise had dark hair, beginning to show streaks of silver. Her eyes were soft and radiated genuine empathy for everyone she looked upon. Her walk was stilted from multiple skeletal issues; from spinal fusions to the ever-increasing arthritis making its way deeper into her joints.

"No getting rid of me," Daly returned her hug with a quick peck on Louise's cheek.

The other couples from the poker group then joined as the cacophony of voices grew louder; the shroud of the dreary, sad day in a cemetery unable to douse their vibrant friendships.

"We'll catch up at Pat's," Louise said over her shoulder as she and Jim exited to their car.

As Mark and Daly broke from the group to go to their car, Daly held Mark's hand tightly. Nothing like losing a friend suddenly and without cause to drive home the brevity of life. And how we need to cherish the time we have. Mark squeezed Daly's hand as he opened her car door and kissed her lightly on the cheek. Closing her door, he strode to the driver's side. They made the five mile drive to Pat's house where the gathering would reminisce of good times had and how much they'd miss Tommy's presence in the future.

Mark and Daly walked up the stamped concrete walk to Pat's front door. They followed Mike and Dianne Gentry by a few steps. Mike was dressed formally from the funeral; his wispy, thinning blonde hair had its usual out of place look. About five foot nine, Mike walked with good posture, but his narrow frame still made his suit hang loosely around his mid-section. His pants appeared one size too large for his waist and hips. Dianne wore a dark purple dress with lavender highlights at the shoulders and neckline, matching belt and a scarf tied loosely around her neck and shoulders. Her make-up was flawless as usual, and tended to camouflage the sharpness of her nose and cheekbones. She looked easily ten years younger than she was.

Pat's younger son, Josh, answered the doorbell and escorted the couples to the open kitchen and dining room area. Vast plates of sandwiches, pasta salads, casseroles, and fruit plus veggie plates were arranged around a serving table. Mark spotted the others of their poker group in the family room beyond the food extravaganza and strolled into the family room to greet them.

Mary Simon was munching from a small plate of veggies and dip as she turned to see Mark and Daly enter. "Hi Daly…Mark," Mary said as she sat her plate on the coffee table, coming forward to hug Daly. "Isn't this just the worst way to get together? I still can't believe Tommy won't come walking in from the patio and tell one of his stupid jokes."

"How have you been? You just got back from traveling didn't you? Somewhere exotic I imagine," Daly questioned as she met Mary's blue eyes. "You look great. How do you travel and never put on a pound?"

Mary was slender, but nicely proportioned with blonde, shoulder length hair. Her face moved from a sad, grieving look to a passing smile as she answered, "I follow the first rule of "eat anything you want, just stop after two bites" -- makes my taste buds think I'm having fun." Then placing her hand to the side of her mouth, she mock whispered, "Works so long as I don't listen to my stomach growl."

Mark stepped in beside Daly's shoulder, "So that's her secret. I thought it was trips to the vomitorium between courses," he whispered into Daly's ear. This prompted a disapproving look as she turned towards Mark.

"And here's my doting husband, whispering "rude nothings" into my ear. Please excuse him. I couldn't find a sitter," Daly said as she moved away from Mark and greeted Michael Simon with a peck on the cheek. "So Michael, what have you been up to recently?"

"Daly, now this is a pleasure. Good to see you brought the ole ball and chain with you. He never seems to know just how lucky a man he is to have corralled a catch like you," Michael gushed as he returned Daly's kiss on the cheek.

At this Mary raised an eyebrow as she turned to talk with Chuck and Linda Kohler.

Michael's occupation as the chief technology officer for a think tank out of L.A. seemed to take him around the world regularly. When they had been married, Mary would join him to seek out contacts for exotic foods or delicacies she could arrange to add to her growing procurement business. Michael used to joke that his job was just a ruse to allow Mary to find just the right caviar, rare herb or exotic flower to compliment the dinner tables of millionaires around the world.

After their divorce, Mary's business had flourished the last few years Mark and Daly had known her. Mary's business, Delicacies Du Jour, had been written up in gourmet magazines of note. Her advice and services were frequently being sought by the finest restaurants in Los Angeles.

"I just finished a South American swing a week ago. Arrived home just a day or so before we got the awful news about Tommy. I still can't believe it. How does someone as full of life as Tommy die in such a senseless way?" Mary sighed as she shook her head and took a sip from her water glass.

"I said the same thing the day it happened," Mark added. "For someone as athletic as Tommy to drown while swimming laps boggles the mind. I talked with Pat after the autopsy. No other causes they could come up with. Guess they say you can drown in a spoonful of water if it goes down the wrong pipe. Just need to focus on helping Pat through it now."

"Yes, that's what matters," Jim Jensen said as he entered the room munching on a carrot from the food plate he'd piled high from all options available. "Pat will need a lot of support from us as the quietness of this house settles in after the relatives and friends are gone."

Louise nodded agreement as she and Jim shared a knowing look.

Jim continued, "I remember how it was for us when our son was in the hospital for months. You don't realize just how quiet a house can be until someone you love isn't there anymore."

Mark knew Jim and Louise's teen-age son had been in a car wreck a couple of years before he and Daly had met them. He didn't know much about the details, other than Jim's son was badly hurt and the other teen in the car had died. Mark had never really had the opportunity to ask Jim more about it.

"Yes, losing your life partner suddenly is going to take time to move through," Chuck Kohler nodded as he squeezed his wife's arm. "Linda and I would be destroyed if one of us…passed on. And we've only been married five years. I can't imagine Pat's feelings of loss after twenty years."

A brief lull came over the conversation. This provided an opening for a medium built man with a business style haircut to step into the room catching the groups attention, "Excuse me, I don't mean to interrupt. I did want to pass along my condolences to Mr. Hemmings' friends."

"I'm Greg Riggsby. I handled the Hemmings' financial matters. He talked of your group very fondly. I understand you all played poker regularly and I know Tom enjoyed your friendships from what he shared with me."

The group made their introductions with Chuck going last. "Well, it's good to know he didn't share his disdain for losing to us. I'm Chuck Kohler and this is my wife, Linda," Chuck said as he reached to shake hands. "We live a couple of hours up the coast in the Santa Maria area, but I used to live in Tom and Pat's neighborhood. We've known them forever it seems."

"It's good to be able to put faces with names. I understood from Tom, you retired a few years back, Mr. Kohler. If I remember correctly you ran a nutritional company in the San Francisco area," Riggsby added.

"Please, Chuck is fine. Yes that's right. Now I volunteer at a food bank in Bakersfield a couple of days a week. Kind of ironic as I helped people supplement their diets to optimize their health. Now the foods I help hand out at the food bank are anything but healthy. But it's a start with folks who aren't predisposed to veggies and the like."

"Yes, I think Tommy mentioned that. I actually know

a few of your names as I worked with Tommy on the joint venture a few of you went together on. I helped Tommy draw up your LLC document so it had all the usual boilerplate for such things. Well, I won't take any more of your time. I'm sure you all have a lot to catch up on." Riggsby half-bowed and nodded his goodbye. He turned and left the room to speak with the grieving widow before departing.

Mary followed him out of the room with her eyes, "Interesting that Tommy would have a financial advisor. I'd always assumed he'd drawn up the LLC thing himself. I thought he handled his own investments." Turning her gaze on Chuck, "And Chuck, how do you live with yourself giving high-fat, junk food to the poor? *Honestly*, you should be better than that."

"Really Mary. And what have you done lately? Caviar on toast for the homeless? Hard to believe someone who panders to the ultra-rich is worried about our more destitute neighbors," Chuck smirked. He purposely picked up a crab cake from his tray, holding it as example A, and popped it in his mouth in one quick motion.

"I'll have you know I do have a heart for the poor. And I certainly don't exacerbate the issue by offering garbage to poor people that don't know any better," Mary shot back with blue eyes flashing a bit more venom than the conversation warranted.

"All right, you two. Let's not lose sight of why we're here. It's certainly not to trade barbs on food choices," Michael interrupted. He continued, "Let's plan to do something fun with Pat once she's had a few weeks to grieve. Jim, why don't you take the lead in planning something. Get back to us in a week or so with some ideas, ok?"

Jim shrugged his agreement as he reached for his sparkling water, "Sure, I'll run with it."

Mary continued to stare darts at Chuck for a long second or two. She rose to freshen her drink as Chuck shared a glance with Linda as if to say, *Man am I glad I married you.*

The conversation moved to stories of Tommy's antics as the poker group's class clown. They remembered the time that Tommy paid off a bet with Mike in pennies, five-thousand to be exact, as it was a fifty dollar bet. Or there was the time Tommy had made an investment in commodity markets while on a road trip where he couldn't get hold of his broker due to no cell service. And finally the time Tommy had lost a poker hand against all odds to Michael, infamous as the poker mind reader of the group.

All good times.

The absence of a friend echoed like the sound of a door closing on fun times followed by the engulfing hollowness of the room exited.

They sat quietly in reverie for a few more minutes. Each couple then made their way to say their goodbyes to Pat.

All that was left, was to head home to continue their thoughts of loss more privately.

Chapter Three

Her eyes scanned the horizon.

She looked through the windshield as the rolling hills and pines of Los Padres National Forest gave way to the flat valley beyond. Bakersfield was a little over an hour up the road, thirty miles beyond where she'd catch Highway 99 from the I-5 she currently was traversing.

The beauty of the forest had been lost on her.

She played her plans for vengeance through her head over and over. Her call a few days after Hemmings' funeral had confirmed that Chuck Kohler would be working his usual shift at the food bank in Bakersfield this Friday afternoon. A smile crossed her face briefly - *actually, his last shift at the food bank.*

She had done more than a little research into Chuck's past as a key manager for Nutraceuticals To Go, Inc. His past allegiance to making money preying on those who believed they could find weight-loss in a bottle had sealed his fate. And now trying to make up for it by working at a food bank. Dishing out high-fat, empty calories to the poor added insult to injury in her book.

She fidgeted in her seat as she conjured up visions of him gripping his chest and falling to the floor, his face contorted in agony. Yes, this would help make the world closer to "right."

As she passed an older style Buick, she glanced to her right. The woman driver had multiple chins and a face that appeared balloon-like in its roundness. Her skin was stretched to the point where a pinprick would surely release her flesh, blood and brains into a spatter on the window.

As she turned her attention back to the road ahead, she found herself slipping into memories of her mother in their small, linoleum-floored kitchen. Her mother was preparing dinner over their kitchen stove. One hand was on her walker and the other held a large wooden spoon stirring something in a large pot.

"So how was your day at school, little flower?" her mother said between labored breaths. She stood with some difficulty over the steaming brew.

"Oh all right I guess. But I'd rather be here to take care of you."

She could see the rolls of fat below her mother's dress disguising the fact her knees existed. Her upper legs were demarcated from her lower legs only by the crease of where the excess flesh and fatty tissue met. Support anklets provided the sense the round torpedoes extending from the bottom of her legs were actually feet. The amorphous appearance of her feet was as if her legs had begun to puddle on the floor in a round mass of human flesh.

Her mother would turn her head to smile at her,

creating more folds in her neck, piled to the side of her three chins.

She would smile back; all the time hating herself for being unable to improve her mother's plight. She had tried to hide the candy bars she'd found in the cupboard, the Slim Jims near the couch, and even left the ice cream out to melt. Her meager attempts never lasted. Her mother was addicted to every form of junk food known to man. She would find a way to replace it or go to many of her back-up stashes when faced with her cravings or boredom.

"So bring me my pills, little flower. I need to take one before each meal is what the brochure said." Her mother nodded toward the large bottle sitting on the counter. "I think these are going to be just the thing. The brochure that came with them says they'll burn away calories. You don't have to do anything but take the pills before each meal. Isn't that amazing, flower?"

The blinking lights in her rearview mirror returned her to the present.

She brought her car into the right lane to let the Porsche behind her pass. The Porsche driver accelerated around her with a flourish of his extended middle finger for her viewing pleasure.

Her sense of helplessness as a child quickly flushed from her system. She focused her mind on how Chuckie Pill-Pushing Kohler was about to pay for all of his years of feeding false hope to the helpless.

The exit for Highway 99 came into view, along with the mileage sign: Bakersfield 35 miles. She continued another ten miles to a deserted rest stop, pulled over, and made her way to the restroom to relieve herself. While there, she transformed from her well-quaffed look to a down-and-out indigent.

Throwing her duffel in the back of the car, she pulled from the curb and entered the highway. She thought to herself, *he won't even see it coming.*

Reaching into her dingy, denim jacket pocket, she fingered the vial she'd carefully prepared for this special occasion. Its contents held the elixir of death, an ounce of lily of the valley extract. Raised by her own hand, she'd passionately cared for her lilies. She'd extracted the venom from the petals, and concentrated this liquid death into just the right dosage to create a massive heart attack when consumed.

It hadn't taken much digging to find Kohler's father had died of a myocardial infarction ten years ago. It made her lily extract the perfect choice. All indications to the coroner would be that a middle-aged, slightly overweight man with a family history of coronary issues had suffered a heart attack.

Nothing too surprising. No reason to look further by any authorities.

One more purveyor of garbage bites it.

The red brick building with the words "Food Bank, Bakersfield" on a sign over the front entrance portico came into view.

It was a one-story building. A few windows faced the parking lot which had room for a half dozen cars, although only two were present.

She pulled her car to the first sidestreet past the Food Bank. Carefully scanning the street for any activity, and seeing none, she exited her car.

To be sure no direct connection with her should something go wrong, she'd had the foresight to rent an older model Chevrolet for cash in San Fernando. She had provided a false address and identity as collateral. After walking a few blocks in the opposite direction of the Food Bank, she would circle around and come in from the opposite direction. Any passers by or nosey witnesses would see nothing out of the ordinary.

Twenty minutes later she entered the Food Bank. She approached the counter where Kohler sat making entries into a computer.

He looked up from his work and smiled, "How can I help you today?"

"Thank you kind sir," she said keeping her eyes averted towards the floor with her posture stooped. "I'm hoping you can help an old lady along her way with something to eat." Her voice cracked a bit and she kept it low. She thought her voice matched the look she'd created. She wore an ill-kept, grey wig under a knitted hat tied around her chin, dirty denim jacket, and baggy sweat pants going down to her mismatched brown flats, with a hole in one toe for good measure. She'd even kept the jacket with her garbage a few days. It provided just the right malodor one might expect from one such as her.

"Not a problem. Just take a look at this list of items we have. Here's a pen to check the ones you'd like. I'll gather it up for you and you'll be on your way."

"Thank you. You're very kind." She took the pen in the soiled garden gloves she was wearing.

Checking a few items, she handed it back to him.

"OK. This will only take a minute. Just write your name down on the log sheet here while I'm gathering it up." Kohler smiled and took a shopping bag with "Bakersfield" emblazoned on the front of it. He headed to the shelves burgeoning with cans, bags and boxes of food staples.

As he turned away, she smiled at the coffee cup by the computer.

She fingered the vial in her jacket.

As he busied himself gathering the food from her list, she leaned forward emptying the contents of her vial into his half-full cup. She was glad to see Chuckie boy used creamer. That should cover any slight off-taste her little potion might impart if he was the sensitive sort.

Kohler returned to the counter with her bag of groceries completed. He looked down at the log she'd signed. "Ok this should do it. And looks like you're all logged in, Lily Hartman."

"Well God bless you in your travels, Lily."

"Oh I'm sure he will," she said as she turned and shuffled out the door. Retracing her steps from the Food Bank, she circled to her car; shedding her jacket, wig and hat combination along the way while no one was watching.

She sat behind the wheel looking at the Food Bank for a few minutes.

Her smile grew as she saw the flashing emergency lights in the distance and heard the wail of the siren.

She pulled from the curb and cruised past the Food Bank.

The EMT's rushed into the doors she'd just vacated a few minutes ago.

You really ought to cut back on the coffee, Chuckie. I hear it's not good for you.

Turning the radio on, she headed towards Chuck and Linda Kohler's house in Santa Maria.

She hummed to Elton John's *Yellow Brick Road.*

She had one more thing to pick up along the way. Wasn't it fortunate Linda wouldn't be home by the time she got there. She might have left the front door open in her hurry to get to her husband's side at the hospital.

Yes, wouldn't that be nice...although too late to say goodbye to poor ole Chuckie.

Chapter 4

Sun streamed through his bedroom's bay window as Mark pried his eyes open, one at a time.

Another glorious summer day in the valley with not a cloud in the sky.

Daly was up, her kitchen noises traveling to him down the hallway.

He rolled from bed, sitting on the edge for a moment and flexing his right arm and shoulder to work out the kinks. He stretched. Wincing at the stiffness in his shoulder, he pondered the weakness of his right tricep no longer able to handle whatever he threw at it.

His mind wandered to a time when he was a young college stud. He had played basketball with his intramural team, racquetball with his best friend five times a week, and had been able to pretty much play any sport of his choice. Then came his Army ROTC stint. Following his graduation as a chemical engineer from ISU, which Uncle Sam had fully funded, he completed his basic training and officer training. His aptitude for science, chemistry and engineering, had made it a natural choice to go into special training. He became an engineering explosives specialist.

Then nine-eleven happened and the war on terror.

His specialty skyrocketed in value to the military. He was now someone they needed in Iraq. Disarming IED's and booby-trapped strongholds in Iraq wasn't something he'd trained for, but now became the job du jour.

Not a bad gig at first given his training had been more than adequate for most of the primitive options used by the Iraqi's. Best of all, he wasn't in direct combat situations…that is until he was checking out a previous Iraqi Sunni stronghold on the outskirts of Fallujah.

He'd been clearing an old hospital that had been used by Sadaam's elite forces as a base for a couple of months. It had been recently deserted. The Iraqi troops had moved away from Fallujah and into the surrounding hills, making them less of an easy target for American hell-fire missiles.

In his initial reconnaissance of the hospital, he'd ensured trip wires were located and disarmed.

He continued into one of the interior rooms. It was used for surgery based on a makeshift operating table in the center and cabinets on the walls containing gauze pads, bandages and miscellaneous medical items.

He had only seen the blinking red light out of the corner of his eye.

He'd dove back through the door into the hallway. This had avoided the deadly intent of the bastard who had set the bomb with a motion detector switch to wreak havoc on the "infidels."

Unfortunately, shrapnel from the IED had torn into

his right shoulder and upper arm, leaving him with more than a nasty memory of his time in Iraq.

His unit got him to a military hospital by helicopter within an hour.

The damage to his shoulder and right arm was significant.

The hospital in Baghdad was able to stabilize his wounds and get him on a plane to Germany where the doctors there repaired his shoulder. The muscle damage to his right tricep would end up being permanent. With his damaged wing having half the strength of his good left arm, he considered himself fortunate in many ways. The Sunni surprise certainly could have left him more debilitated, or dead. But still every once in a while, he went nostalgic; wishing for the physicality he'd known before Iraq.

Snapping out of his unpleasant daydream, Mark stood and headed for the bathroom.

Time to shit, shower, shave and off to the salt mines, he muttered with a half-smile.

Thirty minutes later he joined Daly in the kitchen.

He playfully pinched her butt as she scrambled eggs on their flat top stove. He backed away feigning surprise as she took a swat at him with her spatula.

"'Bout time you got your lazy keester out of bed," she said looking at him over her shoulder as she returned her spatula to the job at hand.

"Oh, nothing like owning your own business. I like not having an alarm clock running my life. So what have you got on the agenda for today?" he asked.

"Once I've finished doing my "wifely" duties, namely taking care of Mr. Ford's breakfast and cleaning the fall-out from his bathroom destruction, I'll probably head to the gym. What's your plan for the day?"

"Well, since one of Mrs. Ford's duties isn't to chase her husband back to the bedroom for unbridled, animal sex…" he paused long enough for Daly to shake her head, then continued, "Guess I'll have to head to work.

"I've got a project a few minutes west of Ventura I should check on. Some movie type that wants full video surveillance added to her security system. Shouldn't take more than an hour or two, then head by the office to see what's shaking. Should be home early today. Maybe we can take a ride up the coast this fine Friday afternoon?" he said with a question in his voice.

"We'll see. I'm doing lunch with some of my old LAPD buddies. If it's a two-margarita lunch, it might take a while. If they've got to get back to work, I could be home mid afternoon."

Daly made it a priority to keep her connections with her old law enforcement friends tight. She had graduated from USC with a psychology degree with an emphasis in criminal justice. This had allowed her to go directly to work for the LAPD as an analyst.

After two years it hit her she'd never be more than an analyst if she wasn't actually on the force. In typical Daly fashion, she took the bull by the horns. She joined the force as a police officer and spent five years working her way back to a desk job in the LAPD behavioral crime unit.

She had shined with her psychological training and a keen sense of what drove people. These skills were finely honed by taking on some of LA's biggest wack jobs. She'd been promoted to Sergeant and was being quietly recruited behind the scenes by the FBI. They wanted her for the elite Behaviorial Analysis Unit.

Then she'd met Mark and decided to chuck it all and join him in his private security firm.

That was five years ago. Daly's skills and credentials had come in handy in those early days. Her insights into client motivations had secured a number of lucrative jobs with the ultra-rich. Their partnership had kick-started Ford and Ford, Esq. into one of the premier private security agencies in LA in half the time it would normally take a new start-up.

"Ok, it's a date. Unless it's not," Mark faked a smile going to a frown. He dished the scrambled eggs from Daly's skillet onto his plate, grabbed a slice of toast from the counter, and wolfed his food. He washed it down with a glass of orange juice Daly had set on their center island for him.

"See you later babe," Mark pecked her on the cheek and headed out the door.

The California sun met his eyes with full force as he pulled from the garage. He grabbed his Ray Bans with one hand as he shielded his eyes with the other. He turned from the gated Sagewood Community main entrance and took back streets to Highway 101.

As he drove, he reflected on the good fortune he and Daly were reveling in. It was hard to believe they had their own security company, and they were doing well.

When he'd returned from Iraq, he'd worked for Procter, a large, mid-western consumer products company. He had started in their security department, but never imagined he would end up in California with a beautiful wife and running his own business only ten years later.

Mark had been successful with Procter, rising to head of security in a record five years. In the spring of 2008, he'd met Daly on an assignment in California as part of a plant investigation.

An employee of Procter had gone on a shooting spree in their Oxnard facility and then disappeared into the community. The plant manager, Dan Norwood, had called to request Mark's help with the situation. Sergeant Daly Dean had been assigned by the LAPD to profile the deranged employee. She did this leading to his arrest a few weeks later.

In the process of the investigation, Daly and Mark had fallen in love.

After trying to make a long distance relationship work for a year, Mark had bitten the bullet. In the summer of 2009, he'd moved to LA and opened Ford Security Associates to be close to Daly. It had taken every last penny he'd been able to save over his time with Procter, plus a substantial loan, to open his own business.

A few short months later Daly had given her notice she was leaving the LAPD.

They were married the Saturday after Daly turned in her badge, September fifth, 2009; thus began Ford and Ford, Esquire.

There had been no looking back as their reputation in the L.A. area took off, causing them to add people to their fledgling company. They now had ten employees with an office in the Santa Monica area. Their central location allowed them to serve the needs of movie stars, business executives, bankers, and sports icons; generally anyone who had a strong need for private security systems, and a bundle of cash.

With their expansion, they had been fortunate enough to hire top-notch IT support as an extra benefit to their clients. Mark had been installing a security system for a free-lance software developer in the LA area, PJ Fettig. PJ had taken an interest in her home's installation, upgrading a few elements of the software. Seeing her improvements to his standard installation, Mark had offered her a part-time job thinking she'd turn it down. PJ found the work interesting and decided she could handle it during her downtime, so she took the job.

Life was good.

Mark finished up going over his Ventura client's project by noon.

He drove to the Santa Monica pier for a quick lunch at one of his favorite taco places, Delgatto's, and then headed to his office around one o'clock.

He began going over the month's billings. This was a paperwork job he enjoyed as much as getting a red-hot poker up his ass so when Daly called he quickly picked up the phone hoping for a reprieve. Her voice was frantic and words came between tears.

"Mark, Linda just called me. Chuck died of a heart

attack," she forced out between halted breaths.

"What? Chuck? But he's healthy as a horse," Mark said incredulously.

"It makes no sense. And on the heels of Tommy…it makes no sense. He just keeled over at the Food Bank he volunteers at."

"Just take it easy babe. I'm headed to my car right now," Mark said as he punched his phone off and half-sprinted to his car. His head spun as he pulled onto the 405 headed for home.

His thoughts jumped to his friend Chuck. Could this really be happening?

How devastated Linda must be.

How hard would Daly take another friend dying so close to Tommy's death?

He couldn't help feeling their little group of friends had become fate's whipping boy.

Chapter 5

Mark goosed his BMW 428 convertible north onto Highway 101 from the I-405. He and Daly were on their way to Chuck Kohler's funeral service in Santa Maria.

It was a Monday afternoon and a sunny day. Unfortunately, that didn't brighten the dark cloud of losing a second close friend, which hung over them.

Mark had taken the opportunity to put the top down for the two-hour drive up the coast highway. He was hoping the California ocean air might blow away some of the melancholy they were feeling.

"Linda must be destroyed," Daly said with her voice raised above the sound of the wind. She looked off into space, not really speaking to anyone.

"Have you talked to her since Friday?"

"I called her Sunday just to let her know I was thinking of her. I asked if there was anything we could do, but she was pretty quiet and just seemed to be in shock. She said Chuck's heart attack was so sudden he really didn't have a chance. The EMTs told her he was already gone by the time they arrived at the food bank."

"I wonder if he had any history in his family of heart issues. He sure seemed to be in good shape. I know he was an avid biker and golfer. Makes you think none of us are as bullet-proof as we think."

"Yeah, I know. It's making me question how two of our best friends can die suddenly within a few weeks of each other. And both from some crazy twist of fate." Daly reached over to put her hand on Mark's shoulder and stared at him until he returned her look.

"The ex-cop in me is *screaming* that coincidences don't happen." Daly continued, "But it's pretty hard to make something out of a drowning and a heart attack."

"Yeah, hard to see any connection, but it's not sitting right with me either."

They rode in silence for the remaining hundred miles up the coast highway. Both seemed lost in their thoughts, feeling like any enjoyment from the ride was pricked and sucked out of their sails by death's bony finger.

Linda and Chuck were only a couple of years into retirement and one of the happiest, and most giving couples Mark and Daly had known. Chuck's passion for helping the down-and-out had exuded from him when he'd talk about what he was doing at the food bank. Linda had a way of telling stories of her volunteer projects at the zoo that were always entertaining to hear. They had travelled extensively since Chuck's retirement and had plans for a European river cruise in late summer.

Now, Linda would be left to pick up the pieces and

somehow move on.

Mark had input the address for the Santa Maria Presbyterian Church to his GPS before leaving home. Now he mindlessly followed the directions through the town of Santa Maria. Making a few turns off Highway 101, they parked in the church parking lot.

They walked towards the back of the traditional Spanish architecture church building. There they saw a sign with "Kohler Funeral" printed on it and an arrow pointing into the double doors at the corner of the church.

They were seated with friends from the poker group who had already arrived. All said their quiet hellos, and then sat soberly through the thirty minute service.

Linda and her kids, a daughter and son, twenty-one and twenty-five, along with Chuck's sister had handled the funeral arrangements. They had taken special care to make the funeral a celebration of Chuck's love of life and the way he shared and passed that feeling onto others…a real tribute to Linda and her family's strength given the shock of losing him so suddenly. Following the graveside service, the poker friends moved to surround Linda to express their condolences. Linda's dad was standing beside her holding her arm. He'd flown in from South Carolina for the funeral to stay a few days to help with all the details of losing his son-in-law.

Greg Riggsby was saying his goodbyes to Linda as the group approached. He turned to greet them, "Don't know if you all remember me from Tommy's funeral lunch. I'm Greg Riggsby. I've been working with Chuck and Linda the last couple of weeks on a financial update. I just can't believe how unfortunate this all is and just hoping I can help Linda in any way possible," Riggsby said as he let his hand fall from Linda's shoulder.

"Well, I'll be on my way. It's clear she's in good hands," he said turning to leave.

"Linda, the service was exactly the way Chuck would have wanted it," Louise Jensen said nodding approvingly.

"How are you holding up?" Daly asked as she reached for Linda's hand.

"I'm doing ok I guess. The kids have been amazing in getting me through. Just not where I thought I'd be on a sunny Monday afternoon," Linda said as she feigned a smile. Her red eyes told the truth.

Mark peeled away from the group when he noticed Chuck's sister, Anna, talking with a few of Chuck's family members. He had a few questions nagging at him around Chuck's death and this was as good a time as any to get a few answers.

"Hello Anna, I'm Mark Ford. My wife, Daly, and I are in a poker group with Linda and Chuck, and have grown close to them over the last few years. I'm very sorry for your loss."

"Thank you. Yes. Chuck and Linda have talked about what good friends you all are," Anna said turning her attention to Mark as he gently touched her arm.

"I know Chuck's death was a shock. He was so active and kept in shape, I'm wondering if there was any family history for this kind of thing?" Mark questioned.

"Yes there is. Our father passed away about fifteen years ago from a heart attack. He was only sixty-one, so

Chuck always worried he needed to take better care of himself. Dad smoked and was pretty overweight. Never saw the value of exercise I guess," she said thoughtfully.

"I never really worried much that we kids would be a health risk if we just stayed away from bad habits." Anna looked back at the flower-covered casket waiting to be interred once family and friends had departed, "But I guess I'll have to rethink that now."

"Thanks for coming today, and for you and your friends being there for Linda," she said as she smiled at Mark and returned to the family escort car. Her daughter and son joined her, and they departed for Linda's house for light snacks and sandwiches with the immediate family.

Mark joined the poker group who had gathered near the line of their parked cars. They were discussing if they should catch an early dinner together on the way back home.

"I'm in if we don't go to some greasy spoon or a place that serves fat on a bun," Mary said. "I don't think I could stomach seeing people stuff themselves with fried whatever and wonder why they've turned into porkers. Or, heaven forbid, have heart attacks like poor Chuck. Especially today."

Michael Simon raised a disapproving eyebrow at his ex-wife, "A bit insensitive aren't you?" Mary shrugged and shot Michael a "who are you" look.

"I know a place Ron and I loved just south of Santa Barbara called Fried Green Tomatoes. It just opened a few weeks ago. Lots of salads and everything is organic," Janice Richmond offered, nodding at Mary encouragingly.

"You'd love it Mary. Although I can't guarantee we won't run into an overweight patron," Ron Richmond added with a fake grimace.

Ron and Janice lived in the Simi Valley area, neighboring San Fernando. With Ron's job at a major grocery retailer, he kept up on all the new restaurant openings that might signal food trends. They were typically the ones in the group to suggest a new eatery.

"Sounds like a plan," Daly chimed in.

The group broke from their huddle towards their cars. Mark caught Jim Jensen by his shirtsleeve, "Jim, wondering if you're available for lunch later this week? Daly and I are having some concerns about the loss of Tommy and Chuck. We thought it might help to talk it out with you."

"Sure, no problem. Let me check my calendar and I'll get back to you," Jim said with a questioning look. "You certainly piqued my interest, but you don't have to be mysterious to get me to do lunch you know."

Daly looked at Mark as they headed from the cemetery, "So what was your little aside with Jim about?"

"I just thought it might be good to talk with Jim about our concern for friends dying in rapid succession. Jim has one of the most analytical minds of anyone I've ever known. Wouldn't hurt to see what he thinks about all this. He'll check his schedule and let me know what day works best. Want to come along?"

"Not sure we should be sharing our paranoia too willingly based on nothing but bad Karma, but you and Jim are close. Maybe it works better if you two hash it out and fill me in later on what devious conspiracies you conjure up."

Mark shrugged, "Probably will play tennis, have lunch and decide the world is just a crappy place sometimes."

Mark continued, "By the way, I did talk with Chuck's sister and turns out their dad died of a heart attack at a pretty young age, sixty-one. Kind of blows a hole in Chuck's coronary being suspicious. Talking to Jim still feels like a chance to air it out with a sharp mind, so I'll see what he thinks."

Daly looked at Mark as though deep in thought. "Yeah that makes foul play less likely doesn't it. Still feels wanky to me though. Call it cop's intuition."

She turned to look towards the sun starting its arc toward the ocean as they drove down the 101. Both quietly mulled over their own sense of "something's rotten in Denmark" as the sun used the clouds to paint a brilliant orange and purple mozaic stretching to the western horizon.

Chapter 6

Mark had pulled up a ridiculously comfortable chair and sat waiting for Jim Jensen to arrive for lunch.

The restaurant was one of Mark and Jim's favorites in the San Fernando area. It was located conveniently off a winding road in the canyons between Calabasas and the ocean. Folded into a tree-filled quadrant of the Santa Monica Mountains, Saddle Peak Lodge sat like an oasis among the cafes and chain restaurants most people saw as San Fernando's primary go-to eateries. The lodge in the name wasn't advertising fluff. The place was a century old, and formerly a hunting lodge. Its three floors were filled with wood paneling and fireplaces, ducks, boats and other outdoorsy gear, bookshelves and leather-and-wood furniture. The tables sported camouflage tablecloths and mason jars for water glasses and, on the walls, LOTS of taxidermy.

A real man cave.

Mark saw Jim sauntering up the steps to the restaurant through the window by his table. Jim was hunched over as usual, appearing lost in thought. Mark couldn't help but smile when Jim stumbled as if the tenth identical step had somehow caught him by surprise. He was the stereotypical absent-minded scientist to a tee: brilliant mind, in fact as brilliant as anyone Mark had ever known, disheveled look with his shirt usually half tucked in, black rimmed glasses from a few decades gone by, and dark black hair, slightly curly. Jim's six foot four inch height seemed less given his stooped posture, but his very long arms gave the impression of a tall man.

Jim hadn't shaved today, causing Mark to wonder if he'd taken the day off from ConGrowth Foods, Co. where Jim was one of the top research and development employees. Jim combined a statistical degree with a Ph. D. in food science as his calling cards. His intelligence and thirty-three years of experience would make him a highly sought after food developer if he ever decided to test his worth in the job market.

Jim was Mark's best friend, tennis partner and his confidant when it came to more private affairs. Mark often sought out Jim to hash over disagreements he might be having with Daly, discuss client concerns, or just share fears about whatever was bothering him. Jim always listened intently and then pulled no punches with what he thought. The perfect makings of a friend.

"Maarrrkkkk!" Jim greeted Mark with his name drawn out to sound similar to the *Cheers* TV sitcom when Norm would enter the bar each episode.

"Hey Jim," Mark said as he stood to shake his hand. "Saw you coming up the steps and wondered if you'd hit a couple of bars on the way here to get a head start," Mark smirked, knowing Jim to be a tea totaller.

"Damn place has too many steps for an ole fart like me," Jim retorted. "Now that I'm sixty-one, I appreciate a nice smooth ramp." He plopped into the heavily padded chair across the table and smiled, "So how's your lovely wife?"

"Daly's doing great considering the last few weeks have hit us all pretty hard," Mark replied as he motioned to the waiter.

Mark ordered a pale ale and Jim asked for a cranberry punch.

"Yeah, Louise hasn't been herself lately either. Kind of moping around when she's not at the hospital. Not sure what she should be doing." Jim shrugged and blew out a long breath communicating a sense of "what are you going to do."

The waiter returned with their drinks and took their orders. Jim asked for the thick styled French toast with bacon as a side while Mark went with the goat cheese and broccoli quiche.

"You know *real* men don't eat that, right?" Jim said as he settled back in his chair. "Now what's on your mind. I don't think you came here to talk about our wives being down in the dumps?"

"No, at least not exactly. Daly and I are concerned at the coincidence of Tommy and Chuck both dying within a few weeks of each other."

"I mean both were perfectly healthy at our last poker game not more than a month ago. Daly tells me her "cop's sixth sense" is ringing off the hook. Honestly I don't know what to think. I mean the chances of a drowning and a heart attack being the work of some unknown assailant is pretty far-fetched. And there's no evidence of a struggle or anything pointing to foul play."

Mark paused for a few seconds looking into his beer, then asked, "But what are you and Louise's thoughts about the whole thing?"

Jim had been listening intently with that stare of a scientist studying a mouse running a maze. "Hmmm. Guess we didn't really have the same sense of something wrong as you two. Tommy's was more surprising and I guess I just presumed Chuck must have had some heart history in his family to die so young."

"Yes. I did get a chance to talk to Chuck's sister at the funeral. She confirmed their dad had passed away at an early age from a heart attack as well."

"So there you have it. What's setting off your "foul play" alarms?" Jim asked as he sipped his drink.

"I don't know. I wouldn't be concerned if it were just me. But when Daly says she's feeling something is wanky, now that gets my attention. I dunno. Maybe losing two friends so unexpectedly is causing me to try to make sense out of the senseless."

They sat in thoughtful silence for a few moments.

Jim steepled his hands under his chin as he lightly tapped his fingertips together. "Ok, let's approach your concern about Tommy and Chuck's deaths being linked like we would any science problem. Let's kick around a few hypotheses assuming they are linked as our base assumption and see where it goes," Jim suggested.

Their lunches arrived and Mark followed Jim's lead in brainstorming while they ate. What possible links might exist between Tommy and Chuck's demise: hidden mafia connections, common ex-girlfriends, vengeful co-workers, some random sociopath. All these and more were considered and fleshed out.

But it was to no avail given the lack of struggle in both cases, and the unrelated causes of death.

As they finished their lunch and ideas seemed to be tapped out, Mark said, "Doesn't seem to be taking us to any viable theories. Maybe we're just confirming there isn't a connection as the only logical outcome."

"That or it's one of those problems you have to sleep on and come back to," Jim offered. "Tell you what. We'll keep thinking it through. I agreed to set up the next poker game at Tommy's funeral lunch and haven't gotten a chance to do it with Chuck's heart attack happening so soon. I'll pull everyone together in a couple of weeks and we can talk more then."

"Sounds like a plan," Mark said as he laid his fork down after the last bite of his quiche.

"Change of subject. Have you noticed the way Mary's been acting the last couple of weeks? Seems out of character. I mean since when did she become the food police? She handles the most exotic delicacies as part of her business, and yet can't handle going to a greasy spoon after Chuck's funeral. What's up with that?" Mark said incredulously.

Jim squirmed in his seat and hesitated before replying, "I think Mary's just showing her stress with the loss of Tommy and Chuck a little differently than the rest of us. I don't see anything with her to be too worried about."

Mark was about to pursue Jim about why he was acting evasive about Mary's behavior when the waiter brought their checks.

They settled their bills and the two friends rose and walked to the parking lot.

Mark stopped by Jim's car as Jim opened his door and climbed in, "You know Jim, the one thing we didn't talk about is what if bad things come in threes?"

Jim looked back at Mark thoughtfully for a moment. "Three points along a similar path usually make for a correlation in my line of work. I'm hoping this time there isn't any."

"Yeah, me too. See you in a couple of weeks."

Mark walked around the back of Jim's car. Unlocking his door with his key fob, he repeated to himself, "Yeah, me too."

Chapter 7

Mike Gentry looked out over Simi Valley. The Los Padres National Forest spread north as far as he could see from his tenth floor office suite. Mike was a VP for ConGrowth Foods, Co. and had overseen the savory snacks division for the past four years. Although CgFC was a multi-national business, the lion's share of its sales were in the US, with increasing amounts in Asia and Latin America. The expanding footprint of the company required extensive travel by its executives so locating its headquarters in close proximity to LAX made a lot of sense. Plus, it helped recruiting with many college grads wanting to live on the west coast.

The pencil in Mike's hand tapped rhythmically on his leather desk pad to some beat in his head.

His thoughts were far away.

He'd been mulling over the losses of Tommy and Chuck from their tight knit group of friends. He and his wife, Dianne, had spent some late nights remembering good times they'd had together over the past several years; wondering how the loss of two from the pride would affect the group.

They hadn't come to any earth-shaking conclusions. Somehow, talking about it seemed to help.

If nothing else, it had reminded them of how short life is and prompted them to make an effort to spend time with each other. As a first step in their new commitment, Mike was meeting Dianne for lunch at Sutter's Mill, one of their favorite lunch places for sandwich and salad type fare.

The phone rang bringing Mike back to the present. It was Jim Jensen.

"Hi Jim. So how goes it in your ivory tower? Any new breakthroughs for our great company?"

"No, not today I'm afraid. I was just calling to see if you and Dianne might be free for poker Friday after next? I had lunch with Mark yesterday and we both felt it would do the group good to get back together; sort of a return to normalcy. So, you think you can make it?"

"Shouldn't be a problem. I'll check it with Dianne. Worst case, she can join us late as usual. Seems *everyone* wants to close real estate deals on Friday nights. Are we doing it at your place?"

"Yes, we'll do dinner at seven. No need to bring anything. We'll just order Chinese as that's everyone's favorite. Nothing like sharing from the same rice bowl."

"Ok. I'm seeing Dianne for lunch today. I'll let her know."

"Sounds good. I'll send out an email later this week

once I hear back from everyone just to confirm. Okay, well take care and say hi to Dianne," Jim said as he clicked off in his usual abrupt manner.

Mike was about to say goodbye, but the dial tone was already buzzing in his ear. He had to smile as Jim would never change. Part of what made Jim such a valuable scientist was always being off to his next thing at the split-second his last thing had ended.

Mike hit the intercom button on his phone, "Shelley, I'm heading out for lunch. Please hold my calls as I'm trying to get a little quality time with Dianne today."

"Sure thing Mike," his admin of ten years replied.

He grabbed his sports jacket from the coat tree in the corner of his office and headed for the elevator. Punching Dianne's stored number in his phone, it rang a couple of times before she picked up. He said cheerily, "Hey Dianne, we still on for lunch today?"

"Oh, yeah I guess it is that time. I'm only fifteen minutes from Sutter's so I'll finish up and be there before noon, okay?" Dianne replied.

"See you there," Mike said as he hit the ground floor button in the elevator.

Exiting the lobby of CgFC and stepping into the bright sun, he reached for his sunglasses in his jacket's breast pocket. Adjusting his Oakleys on the bridge of his nose, he took a deep breath of the clean forest air and strolled to his car.

Unlocking the doors manually with his key, he then unlatched his convertible top and folded it onto the rear cowl of his classic 1990 BMW 325. It was a perfect top-down day for a ride through the valley and along the canyon road. He loved the winding part of the road the most. Each curve would bring him close enough to the edge he could almost touch the valley below, and his little sports car handled the hairpin turns with ease.

Twenty minutes later Mike arrived at the restaurant and captured a table by the window. He ordered an ice tea as he waited for Dianne.

Dianne's car pulled into the parking lot a few minutes later. Mike watched as she walked with quick steps to the restaurant's entrance and past the receptionist, her cell phone pressed to her ear.

A deal in the making no doubt.

Dianne scanned the restaurant as she continued her conversation, nodding when she saw Mike wave his arm back and forth a couple of times. The lunch crowd was beginning to fill Sutter's with conversations filling the air like a soothing hum of white noise. Mike had secured a table for two near the windows sporting a great view of the valley.

"Ok, that sounds low but I'll talk to the sellers and see if they're willing to budge. Can I reach you at this number in the next couple of hours?" she said as she leaned in to give Mike a peck on the cheek. "Right. Okay. Gotta go, but I'll get back with you Frank. Bye."

"So how is old Frank, anyway?" Mike said pretending familiarity with whomever Dianne had been talking with.

"Mike, you know I have to be there for my clients. You don't get into the Million Dollar Club by not taking calls you know." Dianne had been a member of the Million

Dollar Club for Greater LA realtors for the last five years and the top selling realtor in San Fernando for three years running.

"Just kidding my dear. I'm just happy you're able to get away for lunch on this fine California day. Can't think of anybody I'd rather be with," he said as he leaned over the table and kissed her on the lips, holding the kiss for an extra couple of beats just to make his point.

"Well, guess I'll need to do lunch more often if that's how you greet your lunch partners," she laughed, eyes twinkling at his amorous move.

They both ordered their lunches: Mike the Rueben on rye with minestrone soup, and Dianne the Cobb salad, and began catching up on each others' days.

"So Jim called about doing poker a couple of Fridays from now. Sound good to you?"

"Do you think Pat and Linda would make it? Would be great to see them in more pleasant circumstances."

"Don't know who all will make it as Jim is just trying to clear the date. It would be great to see them and the rest of the group to let our hair down a bit."

"Absolutely. I'll check my appointments and move something if I have to. Maybe I'll even turn my phone off for the night," she said raising an eyebrow at Mike.

Feigning a heart attack, Mike grabbed his chest, and they laughed at each other.

The waiter returned with their lunches.

They passed the hour away talking about how lucky they were to have good friends, what vacation they should look into next, and when they should visit their kids' families who now lived in San Francisco and Florida.

As they were finishing up, Dianne's phone rang. She frowned at Mike and he said, "Go ahead. I'll get the bill. See you tonight honey."

Dianne stood up from the table, grazed Mike's cheek with a kiss and was back into her full business mode before she hit the California sunbeams outside the restaurant.

Mike paid the bill in cash and smiled as he casually walked to his car. Leaning back against the car's door, he tilted his head up and let the sun warm his face for a few seconds.

Pulling out of the parking lot he checked his watch; plenty of time to enjoy his winding ride back up the canyon road.

He downshifted and accelerated into the first curve thinking, *not a bad day! Not a bad day at all!*

Chapter 8

Mike Gentry pulled away from Sutter's Mill. He didn't appear to notice the car pulling out behind him and staying a few hundred yards back.

With her red wig and sunglasses, it wasn't anyone he would notice as familiar.

But she certainly knew a lot about him. Following him the last few days had brought her a great deal of info on his habits. She was getting a good idea of just the right way to deal with Mike Gentry.

She followed him as he returned along the winding canyon road to ConGrowth Foods, taking particular note of how long it took him to reach landmarks along the highway. Hesitating along the street outside the company's parking lot, she watched as Gentry pulled into the parking slot bearing his name.

There were more than just a couple of VP's at this behemoth; in fact, several dozen would be more accurate. Gentry's parking spot was about fifty yards beyond the building's entryway and just around the south corner of the building. She would continue to gather details on Gentry over the next week or so as her time allowed.

Her plans to put an end to Mr. Slim Jim were a bit tricky and she needed it all to be perfect.

Gentry disappeared into the building's entrance.

She pulled into the parking lot, maneuvered into an open space about fifty feet from Gentry's car, and slipped her car into park. She made a few notes on a writing pad next to her, capturing dates, times and distances of her reconnaissance.

She looked up at the ConGrowth Foods building's brick and glass facade. She could see banners and posters through the main hallway windows wrapping around the front of the building. Renditions of each of the company's products, along with whatever slogans accompanied their advertising campaigns, were on display: Slim Jims – Original Meat Snacks, Monster Meat Sticks, Snacking Meat Sticks and multiple potato chip brands each with their own slogans covered the hallway like theater marquees.

The onslaught of these gaudy commercial images brought back memories of her mother's pantry from her childhood: Slim Jims, potato chips, popcorn, hard candies of several varieties, peanut butter, and Twinkies had filled those cupboards to over-flowing. She had made tortured trips to those cupboards during her mother's final days. Her mother's bed-ridden state had thrust her into caretaker mode at the tender age of sixteen, which included fetching the slow acting "poisons" her mother craved.

She cringed slightly at the vivid picture her mind

conjured up of her mother

Lying there.

Unable to move; having to be turned to alleviate her bedsores from getting worse.

All the time insisting on eating the garbage from her cupboard.

Propping the pillows under her mother's head and multiple-chinned neck had taken all of her strength.

The body odor had been unbearable even with frequent changes of bedding.

Magazines carrying the most recent gossip had been strewn about her bed. A TV was tuned to some daytime drama focused on dysfunctional families and friends. These were the bedmates for her pitiful mother's existence.

"But momma, you know that's not good for you," the echo of her voice falling on the deaf ears of insatiable gluttony.

"Just bring me what I like, child. Don't worry yourself about what's good for me. Just bring it now so I can rest easy," her mother's words still clearly ringing in her ears.

And she did.

It was horrific for her in those teen years to be complicit to the lingering death of her mother. But it would have been even more unthinkable to not please her, or worse yet, to not be loved by her.

And she had no doubt her mother would have withheld that love to ensure her food jones was met.

How haunted she had been when her mother finally died, at least partially as a result of her spineless actions.

It had left her miserable and despondent for a number

of years.

To deal with her depressed state, her doctor had suggested she take up a hobby, like gardening. At first reticent to try anything beyond her daily regimen of Zoloft, she decided she had nothing to lose. She took her doctor's advice and subscribed to a couple of popular gardening magazines. One of the articles led to her creating a tiered box garden from a pre-fabbed kit purchased at her local garden store.

In those early years on her own, she'd filled her time in her garden raising tomatoes, green beans, peppers of all sorts, sweet corn, melons, onions, multiple herbs for seasoning and a variety of flowers. It had allowed her to pass the time without thinking about anything but the planting and care of her vegetables and flowers.

Her depression had eventually receded.

She had attended college classes in the ensuing years while continuing to take care of her younger brother, Greg; only ten when her mother had died. Her mother's life insurance allowed her to remain in her childhood homestead with her brother and covered their educational and frugal living expenses.

Between college and raising her brother, she moved more and more towards what most people knew as normalcy.

She dated and eventually married an old high school classmate, Bill Davidson. Bill had been the class Romeo during high school; never giving the time of day to her. However, once he'd graduated, his popularity had taken a definite downturn. His derth of female companions in college catalyzed his interest in her when they'd met in a sophomore chemistry class.

Their marriage was to be short-lived as Bill didn't care for her younger brother coming with the package. Plus, his penchant for chasing every skirt that crossed his path became too much for her to put up with.

They divorced.

But in their brief marriage, they had managed to have a son, Danny.

Danny was the love of her life.

With Bill out of the picture, she continued her education and duties as a single mom and big sister using the remainder of her mother's insurance money. As stressful as this might sound to most people, and certainly she had had her moments of anxiety, these were the years she looked back on as the happiest.

She had graduated college and found a job leading to her getting the experience to begin her own successful business.

She had the best sixteen years of her life; and it had begun with Danny's birth.

About the time she'd started her own business, Danny was six, and her brother had gone off to college. From that point on it had been her and Danny. They did everything together: school events, days in the park, bicycling to the local ice cream parlor, homework, trips to the community pool, and life was as good as it could get.

Her business had taken a lot of her time in the beginning, but success had come with persistence and burning the candle at both ends.

Work and Danny were all she needed and all she wanted.

The sudden screech of tires from the street bordering ConGrowth Foods brought her out of her smiling reverie with a start.

Some ass hat passing by had evidently been looking at his cell phone when the car ahead of him had stopped to talk with a pedestrian friend.

"What the hell are you doing?" cell-phone-man yelled out his window. He pulled around the stopped car and flipped the other car the bird as he sped away.

The shrill sound of the tires shattered her pleasant daydreams of Danny. It took her to a dark place where her happy times were ended by one senseless act of teenage bravado. She was suddenly awash in the agony of losing Danny those many years ago.

The pain was unbearable as tears ran down her face staining the writing pad in her lap.

She sat for a few moments collecting herself, vanquishing the memories of losing her son into that deep black hole in her psyche. That darkness which she tried to avoid at all costs. It was the only way she could function when her grief and unrelenting regret overcame her.

Wiping away her tears with the back of her hand, she focused on Gentry's car.

Her eyes narrowed.

There'll be time to avenge you sweet Danny, but this one is for momma.

Chapter 9

The days went by quickly as life returned to routine at Ford and Ford, Esq.

The usual schmoozing with new Valley money. Rich and famous clients looking for ways to protect their extravagant homes and loved ones was a never-ending but lucrative treadmill. The past week, Daly had been scoping out three new properties for potential security issues that would need to be remedied. Mark had busied himself attending to a couple of jobs underway between lunches and dinners with new prospective clients.

Mark was fully immersed with an installation crew in Simi Valley when Daly called him.

"Hey babe," Daly chirped. "Just calling to remind you to be home on time as the poker group is getting together tonight. Seven p.m. at Jim and Louise's."

"Oh yeah. I'd totally forgotten that was tonight. I'm finishing a final systems run-through on a ten thousand square foot McMansion. PJ is doing the final software installation now. Should be done so I can be home by around five o'clock."

"Okay, I should be home shortly after you. See you then."

Daly pocketed her cell phone and continued her walk-through of her client's summer home. She pulled a notepad and pen from her shoulder tote bag and began sketching exit and entrance points. She then did a full circle of the perimeter of the property, noting surrounding terraine features and proximity of neighbors. Checking her watch, Daly saw it was approaching one thirty.

Time for lunch and to catch up with an old friend.

Walking back to her car, she threw her bag in the passenger seat. Settling behind the steering wheel, she punched a number into her phone. "Hey JD. I'm just leaving a job. See you at Murphy's in twenty minutes," she said to JD's answering service, and pulled from the drive.

———•(())•———

Daly saw Mark's car in the garage as she pulled her van into its stall. It was a little after five o'clock.

"Hey babe, so how is the Roberts' job looking?" she said as she came through the mudroom door.

Mark was sitting at the kitchen counter studying his phone.

"Oh it's pretty much good to go. I checked all the systems and only a few minor camera angle issues. I can send the guys over to handle it on Monday. I switched their system on and left Charlie to take them through the basics. How was your day?" he said looking up at her as she pecked his cheek.

"I got out to the Gruber house in Santa Barbara and sketched out what I saw for key entry points. I emailed my notes and sketches into the office so Frank could put together a bid. Got done early so I hit Murphy's for a well deserved pasta salad with JD, an old girlfriend of mine from the CSI lab unit," Daly said as she grabbed a couple of Coronas from the fridge. She handed one to Mark as she leaned back against their center kitchen island.

"Now there's a good idea, but…" he hesitated as he caught the door of the closing refrigerator, reached into the vegetable drawer and produced a lime, "you need this…"

Mark cut a couple of wedges from the bright green fruit with a knife from the counter valet. Reaching into a lower cabinet, he produced what looked like a blue plastic Corona bottle, "…and this to make it a Friday night special."

With a flourish he gripped the top of the blue bottle which separated from the body of the bottle. The top of the bottle was actually a fitted male plunger that inserted into the female body of the bottle which had an opening at the bottom. Placing the blue bottle body on the top of Daly's Corona, he dropped a lime slice into the hole where the plunger had been. With one quick motion he used his other hand to drive the plunger into the fitted body.

"*Voila!* You've been lime bombed," he announced as he removed the Lime Bomber. He smiled and handed the Corona with perfectly squeezed lime slice floating in the top to Daly.

Daly couldn't help but smile back and shake her head.

He had purchased his Lime Bomber on a scuba trip a few years ago. He loved to use it to do what most people would accomplish by just sticking the lime slice into the Corona without a second thought. It was probably one of the stupidest kitchen aids she'd ever seen. However, it was a cherished souvenir to Mark and had become his signature Corona move.

After he'd lime bombed his own beer, she clinked her bottle against his and tipped it to her lips. "Amazing how much better a Corona can be if done the Mark Ford way," she laughed as she eyed his smug look as he took a long swig.

They took their beers to the screened in porch off the kitchen. Sinking into the thick cushions of a wicker love seat, Daly laid her head against Mark's shoulder. He propped his feet on the matching footstool. They sat quietly for several minutes sipping their Coronas and just taking in the sounds of birds singing their territorial songs.

"This is so peaceful," Daly said after a half hour or so had gone by. "I almost want to blow off the poker game tonight and relax here for the evening."

"Yeah, it's tempting. But it would be good seeing the group in a fun social setting for a change."

"Yes, I suppose. I talked with Louise a couple of days ago. She thinks Linda and Pat are planning on coming tonight."

A few peaceful moments went by, then Daly sat up, saying, "Well, need to get myself in the shower if we're going to get there by seven."

Mark laid his head back on the cushion and closed his eyes, "I'll give you a head start as it only takes me five minutes to get ready."

"Just one more example of why men have it made. Enjoy your nap," she said playfully slapping one of his elevated feet as she headed to their master bathroom.

Daly showered, did her make-up and styled her hair using a large roller brush. She created the rounded, just-above-the-shoulder look she was after, turning left, then right, in front of her vanity mirror to check her look. About six-thirty, Mark came into the bathroom, yawned and patted Daly on the butt.

"No. Don't even *think* about it. Get ready or we'll be late," she said without looking at him as she continued to brush her hair in the mirror. Mark made a frowny face and shuffled off to his closet with his head hung down, looking at Daly every couple of steps. Reappearing naked, he made a display of flexing his muscles in the mirror, eyed himself admiringly for a moment and then headed into the shower. As promised, he emerged five minutes later and was dressed and ready to go five minutes after that.

Since Jim and Louise lived four blocks away, they decided to take advantage of the pleasant evening and walk to the party. A few minutes after seven o'clock, they walked up Jim and Louise's driveway and followed the serpentine sidewalk made of red brick pavers to their front door. Louise's landscaping was immaculate and it looked as if they'd just added fresh cyprus mulch.

Mark opened the front door without ringing the doorbell, as was their custom on poker nights. He escorted Daly in with his hand on the small of her back.

"Maarrkkk," Jim bellowed as they made their way through the foyer to the kitchen area at the back of the house. "Damn glad you brought Daly with you, or you'd have to go back and get her. Make yourself at home. The Chinese food is coming shortly. I just ordered what everybody ordered last time, so hope you didn't want to change your minds."

"And what if we did?" Mark said.

"Well…too damned bad, I guess," Jim laughed as he brushed past Mark to hug Daly.

Louise gave Jim her usual disapproving look, "Jim, you really don't know how to act, do you?" Coming forward to give Mark a peck on his cheek. "Why do you all agree to put up with him? I have to, but you could certainly find another way to torture yourselves I'd think."

"Hey Ron, Janice," Mark said to the Richmonds as he slid past Louise to greet the others in the group.

Everyone was there but Dianne Gentry. Mike said she had gotten held up at a house showing so would be coming later, as usual.

Linda Kohler and Pat Hemmings were sitting at the kitchen island. Both looking a bit lost without Tommy and Chuck. Daly pulled up between them, hugged each and began to chat. Nothing much fazed Daly, as she cut through any awkwardness with her sincerity and just being a good friend.

Soon the house was a buzz of multiple conversations,

all happening at once. The poker group seemed like it had been transported by a time machine to a better day, but without two good friends who couldn't make the trip.

The doorbell rang and Jim announced, "Food's here. Help me with the bags, Ron."

A young Asian man could be seen through the glass borders of their main entrance, holding what looked like large paper grocery bags in each arm. Jim opened the door and paid for their take-out food while Ron took the bags from the deliveryman and deposited them on the kitchen table.

"Smells like an oriental mecca to a starving man," Ron said as he sat the bags down.

Louise and Janice began to dig through the bags laying out the different dishes in a buffet style arrangement. Janice announced, "Come and get it," and the group descended on the feast of Moo Goo Gai Pan, General Tso's chicken, Szechuan shrimp, Mongolian beef, sesame chicken, Kung Pao chicken, mixed vegetables with garlic sauce, and several quart containers of hot and sour soup. In the middle of the display was a pile of egg rolls and large containers of steamed rice and vegetable fried rice along with assorted packets of soy and sweet-and-sour sauces.

The conversations continued as the group busied themselves creating their ideal mix of the delights available, heaping their chosen delicacies over their rice of choice. After piling their plates to overflowing, each visited the drink area for wine, beer or bottled waters. With food and drink secured, the men headed into the family room, which sported a big screen TV tuned to the base-ball game. The women detoured to the living room to eat and talk.

Daly sat her plate on the beveled glass coffee table, along with her bottled water, and sat on the edge of one of the large couches. The other women found their own spots on one of the couches or armchairs placed around the coffee table.

"So Louise, do you do all your own landscaping? The beds out front are gorgeous," Daly said, munching on an egg roll.

"Thank you. Yes, pretty much. Jim helps with the mulch by carrying the bags to the edge of the beds, but I really enjoy the arranging and planting. Sometimes when Aiden is home, he'll help me as well. I have my main garden out back and spend most of my free time there in the spring and summer."

"How old is Aiden now?" Janice Richmond questioned. Janice was always the touchy feely one in the group when it came to keeping track of family members and kids. Janice and Ron had three children, two girls out of college and with jobs, while the youngest was finishing up his accounting degree at Xavier University in Cincinnati.

"He'll be twenty-four this coming September. He's two years into medical school at USC, and hopes to start residency somewhere on the west coast in another couple of years if all goes according to plan."

"So what's he planning to specialize in?" Mary Simon asked as she joined the conversation. "My younger brother, Greg, had planned to be a doctor at one point, but then took up finance when pre-med got too hard."

"Oh it changes from month to month as he finds new things he likes or hates in medical school. I just hope he plans to go into internal medicine and avoid the whole surgeon route his mother took," Louise said in her typical self-deprecating way.

Daly knew Louise was a highly regarded gastroenterologist and surgeon in the San Fernando area. Yet she was so unassuming one would be hard pressed to know she was a doctor unless it directly came up in conversation.

"It can be fulfilling," Louise continued, "But sometimes I wonder if I wouldn't have been happier treating runny noses and aching joints. Assisting chronically obese people with by-pass surgery can be pretty frustrating, especially when psychological issues may really be the culprits."

"You know, I can't imagine having to deal with the patients you handle," Mary snorted softly as she picked over her mixed vegetables and steamed rice.

"People too weak to manage their diets to a healthy balance, so they come to you to "fix" them. You'd think they could muster up the will to control their gluttony so they wouldn't have to face the risk of surgery. And I'm guessing that once they get the surgery, most don't change their eating habits and end up right back where they were, right?" Mary asserted.

"Unfortunately, you're not too far off," Louise sighed. "I always make sure my patients understand the need to change lifestyle and eating habits is a prerequisite to being considered a candidate for corrective surgery. But at the end of the day, best intentions only pan out about half the time is my experience."

"As to your question on Aiden's specialty, I really just want him to be happy with whatever he chooses as his field. He's had a pretty hard set of circumstances since his accident eight years ago. It's been particularly difficult for him to move on from losing his best friend," Louise said as she moved a carrot slice back and forth on her plate.

"I guess I hadn't heard about that," Janice Richmond gently prodded in a questioning tone.

Linda and Pat both looked at the floor, seeming to have their own thoughts of missing loved ones.

Mary stood up, looking a bit vexed, "Time for a refill," and abruptly walked through the living room to the kitchen for more cabernet.

Louise continued, "Jim and I don't usually talk about it, and please don't bring it up with Aiden if you happen to see him around here on one of his breaks. Anyway, Aiden and his best friend were pretty much inseparable. In fact, Pat, Mary and Dianne probably remember them hanging around here on poker nights in those early years when we first started playing."

"One night the boys borrowed our car to go out to a movie, and probably drive up and down the street looking for "hot babes." Aiden was sixteen and had his license, but his friend was a few months from getting his. Well, at some point in the evening, Aiden had let his friend behind the wheel. He was a pretty wild kid and from what Aiden told us later, his friend wanted to see how fast the car would go so they had gone out to some of the country roads up the valley."

"Aiden's friend had no business driving like that, but once he was behind the wheel, Aiden couldn't get him to slow down," Louise's voice cracked and she wiped a tear from the corner of her eye. "I guess the road they were on was a gravel one. As they picked up speed, the car fish-tailed, leaving the road, and continuing in the ditch beside the road. The car didn't slow down when it left the road so they were barreling through high grass for several hundred yards. Then there was a culvert…"

Louise stopped and caught her breath with a deep sob, then continued, "Aiden's friend was killed instantly when he hit it head on and went through the windshield. Aiden was spared as his seat belt kept him in the car. Both of his legs and his left arm were broken. He had contusions over most of his body, but he lived, thank God. Aiden had crawled from the car and cradled his friend in his arms when the EMT's found him."

"Oh my," Janice said as she covered her mouth. "I can't even imagine what Aiden went through."

After an uncomfortable pause, Janice's professional curiosity as a psychologist got the best of her. "Did Aiden seek any counseling after the accident?"

"Yes. Once he got through the physical rehab, which took the better part of six months, he agreed to see a psychologist, a Dr. Sheryl Abrams. She specializes in the teen trauma area. It did seem to help, but he went from one of the most happy-go-lucky kids you'd ever meet to such a serious boy. I know the accident still haunts him from time to time." Louise looked down at her hands for a long moment, her eyes beginning to water.

Daly reached out and put her hand on Louise's. "You know Aiden couldn't be luckier to have you and Jim as parents, right? I saw too many cases in my years with LAPD where kids were in similar situations to Aiden, but didn't have the family support. You and Jim are a big part of why he's moving on through med school today, and will keep moving on after that."

"Thanks Daly. Sorry to drag all of you through my family's sad times," Louise said as she looked around the room at each of her friends' soft, wet eyes.

"Let's enjoy our meal and then see if the guys are able to tear themselves away from the Padres' game for a little poker," she said as she smiled, sniffled once and wiped her eyes with her napkin.

A few minutes after eight o'clock, Jim sauntered into the living room. "Well you all look like you could use a little fun. What say we go take as much of Mark and Ron's money as we can for the remainder of the evening? That should cheer everyone up," Jim said as he rubbed his hands together in mock glee.

At Jim's invitation, they moved to the large dining room, depositing their plates in the kitchen sink and re-filling their drinks along the way. The dining table had a couple of card decks in the center of the leather pad which protected the oak table's finish. The dining table easily sat ten, and a matched butler table displayed a metal case of ceramic poker chips. The friends selected chips of blue, white, red and green in exchange for the twenty to forty dollars each anteed in for their stake.

Pat, Linda, Louise, Janice and Daly opted out of the poker game, after mingling for a few minutes as people made their transition to the dining room. They returned to the living room and settled in for some good girl talk.

The rest of the friends found their places around the table. Happy banter began as cards were shuffled, poker chips clinked and the trash talking of each other's hands got fully underway.

Dianne showed up about fifteen minutes into the game. After saying her hellos to the living room klatch, she made herself a plate and poured a glass of wine. Transporting her food and drink to the dining room, she joined the poker fun as she ate her dinner.

Daly engrossed herself with her friends, catching up on family happenings and future vacation plans.

The pall from Louise's earlier sharing about her son's tragic loss of his friend seemed to lift.

The friends talked of better times and good times to come.

Every once in awhile an uproar from the poker go-ings-on would pierce the evening as good hands were won and lost.

Most importantly, the comfort of good friends caring for one another settled back over the group like a warm and familiar blanket.

Chapter 10

She pulled on a runner's vest over her black hoodie as she stepped from her car.

The bright orange reflective tape on the sleeves and two stripes circling the body of the vest provided ample warning of her presence to any passing cars.

It had begun to sprinkle lightly. The encroaching night devoured the dusk as she jogged from the pedestrian side street towards the main drag running in front of ConGrowth Foods.

It was her second such run. She'd hoped to complete her plan for Mike Gentry the previous Wednesday. Unfortunately, a number of the VPs at ConGrowth Foods had decided to catch up on work that evening. She needed the privacy of a deserted parking lot so she'd delayed a week.

Gentry was a creature of habit based on her surveillance the last few weeks. He stayed particularly late on Wednesdays; probably due to his wife having a regular commitment that didn't include him. No reason to hurry home to the little Mrs.

She jogged casually along the sidewalk in front of the building. The south parking lot came into view and she could see she was in luck. The only car remaining in the line of assigned spaces next to the building was the red BMW convertible sitting in front of the sign marked "M. Gentry."

She smiled and continued past the parking lot towards a jogging path, entering a stand of valley oaks off the side of the road. No cars remained in the main part of the parking lot as was typical by this time in the evening. Only a few of the workaholic VP's tended to stay much past six o'clock, and it was nearing eight o'clock as she checked her watch.

Once far enough into the path, she shed the jogging vest. She removed a black knit facemask with a large cyclops hole for her eyes and black leather gloves from the runner's pouch she wore around her waist, also black. Rolling up the vest, she compressed it into her waist pouch. Donning the mask and gloves, she was virtually a shadow along the jogging trail.

She jogged back to the parking lot, being careful to stay along a line of low bushes that rimmed the area. This approach kept her out of the view of the security camera targeted on the empty parking lot.

She reached the south side of the ConGrowth Foods building in less than five minutes. She stayed low and beneath the Japanese Privet hedge which bordered the parking lot edge between the assigned parking spaces and the building about twenty feet away. The hedge was only about three or four feet tall.

She had to crouch-walk her way to Gentry's vehicle on the parking lot side of the hedge, staying out of sight. This avoided her being spotted by the random security guard that might wander the exterior hallway of the building and see her through the large windows facing the parking lot.

She checked her watch as she kneeled next to the BMW. If Mike was his punctual self this evening, she would have about fifteen minutes to complete her tasks.

She removed a Slim Jim car lockpick she had bought online for twenty bucks. It was amazing what you could buy with no question of why you might want something so obviously larcenous. She'd tried it out one night on a similar BMW in her neighborhood. The tool had worked perfectly.

She inserted the tool down the driver's side door and with a few tries, the lock popped up.

Entering the car, she slid into the driver's seat, chuckling at the irony. *Mr. Slim Jim done in by a Slim Jim.*

Reaching inside her hoodie's zippered pocket, she extracted a wide-mouth vial and a pair of latex gloves. Slipping the gloves over the leather gloves she was already wearing, she opened the vial and scooped out some of the thick concoction with her double-gloved fingers. She then rubbed the potent extract into the steering wheel, applying three coats before she was satisfied.

"So I hope you're in the mood for a little English Yew tonight Mr. Gentry," she said under her breath as she slipped back out of the driver's seat.

Crouching, she gently closed the door, leaning her

shoulder into it causing the door to quietly click. Inserting the Slim Jim once more, she re-engaged the locking mechanism.

Returning along the hedge, she retraced her steps to the jogging path. Once fully shrouded in the trees, she exchanged her mask and gloves for the running vest in her waist pouch.

Jogging back along the sidewalk she'd departed a mere twenty minutes ago, she returned to her car and sat patiently.

It would only be a few minutes before her prey fell into her trap. A sense of exhilaration filled her as she stared out into the night with the raindrops beginning to fall more steadily.

Her plan had been riskier than previous ones. The exposed access to Gentry's car presented chances to be seen.

It had also required her to create a new extract from her English Yew leaves and stems. The fine liquid paste she'd come up with could be applied to a surface, like Gentry's leather covered steering wheel. The biggest difficulty then became selecting just the right concentration of English Yew extract that would be effective through skin contact.

She needed it to absorb through the skin slowly, but not too slowly. The perfect timing would be for her toxic paste to take effect five to ten minutes after contact. The extract would then cause paralysis, followed by convulsions.

The added bonus she had not counted on was the rain. If Gentry grasped the steering wheel with wet hands, the absorption of the extract would likely be enhanced; plus the chances of him noticing anything tactilely wrong with the steering wheel went down significantly.

She sat back and waited for her dirt bag fly to enter her web.

Mike Gentry slid his encoded keycard through the automatic security door reader.

It had been a long day as his Wednesdays typically were, and he was looking forward to a cocktail.

He stepped through the door as it clicked loudly and swung open. He searched his cellphone from his inside coat pocket and speed dialed Dianne.

"Hey hon, you done with tennis?" he said as he walked along the front sidewalk towards his car. His steps quickened as the rain seemed to intensify.

"Yes, just finished up and having a drink with a few of the girls before I head home," Dianne answered.

"You want me to bring something home for you?" he offered as he reached in his pocket feeling for his car fob while holding the phone under his chin.

"No, I ate earlier. Pick yourself up something if you want."

"Ok. I'll see you in a half hour or so. It's started to rain here so may take me a bit longer. See you at home." Mike slipped the phone back in his coat pocket and thumbed the key fob to open his car door. Throwing his briefcase in the passenger seat and sliding behind the wheel, he pulled the door shut behind him as the rain began to pelt the windshield.

He backed his car out of his space, and with a quick

turn of the wheel goosed his BMW towards the parking lot exit. Turning onto the main road heading back down the canyon, he switched the radio to a news channel.

Noticing his hands felt a little greasy on the steering wheel, he looked at them to see if he'd accidently gotten into something. His palms looked slightly wet from the rain, so he rubbed them together as he steered with his knees.

It was about eight-thirty. He'd had one of ConGrowth Food's new meat snacks around five o'clock to get him through until dinner, but now he was starving. On cue, his stomach growled.

He listened to the news as he drove. No other cars were out. He guessed the weather turning rainy had probably kept people at home.

He wound his way down the canyon road.

He noticed his hands were beginning to tingle, almost like they had fallen asleep. *Must be hungrier than I thought.*

He took one hand off the steering wheel and shook it to bring the feeling back, but now the tingling was spreading through his arms at an alarming rate. Mike's arms felt like they suddenly weighed a ton and his legs were quickly losing feeling as well.

He was into the winding part of the narrow road at this point; no place to pull over and let what he assumed to be low blood sugar pass.

He tried to raise his right foot from the accelerator to brake the car.

His leg was like concrete.

His hands were losing all strength to the point he

couldn't grip the steering wheel. He weaved around the next hairpin turn mustering all of his remaining strength to keep the car in the road by leaning forward using his forearms to steer.

He could feel his body shutting down on him.

Then he began to convulse, losing any control he had over his extremities.

The car had accelerated to where it was now going over fifty miles an hour towards the next curve. Even on a dry day, he never took that curve at over twenty-five.

He felt the car smash through the guardrail and leave solid ground. His wingless red chariot flew out over the sheer wall of the canyon.

After a couple of seconds of weightless flight, he felt a split second of brain-numbing pain. Then nothing.

———— ((())) ————

She followed a few hundred yards behind Gentry, keeping his taillights in view through the now steadily falling rain. Her plan was falling into place better than she had hoped. No other cars were around so she could actually watch Gentry meet his destiny on this rainy California evening.

She knew he would be feeling the effects of his English Yew hangover within a few minutes of entering the winding canyon road.

The question in her mind was if he would be lucky enough to get the car to some point of safety before his drive home became lethal. She couldn't be sure he'd leave the highway at just the right spot with the number of variables left to chance.

If he were able to pull his car to the side of the road, her back-up plan was to help him over one of the more dangerous precipices while he was still in an incapacitated state.

She saw him begin to weave ahead of her causing her to grip her steering wheel tighter in anticipation.

Just hold on a little longer Slim Jim king. Just keep it together a little longer.

The BMW disappeared around a curve as she sped up to get closer.

She rounded the sharp turn just in time to see the taillights disappearing over the edge of the sheer roadside.

Pulling up to the spot where Gentry's car had disappeared, she jumped from her car, excitedly rushing to the edge of the road.

The BMW had evidently left the highway at a good enough speed to go airborne for several hundred feet before crashing into the hillside. It was still tumbling bumper over bumper down to the valley's floor when she approached the ruptured railing.

The car came to rest, partially visible through the murky haze of the falling rain.

Its headlights illuminated the scrub brush as it lay on its mangled side.

There seemed to be an orange flare for an instant somewhere beneath the undercarriage. Then the car exploded in a burst of flame sending several blazing pieces arcing into the rainy night.

She stood at the road's edge for a few moments taking it all in.

This had truly been her best work to date. Not only was the Slim Jim garbage man dead, but any evidence of the English Yew that had helped him to his fiery demise would be incinerated.

Just an unfortunate car wreck on a rainy, slick night.

Her plan, with a little help from the weather, had gone beautifully. She seemed to revel in the flames as they consumed their incapacitated prisoner.

She smiled and murmured to herself, "That's for you momma. That's for you."

Her gaze turned from a look of satisfaction into a dark glower as her eyes reflected the flame's fierce red glow.

Part II

"...And pretty maids all in
a row."

Chapter 11

News of Mike's accident went through the poker group like a raw nerve plunged into an antiseptic bath. Another of their tight-knit group dying tragically set off a wave of emotions. The shock of losing their friends unexpectedly and at such an alarming rate was taking its toll.

Mark was quick to call Sergeant McClarey using the private number he'd kept from their meeting at Tommy's house several weeks before.

"Sergeant, I just got off the phone with Dianne. She said the police are investigating the cause of Mike's accident, but wouldn't say anymore. What can you tell me?" Mark begged into the phone as his voice trailed off.

"Mr. Ford, I'm not at liberty to tell you anything even if I had the wee details, which I don't. The investigation hasn't released the accident scene. What I told m'lady Gentry is his car appears t' have lost control and crashed, resultin in the gas tank catchin fire. Whether Master Gentry died from a bad ticker at the wheel, from the impact o' the crash or in the fire dat followed will require the full medical, so I just don't know. There are no signs o' foul play and no witnesses t' the incident, so all we 'ave is the accident scene as our evidence and not much else t' sort this out."

The Sergeant hesitated, then added, "Sorry I don't have more for you. I know how close you and yer mates were t' Master Gentry, so I'll be sure t' let you know what shows up from the investigation o' the scene...after we've informed m'Lady Gentry, o' course."

Mark turned to Daly as he disconnected from the call, "Looks like no information beyond what we already heard from Dianne, assuming the good sergeant isn't holding back on us."

"Mark, my cop's intuition was already on high alert. Now it's *freaking* off the scale!" Daly paced back and forth in their kitchen looking at Mark every few steps. She appeared ready to punch something if she didn't get some kind of resolution.

"We can't just sit here and wring our hands anymore. It's time to take this to the next level, whether the police want us to or not." Daly locked eyes with Mark, and declared, "This is bullshit! Total eff'n bullshit, and I want to talk to Sergeant "No Answers" myself."

Mark grabbed his keys from the kitchen island as he followed Daly to the garage. The kitchen door nearly caught him in the face as it slammed behind her.

She marched to the car, opened the passenger door and sat staring bullets at Mark. "Well. Are we going or not?"

Mark climbed in and started to say something, but thought better of it. He started the car, pulled out of the driveway and started towards the police station.

It was time for a come-to-Jesus meeting with Sergeant McClarey, hosted by his lovely wife, the exorcist lady of L.A.P.D.

God help you Sergeant McClarey. God help you.

Daly was out of the car and headed into the police station as Mark shifted into park. He'd pulled into one of the visitor spots directly in front, which allowed Daly to enter the staion in a few quick strides.

He wasn't sure what his role was to be in the discussion with the police detective, but it was clear that Daly was running the show. He'd just follow her lead at this point and see where it got them.

Daly approached the duty sergeant and asked to see Sergeant McClarey. Before the duty sergeant could begin his routine of "what seems to be the problem, little lady," Daly spotted McClarey at his desk.

She pushed through the swinging stanchion gate and approached McClarey for a more direct how-do-you-do. "Sergeant McClarey. Sergeant McClarey," she called out as she strided towards his desk.

The half-dozen or so cops in the bullpen area were all looking at her. They seemed to be trying to decide what kind of threat this female terrier posed to their general health.

"I'd like a minute of your time to talk the Gentry case, Sergeant. That is if you think you can pull your head out long enough to talk to someone who's trying to do more than wait for clues to drop out of the sky and hit them like a ton of shit," she said as she locked eyes with McClarey.

Mark was trying to stay close to Daly, but it was clear she was on a beeline to McClarey that would not be detoured.

Arriving at his desk, she stood over him, looking at him expectantly.

His eyes widened, then narrowed at this female juggernaut, "M'Lady Ford. Why top o' the mornin t' you. Why don't we take this into one o' the meetin rooms where we can talk more private-like?"

Daly looked at the adjoining room that McClarey motioned towards, back at him and then marched into the room and took a chair.

McClarey stood up slowly, looked questioningly at Mark, and followed Daly into the room.

Mark followed.

"So I take it your husband did'n tell you we had no further detail on the Gentry case?"

"My husband told me *exactly* what you said and I say it's Bull Shit," Daly stared to the back of McClarey's skull through his eyes making sure he got the full intensity of the "bull" and the "shit."

"You are now looking into the third death of very good friends of mine that have all died under suspicious circumstances in the past three months. Based on the lack of any apparent activity on your part, I assume you don't have a clue if or how these "coincidental" deaths may have happened."

She continued, "I'm an ex-cop and spent several years

investigating some of the nastiest crimes you can imagine. My ex-cop spidey senses are going off like an eff'n five alarm fire. What are your cop instincts telling you, Sergeant?"

McClarey looked at Daly for a few seconds saying nothing, then relaxed back into his chair and cleared his throat, "M'Lady Ford, I assure you I'm takin the death o' yer mates very seriously. I've looked at all the findings for Tommy Hemmings and Chuck Kohler, and I'll be the lead detective for Mike Gentry if any inklin o' foul play pops up in his death."

Clearing his throat again, he continued, "However, until I have some connectin pattern, cause o' demise, or motive dat links these passins, there's nothin t' investigate beyond a series o' very unfortunate incidents. And maybe in the case o' Chuck Kohler, natural causes due t' a faulty ticker. I'll agree it's a mite coincidental how it's impacted yer circle o' mates, but dat's all I can say about it at the present."

Daly stared hard at McClarey.

Mark could see her frustration was ready to boil over. Not having any credible counter-theories to put on the table, she was left to stew in a speechless stare.

Mark felt her pain and helplessness as they sat there a few moments longer. He then broke the silence and offered, "Sergeant McClarey, we know you're doing your best and there's no clear path to connect our friends' deaths. At the same time, I've come to know my wife's sixth sense in these matters is reliable. If she feels there's something more here, then believe me, you ought to take notice and dig deeper."

"Master Ford, I appreciate your wife has a particular set o' experiences and trainin dat make her more than the average person who comes t' me with concern. Believe me, I will keep an open mind t' whatever we uncover, and I'll be lookin for the connections she's suggestin. At the same time, I think you both could take some time t' consider how strongly the loss of three mates in a short timeframe is affectin you and your ability t' be objective-like."

At the word "objective," Mark felt Daly's blood pressure spike from across the room.

She stood up and stormed from the room muttering something about eviscerating a miserable, eff'n bureaucratic leprechaun and the horse he rode in on.

Mark shrugged at McClarey, and stood to leave, "I'm really serious about Daly's sense for these kind of things. She has a good track record for her time in LAPD and their Behavior Analysis Unit. Please do keep an open mind as you say. It's a given this is close to home for her, but I wouldn't ignore her instincts when it comes to bad guys."

Mark exited the police station with all eyes glued on him as he followed Daly's jet stream out of the station.

Climbing into the car he could see Daly focused through the windshield looking at nothing, but doing it very intently. He said, "Well, I think that went well, don't you?"

"Not the time, Mark," she shot him a glance indicating his attempt at humor was not appreciated. "We're *not* going to let this sit on some bureaucrat's desk gathering dust. We're going to use all our resources as Ford and Ford to figure this out. I'm eff'n *sick* of attending friends' funerals and we're going to make sure there aren't any more in our near future."

They sat in silence for a few moments.

"I've set up a meeting with Jim tomorrow to hash over possible connections, motives and generally talk anything he might see using that big brain of his. Maybe something will come out of that we can sink our teeth into," Mark said as he reached across the seat and put his hand on Daly's shoulder. "You know I'm with you on this, right?"

"I know, I know. I just need somewhere to look so we can start turning over rocks and see what kind of scum crawls out."

"That's my girl. The scum kicking babe I could never get enough of, so I married her," he said as he patted her leg.

She couldn't help but smile a little.

He started the car and reached for her hand, saying, "Let's put our heads together tonight and come up with every wild option that hits us. We can bounce our ideas off Jim tomorrow and see what he can add."

Chapter 12

Mark and Daly pulled up in front of the Saddle Peak Lodge around noon. The sun was in full glory, blazing down from a pure blue backdrop; a cloudless sky and moving from warm to hot on this first day of May

Daly and Mark walked hand-in-hand up the front steps. Mark sought out the hostess to ask for one of the private rooms off the main dining area. He asked the hostess to send Mr. Jensen back to them when he arrived.

They settled back into their chairs, not as plush as the main dining room's and straight-backed for more practical business meetings. Daly brought out her writing pad where she had captured their notes from the previous evening's brainstorm session.

They'd been up until past midnight trying to come up with potential theories they could rationally consider, plus a few that were outside the rational box; like alien conspiracies or supernatural phenomenon. In total they had listed over two dozen possibilities linking their friend's untimely deaths. They'd then eliminated all but the top five options. These were the ones they wanted to present to Jim when he arrived as starting material.

Daly was relooking at her list and the order they'd created for most likely to least likely when Jim arrived.

"Daly and Doofus, so good you could meet me in my private office," Jim smiled as he bent to kiss Daly on the cheek and gave Mark's shoulder a playful punch.

"Yeah, thought it might be easier to talk freely. Plus I don't really want to be seen with you in public," Mark said as he looked out the corner of his eye at Daly for encouragement.

Daly raised her eyebrows and sighed, "Why do boys always have to be boys?"

"Just our way." Jim shrugged and then turned serious. "So what are you laboring over with all that investigative genius? Mike's death supplies the third point in a curve Mark and I were discussing a few weeks ago. We need to consider if there's any sense to be made from these awful circumstances."

"Exactly," Mark agreed. Let's order our food and we can take you through some thoughts Daly and I came up with last night. Hopefully some will hit you as plausible, or you'll come up with new angles."

The waitress entered the room with glasses of water and efficiently took their orders. Mark ordered a bleu cheese burger and beer-battered onion rings, while Jim went with his standard waffles and bacon, and Daly with blueberry pancakes with a fruit salad on the side.

After ordering their lunches and drinks, they talked

for a bit about how Dianne was doing. A few minutes later their food arrived. They asked the waitress not to disturb them for a couple of hours while they worked. The waitress nodded and pulled the double doors to the meeting room closed behind her as she exited.

As the waitress closed the door, Daly produced her writing pad with the list she had developed with Mark for their group's perusal. "We developed a lot more ideas, but we think these five are the most likely places to start as we're working against the general theory that all the deaths are related."

The list was numbered one to five:

1. Psychopath who is targeting a circle of friends for unknown, but related reasons
2. Family member(s) deciding to get vengeance
3. Ex-girlfriends or lovers that crossed paths with all three
4. Business deal(s) that are related and went bad
5. Government conspiracy plot that crossed paths with all three

Jim studied the list intently for several minutes without saying anything.

Finally, he looked up at Daly and Mark, "Good list. Covers the basic motivations of love, greed, revenge, and a good dose of paranoia. That's a good start. I also like starting with the premise that the deaths are all linked. That forces us to think through connections using critical thinking, before going to the police assumption of a series of unrelated and unfortunate deaths."

Jim continued, "So given the base premise of connections between the deaths, let's consider if the murders could be connected by their mechanisms. On the surface we have a drowning, a heart attack and a fatal car accident. No obvious murder weapon connection."

"However, in each case we have a relatively healthy person with no predispositions to suicide, drugs or alcohol to excess. And the deaths appear surprising in each circumstance," Jim said thoughtfully.

"What if we assumed the murderer has a particular penchant for hiding his method of killing?" Daly suggested.

"Yes that could be plausible. A good way to cover your tracks would be to bring new methods to each crime. Of course that also presents the most complex route for our killer. For now let's assume there is a connection that simplifies the killer's planning process," Jim proposed.

"If we consider Chuck as being killed by the same murderer as Tommy and Mike, it might simplify the method side of this," Mark offered. "Chuck had to be poisoned or drugged to induce a heart attack."

"Excellent thought," Jim commended. "And I always thought you were a mere reflection of your brilliant wife. Let's go with that thought for a minute. If we assume drugs or poison is at the heart of the killer's modus operandi, then how would that fit for Tommy and Chuck?"

"Drowning could be induced by many drugs if the person ingested them then was incapacitated in a pool, " Daly surmised.

"Yes, and in Mike's case, if drugged at just the right

dose and timing, it could have led to a car crash on the winding road between his work and home," Jim said placing his hands in his familiar thinking pose, inverted V-shaped and tapping his fingers against one another below his chin.

"Of course, you'd think the coroner's reports would have ruled out most drugs as a standard toxicology analysis during the autopsy," Daly said with a puzzled tone. "In both Tommy and Chuck's cases, McClarey indicated the tox screens came back clean. Only a couple of drugs that were prescribed medications and not related to CoD."

"Well, continuing down the path of assuming they're connected and common methods, it is possible to introduce a bioactive agent that wouldn't show up in normal tox screens," Jim offered.

"How is that possible?" Mark asked. "With the technology of our police labs these days, they can find the most minute quantities of anything."

"True if the analyst uses appropriate control chemicals to identify the culprit baddies. But if non-standard bioactive agents are introduced, the high-tech machines can be blind to what's there if not calibrated appropriately. Especially if the preliminary report indicates the victim died of natural or accidental causes. Then nothing out of the ordinary is screened for." Jim's voice trailed off as he thought about his hypothesis.

"If someone had a good working knowledge of how to use non-traditional chemicals or drugs, they could make natural or accidental causes the first and obvious choice." Jim said and suddenly looked lost in thought. He stared out one of the multi-pained windows of the lodge.

"Jim, what are you thinking?" Daly prodded as the silence grew for several minutes.

"Well, I don't want to jump too quickly to any conclusions, but that could point to someone with significant pharmacology training, or even a medical doctor."

"Someone who had intimate knowledge of and access to all the victims. And potentially had suffered some kind of trauma creating a psychotic break," Daly mused out loud. "That could be a pretty good start towards a profile if this is a serial type murder. It would tend to favor a female suspect, given the use of poison or drugs tends to be the choice for the fairer sex."

Jim stood up and walked to the window he'd been peering out earlier. He began to pace a few steps, reversed direction and returned to the window; obviously deep in thought and becoming a bit agitated.

"What is it Jim? You look displeased with something you're thinking," Mark prodded.

Jim looked at him, then at Daly. He started to say something, then returned to looking out the window in disturbed silence.

"Jim, we're just spit-balling ideas here, so you don't need to be concerned we'll go too far with something you're thinking. Just spill it." Daly implored.

"What I'm about to tell you needs to stay in this room as it could be damaging to friends close to us. I'm sworn not to share any specifics with anyone. Is that understood?" Jim stared hard at Daly until she nodded agreement, then moved his gaze to Mark for the same confirmation.

"Ok then. You may not know this but Mary Simon was married before she met Michael and had a son and daughter from that marriage."

Jim continued, "They lost their teenage son in a tragic accident that Mary has never been open to talking about. The loss of her son destroyed her. She blamed her husband for not being more protective to the point where they became irreconcilable and divorced."

Her daughter blamed Mary for the divorce. She made Mary's life miserable until she was old enough to be on her own, at which point she left. Once on her own again, Mary moved on and rebooted her life. She attended college and became a registered pharmacist, which is when she met Michael. This was all before she started her Delicacies du Jour business. It was before the poker group began."

Jim hesitated and sipped his water. Clearing his throat, he continued, "Mary and Michael began having problems and eventually divorced. During that time, Louise became a confidant with Mary and they became very close; a shared connection with their medical-pharma training and all, I suppose."

"A couple of years ago you probably remember Mary taking a three-month extended trip overseas. In confidence, Mary told Louise she was not going overseas. In actuality, She had breast cancer and was going to have a double mastectomy performed. She talked this with Louise to get advice and a referral to an oncologist at the hospital where Louise worked."

"The surgery was a success in conjunction with the

follow up radiation and chemo treatments. From the experience and a lot of Mary's own personal research on cancer, she developed very strong feelings on junk food, unhealthy eating habits, etc."

"As a result, she decided to change her eating habits radically."

"Along with these dietary changes, Louise noticed Mary's personality shifted as well. She turned into someone less tolerant. Fanatical about food choices, and almost vengeful when other people made unhealthy choices. You probably have witnessed this at some of our poker group get-togethers," Jim looked at Daly to Mark as they nodded this was true.

Daly added, "Yes we have noticed her overreacting a couple of times over the last several months. We thought it was just the overall stress from losing good friends showing up in weird ways."

"Yes, and that's probably the right answer," Jim said with concern still in his voice. "I'm probably letting our profiling session lead me in directions that over-step any facts we have. It's just that as we developed the specifics of who might be our killer, Mary popped into my head as someone who would fit the profile."

"You know another aspect of this is developing a common motive across Tommy, Chuck and Mike," Mark offered. "It is interesting that all three were in similar businesses; all related to food or snack companies. Mary's newfound obsession with healthy eating wouldn't exactly endear them to her or her advocacy for healthy eating, would it?"

"I don't know, we're probably stretching coincidental happenings to fit the specifics of a friend we're too familiar with," Jim said as he waved his hand as if to brush the conversation into the corner of the room. "Thinking a good friend could lose her sanity and become a cold-blooded killer out of a zealousness for better eating is pretty far-fetched I'd say. And she certainly isn't the only person around with pharma-type training or expertise."

"Agreed," Daly said. "Let's continue working some other angles in our remaining time and see if any more likely scenarios appear."

"One connection I'll need to talk to Louise about comes to mind," Jim said thoughtfully. "A little over a year ago, Louise received a large bonus from her hospital. About the same time, Mary's business had been doing quite well, and she talked Louise into investing in some venture Tommy Hemmings was pulling together; a joint venture of some kind. Pretty speculative, but something Louise and Mary decided to do with part of their windfall cash."

"That could be an interesting coincidence if Chuck and Mike were investors, too," Daly mused.

"Kind of points another finger at Mary being a suspect if there's some financial angle benefitting her," Mark added.

"I'll check with Louise when she gets home to see if anyone else invested in Tommy's venture, and what it was all about," Jim offered.

They worked through several other potential theories over the next hour. They were sadly lacking in facts on family, ex-lovers, or even business dealings. They were left with baseless speculations. These alternatives didn't lead to any fleshed out hypotheses. When it became clear discussing other options was leading them nowhere, they returned back to the premise that one of their own poker club friends was their most promising suspect.

"I think we've done all we can do today," Mark conceded as he began collecting the multiple pages of notes they'd created. "Let's give our thinking some time to gestate. See if anything hits us as more credible over the next few days. Then we can regroup and assess where we are."

"Sounds right. I can do some discreet digging on Tommy, Chuck and Mike to see if anything turns up as connections along the family, ex-lover, or business lines," Daly said as she pushed her chair back from the table.

"Remember, not a word about the "Mary hypothesis" until we have something more to go on. Louise would absolutely eviscerate me and let the buzzards feast on my entrails if she learns I broke her confidence with Mary," Jim admonished them while making a long slicing motion with his finger from his chin to his belly button.

"No worries old friend, we'll keep working the scenarios to find a better match to all the facts. Ones we can feel confident are on the right track," Mark assured him as he opened the door and motioned for Jim and Daly to go through.

In the parking lot, Mark and Daly climbed into Mark's convertible.

Daly looked at Mark holding his eyes in her intense gaze. "You know we can't just assume Mary is not a suspect because she's our friend, right? We have to keep things moving forward. Who knows who might be next?"

Mark nodded, pressed the ignition button and sighed deeply, "And you and I need to tread carefully. We might be on that list too."

Chapter 13

At the back of her office was a six-panel door leading into a separate alcove area.

This inner sanctum was long and narrow. Its only illumination came from a fluorescent ceiling panel which revealed shelves and cabinets lining the areas above and to the sides of a wet bar. Faux-painted tropical ferns against a light green background covered the walls. A two-burner gas stovetop was to the left of the sink, and a black granite counter area to the right, with closed oak cupboards and a mini-refrigerator below.

The shelves were overflowing with canisters, jars, and tins of all sizes along with a few coffee and soup mugs. A small coffee grinder and a French coffee press were at the back of the counter top.

Closer examination revealed the shelved containers carefully labeled with their contents: green tea, oolong tea, white leaf tea, lemon extract, garlic cloves, cinnamon sticks, coffee beans of various varieties and a plethora of other natural and organic items arranged in alphabetical order. The refrigerator contained a labeled mason jar of honey and what looked like antique quart milk jars; reminiscent of those delivered fresh from a dairy in the 1950's to your front porch.

No sugar, no sweeteners, no pre-packaged or processed foods of any kind trespassed in this all-natural retreat.

The items on her shelf were a stark contrast to her mother's pantry from her childhood. Slim Jims, cookies, caramel corn, assorted candy and Twinkies had filled those cupboards.

Her thoughts turned to that day of her revelation so many years ago.

Following the loss of her son, her love of gardening had returned to fill her empty life and brought her back from the deepest depths of depression.

But this time, her guilt could not be assuaged. The guilt she felt for not being able to intervene to save her mother still weighed heavy on her heart. Only now it was multiplied a hundredfold by her helplessness to save her son from death at the hands of his best friend.

Then as if God himself had taken pity on her and her plight, she came across an article about exotic vegetables and fruits she might try next. As part of the article there was a warning against the toxic nature of many of these plants, flowers or even parts of vegetables that might prove harmful to your health; like the leaves of rhubarb being quite poisonous even though the rhubarb stalks make an excellent pie.

This had led to her epiphany.

She no longer needed to wallow in self-pity, feeling helpless to do anything about the afflictions of her mother. The secret was in her garden if she just turned her attention to these toxic beauties of nature. She knew this knowledge hadn't accidentally made its way into her hands, but was given to her for a purpose.

She studied which plants were toxic and it became clear this was the road to her redemption from the awful guilt she'd suffered since her mother's death. Most of the plants she sought were readily available through mail order houses specializing in gardening. This made the materials for her vengeance abundant and inexpensive.

The burden of her bottomless guilt lifted from her.

She now had the means to make those who had led to her mother's lingering death pay for their atrocities.

And seek retribution for Danny as well.

Now, eight years into her quest for vengeance, she had built up quite a potpourri of deadly or incapacitating options for her use.

Five years ago, she'd purchased an upscale house in Simi Valley with a small green house at the back of the property. The secluded nature of the property gave her more privacy to pursue her botanical endeavors.

It also provided the ability to keep her specifically designed laboratory in the same location and away from anyone's notice. Her more challenging extracts required the use of basic glassware items, Bunsen burners and an array of distillation gear allowing for gentle removal of the more sensitive components. This setup had enhanced her ability to not only create the toxins for her purpose, but also transform them into tailored delivery mechanisms: liquids, powders, salves, or even hand lotions were possible means to her ends with this capability.

She set down the small shopping bag she'd brought with her.

Crouched in front of the cabinet on the right side of her kitchenette, she dialed the combination to an inset lock. She used these hidden shelves to keep her treasures away from prying eyes that might make their way into her secret space. Behind the cabinet's front was a series of pull-out shelves, allowing her to store her canisters, jars, vials and zip lock bags.

She admired her menagerie of death-inducing agents as she ran her finger across some of the labels: castor beans/ricin extract, rosary peas, monkshood, winter-sweet, Angel's trumpet, hemlock, English yew, snakeroot, strychnine tree fruit seeds, daphne, narcissists, oleander, rhododendron, choke cherry leaves and nightshade.

It had taken her years to perfect her sinister garden's delights. It nearly overwhelmed her with a feeling of accomplishment every time she visited the many choices for her mission.

And that mission burned in her: to rid the world of human garbage purveyors, one scoundrel at a time.

She pulled out the bottom shelf. Her mementos of past conquests were displayed in a felt-lined case. She smiled as she touched her most recent additions. Each was labeled with block letters underneath it; TJH, CLK and MRG.

Monkshood

Lily of the Valley

Angels Trumpet

Water Hemlock

Castor Beans

Oleander

She gazed at her trophies and was transported to her mother's bedside. To those last days of spoonfeeding her when she had grown too morbidly obese to manage it herself.

At the tender age of eighteen, she had okay'd the doctor's desire to try gastric bypass surgery as a last resort to help her mother control her weight gain.

Her mother, barely able to understand what was happening, was led to her slaughter by these supposed doctors there to help the helpless. Instead, these leaches fed off their patients' desperation and ignorance to pad their retirement funds with no thought of whether their victims lived or died.

She still remembered the gastroenterologist's hollow sympathy as he came out of surgery. The haughty doctor hadn't given her mother a fighting chance and hadn't really cared. He felt she was "too far gone to save."

Not worth saving. That's what he should have said if he'd been truthful about how he really felt. He was just like all the other filthy surgeons taking huge amounts of money while doing shoddy work with no real sense of caring.

Her next victim wouldn't be preying on any helpless innocents any more.

She removed the gardening gloves she'd recently bought from the shopping bag. *What's the perfect little surprise from my garden to escort you to your rotting hell?*

Her eyes traced over the many vials and came to rest on an emulsion she'd prepared and labeled as, "Hemlock Root Sap."

This should do nicely.

She had come across this plant extract a few years ago as a particularly deadly addition to her menagerie. It could be ingested or absorbed through the skin, if properly reduced to the emulsion type she'd chosen. With extended skin contact, the emulsion would enter the victim's nervous system leading to a grand mal seizure. This was usually followed by a quick death involving convulsions so strong bones could break. In many cases the victim might swallow their tongue and asphyxiate.

She reached into one of her cabinet drawers and extracted a set of thick chemically resistant gloves. Putting them on, she reached for the targeted vial. She turned the gloves she'd purchased inside out and spread them out on the counter on a disposable plastic sheet. She then reached into the same drawer she had retrieved the gloves from and withdrew a small basting brush.

She proceeded to brush the deadly liquid onto the gloves interior lining. As she patiently worked to fully saturate the gloves' linings, a deep feeling of completion, almost sexual in nature, welled up in her causing her face to flush.

In a few hours you'll be dry and ready to meter out justice, removing at least one elitist doctor from this world.

Rest in peace mother, your little flower's making them pay.

Chapter 14

Louise stepped through the door of the Santa Monica General Hospital into streaming sunlight so bright she had to shade her eyes.

She took a deep breath and smiled as she walked down the steps to the parking lot. Her unassuming Prius awaited her in the parking space marked "L.A. Jensen."

Louise loved Thursday afternoons. These were her mid-week breaks from the hospital. She was always done with her rounds and final paperwork by eleven o'clock and ready for some needed "me time."

As she pulled away from the hospital heading for the 101, her thoughts turned to the loss of Tommy, Chuck and Mike.

As a doctor, and more to the point, a surgeon, she was accustomed to dealing with patients in dire circumstances. On rare occasion she'd lost a patient when her skills had not proven adequate, or fate took the steering wheel from her hands. But losing close friends in rapid succession was beyond any work-related grief she'd had to face. She knew the wives of these good men. All the plans that would now go unrealized were just too much for her to dwell on.

Even more disturbing, Jim had questioned her concerning her and Mary's involvement in Tommy's joint venture. She couldn't imagine how dabbling in a speculative upstream investment could be linked to Tommy's death. Tommy had kept information on the venture very close to the vest so she didn't know who beyond her and Mary were partners. Jim had seemed suspicious of Mary's intentions, but she knew her best friend had been well intentioned. Mary had not pressured her to invest, seeming to see it as an opportunity to share with a good friend.

She sighed, *Louise, the day's too nice to crawl into dark places where no light can reach. Enjoy the day and the time you have as life is certainly too short.*

Her little self pep talk seemed to drive away the sadness she had been chasing down a rabbit hole. Her thoughts turned to the new plantings she had waiting for her in her garage portico. *Surely giving nourishment and a good home to daisies, chrysanthemums and roses is a way to celebrate the full glory of this beautiful day.*

A small smile returned as she signaled to merge onto the 101. She switched on the radio which was playing Pharrel's *Happy*. Her eyebrows raised in approval and she let out a small snort, "Guess you agree," her fingers beginning to tap along.

Twenty minutes later, Louise pulled into her garage.

Anxious to begin her gardening, she quickly gathered up her briefcase from the passenger seat floor, and headed through the garage portico area and into the house. She donned her favorite gardening gear: capris, flowered blouse tied at the waist, garish hot pink clogs and a floppy hat with "Born to Bloom" emblazoned across the front brim.

Her new plantings seemed to greet her as she re-entered the garage to gather up these beauties along with her small gardening spade and gloves. She thought it strange that only one pair of her gloves was lying across the workbench. She typically left two or three pairs out where they could be easily accessed. *Could Jim have moved my gloves or stored them somewhere?* she puzzled as she slipped the gloves on. She'd have to ask Jim if he'd been doing some organizing in the garage when he got home.

She exited the rear garage door to the large flowerbed she'd be embellishing today.

The bed was already in full bloom with assorted flowers, geraniums, rose bushes, hostas, and ground-covering phlox bordering the bed in vibrant purple. A section of the bed farthest from the house was already cleared and awaiting the new recruits Louise would bring to it with loving care.

Louise placed the tray of flowers down next to the tilled black dirt swatch, about three feet by three feet in size. Kneeling beside her treasures, she carefully placed the individual flowers into the open space. She began rearranging them until she had the desired balance she was seeking. Grasping her garden trowel, she began digging holes to receive the plantings from their temporary plastic sleeves.

The afternoon sun felt wonderful on her arms and calves as she patiently tucked the flowers into their new environment. The temperature was creeping into the eighties and Louise could feel the sweat forming on her forehead and dripping down her nose. She brushed it away with the back of her gloves and from time to time straightened her back to stretch out the kinks before continuing her task.

Louise stopped to drink from the plastic water bottle she'd placed beside her work area, and noticed her hands seemed to be cramping as she twisted the screw cap off the bottle. She thought this strange as her hands were particularly strong, being a surgeon. She'd only been gardening for thirty minutes or so.

As she sipped the water, she felt her throat constricting, making it difficult to swallow. She assumed the heat had been more intense than she had assumed, and started to get up to go inside.

Her legs began twitching uncontrollably.

Unable to bear any weight on her failing legs, she began belly crawling towards the house. She had left her cellphone in the kitchen as it was her way of declaring this as her private time. She hadn't wanted to take any calls from the hospital, which were almost nonstop if she made herself available.

Now her phone was her only friend. She needed to make her way to it as something very wrong was afflicting her.

Her medically trained mind started to run through all the possibilities. She began crawling across the thirty feet to the garage, turning the options over in her head; stroke, heat exhaustion, or some unknown allergy to something in the dirt.

None of these made sense from her knowledge of typical symptomology.

About ten feet from the garage door, Louise's whole body was cramping. She could no longer move forward and went into a fetal position with her limbs jerking and her hands cramping into tightly wound balls.

The pain was excruciating and her neck muscles began contracting with strong, uncontrolled spasms causing her to beat her head against the ground.

She felt all the blood drain from her face and she knew she was about to lose consciousness. Then she thought she saw a figure standing over her.

Oh thank God! Someone's here.

And all went black.

———————◦《◉》◦———————

She stood over Louise's unconscious, but still twitching body and glowered down at her.

Her plan had worked beautifully. Earlier this morning she had entered the Jensen's garage after they'd left for work and left her hemlock tainted gloves on the workbench. She'd made sure to pick up the three pairs already there to ensure Louise would be left with only one option.

She'd then left and returned about thirty minutes before Louise had arrived home for her typical Thursday afternoon time off.

Parking in the alley behind the house, she'd positioned herself behind a hedge at the back of the Jensen's yard. She had a front row seat for Louise's slow and painful demise.

It couldn't have gone better. Hearing Louise happily humming away as she planted her flowers with no sense of her impending doom...until the hemlock penetrating her skin began to have its effect.

Such a painful death she'd never witnessed. A rush came over her as she looked down at Louise's twitching muscles. "So Doctor, it looks like there's no one here that can help you. Guess you're "too far gone to save." Oh well, one less butcher in the world is a good start if you ask me."

Louise's breathing became ragged. She convulsed, arching her back. Her eyes opened, rolled back so only the whites were showing. Her tongue lolled out the side of her mouth with blood dripping down her cheek from where she had bitten through the protruding muscle.

Her seizure took on all the appearances of a grand mal, continuing for about three minutes.

Then Louise's body went limp as she let out one last breath.

She bent down over Louise, nudging her roughly to make sure she wasn't going to catch a second wind and suddenly revive.

Putting on the rubber, chemical resistant gloves she'd brought with her, she leaned over the body. She removed the tainted gloves from Louise's tightly clenched hands, still rigid from the poison's effects. Taking Louise's original gloves she'd purloined earlier in the day, she now placed these onto Louise's hands. She rubbed a bit of fresh dirt on the gloves to make them appear to have been recently used.

"There that ought to do it."

She placed the other gloves she'd taken earlier on the workbench. Looking around to ensure no neighbors seemed to be nearby, she slipped into the house making her way to the kitchen area.

Opening a few drawers, she found the prize she was looking for. Smiling at her treasure, she exited out the back garage door, across the lawn and through the hedge to her waiting car.

As she stepped through the hedge, she looked back at Louise's lifeless form. Something ironic suddenly occurred to her.

"You're in good company Louise. As your fellow lover of hemlock, Socrates, said, 'Death may be the greatest of all human blessings.'"

Chapter 15

"Mark, got to…come now. Found Louise unconscious…not breathing. Come now!" Jim sputtered into the phone.

"Jim what are you saying? I can hardly understand you. What's wrong with Louise?" Mark said as he gripped his desk phone tighter, leaning forward with creased brows.

"Just come to the hospital. *Now!*"

Mark heard the click of Jim's phone go dead and dropped his phone into the desk cradle. He stood and reached into his pocket for his cellphone. Giant striding his way to his car, he speed-dialed Daly and got her on the second ring.

"Daly honey. Something's happened to Louise. Jim wants me to meet him at the hospital right away."

"Oh my god. Did he say what happened?"

"He was totally panicked on the phone so I couldn't get anything other than to meet him at the hospital. I'm on my way there now."

"I'm coming too. I've been at the LAPD central

station doing some research, so it will take me about an hour with traffic. Call me if you learn anything before I get there." She clicked off.

Mark screeched his tires as he pulled from the parking lot and used a combination of his BMW 428's paddle shifters, medians and bike lanes to make his way through the beginning of rush hour traffic.

He pulled into Santa Monica General Hospital fifteen minutes later. Rather than look for a parking place, he just wheeled into Louise's reserved space in the front of the hospital.

He half-sprinted to the lobby receptionist. Looking at her with wild eyes, he breathlessly asked, "I'm a friend of Louise and Jim Jensen, can you tell me which room Louise is in?"

The receptionist, Lindsay H. based on the nametag on her left shoulder, looked up from her screen at Mark. Doing a double take of his anxious expression with sweat starting to bead on his forehead, Lindsay H. said, "And you're who again?"

"I'm Mark Ford, a good friend of Louise Jensen who is a surgeon here. Her husband called me and said she'd been brought here and I need to locate them both. Please hurry."

Lindsay H. looked skeptically at Mark, then returned her eyes to her screen and began punching a few keys to bring up patient information. "I don't see any Louise Jensen being admitted. I'm sorry. Maybe you should call your friend to see if it was this hospital."

Mark spun away from the receptionist's desk and

clawed his phone from his pants pocket, hitting the redial for Jim's last call. The phone rang and rang but Jim wasn't answering.

That couldn't be good.

Mark glared at the receptionist, then strode away from her desk towards the Emergency Room. Surely they would know if Louise was still being treated there or had moved on to another wing of the hospital. Mark pushed through the double doors to the ER clearly marked with "Authorized Personnel Only." Stepping through the doors, he grabbed the first orderly he could lay hands on.

"Did you receive a Louise Jensen here in the last half hour?"

The orderly looked blankly at Mark and said, "You know you're not supposed to be in here, right?" Seeing Mark wasn't budging, he let out an exasperated sigh and pointed to a busy receiving desk about halfway down the corridor.

"Check with them. They'll know who's come through here."

Mark sprinted down the corridor and draped himself over the desk of the head nurse running the station, "Can you help me please. I need to know if a Louise Jensen just came through here. Her husband, Jim, called me and asked me to meet him here."

The nurse looked into Mark's face, only a few inches from her own, and said, "Sir, please step back or I'll have you removed from this ER."

Mark complied but kept his gaze fully locked on the nurse, "Please can you tell me if Louise Jensen was just here or admitted?"

Before the nurse could compose herself to deal with his request, Mark saw Jim through a small window in a waiting room door just down from the reception desk. Stepping away from the desk, Mark walked up to the door's window and felt his heart fall through his stomach.

He could see Jim had his head in his hands and was sobbing uncontrollably.

He knocked lightly on the door, getting Jim's attention, and then pushed it open knowing he didn't want to hear what was about to be said.

It took several minutes for Jim to compose himself enough to relay the horrific news to Mark.

Louise didn't make it, and had been declared DOA.

Mark placed his arm around Jim and just sat there.

No words.

Just numb.

Daly arrived an hour later, already knowing Louise had passed away from an earlier phone call from Mark, and joined them in the waiting room.

"Jim, I'm so sorry," she said with tears streaming down her face. She hugged him and sobbed.

"No cause of death from any of the EMT's or doctors in ER. I guess they'll have to run tests to know what happened," Jim finally offered with a flatness to his voice. "All I know is she's gone. The love of my life is gone and it doesn't make any sense."

Daly's eyes began to tear again, and the hollowness inside of Mark was heavier than he'd ever felt.

As they sat in numbed silence, there was a knock on

the door. Mary Simon swung the door open and stepped into the waiting room.

"My god Jim. I just heard from neighbors who saw the Life Squad at your house. They said it was Louise. Is she ok?"

As Mark and Daly looked expectantly at Jim to let Mary know of Louise's passing, Jim stood up. His face moved from one of total grief, to a reddening anger taking over his cheeks. He reached for Mary's shoulders and held them in his vice-like grip.

"Did you do this? *Did you?* Louise helped you when you needed it most and *this* is how you repay her?" Jim's words came out like venom as he looked at Mary in disgust and loathing.

Mark stepped in to release Jim's grip on Mary, inserting himself as a barrier to Jim's burning anger.

"Jim, what are you talking about? Mary hasn't done anything." Mark pleaded as Jim stepped away.

Jim seemed unable to remain in Mary's presence as he was almost shaking with anger. He moved towards the open door, then turned and glared at Mary. He coldly spat out, "Just stay away from me! Louise was *everything* to me and you've taken her away."

As Jim exited the room, he brushed past Sergeant McClarey who had been about to enter when Jim's accusation of Mary had occurred. With a very puzzled look on his face, he looked at Daly, then Mark, and finally Mary, letting his gaze sit for a few seconds on each. "I heard dat m'Lady Jensen was brought up here and thought I should come by t' see if anything I could be a bit o' help with."

Mary, still reeling from Jim's accusation, said, "I need to go. This makes no sense. I can't believe she's gone."

Mark reached for Mary, "Jim is obviously too distraught to know what he's saying."

Mary looked through Mark. She shrugged past him and the puzzled Sergeant McClarey to exit the waiting room.

Left alone with Sergeant McClarey, Daly and Mark shifted uncomfortably in the silence. After a moment, Mark said, "I guess you heard that Louise didn't make it. No explanations yet for what happened. They'll need a full autopsy to get to a cause of death is what they're saying."

"Yup, I got dat much. What I didn't catch was why Master Jensen would be blamin his lady friend for his wife's demise. You think you could shed a bit o' light on dat for me?" McClarey's voice lilted up with his question.

Mark and Daly looked at each other uncomfortably for a second.

Then Daly said, "I think you'll need to talk to Jim about that. Good day Sergeant."

They exited past the sergeant's arched eyebrow as he held the door for them to pass.

Chapter 16

"Sergeant McClarey?"

"Speakin."

"My name is Barry Allen, I'm a toxicology analyst for the Santa Monica Medical Examiner's Lab. You asked us to get to you as soon as we had any toxicology results on a Louise Jensen. Looks like significant traces of some kind of natural poison in her tissues, especially through the arms and hand areas. We're doing more tests to more definitively say what it was, but enough here to say she didn't die of natural causes. The toxin was definitely the CoD."

"When will you 'ave more on the exact source o' the poison, son," McClarey said.

"We should have it within the next couple of days, Sergeant."

"Well, keep at it. Important t' have anything you can. It's lookin more like a murder case now you know." McClarey hung up the phone and leaned back in his chair as he studied the ceiling lost in thought.

So the plot thickens and maybe m'Lady Ford's instincts are lookin a wee bit t' the better.

McClarey pushed back from his desk, turning to one of the policemen near him and said, "I think it's time t' knock up the grievin widower and see if he can enlighten me day."

His fellow officer looked questioningly at him, shook his head and returned to the report he was working on.

McClarey grabbed his tweed jacket and headed out the door to pay Jim Jensen a visit.

McClarey exited the police station and climbed into his late model Ford Taurus provided by the bonnie taxpayers of Santa Monica. He drove out of the lot, headed for San Fernando. He'd plucked Jensen's address from the file he'd started the day before when Louise Jensen's death appeared to be less than natural.

He was starting to feel more alive than he'd felt in quite some time. There was nothing like a knotty murder case to get his juices flowing again.

As he drove he reflected back on the circuitous path that had led him to this mecca of sunshine and tans. It was so different from his previous thirty years on the damp isles of Ireland and England.

He'd been driven from his earliest days in Belfast to be a policeman, and beyond that to make his mark as a detective. After five years with the Belfast constabulary, he'd tested and become a detective. A few years after that, he'd transferred to London's east end. There he'd continued to excel as a detective with particularly good instincts when it came to the more serious crimes involving murder and mayhem.

That was also where he met the love of his life, Lottie Wainwright.

They'd fallen madly in love and married within a few short months after first meeting.

He had continued his penchant for solving difficult cases, and was promoted to Detective Sergeant after three years. Given his success and stock was rising with the London constabulary, he reached for the brass ring. He applied for a post with Scotland Yard. With the strong support of his chief inspector, he was accepted; Sean McClarey, Sergeant Inspector of Scotland Yard.

He had reached a pinnacle he'd only dared to dream about.

Three years into a successful career with The Yard, he and Lottie decided they could afford a family and Lottie became pregnant. It was a difficult pregnancy and seven months into it, he needed to take a sabbatical to tend to Lottie and the baby-to-be.

But it wasn't to be.

His eyes teared as he looked out through the windshield at the sunny day surrounding him. His breath caught in his throat every time he went back to those darkest of days. Losing Lottie and the baby in a breach birth had brought him to his knees. Every time those dark days revived in the recesses of his mind, he felt the pain return as if it was yesterday.

He'd gone into a dark hole back then. He hadn't been sure at the time if he'd ever find a way to move on.

After months of despondency, his supervising chief at Scotland Yard had approached him about an overseas assignment. He suggested it would be a chance for him to get his head straight and be in less familiar surroundings; a place that didn't constantly remind him of his loss as a way to move forward.

He knew he couldn't continue to wallow in his misery so he agreed to accept the long-term assignment in southern California. His chief had an old friend who was now the chief of police for Santa Monica.

A favor was asked and granted.

He became the resident Irishman of the Santa Monica PD. That was two years ago and he'd definitely done some personal healing in the new role. It still hadn't stopped the memories of Lottie from flooding his world every few days; especially when he had to deal with a poor bloke like Jim Jensen losing the lady of his life.

Nonetheless, he was returning to the chase; being one of the good chaps. Bringing those who buggered up others lives to justice was what he knew he was meant for in this life.

As he pulled onto the Jensen's street, he took a deep breath and shook off the memories. They wouldn't serve him well in a murder investigation. He needed to be sharp. He needed to make Lottie proud again, whenever she happened to be looking down from above.

On the third ring of the doorbell, Jim opened his front door. He looked at McClarey with hollow eyes. "What do you want?" he said with the inflection of someone looking to be left alone.

"Master Jensen, sorry to knock you up, but I wanted t' let you know how sorry I am about yer lady." McClarey studied Jim for a few seconds and noted Jim seemed tired beyond words. "And I'd like t' share some details from the Medical Examiner's Office that came t' me attention if you have a bit o' time."

Jim motioned the sergeant in and led him through the foyer to a family room with leather couches and chairs set in front of a stone hearth fireplace. A coffee table centered in front of one of the couches was strewn with take-out food boxes, Coke cans and a half-gone bottle of Jack Daniels. Jim sagged into the couch with the debris around him. Sergeant McClarey took a well-padded and worn chair to its side.

"So what details did you want to discuss?"

"Master Jensen, may I call you Jim?" Jim nodded but didn't look to care about much of anything, let alone what someone called him. "Good. Then, Jim, I had asked the medical examiner t' run their chemist tests on yer wife on a rush basis and they came back with some disturbin results."

Jim sat forward, now staring intently at the sergeant and asked impatiently, "So what have you found?"

"It appears a biologic toxin o' some kind came in contact with m'Lady Jensen's hands and arms. They need t' run it through a bit more t' know exactly the source, but it's enough t' know it's the cause o' her affliction." He let this information sit there for a minute as Jim seemed to be mulling it over. "I also need t' ask you somethin. I couldn't help but notice you were a might bit upset with yer lady friend at the hospital. Would you care t' shed some light on what dat was about?"

Jim sat back into the couch and seemed to be conflicted on how he might answer the question posed, then sat forward and said, "I do have some thoughts on who might be behind this and potentially other recent murders that have been cast aside as accidental in nature." He let this assertion hang in the air for several seconds.

"I've been working with the Fords to see if we could come up with anything to explain the losses of some very close friends I'm sure you're aware of." Jim looked at McClarey to ensure he was tracking with him.

McClarey nodded for Jim to continue.

"We'd established a basic hypothesis that seemed to be consistent with the facts we had. Maybe even more so with what you've just shared with me on Louise. We're working under the assumption that our friend's deaths are linked through one common killer. Beyond that we think the use of biological agents could account for the deaths of Chuck Kohler and Tommy Hemmings, and potentially Mike Gentry."

"And I would now add to that list...my wife." Jim breathed in deeply and exhaled, continuing his train of thought, "Further, we believe someone skilled in medical areas and knowledgable of chemical and biological effects on the body could be behind these crimes."

"Interestin theory. Dat still doesn't explain why you took such exception with yer lady friend?" McClarey let his half-question linger in the air.

Jim looked down at his hands as he rubbed his fingertips together distractedly. "I was distraught...looking to strike out at anyone when you arrived at the hospital. I overreacted to Mary showing up. She is a potential person who could fit the profile we created for the killer. She's also gone through some very serious issues which seem to have changed her in the last several months."

"Would you care t' elaborate a bit more on what you mean by "issues" and "changed her," Jim?" McClarey said patiently as he leaned forward in his chair to study Jim more closely.

"I want to be clear. I don't have any proof Mary has done anything wrong. I'm feeling quite out on a limb pointing the smoking gun, or in this case, poison potion, in her direction. In any case, what had drawn me to consider her as a suspect was shared in confidence with me by Louise. I'm not really comfortable talking about it any further. Just let it suffice that she went through some medical issues. Her personality seemed to take on a harder edge in certain areas; especially around the topic of eating healthier. At times, she seemed almost zealous about her newfound diet. She was equally zealous, but in a negative way, about others who didn't share her beliefs or contributed to the nonhealthy diets of others."

"I only tell you this as it seemed relevant at the time. Tommy, Chuck and Mike were all associated with different aspects of the food industry which Mary had issues with. Honestly, I'm not sure how Louise would fit into that hypothesis. She was as much about healthy eating as anyone I know given her work to help people afflicted with eating disorders. It doesn't really fit our proposed hypothesis at all anymore," Jim sighed as he leaned back. He looked at McClarey as if hoping the sergeant might be able to help fit the pieces together.

"I see. If I'm understandin you then, yer thinkin this Mary Simon might not be the culprit you thought she was yesterday as you don't see her motivation t' do m'Lady Jensen any harm. Is dat about right?" McClarey looked at Jim letting his question sink in for a minute.

"Well, I don't know what to think at this point. I suppose there could be some other motivation to hurt Louise. I just can't fathom what it would be as they were good friends and even confidants. I don't know anymore," Jim said as he shook his head.

"Ok then, well you've been through the wringer and out the other side, so I'll be takin me leave and let you get some rest," McClarey rose and stretched out his hand to Jim. "I truly am sorry for yer loss Jim. I lost me wife just over two years ago. All I can say izza does get better if you give it some time."

Jim shook his hand and looked at McClarey. His features softened a bit and he asked, "How did you get through it?"

"You never get totally through it. But you know in yer heart yer little lady would've wanted you t' move on with yer life. And dat's what you do." McClarey half-smiled and gripped Jim's shoulder with his free hand and added, "One step at a time."

McClarey climbed into his Taurus and he gave a call to the desk sergeant. "Sergeant, would you do me a favor and look up the address o' a Mary Simon?" McClarey pulled out his note pad from his inside jacket pocket and jotted down the address. "Thank you sergeant. Only a few blocks away."

McClarey wheeled his car from the curb and wondered what Mary Simon would have to say about all this.

Would she be the grieving friend of Louise Jensen?

Or a cold-blooded tart in a merino wool jumper.

Chapter 17

Mary Simon lived three blocks from the Jensens. McClarey pulled to the curb outside her house about three minutes after he'd left Jim Jensen's.

The house presence was quite striking with a circular driveway nicely appointed with decorative trees and shrubs. A hanging bougainvillea trellis with mature vines formed an entry tunnel from the driveway. Snow in Summer groundcover hugged the edge of the walkway with their delicate white blooms. Three large steps led up to the front door.

He rang the doorbell.

After a few unsuccessful attempts to raise anyone, he noticed a sidewalk leading to the back of the house. He decided to see if anyone was home and hadn't heard the doorbell.

He followed the exterior of the house, passing landscaped beds of differing sizes and shapes, each tastefully planted with bright flowers, phlox and miniature shrubs. As he cleared the corner of the house, he could see Mary was on her knees with her back to him, working in her garden.

She appeared to be weeding a row of kale, set between various rows of assorted vegetables and herbs: spinach, cabbage, zucchini, tomatoes, onions, lavender, basil, cilantro, rosemary, thyme and a few more unidentifiable greens. All laid out meticulously throughout the twenty by thirty foot space. A three foot, white lattice fence enclosed her garden space, and an arched trellis stood at the end facing the rear of the house.

Before he could say anything, she must have sensed his presence and turned with a startled look on her face.

"What…what are you doing here? Who are you?"

"Beg yer pardon m'Lady. I rang at the front, but no one seemed t' hear the chimes. I'm Sergeant McClarey o' the Santa Monica PD," he said as he held his shield out to calm any concerns of an unwanted intruder with malintent on his mind. "Would you mind if I asked you a few questions while I'm here, or would you like me t' come back at a more convenient hour?"

Mary stood up, looked closely at his detective's shield. Appearing satisfied, she nodded and said, "No, no. This is as good a time as any. Let's move to the patio where we can sit."

Exiting her garden through the vine-covered arch, she moved to a glass tabletop under a large sun umbrella on the patio. She had a pitcher of ice tea and glasses on the table from which she poured a glass and offered McClarey the same. Mary pulled up one of the metal patio chairs with a bright orange seat cushion. Settling into it as she took a long sip of her iced tea, " So why would the Santa Monica police want to talk to me anyway?"

"Thank you for allowin me t' interrupt, m'Lady Simon. I promise not t' spoil too much o' this beautiful day for you. I'm followin up a few items from Louise Jensen's unfortunate demise and thought you might be able t' fill in a few blanks for me," McClarey said as he pulled up another of the patio chairs and sat down.

"Please call me Mary. Although I might like the sound of m'Lady, seems a bit pretentious for a California girl, don't you think?" She sipped her tea again as a slight smile creased the corners of her mouth.

"Please excuse my appearance as I've been a bit under the weather with Louise's passing so haven't put on my makeup or dressed for the day. Working in my garden helps lift my spirits, and god knows I need some of that right now. I thought I'd spend some time tending it as a pick-me-up. It was one of the hobbies Louise and I shared."

Sergeant McClarey took in her appearance as he took a sip of his ice tea. She was in what appeared to be running sweats, her blonde hair pulled back into a ponytail, blue eyes encircled in red and her facial features drawn. She looked like she was in mourning; hiding from the sharp edges of the world that had recently cut her deeply. "Not a problem, Mary. I understand you and Louise Jensen were close mates?"

"Louise and I had a very special relationship. Most people are never blessed with a friend they can go to with anything. Louise was that for me. I'll miss her terribly…"

her voice cracked and faded as she gazed unseeingly at the melting ice cubes in her glass. She sighed heavily as tears started to form at the edges of her eyes accentuating the redness.

"I couldn't help but hear Jim Jensen at the hospital have a few words with you. I wondered if you had any thoughts as t' why he might think you wished his lady harm?" he asked as he studied her reaction.

She looked up and met his eyes with a questioning look.

"No. I can't imagine why Jim would say such things. He knows Louise and I were close. Believe me, it tore me up all last night wondering why he would say something so hurtful. I can only assume his grief made him lash out at someone close to Louise, and I was there I suppose. I can't blame him really. It's a tragic loss and he must feel it beyond what I can imagine."

"Have you talked with him to see why he was so angry towards me?" she asked seeming to be genuinely looking for McClarey to help her resolve this painful cloud she was living under.

"Well, as a matter o' fact, I've just come from talkin with Master Jensen exactly t' dat point." He let his words sit for a moment as he continued to watch her reaction. Her eyes were fixed on him expectantly with no sign of calculation or guile.

"It seems Master Jensen has been lookin into the loss o' yer circle o' mates, and has a theory dat someone might be targetin them for manky purposes."

"Are you saying that Jim suspects someone is

behind the deaths of Tommy…Mike…Chuck?" she said incredulously.

As she thought for a few seconds, the connection started to sink in and her questions began to flow. "So are you saying that he thinks they were murdered? And what does that have to do with Louise? Do you know something about how she died?"

McClarey hesitated before answering. Normally, providing too much information to a potential suspect was unwise. In this instance, a little more information might provide just the right amount of rope to see if she followed it to a noose or a lifeline.

"Aye. We 'ave a pretty good idea dat Louise Jensen's demise might be an intentional act," he offered, watching and waiting to see where she went with this bit of info.

"What do you have? I know she came in unconscious and never revived. Do you have something showing someone was there with her and responsible for this?" she said as she leaned forward staring hard at him. "Tell me what you know."

"Well, I can't really get into the wee details of an investigation you understand. Confidentiality and all you know. But there's evidence m'Lady Jensen succumbed t' some kind o' poison she might have come in contact with when she was in her garden."

"You're making no sense. What does her gardening have to do with poison? Why would that make you suspect foul play?"

He studied her reaction. He was having a hard time reading her. Was she legitimately trying to make sense of what he'd shared, or was she practiced at hiding behind the mask of a murderer in a game of deception?

"Well, as I said, I can't really divulge anymore without compromisin me case. But Jim Jensen shared he might have wrongly accused you in the hospital in a moment o' grief. In the heat o' it all, he was linkin your knowledge as a chemist with how his lady and other friends had been dispatched."

"He felt his accusation was wrongly placed when I talked with him today, agreein your relationship with his wife made dat unthinkable," McClarey said as he paused, waiting to see her reaction to this explanation.

Mary sat back in her chair as the realization slowly hit her, "You mean my training as a pharmacist makes me a potential suspect. So Jim thought I somehow poisoned Louise with some chemical concoction...and maybe did the same with Tommy, Mike and Chuck."

Her face took on an incredulous look as she stared out over her backyard, continuing to let the realization of Jim's theory fully sink in.

"Unbelievable," was all she said as they sat for a few moments.

She finally returned from her thoughts and said resolutely, "I guess I shouldn't be too harsh on Jim with what he's going through. Certainly he and Louise had issues before this that probably are weighing heavily on his mind as well."

"Would you mind enlightenin me on what issues yer referrin t', Mary?"

"He probably didn't mention their son Aiden, I

suppose. The loss of Louise has got to make dealing with Aiden's on-going issues even more difficult."

"Issues?" McClarey prodded.

"About eight years ago when Aiden was sixteen he was involved in a horrible accident. His best friend was in the car and was killed. Aiden was cleared of any charges."

"Just a bad luck situation where his car caught some loose gravel on a country road. He lost control, left the road and ended up crashing into a culvert. Aiden hadn't been drinking or anything. But his friend didn't have his seatbelt on and went through the windshield as I understood it from Louise. Aiden really struggled with his friend's death. He was in counseling for years. Louise felt it had changed him from the carefree son she'd known into a more serious and troubled boy."

McClarey pondered this new information for a few seconds, then said, "So you're thinkin Jim Jensen is a bit over-wrought with losing his wife and his son's on-going issue. I suppose yer probably right about him being a bit sideways with all dat."

"I mean what reason would I have to hurt any of my friends, especially Louise?" she said imploringly.

"Well, without gettin into any specifics, Jim Jensen mentioned you had a rough patch a while back. He thought you might have had a change o' heart on some things because o' it in the area of your health," McClarey let this sit seeing where Mary might take it.

"I guess Jim was in a sharing mood when you saw him."

"Yes, I did go through a "rough patch" as you call it;

breast cancer to be more specific. It was life changing to be threatened with cancer at your doorstep. I have made many changes coming out of those very scary times. I don't see how that provides a motive to kill my friends."

"If anything I've been more outspoken on how they might eat better, exercise and stay away from all the junk the world wallows in. But my purpose in chastising them was so they wouldn't have to repeat the mistakes I made that brought cancer into my life," she said indignantly, her voice raising slightly with her agitation.

"Honestly, I think Jim is teetering towards paranoia. I also think he deserves a "pass" with all that's hit him. Nonetheless, I don't see how any logic leads you to my doorstep," she announced with an edge of indignation in her voice.

"Well I can see I'm upsettin yer afternoon, so I'll apologize if I've caused you any grief in me visit and be gettin on," McClarey said as he rose and tipped his cap to Mary, turning to leave.

After taking a few steps, he turned back and said, "By the way, I didn't compliment you on yer garden. Ye've got quite the green thumb by the look o' things."

"Please enjoy the rest of dis glorious day m'Lady," he said as he smiled, tipped his cap a second time and disappeared around the corner of the house.

Chapter 18

Finally giving up on getting any sleep, Daly threw back her rumpled bed coverings.

She had tossed and turned for most of the night like an eight-year old suffering from too much cotton candy, plus a strong dose of unknown phantoms chasing her into some dark abyss.

She quietly shuffled down the hall to the kitchen.

The clock in her coffeemaker glowed "5:00 a.m." She hit the "Brew" button to deliver her morning elixir. Mark had filled the reservoir with water and measured the coffee into the paper filter the night before as one of his standard household duties. A large splash of hazelnut creamer and four sugars later, Daly had her giant sized mug emblazoned with "Badass" on it.

She shuffled towards the front door to get the morning paper.

It was Tuesday, the day after Louise's funeral. Bidding her friends farewell from this celestial blue ball was becoming a real downer. Seeing Jim so destroyed had really impacted Mark as well. She rarely saw her husband in a down moment, with the exception of when he decided to engage her on the subject of having kids.

Mark wanted desperately to start a family. They were approaching their forties, bringing the looming specter of "women too old to have kids, having kids with disabilities" into clear view.

She just couldn't see herself bringing an innocent into a world where she'd seen man commit terrible evils against his fellow man for little or no reason. She knew it wasn't fair to gauge the human race by what she'd seen as a cop and profiler in the serial killer unit of the LAPD; but it was equally hard to pass it off as something she or her offspring could never experience.

The world owed her no passes.

Senseless pain and anguish was passed out regularly. It was like the universal gods were playing bowling for dollars with people's lives; gleefully knocking the pins into the gutter, where they were collected later to be set up for another rousing game of "shit happens."

Mark saw kids as just "part of living a full life," so they'd agreed to disagree.

She didn't stress too much about it as she had the ultimate veto power on this one; a little pillbox she visited regularly to guarantee no surprises.

She retrieved the paper from the front step and returned to their family room. Making herself comfortable, she nested in the corner of their plush suede couch, switched on the tabletop reading lamp and laid the paper beside her.

Staring out into the dark beyond the large floor to

ceiling windows, a feeling of morose helplessness began to consume her. The hard truth of Louise's death hung there in the room. Her morning routine was sacrosanct: coffee, crossword, and Sudoku, but she couldn't work up the interest out of her malaise to follow this hallowed routine.

She didn't have a sense of how long she had stared out into the darkness. The shifting pale light of the sun starting to rise broke through her numbness as she realized the crossword puzzle from the paper laid next to her, untouched. She shifted out of her near-fetal position she'd instinctually gone to with knees tightly curled under her. Sitting up and leaning forward with her elbows on her knees, she became agitated.

I need to pull myself out of this funk. Being Daly the bereaved friend is doing no eff'n good for me or anyone else.

She seemed to have a sudden realization as she sat up straight, *so let's see what Daly the cop can do.*

She stood up with a sense of purpose. Walking back through the kitchen to the main hallway where the basement entrance led down to their finished movie room, bar area and storage room, she flipped on the basement lights from the top of the stairs. Quickly she descended to the lower floor, through the movie room and to the large back storage room.

Rummaging in the far corner, she side-stepped empty boxes and items that were either out of season or of no further use, but not quite ready to visit the garbage can. She found what she was looking for next to a file cabinet.

Extracting a four foot easel with a flip chart, she

hoisted this remnant of playing Pictionary™ from its dark corner. The flip chart was attached by a couple of machine head screws with wing nuts matched to the spacing of the flip chart's pre-punched holes. Grabbing her treasure by the edge of the metal easel's surface, she returned up the stairs to the family room.

Snatching a marker from the pewter mug turned pen-holder on the kitchen desk, she said resolutely and aloud, "Now *this* is what Daly the cop would do."

She reached into a drawer where she had placed Mark's notes from their brainstorming session with Jim the previous week. Retrieving the legal pad along with the marker she went back to the family room.

Now where to begin, where to begin.

She tapped her chin with her finger and thoughtfully reviewed Mark's notes from their meeting.

She wrote headers on five separate flip chart pages. Tearing them from the pad, she hung them on the walls around her by the two inch wide adhesive strip located at the top of each sheet's backside.

Her headers were: Psychopath, Family Member, Ex-girlfriends, Business Deals, and Government.

With the sheets surrounding her on all sides, she began filling in questions she had and any known details under the respective subjects.

At seven thirty, Mark stumbled into the family room rubbing the sleep from his eyes. "So what the heck is all this? You must have gotten up at zero dark thirty."

Continuing to scribble items on the sheets as she moved back and forth between the five charts, she replied hurriedly, "Yeah, I couldn't sleep and moping around was just making me feel worse. I decided to organize our theories from last week with Jim. Plus, I added some of my own research I was working on with my LAPD friends to see where all that might take me. Just the cop in me coming out I guess."

Mark nodded appreciatively at her work. "Not bad," he said as he yawned and moved forward to review what she'd written on the charts. "I didn't realize you had collected this much info since our meeting with Jim."

"I hadn't gotten a chance to bring you up to speed with all the craziness around Louise's..." her voice trailed off not needing or wanting to reiterate the loss of her friend.

"Anyway, this is how my mind works. Laying out all the things we know or want to know helps me keep focused on trying to get to something we can use. And it beats being a useless slug crying in my coffee."

"So, any insights or revelations from your dawn patrol efforts?"

"Biggest thing so far is what the unlikely theories are. My snooping around through public records and any police records makes the ex-girlfriend option not very likely, or extremely well hidden. No unexplained properties or apartments being bankrolled. No suspicious bank transactions. No recurring phone calls to unknown numbers or potential whores in waiting. Nothing that would indicate Tommy, Mike and Chuck were anything but the good husbands we believed them to be."

"Of course that doesn't mean they weren't very good at hiding an extramarital liaison?"

"Sure, but if we assume the same person is behind all the murders, the fact that none of them called some common phone number or crossed paths in parallel ways makes me skeptical an ex-girlfriend is involved. Let alone the improbability that all three would have had relations with her. Somehow that would come out in casual discussions or a reminiscing session of the past given they knew each other for years."

"Ok, let's put that to the bottom of our probable theories list. Any others we can eliminate?"

Daly tapped her chin and moved to the chart titled Government. "This one seemed like a longshot at the time we brought it up. I didn't find any historical issues with government agencies, even the IRS. None of them had early careers that intersected any government agencies directly or indirectly from any records I came across. I think this can join the "ex-girlfriends" discard pile for now."

"That leaves us with Psychopath, Family Member, and Business Deals," Mark mused as he skimmed over the notes and questions Daly had scribbled beneath each category. "Our meeting with Jim mostly focused on the Psychopath option with a penchant for poison as you've captured here."

"Yeah, I need a lot more basic data gathering. For the Business Deal option, I'm thinking of contacting the spouses to cross-check business deals they might have had in common. If they agree to give me access to their financial portfolios that would be a place to start. We met the guy at Tommy's funeral, Greg something, who said he handled Tommy's planning and was working with Chuck. He might be helpful if Pat and Linda are okay with me talking with him."

"And for the Family Members?"

"On the family side, I could do some more digging through public records to see if any court documents or legal disputes. Otherwise I think I'm looking at some tough interviews with the bereaved widows and Jim," Daly's tone conveyed her lack of enthusiasm for the difficult task of interviewing good friends about their loved ones; especially about the ones that might be cold-blooded murderers.

Mark stepped closer to the chart with Psychopath across the top, "Louise's murder throws a new wrench into our Psychopath food terrorist theory. She wasn't in the food business and she probably had the healthiest eating habits of anyone I know."

"It also casts doubt on our lead suspect for that theory. Mary was Louise's best friend and soul mate." Daly did a full stretch up on her toes with her arms to the ceiling, and turned to Mark announcing, "I'm going for a morning run to let all of this percolate and see if I can shake anything out of the coconut tree. Want to join me?"

"Sure, why wouldn't I want to be there when the coconuts start dropping. Let me grab a slurp of coffee and we can head out to do some shakin'."

"OK, but be quick. I still need to make that tuna casserole that Jim loves and get it over to Pat who's coordinating the meals for Jim," she said as she headed for their bedroom to pull on some running gear.

Mark raised his eyebrows and smirked under his breath, "Better that Jim suffer the slings and arrows of Daly's casseroles than I."

Chapter 19

Sergeant McClarey sat at his desk puzzling over notes from his conversations with Jim Jensen and Mary Simon on Tuesday, the day after Louise's funeral. It had been useful to talk to them while they were in shock over Louise's passing. He felt their guards had been down a bit.

He was still in a quandary on what to think about Mary; was she a master deceiver or a mourning friend to Louise? He hadn't picked up any inconsistencies in her questions to him or the paths of logic she'd followed.

Sometimes murderers tried to pry facts from the police during questioning. Hoping to tell if they'd covered their tracks well, or to see how much the police had pulled together from clues. Mary's questions had seemed to be more of the concerned friend genre.

The one aside with Mary he'd not expected was her sharing that Jim and Louise's son had been in a tragic accident several years ago. This seemed like something he should learn a bit more about. Maybe a new ray of light might come from a past tragedy of the victim.

He tapped a few keys on his desk computer and pulled up a direct link to the Santa Monica on-line library. His file on Louise Jensen indicated her son, Aiden, was currently attending college at USC's med school. He was twenty-four years old according to his driver's license. Assuming his accident was at sixteen as Mary had indicated, he'd be looking for an article from seven or eight years ago.

In a few minutes, he found the article of interest, *Unlicensed Teen Killed, Passenger Survives.* Reading the short article through a couple of times, he pulled out his notepad and wrote down "Danny Davidson, survived by mother, Kimberly Davidson."

The article was sparse on any facts surrounding the accident. Evidently Danny Davidson had been driving Aiden Jensen's car, or more likely, his parent's car. He'd lost control on a small side road in a country area of the Santa Monica Mountains, off highway 27. No drugs or alcohol were suspected, but the coroner's report was still pending at the time the article was written.

With the date from the article confirming when the accident occurred, he was able to pull up the police report electronically. It confirmed the article's facts, plus added details from the accident scene.

The accident had taken place on a gravel road. The car had left the main roadway and crashed into a culvert in the ditch traveling at an estimated fifty miles per hour at impact. The driver was thrown through the windshield sustaining major head trauma and multiple broken bones. The blow to the head was listed as the CoD in the coroner's attached report. No drugs or alcohol found in the driver's or passenger's systems. The passenger, Aiden Jensen, sustained major contusions, two broken legs and a collar bone fracture. He was admitted to the hospital.

McClarey sat back in his seat puzzling over why the unlicensed Danny Davidson was driving the car. Had Aiden been unable to drive for some reason? Was it a friend letting a friend indulge in some driving practice?

As he turned this over in his mind, he looked down at his notes at the surviving mother's name. Kimberly Davidson. Tapping a few more keys he pulled up his link to the DMV for Santa Monica and found the files for Kimberly Davidson. A name change was registered as occurring about one year after her son's accident. She was now going by Kimberly Riggsby, her maiden name. Her home address was listed in Simi Valley with a business address in San Fernando on Hubbard Street, Exciting Designs for Life.

McClarey grabbed his suit jacket from the back of his chair and snatched his cap from the miniature hat tree. The quirky hat tree made his desk stand out in stark contrast to any of the other desks in the bullpen. He headed for the door.

He'd pay a little visit to Kimberly Riggsby at her office. It was now mid-day on this fine Wednesday, so he'd catch lunch at a particular pub he liked to frequent near San Fernando on the way. Some fish n' chips, a non-sanctioned pint o' Gat, or Guinness to the non-Irish, and Riggsby's studio as his next stop.

McClarey made the trip to the San Fernando area in

about an hour, enjoyed his lunch and Gat, and arrived at Riggsby's office around two o'clock. The office complex housing Exciting Designs for Life was part of a modernlooking circle drive. It was located across from a gorgeous park of crab apple trees, Bradford pears and some red maples. Park benches were strategically placed along the walk and under some of the larger shade trees.

McClarey walked up the central sidewalk and entered the office complex's lobby. A check of the businesses displayed in the glass framed directory outside the building had indicated Exciting Designs for Life was on the first floor, room number 66.

McClarey strolled down the hall to the beveled half-glass door with the number "66" at the top, and under it *"Kimberly Riggsby – Exciting Designs for Life"* scripted onto the glass with a frost-like finish. He knocked at the door and simultaneously turned the knob to enter.

Kimberly looked up from her desk, a bit startled. She composed herself and smiled as she began to stand, "Hello, may I help you?"

"Good day m'Lady. I was hoping to talk to a Miss Kimberly Riggsby. Might you be her?"

"I'm Kimberly. Please come in."

Kimberly's heart shaped face was framed by golden blonde hair; her facial features were nicely proportioned, and they seemed centered around her blue pearlescent eyes. She wore a black skirt and a white blouse with a blue silk scarf at her neck. She radiated an "all business" look. An expensive-looking leather portfolio bag with a long carrying strap sat against the leg of her desk.

"Grand, I don't think I'll need t' take up much of yer time. I'm Sergeant McClarey o'the Santa Monica PD and I'm followin up on a few details for a case o' mine," he said as he produced his detective's shield for her to examine.

Kimberly's office was located at the south end of the five-story office building. The architecture was a tiered modern motif so her first floor office jutted out from the main building like the first of four stepping-stones for some giant to access the roof. In the southwest corner of her office, she had her own private door exiting to the surrounding grounds and parking lot.

The interior decorating studio had skylights placed strategically to catch the morning and afternoon sun. Sunshine could illuminate the room, then quickly flee the scene as passing clouds threw the room into sudden shadow. The ceiling was augmented with cylindrical track lights pointing into the various recesses of the room for days when the sun proved unavailable.

He crossed the room to one of two chairs positioned in front of Kimberly's desk and sat down. He casually surveyed his surroundings.

The furniture had sleek lines in gunmetal black, starkly jutting from the pure white plush carpet. The work area appeared Spartan with a drawing table in one corner and Kimberly's desk and executive style chair in the adjoining corner. A receiving area on the opposite side of the room had a chaise lounge ensemble arranged in front of a stone fireplace with a black onyx mantel. The stones of the fireplace were a mix of black agate, obsidian, and granite placed in perfect symmetry around the three foot square opening. The maw of the fireplace was covered with a mesh screen akin to the mail knights might have worn into battle.

The artwork items displayed on the wall were an extension of the futuristic furniture: a Picasso print, an abstract version of a grassy meadow at dusk, and a re-print of The Scream.

"Nice studio you 'ave here." He hesitated looking for a word other than stark and said, "Very modern and all."

"We try to give our clients a feel for the kind of clean design we strive for. Our office is our first impression." She glanced up from his badge with a forced smile and asked, "So what can I help you with sergeant?"

The desk and chair at which Kimberly sat were in the corner of the room with her back to the outer wall. The desk had a thick oval glass top, beveled at the edges, and supported by metal legs attached to the desk's edges. The legs crossed through a focal point under the center, forming four curved supports shaped like talons.

The chair behind the desk was black leather with raised stitching. The chair's armrests curved inward towards Kimberly at either end giving the sense it could grasp and hold her victim.

Centered on the desktop was a leather writing pad with the edges detailed with richly embossed caricatures of knights on horses battling one another. A desk valet with an onyx pen sat just to the pad's right and a cantilevered LED desk light hovered over the writing pad. A black organizing tray holding invoices and current correspondence of interest was in the upper right corner of her desk.

The only decoration on the desk was a six-inch diameter crystal ball in a round, blood red stand to the left of her writing area. Displayed in the center of the orb was a sky blue flower: exotic in the detail of the hooded bell-like petals, hanging along the stem, suspended weightless in its glass prison.

McClarey's eyes fell on the glass orb on Kimberly's desk as he commented, "Your desk ornament is a bit unique. Don't think I know what kind o' flower dat is?"

Kimberly met his eyes intensely for a moment. "It's monkshood," she said as she leaned back in her chair. "Are you interested in flowers as a rule? I wouldn't think someone in your line of work would find such things of much interest."

"Oh not really. It's just nicely displayed. I thought it might be o' some significance," he said.

Kimberly straightened up a bit more in her chair at his assertion. "No, not really. I think I picked it up at a home decorating show. I thought it would be a good accent for my desk," she said as her piercing blue eyes broke contact with McClarey, her brief interest gone.

"I'm sure your case doesn't involve questioning me about my desk decor, does it?" she said with an impatient edge.

"No m'Lady, not at all. Just found it strikin." He produced a photo from his inside jacket pocket of Louise Jensen and pushed it across the desk. "I believe you might have known the unfortunate lady who passed away last Thursday. A Louise Jensen." McClarey watched as

Riggsby's look of mild annoyance turned to a darker shade. A frown formed at the corners of Kimberly's mouth and her eyes seemed to flash as if electrified in her sockets.

"Yes, of course I remember her. She's the mother of a derelict son who cost *My* son his life," she spat as she stared hard through the centers of McClarey's eyes.

"Me apologies m'Lady for bringin up such a sorrowful time for you, but I was wonderin if you'd had any contact with Louise Jensen since the time o' yer son's accident?"

Riggsby continued to stare bolts of lightning at McClarey for a few seconds, and then looked away. Composing herself, she pulled at her jacket as if to straighten some unseen wrinkle that was bothering her.

"Oh, I see," she said as she returned her cold gaze to his. "You think I might have something to do with her murder? Well I haven't seen her since her pitiful try at empathy at my son's funeral. Sorry to disappoint."

"Pardon me m'Lady, but I didn't say she'd been murdered at all. Why would you think dat?"

"I don't assume the Santa Monica Police would drive to San Fernando to let me know that a person I have no contact with, and serves only to remind me of the worst day of my life, had died of natural causes."

"No I s'pose not," he nodded as he continued. "Well I'd like t'know a little more about how yer son acquainted himself with the Jensens. It might help me fill in a few blanks around Louise's history. I understand dat your son was a good friend o' Aiden."

She visibly winced at the name, "My son, Danny, was best friends with him from the time they were twelve.

They did everything together."

"I didn't see any harm in the friendship, at least not until my Danny didn't come home." She looked away as tears formed in the corners of her eyes. "Danny worshipped Aiden. When Aiden got his license, I should have known Danny wouldn't be safe. He never should have let him behind the wheel of his car. What the *hell* was he thinking?" she sighed in exacerbation as she seemed to stare off into space. She dabbed her eyes with a tissue plucked from the leather portfolio beside her desk.

"If you don't mind me askin, I would o' thought you and m'Lady Jensen might 'ave become closer over yer loss? You know her son suffered both from his injuries dat night, but also has been fightin with the guilt he feels mightily from the accident," McClarey queried as he studied her closely. He knew this was shaky ground for a line of questioning. He had been trying to get a feel for what Louise Jensen might have filled those difficult years with after the accident. It now occurred to him that he might also get insight into Kimberly's mourning period.

Riggsby's eyes flared again as the wet softness turned to stone. "And why would I want anything to do with the bitch-mother of the boy who led my son to his death? I hope she got just a taste of the torture I went through before she died. I hope her son's guilt gives him nightmares *every night* for the rest of his life."

She met his eyes with pure hatred on full display, her face contorted with anger.

"I see yer still feelin the sting o' your son's passin. I'm sorry for what must have been a painful time." He hesitated and then continued, "Just one more question. Do you have any connections t' a Mary Simon? Jim Jensen had some reservations about her and his wife, so I'm wonderin if you had crossed paths at all and could shed some light on their relationship."

"I vaguely remember the name as one of Jensen's friends. Part of a card group or something from what Danny had told me. No one I would have any reason to know."

"Very good m'Lady Riggsby. I'll be needin you t' provide me with where you were Thursday last, around midday t' make sure all me facts are in order."

She seemed to lose the hardness in her eyes as she realized he was asking her for her alibi. "Yes, of course."

She reached into her portfolio producing her phone. She swiped at her phone's screen a few times and seemed to be looking at her calendar. "I was with a client that morning, got lunch on the way to an install site, and then was at the client's installation for the rest of the afternoon."

"If you wouldn't mind emailing me the client's information so I can follow up, I'd greatly appreciate it. Just so I don't bother you further," he said as he slid his business card across the desk to her. "Well, I'll be takin me leave now. I'll confirm back we've got no further questions once I get your information. Good day t' you."

McClarey got up to leave the office.

He could feel Kimberly's eyes steadily boring into his back, but he didn't want to turn to confirm his paranoia. He just walked to the door, pivoted as he opened it, and looking over his shoulder, gave her a cursory goodbye tip of his cap.

She was now sitting behind her desk with her fingers steepled together and touching her chin as if studying him as he left. She half-nodded when he caught her eye.

He stepped into the hallway closing the door behind him.

Walking to his car, McClarey couldn't help but feel she had acted a bit strangely. Even though her distaste for Louise Jensen seemed rooted in the loss of her son, it seemed a bit too over the top after eight years.

He settled into his car. Turning the ignition, he mused to himself, *there's somethin a wee bit different about m'Lady Kimberly, and not in a good way.*

Chapter 20

Jim had been spending time with Aiden, who had come back from school for the funeral. Together they were trying to make sense of it all, but to no avail. Their last few days together had been a roller coaster of remembering the good times to lows thinking of how much Louise would be missed.

Jim had shared how he'd met Louise. He had returned from Vietnam in April of 1974 and entered college on the GI Bill, graduating with a Ph.D. in Food Science in early 1981. Hired out of college by ConGrowth Foods, he was just starting his career when he met Louise.

On one of his checkups at the Veteran's Administration hospital, he had tripped over an emergency crash cart left in the hallway. This made a horrendous noise as he sprawled out with all of the lifesaving elements of the cart scattered around him; an IV tube hanging from one ear.

This lovely young vision of a woman named Louise had helped him to his feet. He'd looked so awestruck as she helped him up. She wanted to check him out to make sure he hadn't injured anything.

It turned out she was doing her residency at the VA. After a quick once over, she declared him fit to go trip somewhere else, *but please after her shift.* This had led him to ask when that shift might end.

That had been in March of 1981. The rest was a storybook romance; a dream which he had never wanted to wake from. They were married in June of 1983 when Louise finished her residency. Aiden had come along six and a half years later.

Aiden shared his regret for how hard he'd made it on his mom, especially after his accident. "Mom never once complained about taking me to therapist appointments or said she was too busy to listen to my journeys into self-pity and regrets."

Aiden had sighed deeply, then lamented, "Now I wish I'd spent the time getting to know her better; hearing about her dreams, fun times she looked back on, or things she was looking forward to. I can't believe how selfish and needy I must have looked to her."

When Aiden had said this, Jim had reached out and grasped his shoulder as they sat on their family room couch. He locked eyes with his son. "Aiden, your mom never regretted a single moment she spent with you. She lived to hear what you were feeling or what you wanted from life. It may not seem like it to you, but your biggest gift to her was the time you spent with her. It really didn't matter what you were talking about. She just wanted to connect with you on things that you cared about or needed to say."

They'd had several good cries between their fond memories and a few laughs.

Like the time Louise had been beside herself when she'd found out Aiden had smuggled a puppy into their house. He'd come across it on his way home from school. The puppy had been stashed in his gym bag. Louise had started up a conversation with Aiden as he came through the front door. He'd desperately tried to end the discussion so he could get his uninvited houseguest up to his room and stowed away before being caught.

As they talked there in the entryway, Louise noticed a stream of liquid coming from the lower corner of his gym bag.

"The coach really worked us today. Guess my gym clothes were wetter than I'd thought," Aiden had lamely offered.

Louise had stared unbelievingly at the puddle growing at his feet and finally said, "Did your coach work you so hard you peed yourself, because that's not like any sweat I've seen?"

Aiden and Jim laughed as they remembered how that puppy had become Louise's pet more than Aiden's. She had called him Bold Move, or BM for short. This was in homage to Aiden's try at sneaking him past her, but also made her laugh given her chosen field of gastroenterology.

As if on cue, they'd heard a scratch on the back door. There was the large golden retriever begging to be let in after an afternoon of chasing birds and butterflies in the backyard. They'd looked at BM's questioning face through the patio door as if he were wondering what fun he might be missing and laughed again until they cried.

Louise was so much a part of both of their lives it seemed surreal to imagine going forward without her.

Now it was late in the afternoon on Wednesday, two days after Louise's funeral.

Aiden came down the stairs with his backpack, suitcase and his computer bag slung over his shoulder. "Well guess it's time to be heading back to the heart of LA. I'll need to hit the books and do some catching up," he said as he deposited his items in the hallway. Aiden was in his second year of med school at USC in downtown LA.

Jim rose out of his chair and walked to Aiden. Giving him a hug that lasted a bit longer than their usual embrace, he said softly, "I love you son. Drive careful and give me a call when you get to campus."

"Love you too, Dad."

Jim opened the front door to help Aiden move his bags from the house to his car waiting in the driveway.

A startled Pat Hemmings stood on the front stoop wrestling a large covered box and reaching for the doorbell. "Oh Jim! You gave me a scare," she gasped.

"Sorry Pat, let me give you a hand with that," Jim offered as he swung the door open and wrested the box from Pat. "What is this anyway?"

"We thought you might be needing some meals for a few days with Aiden home and all. It's from Daly, Linda, Mary and me. The least we could do. Mary included some kind of goodies with a note in here somewhere so you can indulge yourself a bit."

Pat forced a smile. She stepped forward to hug Aiden,

asking, "On your way out?"

"Yeah, school must go on, and they need me for my shining personality," Aiden said as he chuffed a laugh.

"Well, don't undersell yourself. They do need you. I'm not kidding. You're going to be somebody great, I just know it." Pat gushed as she reached towards Aiden's cheek. She stopped herself short of pinching it, and just patted it lightly. "Why don't you take some of this food with you? Growing boy and all," she offered.

"Thanks Mrs. Hemmings, but we've been eating like horses here with all the food left over from mom's…anyway I've got a great food plan at school. But thanks anyway," he said as he hoisted his bags and headed towards his car.

Jim put his hand on Aiden's shoulder and said, "Drive safe son, and call me. By the way, next time you're back I'll regale you with war stories from my days with the Cong."

Aiden nodded and faked a pained smile, "Looking forward to it, Dad."

Turning to Pat Jim made a sweeping motion with his arm toward the inner hallway, "So Pat, come on in and stay awhile."

"I would, but I'm on my way to an early dinner with Linda and then book club. Linda suggested she and I join a book club. They call themselves The Guernsey Wannabes, named after a favorite read about a World War II literary society. She's really been a help to me after losing Tommy." She caught herself just a beat too late, and stammered, "I didn't mean to bring up my problems, Jim. You need to stay focused on getting through your own loss. That's what matters most."

"Thanks Pat. It's not something I ever thought about, being without Louise and all. Guess I'll be lost for a while."

"Let me help you put this food away," Pat said as she motioned Jim towards the kitchen.

He took the lid from the box and began unloading it onto the counter. "Looks like you all didn't let me down. I see Daly's famous tuna casserole, your pasta salad, and Linda's chocolate chip cookies. All my favorites."

"Plus the fancy little bag is from Mary. Chocolates I think," Pat said with a bit of longing in her voice. "She left them on my front porch in a cooler with the note you see there."

The typed note said, *Jim, so sorry for your loss. Hope you enjoy these. Mary.*

"A little formal don't you think," Pat said as she raised an eyebrow. "Who says that to a close friend, anyway. And not even signed. Oh well I'm sure she was well intentioned."

"I'm sure she was," Jim said in a flat tone as he began moving the casserole and salad to the fridge. "Looks like I'm covered for the next several days with all this. Pass along my thanks to everyone. You really didn't need to do all this."

"Not a problem at all. You know, busy hands and all."

Not really knowing what this meant, Jim just nodded and stepped forward to give Pat a hug. "Thanks Pat, very appreciated."

Keeping his arm around her, they walked to the front door.

DAN BLAIR

"Well, Linda will be saving me a table so I better get going. We're trying out a new place on the west side of the Valley. Called Oysters and Brew, or something like that," she said as she stopped on the front stoop, then turned to face Jim. "You know you can call any of us if you need anything, right?"

"I know Pat. Louise would be happy to know her friends are every bit as good as she thought they were." Jim waved as Pat walked to her car parked in the drive, next to the spot Aiden had just vacated.

Jim shut the front door and felt his stomach growl.

Guess it's time to break open the pity food buffet and watch some Jeopardy.

———◦《◉》◦———

At three a.m., Jim woke to the most intense stomach cramps he could remember.

He lumbered to the master bathroom barely in time to avoid defecating all over the floor. He moaned to the sounds of explosive diarrhea. Leaning forward on the toilet over a bathroom trash bin placed there for tissues and the like, he began to wretch.

So this is what spewing from both ends feels like.

Waves of nausea came over him. After several minutes the nausea seemed to subside. He cleaned himself and started back to bed.

Halfway there, he fell to his knees on the tile bathroom floor and began to vomit blood.

Reeling from the sight of a puddle of his congealing blood and the extreme nausea, he rolled onto his side and passed out.

——⸺«(●)»⸺——

He felt his eyes flutter open.

He wasn't sure where he was.

He rolled onto his back and could see the wall clock with hands indicating 4:15. Rolling onto his stomach, he pushed himself up onto his knees. Holding his stomach with one hand, he grasped the lavatory top with his other hand and leaned heavily across the makeup area bench top. He felt like the fires of Hades had been stored in his gut temporarily.

Releasing his stomach for a moment, he knocked the bathroom phone from its cradle and punched in 911.

After two rings the dispatch officer picked up and asked, " What is your emergency?"

Jim started to speak as another wave of pain came over him and his bowels released where he was standing. He weakly gasped into the phone, "Help me. Send an ambulance."

"Sir, can you tell me what is wrong? Are you able to give me your address?"

Jim collapsed to the floor, dropping the phone.

The 911 operator urgently tried to get a response from the phone hanging in space by its cord, "Sir, are you there? I'm sending help. Can you hear me? Stay on the line."

Jim tried to focus on the phone penduluming over his head. His eyelids felt like they'd been weighted with lead.

The sound of the operator seemed to disappear into a deep well.

Jim's head fell back onto the tile floor with a soft thump as he slipped into unconsciousness.

———◦((◦))◦———

At five a.m. Mark sat up with a start as the bedside phone rang. "What, who is this?...What?...Ok, ok. I'll be there in thirty minutes."

Daly roused and in a sleepy voice said, "Who was it?"

"Go back to sleep. I'm going to head down to the hospital. Jim was admitted with some kind of severe flu symptoms. He gave me as his emergency contact so they want to talk to me."

"Probably from all the stress of losing Louise. I'll call you from the hospital when I get there and know something," Mark yawned as he rubbed his eyes.

Dropping his pajamas to the floor, he clambered into their shower letting the cold water bring him out of his sleep-induced haze. Toweling off, he quickly dressed and headed through the kitchen and out the garage door.

He pulled up in front of the Santa Monica Hospital twenty minutes later.

The nurse who had called him, had indicated Jim was in room 704. Mark entered the lobby and headed for the elevator. It took him a few minutes once he arrived at the seventh floor to get his bearings and locate the head nurse's station. It was just down the hall from Jim's room.

"Hello, I'm Mark Ford. I received a call concerning Jim Jensen who's in room 704."

A plump nurse with a pleasant face, especially for someone there at five thirty in the morning, looked up and smiled. "Yes, Mr. Ford. I'm Nurse Kentner. I called you as Mr. Jensen indicated you were his emergency contact. I understand his wife is deceased."

She rose from her desk, pivoting around the counter to join him. "Mr. Jensen appears to be suffering from severe flu or possibly food poisoning. He reported severe vomiting and diarrhea, with significant blood in both. We've given him the appropriate drugs to ease his symptoms. He's resting comfortably right now. We've also begun an IV to keep him hydrated."

"Do you know what's causing it?"

"Not at this point. We're running fecal tests and stomach fluids to see if anything shows up. It may just be a severe flu bug, but I thought I should talk to you to see if you might have any thoughts on what it could be. We would normally talk to the spouse, but…"

"Yes, I understand. Jim lost his wife a week ago, Thursday, and I'm sure his stress level is high from that. I don't know of any medications he was on, but his records are likely here. His wife was one of the hospital's doctors on staff. I don't know what he'd been eating, but I could call his son, Aiden, as they were together the last few days."

"That would be helpful. As I said, we're running a

whole barrage of tests. Something may turn up there. You're welcome to see your friend. He's sleeping now. When he wakes up, please ask him if he has any idea what might have caused this severe of a reaction," nurse Kentner said as she motioned to Jim's room. She returned to her desk and began punching keys.

Mark walked the thirty feet or so to Jim's room and knocked lightly on the partially open door. When no one responded, he stepped into the room.

He was met by Jim's pale, sleeping face. Oxygen tubes were inserted in his nose, multiple IV bags were hung from a metal dispensing tree, and a probe was attached like a clothespin to Jim's left index finger. A vital functions monitor beeped away at his bedside.

"Well old friend, this has not been your week," Mark said softly as he settled into the visitor's recliner by Jim's bed.

Chapter 21

Mary Simon was having a hard time shaking off a feeling of deep hopelessness.

She heated her tea kettle for her morning wake-up; a hibiscus and green tea blend she had come to favor.

She shuffled to the kitchen island and began to select fruits for a smoothie; a banana, fresh strawberries and a peach were quickly peeled or cleaned, sliced and placed in her state-of-the art blender. She hit the "Puree" button. The high-pitched whine of the blades tearing at the flesh of the medley of fruits set her teeth on edge. She poured the blender's contents into a large frosted glass and stared blankly out the window as she waited for the kettle to boil.

It was Thursday, three days since Louise's funeral. She still couldn't shake the strong sense of loss.

Her last few days had been a blur. Sleeping too much, reading mindless magazine articles on how to decorate your bathroom to be more European, and frequent trips to weed and reweed her garden had filled her time. She knew her depressed state was mostly based on her inability to deal with losing her beloved friend.

Of equal weight was how it reminded her of losing her son, Lesley.

Louise's death had catalyzed all the memories Mary tried so hard to bury; to place in the most remote areas of her mind that no archeologist could dig out with precision pick hammers and brushes. But the overwhelming feelings of loss and a life cut short would not stay in their sepulcher.

She had not slept well the last several nights as images of her Lesley visited her. Sometimes he'd been playing in the yard with their dog. Sometimes he was gasping for air as he went under the waves with a look of stark fear and desperation on his face.

Her vivid memories of Lesley's death by drowning were purely of her imagination as she had not directly witnessed it.

Her first husband, Will, had wanted to take the family on a beach vacation to Padre Island near Brownsville, Texas. Averly and Lesley had never been on a beach vacation so it had seemed like a good idea to her.

Will and Lesley had decided to try boogey boarding as Lesley wasn't a particularly strong swimmer. Riding the surging, breaking waves on a floating foam-composite board sounded like fun.

Their fourteen year old daughter, Averly, had decided to walk the beach checking out any teenage boys she could get to ogle her new, skimpy bikini. After an hour or so, Will had tired of the raging sea and returned to the beach to soak up the intense Texas sun. Lesley had continued to ride the waves with sixteen-year-old glee.

Mary had split her time watching Averly to guarantee no beach trysts got out of hand and Lesley paddling out towards bigger and better waves. Lesley had seemed to be resting on his boogey board and enjoying the beautiful day under clear blue coastal skies. Mary nudged Will saying, "I think Lesley's getting too far out."

"Hmm, what?" Will had murmured in a sleepy voice.

"Will, go get Lesley," she said more firmly as she nudged him, rolling him onto his side.

Will blinked a few times as the bright sun accosted his sleep filled eyes, "Ok, ok. I'm going."

Mary had stood and watched with a growing feeling of trepidation as Will picked up his boogey board, entered the waves and began to paddle towards Lesley. Lesley had fast become a receding formless speck on the horizon.

Will had told Mary he'd almost reached Lesley that day when his son had suddenly rolled off his boogie board as if deciding to swim alongside it. Only twenty yards or so from Lesley, he'd not been terribly concerned at first.

Then Lesley lost his grip on the board and began to thrash in the water.

Will paddled urgently towards him. He had been only a few yards from him when Lesley disappeared beneath the roiling waves.

Will had immediately left his own board and swam to Lesley's last position. He began diving beneath the waves to search for Lesley and bring him back to the surface.

Between the murky water, waves, and the strong current, he'd found himself quickly tiring and unable to locate Lesley. He'd thought he had felt Lesley's fingers briefly on one desperate attempt. The current had pulled Lesley away with a force Will was unable to overcome.

As Will realized he would be unable to save his son, he began to yell for help, waving his arms wildly.

Mary yelled for the lifeguard in his perch a hundred feet away, but he had already seen Will's waving arms. In her growing hysteria, she now saw the beach signs posted near the lifeguard stand warning of strong rip tides.

The lifeguard ran into the surf with a life preserver on an ankle rope. He dove into the surging sea, taking long steady strokes towards Will's flailing arms.

It had been too late.

Lesley had been swept away in the silent riptide that lurked beneath the foamed surface.

He'd been taken from her forever.

It had been several hours before the Coast Guard had been able to find Lesley's body several hundred yards away; lifeless and drained of all the future basketball and baseball games, dates with girlfriends, college friends and hopes for good times that Mary had envisioned for him.

She had been unable to forgive Will in her grief and the anger that had followed.

Will had bravely tried to shoulder the blame for Lesley's death. That had not been enough for Mary's unquenchable need to have Lesley returned to her. She knew that Will sensed she had wished more than once that Will had drowned that day, rather than Lesley.

The darkness Mary descended into was implacable and had led ultimately to the end of Will's patience.

They'd divorced six months after losing Lesley.

Mary jolted out of her daymare. The whistling of the tea kettle sounding more to her like the gurgling scream she'd never heard as Lesley disappeared below the waves. She poured the boiling water over the dried tea leaves in her cup and set it aside. The smell of the hibiscus filled her nostrils as the tea steeped and cooled, returning her to a state of calm acceptance.

Her life had changed so radically since Lesley had been taken from her. Not just her divorce with Will. That had been more her fault than his. But also in the estrangement of her daughter, Averly.

After Mary divorced Will, Averly had grown to strongly resent her for driving Will out of their home. Averly's zealous teenage desire for accountability when things were not going her way had fallen squarely on Mary. She'd been at those soul-shaping years when Lesley, the brother she looked up to, had been snatched from her. Then six months later her father whom she adored, was booted out the door.

The following teen years were truly brutal on Mary.

Averly had not grown through her losses. Rather, she seemed to seethe in them like being bathed in acid whenever she was in Mary's presence.

Mary had returned to school to get a pharmacy degree. She found immersing herself in books and classes was far easier than healing the rift with her daughter. The distance between them continued to grow to epic proportions. At eighteen, Averly had finally declared herself free of any more parenting from her mother.

She left Mary to a life of loneliness and regrets.

As she sipped her soothing tea, she decided it might be better to get out of the house; do some paperwork at her office. She'd been ignoring messages and emails for a week now. Catching up could easily fill the rest of her day, and hopefully return the memories to the depths of her consciousness where they could fester and await some future pity party.

She slugged down her fruit smoothie. Carrying her tea cup with her, she retreated to her master bath to shower and see if her makeup still lurked within her vanity after being untouched for days.

An hour later she emerged from her front door into brilliant sunshine. It was another cloudless California day. She thought, *today's the first day of the rest of your life*, and then, *if I feed myself enough horseshit, I'll learn to like the taste.*

She threw her soft, satchel briefcase into the passenger seat of her Mercedes SL, and headed to her office in east Santa Monica.

After clearing out a few hundred emails, answering phone messages and checking in with a few clients, Mary looked at her wall clock. The clock was her favorite wall decoration; shaped like a splayed-out globe with all the continents represented. A set of timekeeping hands anchored by a stem somewhere in the western US, indicated it was three p.m.

She felt a pang of hunger, and looked hungrily at her refrigerator, *so what have you got for me to munch on?* Opening the door she pulled out some snack sized specialty cheeses, a package of Greek yogurt with real strawberries, and a small bottle of milk shaped like the old-fashioned milk bottles dairies used to deliver to people's doors in the 1950's. She had a six pack of the milk special delivered from a local dairy farmer each week, along with cream for her coffee.

She noticed a soft-sided lunch pail in the back of the refrigerator that was not hers. She started to reach for it to investigate, then realized it must belong to Margie. Margie was her part-time assistant who helped her out with special events or deliveries from time to time when she was in a bind.

Carrying her edible treasures back to her desk, she sat and munched her growling stomach into submission. She continued to thumb through her snail mail, which had also stacked up in the week she'd been out of office. Her cell phone rang and she answered, "Delicacies Du Jour, Mary speaking."

"Hi Mare, it's Pat. I just wanted to follow up and let you know Jim really appreciated the food we dropped over at his house the other day. He was eyeing that little bag of chocolates you dropped by my house pretty lustfully. I called to see if he needed anything else, but no answer so guess he must be out and about today."

Pat Hemmings paused for a nanosecond and continued, "So are you doing any better? I tried calling you several times, but guess you were busy."

"Yes, I've been taking a few days for myself so turned the phone off. I'm back at work today. It seems to be helping a bit," Mary said as she took a sip of her milk. "I'll be heading home in a few minutes. Just catching up from being out. Why don't I give you a call later and we can figure out a time to get together?"

"Sounds good, Mare. Ok, I'll let you go but do give me a call. Bye."

Mary was puzzled over Pat's call. She hadn't sent any chocolates to Jim. Maybe Margie had handled it for her since she was out of office. That would be like Margie to be thoughtful enough to send something in her stead. She'd have to ask about it when she saw her in the next day or so.

Mary gathered up the remaining mail she'd not gotten to and stuffed it into the side pocket of her briefcase. She rinsed the milk bottle in a small sink next to her refrigerator, and placed it in a cardboard carton she kept for return of the empties to her dairy farmer connection.

Looking around her office she said, "Well, life goes on," and headed out the door for home.

Around eight o'clock Mary started to feel her stomach rumble.

She'd gotten home around four that afternoon after picking up a dinner salad at one of her favorite local restaurants, The Green Palace. She'd only finished eating about an hour earlier and had settled into a good book for her evening's entertainment. It didn't make sense to her she could already be feeling hungry.

She rose to get a glass of water. The rumbling descended from her stomach to her abdomen.

Dashing for the bathroom off her kitchen area, she barely made it over the toilet as her bowels erupted.

The accompanying abdominal cramps seemed to turn her inside out. It was as if her intestines were about to leave the security of her body and seek some less hellacious abode.

She sat hunched over in pain, hoping for a reprieve long enough to get to her medicine chest. The waves of abdominal cramps came one after the other. A cold sweat formed on her face and the moans coming from her seemed to be outside her physical being. She wondered if some paranormal apparition had assumed control of her bathroom and decided to make its presence felt in a most debasing way.

After an hour or so had passed, Mary decided her illness was well beyond something she should be self-medicating. Pepto Bismol™ or whatever else she had in her medicine chest was no match for the monster in her gut.

She reached for her smart phone, snaking it out of her pajama pocket, and pulled up her Favorites list on the glowing screen. Suddenly it hit her, calling Louise wasn't an option. "Damn you Louise, *why* did you have to leave me," she moaned.

She stared at her phone as another wave of abdominal cramps and the accompanying explosive diarrhea hit her. She closed her eyes. Feeling faint and knowing she had to call someone, she touched Michael's name on her speed dial list.

"Hello Mary. To what do I owe this pleasure?" Michael said as he answered after a couple of rings.

"Michael, I'm sick. Really sick. Can you come?" Mary gasped out her request, drawing short breaths. "I need a

DAN BLAIR

hospital." She dropped the phone to the floor and leaned against the sink cabinet adjacent to the toilet to keep her from falling to the floor.

"Hurry Michael. Hurry," she whispered as she felt the blood draining from her face.

Mary remembered Michael holding a cold cloth to her face, cleaning her up and helping her to his car. She realized she must have passed out at that point as the next thing she remembered was waking up in her hospital bed.

Michael was standing beside her and holding her hand. A nurse busied herself at a portable computer station to the other side of her bed. An IV tube protruded from her right arm leading up to a clear bag dripping fluid into a metering valve suspended from a metal pedestal.

"Wow Mary, you really gave me a scare," Michael said as he forced a smile.

"Where are we?" Mary said groggily.

"We're at Santa Monica General. You're going to be fine, but the doctor wanted to talk to you as soon as you were awake." Michael turned to the nurse, "Can you get the doctor? I think she's back with us again."

The nurse logged out of her computer screen, nodded at Michael and left the room.

"So by the looks of things when I got to you, Montezuma's Revenge appeared to have taken you for a wild ride. Can you remember what happened at all?" Michael gently prodded.

"I don't know. I had just finished dinner and was reading when it hit me. Worst case of cramps and the runs I've ever had. It just didn't let up. I couldn't leave the bathroom to take anything, and then I was too weak to..." Mary paused and a pained expression returned to her face.

"Another cramp?" Michael asked as she nodded.

The door opened as Michael held Mary's hand, "Hello Ms. Simon, I'm Doctor Prakesh. I understand you're having severe abdominal cramping and earlier in the night you suffered diarrhea. Is that right?"

Mary looked up with glazed eyes as the cramp subsided, answering, "Yes that's right."

"Can you tell me what you've had to eat in the last eight hours or so?" Dr. Prakesh asked.

"I had an avocado and chicken salad for dinner around six o'clock or so with water. I only snacked earlier in the day; some cheese, yogurt and milk."

"I see. Do you know if the cheese, yogurt and milk were pasteurized?" the doctor queried.

"I think the cheese and yogurt were. They come in commercial packaging at least. The milk is natural, straight from a local dairy farm."

"OK. I think we need to get a culture run on your BM. That should tell us a lot more about what's causing the problem," Dr. Prakesh said. He turned to the nurse, asked her to collect a sample and ordered a series of lab tests to be run. "I'll be back to talk in the morning when we get the lab tests back. I've prescribed fluids to keep you hydrated and you can ask for pain medication if the cramps become too severe. Any questions for me?"

"Do you think it's food poisoning doc, or something else?" Michael asked.

"It looks to be food poisoning based on the symptoms

and the rapid onset. We'll know more as soon as the lab tests come back. If it's a common foodborne pathogen, the lab results will identify it and we can work from there. The best thing for her now is to rest and take in as much fluid as possible." Dr. Prakesh shook Michael's hand, and smiled at Mary, saying "You've had a rough night. Just relax as best you can and get some sleep."

As Dr. Prakash exited the room, Michael turned back to Mary, "I can stay tonight if you'd feel better with me here."

"No, no. I just need to rest. If you can make sure everything is turned off and locked up back at my house, that would be great." Mary's eyes began to droop as the stress and strain of her evening began to catch up with her.

"I just need to sleep it off. I'll be fine. You can come see me tomorrow," she said as she weakly smiled and looked up at him with half-open eyes. "Michael, I really don't deserve you, you know. I never should have pushed you away."

"Shhh. Yeah, I know," he whispered as he returned her smile. "Now get some rest," he said as he squeezed her hand and watched her eyes flutter, then close.

Chapter 22

Mark Ford had spent the last few hours sleeping on and off in the recliner next to Jim Jensen's hospital bed.

It was now eight a.m. Thursday morning.

Mark reached down for the recliner release lever and quietly returned his chair to an upright position. Jim was still sleeping, and from the sound of his deep breathing, he wouldn't be waking anytime soon.

Mark stood and stretched as he looked out over the hospital park directly beneath Jim's window. The day was a bit gray and overcast. It looked as if the sun might burn through the mantle of thick clouds. A few brighter spots were beginning to glow in the eastern sky. He turned and looked at Jim resting peacefully and remembered he was to give Jim's son, Aiden, a call. The doctor had asked him to check what Jim might have consumed the previous day.

He stepped out of the room and into the brightly lit corridor. The sounds of the next hospital shift coming on and the business of the day getting fully underway surrounded him. Breakfast trays being delivered, multiple doctors starting to make their rounds, and night nurses covering the previous evenings events with their day-shift counter-parts created a background noise signaling a new day.

Mark walked a few doors down the hallway to a visitor's lounge. He looked inside and saw no one was currently in this oasis for loved ones thoughtfully provided by the hospital.

He stepped through the door, closing it behind him. Crossing the room to the beverage station, he poured a cup of coffee from the full carafe provided. He topped the black brew off with hazelnut creamer from a large push-top bottle and a package of sucralose sweetener.

Stirring his caffeine-laden concoction with one of the small plastic straws provided, he crossed the room to a private cubicle with an adjustable office chair.

The workstation had a general use desktop computer, phone, and a small writing pad with pens provided in a cup with a Santa Monica General Hospital logo. Sitting in the chair, he felt below the seat and found the knob to adjust the height to a more comfortable position.

He pulled out his phone. A quick search of the student directory at USC produced Aiden's campus phone number. He punched the number into his cell.

Five rings later, a sleepy, somewhat annoyed, voice answered, "Hello. Who's rattling my chain this early in the morning?"

"Hi Aiden. It's Mark Ford, a friend of your Dad."

"Oh, sure Mr. Ford. Is everything OK?"

"Aiden, your dad's in the Santa Monica hospital. I just left his room. He suffered some kind of severe stomach and abdominal pain last night, but he's resting peacefully now," Mark explained, then waited a few beats to let Aiden process this information.

"Your dad's doctor wanted me to find out a few things from you concerning your time together yesterday before you left for school if that's OK."

"Sure, sure Mr. Ford. Wow, I just said goodbye to him around six yesterday afternoon. Must have hit him after that. He was feeling fine when I left," Aiden said, now fully awake.

"The doctor is thinking he might have some kind of food poisoning based on the severe vomiting and diarrhea he suffered last night. I assume you're feeling ok this morning, right?" Mark queried.

"Yeah, I'm a little tired from staying up last night after getting back to my dorm, but no problems like that."

"Did you and your dad eat lunch and dinner together yesterday?"

"We had a pizza for lunch, but I headed back to school before supper. Mrs. Hemmings stopped by with some food for dad just as I was leaving and offered some to me. I was already on my way out the door so I passed. Do you think something in the stuff she brought made my dad sick?" Aiden said as the concern in his voice went up a notch.

"I don't know, but sounds like I should check it out. Okay, nothing else from yesterday you can think of that was out of the ordinary?" Mark asked as he made a few notes on the writing pad.

"No, nothing. We were just hanging around home and talking most of the time. Just remembering Mom and all, you know. Do you think I should come down and see Dad at the hospital?" Aiden asked.

"Your call Aiden, but he's pretty wrung out after last night. I'd say give him a day and maybe come down for the weekend. I'm sure he'd appreciate that. I'll tell him we talked when he wakes up," Mark said.

"Ok, tell him I love him and I'll be down to see him soon."

Mark provided Aiden with Jim's room number so he could call Jim later that day if he wanted to say hello in person. Mark assured Aiden everything would be fine and thanked him for his help.

Upon hanging up, Mark immediately dialed Daly. She picked up after the first ring.

"Hey babe, just checking in," Mark said.

"So what's the story on Jim? Is he doing Okay?" Daly asked with more than a little uneasiness in her voice.

"Yeah, he's resting comfortably. The doctors aren't sure what it is. Probably some kind of food poisoning is their best guess right now. I talked to Aiden and he said he left Jim at six o'clock yesterday and all was fine."

"Pat Hemmings had brought by some food for Jim just as Aiden was leaving. I'm thinking we ought to get to Jim's house and check that out as a possible culprit," Mark explained.

"Oh no. You're telling me my tuna casserole put Jim in the hospital?" Daly sounded horrified at the thought she might have contributed to Jim's maladies.

"Let's not jump the gun just yet. I've survived many of your tuna casseroles, and only thought about going to the hospital a couple of times," Mark smiled at himself as he waited for Daly's comeback.

"Not funny mister! Everyone loves my casserole." Daly paused as if in thought, then continued, "I can pick up Pat and go by Jim's house to collect the food she dropped off for testing. I've got a friend, JD Kruger, in the LAPD CSI lab that will rush it through for me."

"Great. That sounds like a good plan. Given the severity of Jim's symptoms, getting a handle on what might have caused it sooner rather than later has got to help the doctors," Mark agreed. "They've ordered several tests, but I haven't heard if anything definitive yet."

"OK, I'll give Pat a call right now. I'll let you know when I have the samples." Daly clicked off as Mark was about to say something witty about her casserole. Typical Daly, always on the move.

Mark returned to Jim's room. Jim had been roused by his doctor making his rounds. The doctor was questioning Jim on his previous day's activities trying to get a handle on what might be causing his severe digestive issues.

"So your tests are not showing anything in the normal food poisoning realm that we run as a standard battery of tests," the doctor explained. "I'm wondering if you might be exhibiting severe symptoms of stress with the recent passing of your wife."

Jim seemed quite groggy, probably from the pain medications they had administered for his severe cramping, "I dunno. I was feeling okay physically until last night. Just kind of down and still processing Louise not being there and all."

"Your vitals are a bit weak so I'll continue to keep you on fluids and a bland diet for now. I'll order some more blood work so we can rule out a few other options and go from there," the doctor said as he made a few notes on Jim's hospital chart. Returning the chart to its hanger on the end of his bed, the doctor turned to Mark and asked, "Mr. Ford, can I speak with you for a moment outside?"

Mark followed the doctor into the hallway.

"I'm Dr. Miller. I understand you have permission from Mr. Jensen to receive any medical information or diagnoses concerning his condition." Dr Miller's clear green eyes penetrated Mark who nodded.

"I don't want to sugarcoat his condition. I'm quite concerned we haven't been able to pinpoint what's creating his illness."

"Yes, doctor. My wife is collecting some food samples from Jim's house for testing through the LAPD. Maybe that will tell us something." Mark offered.

"It's possible, but we ran the standard bacteriological battery for salmonella, e-coli and a few other typical foodborne pathogens. There's nothing out of the ordinary from the lab results. We'll rerun these of course, but I'm not hopeful that's the issue." Dr. Miller looked at Mark as he cocked his head questioningly and asked, "Is there something more going on here that I should know about? Drug use maybe? Or something out of the ordinary that Jim is involved with?"

"Doc, Jim is a straight arrow. I'm totally baffled by this. Yeah, he's under a lot of stress, but he spent the last few days with his son and he didn't notice anything out of the ordinary either," Mark said with exasperation showing in his tone.

"Well if anything comes to mind, please have one of the nurses page me. I'm hesitant to start him on any regimen of treatment beyond IV fluids if we don't have a handle on what's behind his basic symptomology," Dr. Miller said as he shook Mark's hand.

Mark nodded and watched Dr. Miller stride down the hallway to his next patient stop.

Mark's mind was churning like a whirlpool trying to suck any piece of hope from the flotsam surrounding him. He was coming up empty. He'd placed all his eggs in the "food poisoning" basket and now it wasn't clear that was the problem at all.

Returning to Jim's bedside, Mark took up his position in the recliner. It was approaching ten o'clock and Jim had fallen back into a restless sleep as his monitor beeped ominously in the otherwise quiet room. Mark leaned back into the comfortable faux-leather chair and closed his eyes as he rubbed his temples.

The smell and sounds of the room cast a spell on Mark in his semi-conscious state. He found himself returning to a military hospital in Baghdad. It was just after he'd been medivac'd from the blast site in Fallujah where he'd stumbled onto an IED.

He remembered the dull, but tolerable pain that had traveled from his right shoulder down through his wrist.

The pain was significantly better than the searing branding iron version he'd felt prior to a heavy dose of morphine the field medics had administered. The military doctors and nurses had hooked him to every tube at their disposal and were pumping him full of a brew of fluids, pain killers and antibiotics.

He had gazed up at the fluorescent ceiling lights wondering if this was the way his Iraqi beach vacation would end; no pretty umbrella drinks, no scantily clad women, and no gently lapping ocean waves to be seen. He'd floated in and out of consciousness for the next few hours wondering why they weren't doing anything.

Why wasn't he being prepped for surgery?
What the hell were they waiting for?

Of course now he knew they had been stabilizing him prior to putting him on a transport to Frankfurt. There he had received the more advanced medical care he'd needed.

He couldn't help but return to that feeling of helplessness and impatience. Of wanting someone to do something as Jim laid there abandoned by medical science.

Mark woke from the sound of the on-duty nurse bringing in Jim's food tray around noon. She asked if he would like anything from the commissary brought up, but Mark decided he needed to stretch his legs.

He left to seek out the lunch area of the hospital. After treating himself to the hospital version of a grilled ham and cheese with a cold glass of milk, he returned to Jim's room. Jim was wavering between a restless sleep and opening his glazed eyes from time to time trying to take in his surroundings. A few unintelligible words were mingled between his low groans. He seemed to be walking the tightrope between conscious and unconscious realities, lost in a drug-induced mist that had to be difficult for someone as mentally sharp as Jim to tolerate.

Mark flipped through a few magazines sitting in a rack near the window, and finally flipped the TV on to pass the time. He hadn't brought a book or his Kindle so he was at the mercy of daytime television. Something he never watched if it could be avoided.

After about three hours or so of dysfunctional families forced to face siblings, or mothers, or fathers, or children they had long ago estranged themselves from, Mark was nearing the end of his rope. Jim had not stirred. He seemed to be retreating more and more into a sleep state with minimal lucid moments. No communication with Mark indicated any improvement.

It was nearing the hospital dinner hour, six o'clock, when Mark stepped into the hallway. He called Daly to see if any news from her LAPD contacts on the lab tests.

"Hey hon. Any news from LAPD on the samples?" he asked.

"No. I was just getting ready to check in with JD. She thought they'd have something by now," Daly answered. "I'll give her a call and let you know as soon as I hear anything."

Mark settled back into his chair. Switching the channel to the local news, he waited, drumming his fingers on the chair arms.

Around seven p.m. Mark's phone buzzed. It was Daly. "You're not going to believe this," Daly said breathlessly.

"What?"

"I had JD at the LAPD lab run the usual series of tests they might look for in a food poisoning case. But she added a few tests they use for terrorist chemical agents just to cover all the bases. JD found ricin in the chocolates at Jim's house. *Eff'n ricin!*" Daly yelled into the phone.

"The shit has hit the fan here. They've contacted Homeland and the FBI to let them know there's a chemical weapon in play."

Mark sat back in his chair, "So you're telling me Mary spiked Jim's chocolates with a chemical weapon?"

"Exactly. The chocolates still had the note from Mary attached to it so we know they were from her. How the hell does a foodie like Mary get hold of a chemical agent like ricin?" Daly said in disbelief.

"Ok. I need to get to Jim's doctor with this info. He needs to know what he's dealing with," Mark said as he disconnected.

Mark practically ran to the nurse's station and had Dr. Miller paged. Dr. Miller called Mark within a few seconds of his page. After an urgent conversation with Mark, the doctor asked him to hand the phone to the head nurse. As she talked to Dr. Miller, her eyes grew round.

When she handed the phone back to Mark, all hell broke loose.

The head nurse ordered Jim moved to a special containment room. The hospital had set up a room for the potential of ebola patients or other highly virulent diseases. All personnel dealing with Jim's transport to his isolation room donned full HAZMAT gear.

The area surrounding Jim suddenly became some-thing out of a science fiction movie. Complete with the unnamed government agency sweeping into an area sporting possible alien beings, locking down all access and whisking the ET, in this case Jim, to a secure holding area.

Mark was asked to retreat to the visitor's lounge where Dr. Miller would find him when Jim's situation was fully under control. From the lounge, Mark dialed Sergeant McClarey to let him know the most recent development of Jim's ricin poisoning.

"Sergeant, it's looking like Mary was behind poisoning Jim," Mark explained. "That begs the question of whether Mary was getting rid of Jim given his concern she was a potential suspect in the murders of Louise, Tommy, Mike and Chuck."

McClarey didn't answer immediately, "Master Ford, I can't really comment on what it's lookin like at the pres-ent. I've just hooked up with Homeland and the lead FBI agent, Special Agent Bernie Eagleman, who's ordered a warrant be issued t' search Mary Simon's house and of-fice. We should know a lot more in the next few hours. I'll keep you in the loop as I learn more. Goodnight Master Ford and let yer lady know her spidey senses appear t' be spot on."

Chapter 23

It had been a long night.

After Mark had called McClarey from the hospital around nine p.m., he'd returned home.

He and Daly had sat up talking most of the night. There was no making sense of how Mary could have turned into a cold-blooded psycho with her most trusted friends. Mary's medical difficulties and fixation on a healthy lifestyle just seemed too weak a motive to Daly. She felt from her profiling experience there should have been a triggering event for this kind of extreme psychotic behavior. Especially since the victims were wellknown friends. A longer-term medical crisis like breast cancer wouldn't be a typical trigger for the extreme retribution carried out over the last several months.

It was now nine a.m., Friday.

Daly and Mark had decided they should go check on Jim at the hospital. Mark had called Dr. Miller earlier in the morning. He'd informed Mark that Jim was resting comfortably, receiving fluids, and had undergone an activated charcoal purge to remove any remaining ricin in his system. Dr. Miller had explained there wasn't an antidote or direct medical treatment for ricin. They would administer supportive care to keep Jim hydrated and nutritionally whole while his body excreted the poison from its systems. Jim was showing signs of feeling better as he'd talked with Dr. Miller during his morning rounds and asked when he could go home.

Mark backed his car out of the driveway with Daly riding shotgun and headed for the 101. They pulled into the Santa Monica Hospital's visitor parking lot thirty minutes later.

The same head nurse was outside the special unit where Jim had been isolated the night before. After receiving their hospital gowns, masks and gloves, they were allowed to enter Jim's room. Sergeant McClarey was already in the room with Jim. Mark nudged the hospital door open, peeking around the door like a curious child who wanted to join the group.

"Well hello Sergeant. I see you and Jim are already catching up on last night's craziness," Mark said as Daly pushed the door open wide and stepped past him.

"Craziness is a good word for it, or maybe eff'n Nuts with a capital N," Daly added as she moved to Jim's bedside.

"So how are you feeling Jim?" she asked, her voice softening.

From behind tired eyes and a gaunt face, Jim answered, "A little better, but not on solid food yet. The doc says it will be a few days before I'm likely to get my shore pass," Jim smiled weakly at Daly who was squeezing his hand. "The good sergeant here was filling me in on all the excitement I missed yesterday."

"A good mornin t' you, Master and m'Lady Ford. There's been quite a flurry of actions as you might 'ave guessed with Homeland and the FBI gettin involved in a ricin poisonin. I was just lettin Master Jensen know dat the search o' Mary Simon's house didn't turn up anythin, not even m'Lady Simon," McClarey said as one eyebrow raised.

"However, the search o' her office found all we might 'ave guessed at and a bit more. Homeland found a few chemical type vials o' some real nasties in her office cold box. Overnight testin confirmed one o' the items was ricin, at a pretty high concentration, and matchin the chocolate samples m'Lady Ford had provided the LAPD."

"One o' the other vials appears consistent with the poison found on Louise Jensen's hands, while another was an extract from flowers." McClarey checked his note-pad and added, "Lilies o' the valley. Which I'm told by me Homeland lab chaps, can bugger a person enough t' bring on a heart attack similar t' the one Chuck Kohler suffered."

McClarey turned to look at Jim and said apologetically, "We'll likely need t' exhume m'Lady Jensen and Chuck Kohler t' confirm the chemicals are a match with the ones we found at Mary Simon's office."

"Yes, I understand. Let me know what you need," Jim said resignedly.

"I want to do all I can to make sure Mary is behind bars. Or better yet, on her way to some super-Max for a lethal injection cocktail; her last stop on the way to hell," Jim said as his eyes flashed with the vengeance he felt on full display.

"I appreciate yer willingness t' help me build the case against Mary Simon. I know it's not easy t' revisit wounds so fresh," McClarey said as he placed a hand on Jim's shoulder.

Jim's features morphed from anger to grief and then finally to weariness.

The quietness of the room was palpable. Mark and Daly had no words to salve Jim's pain. Their dear friend seemed to be getting some level of closure from Mary's implication in Louise's murder. The deep level of loss Jim felt, and that they shared in as good friends, seemed to be a black hole with no bottom. And no ladder led back to the light of loved ones lost.

"Well, I should be gettin on. We'll be needin t' locate Mary Simon. Plus the paperwork'll be an avalanche o' forms fallin around me head with Homeland and the FBI involved," McClarey grimaced as he nodded to Jim and headed for the exit. "I wonder if I could speak t' m'Lady Ford and you, Master Ford for just a wee bit?" McClarey motioned toward the hallway.

Once outside Jim's room, McClarey turned to Mark and Daly, "I left the Homeland blokes around six this mornin after they'd shared the findins o' their search of Mary Simon's office. They asked me t' let you know they'd like t' debrief with you; today if possible. Given you two led 'em t' the goods and all, I'm guessin they'll want t' get all their chickens in a row."

"No problem, Sergeant. We can swing by there after we visit with Jim," Mark said.

"Sergeant, does anything about Mary being the murderer strike you as wanky?" Daly said as she cocked her head at McClarey.

"Well, m'Lady Ford, we're pretty early in the data gatherin stage. I'd agree we should get all the facts t' the surface before slammin the cell door shut on Mary Simon. What're yer spidey senses tellin you now?" he asked.

"Mary going over the wall to psycho land doesn't fit any of my previous experience profiling serial killers. There doesn't seem to be any triggering trauma or violent loss in her life capable of creating this kind of break with sanity. Especially acting out against long-time friends. Yes, she is a breast cancer survivor, a two-time divorcee, and did lose her son many years ago, but the timeframe for these events was almost a decade long. Usually, there is an acute crisis that leads a person to kill a close friend." Daly paused waiting for McClarey to respond.

"Mind you, we don't know Mary Simon didn't go off her cracker some time ago. It just might o' took her this long t' plan her deadly mischief," McClarey mused. "Poisonin takes plannin and gatherin all the needed concoctions. Then there's gettin the pieces t' fall together if yer not o' the mind t' get caught, you know."

"Yes. The planning for these murders does seem quite calculated," Daly agreed. "And using poison isn't a crime of passion. More often it's a woman's best chance at revenge or the convenient disposal of a spouse who's lost that loving feeling."

They were all mulling over these thoughts when Sergeant McClarey's phone buzzed.

"McClarey here. Yes. She's where? Any idea of what she might have eaten to set it off?" he asked as he pulled out his small note pad and jotted something down.

"Hmmm. This mornin, eh? All right, I'm at the hospital now. Just finished updatin Jim Jensen and the Fords on last night's findins. I'll secure Mary Simon's room with hospital security and get back t' you," McClarey said as he ended the call.

McClarey turned to Daly and Mark, "If you thought yer spidey senses were tinglin before, this ought t' give 'em a real shocker. Turns out Mary Simon came down with food poisonin and her ex, Michael, brought her t' this very hospital around eight last night."

"Mary's *here*?" Daly exclaimed.

"Well, she was. Evidently, she passed away early this mornin due t' complications," McClarey said in a puzzled tone.

"Dat was one o' the boys at Homeland who had tracked her down by finally callin her ex," McClarey paused as if thinking through what had just been relayed to him by his Homeland contact. "Michael was quite upset as you might imagine. He said he'd gotten the call from the hospital dat his wife had passed in the early mornin hours."

"Even stranger, the Homeland lab boys found a particularly nasty bug in the bottles o' milk at Mary Simon's office refrigerator." He consulted the note he'd just written, "E-coli O157:H7 they called it. It's the one you see in the papers every now and again dat can wreak havoc on kiddos or immune compromised people. Evidently it's found in buggered up raw milk or under-cooked hamburger," McClarey explained as Daly and Mark looked at him with mouths agape.

"So the prime suspect poisons herself, *or* is this some perfect eff'n twist of fate delivered by Elsie the Cow?" Daly said in stunned disbelief as she looked questioningly at Mark and McClarey.

Part III.

Vengeance blooms, and the petals fall.

Chapter 24

Mark sat his coffee cup on Sergeant McClarey's conference room table.

It was Monday morning around nine.

He and Daly had come to the Santa Monica PD station. Sergeant McClarey had offered to share the evidence collected over the weekend, a courtesy given their help with the case. Daly sat next to Mark and across from Sergeant McClarey sipping from her "Badass" mug. She was looking through a stack of files sitting in the middle of the table.

"So looks like you and the Homeland crew had a busy weekend," Daly half-smiled at McClarey as she continued to thumb through the evidence files.

"You could say dat m'Lady. I don't think the Feds punch a clock when it comes t' more serious matters, like chemical terrorism," McClarey said reaching into a box of assorted doughnuts on the edge of the table. He held one towards Daly who waved him off, then reoffered it to Mark.

"Thanks," Mark said as he accepted the glazed gift.

"Did anything show up explaining what Mary's motive might have been?"

"There's still a wee bit o' work t' do goin through Mary Simon's computer files dat may take a few days. Nothin from the initial looks at physical home and office files. No records o' purchasin any nefarious type materials either. Her phone records'll be checked as well over the next few days. Basically nothin at first blush."

"She traveled extensively for her business. I suppose she could have purchased just about anything she needed while abroad. There wouldn't be a record if she used cash," Mark said as he glanced at a few of the evidence files.

"Yeah. Dat's what the Homeland boys are surmisin at this point. Though they'd really like t' turn up a smokin pistol t' put this babe in the crib," McClarey said as he leaned back in his chair and stretched. "I've gotta say I'm feelin the same."

Daly looked up from the files detailing the lab results of the poisons found at Mary's office and said to McClarey, "So our best explanation of the evidence is Mary somehow obtained a highly controlled substance while on some trip to east eff'n Googlestan. She spikes it into Jim's chocolates and leaves a note on the gift saying it's from her. Seems too pat to me. How do we explain Chuck's poisoning, turned heart attack?"

"The Feds were able t' go back and check the video and visitor registration at the foodbank from the day he had his heart attack. Appears they had a few visitors dat mornin. Nothin conclusive. A lot o' the visitors t' dat place use aliases and don't have mailin addresses and the like.

Hard t' know if one o' the visitors might 'ave been Mary."

"There was a woman who signed in as Chuck Kohler's last customer. Used the name Lily Hartman in the registry. Dat's a wee bit ironic if it's the killer boastin she used lily o' the valley extract. The video doesn't get a good look at her face. It's possible it was Mary Simon dressed up as some down-and-out 'omeless woman," McClarey said shrugging.

"What about connections to Mike's and Tommy's deaths?" Mark asked.

"Well, we're bein a bit speculative in tryin t' tie their demise into Mary Simon," McClarey said as he paused to blow on his hot coffee. "We need t' exhume their bodies for a more thorough autopsy as the next step. Assumin we find a basis from dat t' suspect foul play, we can follow the evidence t' see where it takes us."

"There's got to be something we're missing that makes Mary the clear killer, motive and all. Or there's some whole other explanation we haven't even begun to understand," Daly said as she slapped one of the evidence files on the desk and stared at Sergeant McClarey.

"Given the deadly little smorgasbord the Feds found in her office, maybe she just snapped. Decided to take out those closest to her. Who knows, we might have been next on her dine and die list," Mark offered as he reached out to touch Daly's hand.

"I don't buy it. At least not without some ulterior motive we haven't uncovered yet. You don't just kill your best friend without something triggering it. I just don't buy it," Daly sat back in her chair. She crossed her arms in annoyance with the obvious facts surrounding her.

Sergeant McClarey shuffled through the folders and pulled out the one marked "Mary Simon Lab Results." "As I mentioned Friday, Mary Simon appears t' have succumbed t' a particularly nasty form o' food poisonin. The doctors think her immune system was still a bit compromised from her previous bout wit cancer. She had finished her chemo treatments about six months ago, but she was still vulnerable."

"The samples o' her special ordered milk appear t' be the source. We'll be lookin into the dairy farmer's operation over the next few days. The bottles had rubber resealable caps, so no real way t' know if they were intentionally buggered. We'll be checkin the dairy for this kind o' e-coli. I'm told it wouldn't be dat uncommon t' have this particular bug show up in a raw dairy situation. We'll see what we find at the farm."

McClarey hesitated and then continued, "It's probably nothin, but there is one other thing I'll be lookin into for me own purposes. As part o' tryin to better understand the background on Louise's case, I interviewed Kimberly Riggsby concernin the death o' her son."

"You may know this already. Jim and Louise's son, Aiden, was in a serious car wreck as a teenager. Kimberly Riggsby's son was the driver in the wreck and her son was killed. When I went t' talk t' her about Louise Jensen's murder, she was none too sympathetic over her demise. I came away thinkin there's more t' her story I need t' know."

"Even if she did have it in for Louise, what are you

thinking her connection to Chuck and the others might be?" Daly asked with a raised eyebrow.

"I dunno. Dat's why I'd like another chance t' see if anythin under the surface shows up. Especially now dat Mary Simon is implicated in Louise's and Chuck Kohler's murders. By the way, have you checked in on Master Jensen t' see how he's doin?" McClarey asked Mark.

"Yes, we stopped by the hospital this morning and he seemed to be doing much better. Aiden got home from school Saturday and stayed with Jim at the hospital through Sunday night. Jim's hoping to be released in a couple of days, so Aiden is planning on comng back later in the week to move him home." Mark paused as he looked at Daly, "I think having Aiden there lifted his spirits considerably, don't you hon?"

"What? Oh, definitely," Daly said distractedly as she began shuffling back through the folders again. "Do you think I could get copies of these files to look over? I tend to work better if I can spread my work around me."

"I can check dat out with me Fed boyos, but I don't think it should be a problem given yer help so far," McClarey said as he squinted at Daly. "I can see yer not feelin we've got the bad guy on this one, right?"

"No, I'm feeling there's a piece in the puzzle we aren't seeing. Depending on what that piece looks like, I'll know if we've got it nailed or if the screen door's still open."

"Good enough for me. Well let me know if yer spidey senses give you a tinglin. They've been pretty spot on up 'til now," McClarey said smiling as he stood up and opened the door for Daly and Mark to exit.

Mark pulled Daly's chair out for her and followed her out of McClarey's conference room. As they reached the parking lot, he turned to Daly, "I'm getting that sense you're not about to let this go. What's next?"

"I don't know. I'd love to just take it all at face value and put a big sign on Mary's grave saying, "She Did It." But the detective in me needs more. I feel like there's another shoe to drop."

Mark opened Daly's car door, "So I guess we wait to see what turns up in the next few days as the feds comb through it all. Maybe that's the shoe we're waiting for."

Mark closed Daly's door and walked to the driver's side of the car.

He couldn't help but feel the shoe Daly was waiting for was a size fifteen, steel-toed shit kicker. Her cop's intuition was usually right, and she'd kicked more than one turd into a cloud of look-what-I found-here dust.

Chapter 25

S he approached her office down the tiled corridor. Her black Louboutin heels clicking with each step in a rhythmic staccato beat, a sharp echo from the corridor walls following her.

Her arms swung slightly with each step giving a sense of balance to her stride. The purposeful pace announced she had somewhere to be.

She wore a form-fitting black skirt revealing her legs from just above the knees. Her athletically shaped calves tensed with each step, showing the muscle and sinew beneath her lightly tanned skin, melting away to smoothness between steps. Shoulders square and sculpted beneath a black short jacket, darts sewn in front, a white blouse and a knotted black and gray patterned silk scarf at her neck, completed the professional look she strived to create. A leather portfolio bag with a long carrying strap slung over her shoulder punctuated her being on her way to something that mattered.

She approached her office door. The corners of her

mouth turned up slightly at the frosted glass script on the door: *Kimberly Riggsby – Exciting Designs for Life.*

Her long fingers searched the side pocket of her portfolio bag. She took the last couple of steps toward the entrance, and without needing to direct her gaze away from her scripted name, she produced a key chain. She inserted the key labeled "Office." A quick half turn to the right, the clack of the lock welcoming her, and she stepped through the door projecting an air of confidence and control to the space beyond.

Silently she crossed the room with her stilettos stabbing the plush white carpet with each step. Placing her bag by the talon-like leg of her desk, she settled into the comfortable executive chair; a queen on her throne.

She reached out to touch the glass orb on her desk containing the monkshood flower suspended in its crystal clear sarcophagus. Smiling, she remembered the previous few days' events.

It had been so nice of that putz, Sergeant McClarey, to visit her with his clueless questions and suspicions thinly veiled. She'd shared her true feelings of disgust and loathing directed at the dead Jensen woman. Her feelings were justified given the loss of her precious Danny from the carelessness of the bitch's son.

McClarey had unknowingly laid a present in her lap that day; his suspicion of Mary Simon as a potential suspect in Louise Jensen's murder.

It had required some quick thinking on her part. After McClarey's departure she'd decided to take full advantage of this new morsel of knowledge. A check of the poker group's Facebook™ posts revealed Pat Hemmings was arranging post-funeral meals for Jim Jensen. This provided the perfect opportunity for her to pull together a gift for poor Jim to help assuage the loss of his wife.

Her plan had taken shape easily with the help of Jim's doting friends trying to soften the loss of Louise: preparing her specialty chocolates, including a nice note from Mary, and leaving the ricin tainted chocolates on Hemmings' porch. The gift would provide the perfect trail to Mary Simon, specially delivered by Jim's dear and trusted friend, Pat.

A few search warrants later, the authorities would find the highly toxic concoctions in Mary's office. Not only the ricin used to spike the tasty confections, but lily of the valley extract and hemlock sap. These should give the police more than enough evidence to connect Mary to Chuck Kohler's and Louise Jensen's deaths.

Unfortunately, the much maligned Mary Simon wouldn't be able to chat about her murderous ways, or be questioned about why she had highly controlled, illegal substances in her possession. She would prove to be a *dead end*, literally.

Kimberly remembered sitting patiently in the hospital parking lot last Thursday night.

The blazing "Emergency Entrance" red letters lit up the windshield of her car. She had entered the hospital as a candy striper. Although a bit after hours for a volunteer to be brightening a patient's stay, no one had seemed to pay her any attention. She had checked the logs to find Mary's room. Smiling at the night shift orderlies and nurses had seemed to be the only hall pass she'd needed.

Entering Mary's room had seemed too easy. The only delay she had encountered was one of her own making.

She'd entered the hospital room with the droning beep of Mary's heart monitor as the only sound. The high-pitched sound echoed off the walls while the dull green light from her monitor cast a strange hue over the room.

This ethereal combination had transported Kimberly to the bedside of her mother so many years ago. Those painful last days sitting with her mother. Waiting for the hooded specter of death's merciful visit to end the barbaric dance of a body unable to sustain itself. A body being urged on by tubes inserted into all orifices, ventilators pumping oxygen to tired lungs, and a soup of drugs designed to ease the passage from this life to the next delivered through her IV.

Those painful, languishing hours with her mother had provided ample time to live and relive the guilt she felt. Her inability to intervene in what was an obvious path to destruction. The perpetual ingestion of junk food and empty calories. The misguided belief in "easy fix" pills or fat-burning supplements.

Finally giving in to the gastric by-pass surgery to overcome her mother's obesity; a disease which easily overwhelmed any sense that discipline and willpower might win the day. Her mother's extreme obesity had happened in baby steps and over years of acclimation to poor eating habits becoming the norm.

Kimberly's guilt had descended on her psyche like a

cold draft of frigid accountability. It had traveled up her spine and entered her cerebral cavity exposing her brain to the harsh realization of her complicity in her mother's suffering and ultimate demise. And with these cold thoughts as her companion, she had awaited death's visitation.

A shiver had pierced Kimberly's consciousness that night, returning her to the task at hand. Removing the vial of aconite from her striped apron's front pocket along with a small syringe, she had injected the potent extract into Mary Simon's IV. The fatal dose had been delivered over the next few minutes, and would appear to be a complication of her severe food poisoning and an unfortunate by-product of her weakened immune system.

She hoped the sweet irony of her plan would not be lost on those investigating Mary's heinous actions. How sweet for Mary to die from complications of adulterated natural milk, and be tagged with the murders of her ex-friends via "natural" poisonings.

She had been able to slip out of the hospital unnoticed after tying up her remaining loose end.

The coup de grace had been her brilliance in killing two birds with one visit to Mary's office that previous Wednesday. She had not only planted the poison evidence in Mary's office, but at the same time had injected the bottles of Mary's raw milk with a particularly virulent strain of e-coli; one carefully chosen to create extreme hemorrhagic diarrhea. This had resulted in Mary's hospitalization and the opening for her to ensure Mary wouldn't be available for any probing questions. The final step in setting Mary up to be her foil and a very guilty suspect.

Reflection on the last few days' activities brought a cruel smile to Kimberly's face. She felt the satisfaction of a well-woven web of vengeance straining towards fruition. And best of all, no one seemed the wiser to her culminating her revenge.

All this left her able to pursue her last and most important victim on her own timing.

As she pulled a writing tablet from her portfolio to begin brainstorming her plans and next moves, her phone rang. Picking up the receiver after a few annoying rings, she answered, "Exciting Designs for Life, Kimberly speaking. How can I help you?"

"Hey sis. I just checked in with Pat Hemmings to see what's being said about all the excitement at the hospital over the weekend," Greg Riggsby announced, then paused, seeming to enjoy the suspense.

"Looks like everything has gone perfectly. Mary is the prime suspect in the murders. Her own death is being blamed on complications of her accidental food poisoning. Hemmings has been burning up the phone lines with the Fords who seem to have an inside hookup with the detective handling the case. Hemmings is all too happy to share anything and everything she knows with her friendly neighborhood financial advisor, namely me." Greg laughed, and continued, "So what's next with all the heat nicely pointing away from you?"

"Little brother, I agreed to handle the low-life poker klatsch as you and I wanted, and on your timing. Now I need to plan how I'll end the one who's devastated MY last eight years. And do it on MY timing," Kimberly said, hissing her last assertion into her cell.

"Fine. Fine. As well as this has gone, you deserve to focus on your own unfinished business. I'd prefer it if you gave everything a few weeks to cool off. You know, make sure the Feds have returned to chasing their top ten list before you create any more bodies by the side of the road."

"You know me. Careful to a fault."

"Well, momma would be proud of her little flower if she's looking down on your handiwork. Very proud. Take care sis and let me know if you need me for your upcoming plans. Love you."

"Love you too, little brother. I'll give you a call when I'm ready to share."

Hanging up the phone, she felt her momma was looking down on her proudly as her brother had speculated. It had been a long and grueling undertaking to plan out the last several months. The sense of fulfillment she was experiencing in avenging her mother's wrongful death made it all worthwhile. The sweetest tasting fruit she could imagine.

With a satisfied sigh, she took the pen from her desk valet. She began meticulously planning the next moves in her desired end game. She had fantasized about achieving justice and peace dozens of times; of reaching a sense closure. The pain from the many tortured and sleepless nights she'd endured these past eight years was about to be repaid in full.

The anticipation of revenge was intoxicating.

And now, it was time to act.

Chapter 26

M cClarey sat at his desk sipping his third cup of PG Tips, his thinking beverage. He'd wet the tea in a portable kettle and hot plate combo positioned at the corner of his desk at six a.m. Over the last few hours, he'd been poring over multiple reports and analyses from his Fed counter-parts on the Mary Simon case on this fine Wednesday morning.

He had to admit he was pleasantly surprised by the amount of information and the thoroughness of what he was seeing. Most astounding to him was the speed at which it had been pulled together by the Homeland and FBI teams descending on the case the previous Thursday. The threat of a chemical agent set loose in a metropolis like L.A. garnered no lack of resources. The urgency went to DEFCON 5 at the blink of an eye.

The evidence of the use of ricin and other toxic chemicals along with the immediate demise of the perpetrator, Mary Simon, appeared to make this case a very short crisis for the Feds. However, they were fastidious by nature.

Reports and background information they'd gathered still needed to be tied up with a proper bow and filed for future reference.

A few discoveries that were brought to the surface via these reports gave him pause. He was trying to match the facts to the three Simon victims, and assumed friends from past years.

His first concern centered on the emails acquired from the laptops of Mary Simon and Louise Jensen, now logged into evidence. In looking over the significant correspondence between the two, there was nothing to indicate they were anything but good friends. In fact, all pointed to them being BFF's if the notes back and forth could be taken at face value.

Mary's bout with cancer had shown up in the subject matter along with Louise's concerns about her son's psychological scarring and feeling of helplessness about it. Even more recent items concerning the losses of Chuck Kohler, Tommy Hemmings and Mike Gentry seemed to be grief stricken or sharing concerns for the spouses left behind.

Beyond the emails with victims or spouses, there was no indication from Mary's files of any plans or correspondence concerning harm to any of the suspected victims of her killing spree. Phone records and forensics on Mary's cellphone were also clean of any suspicious calls or messages.

Secondly, Mary's car had also been brought into the Santa Monica PD forensic geek squad for a once over. This included a download of her GPS system to track her whereabouts of the last couple of weeks.

Of particular interest was the day of Louise Jensen's murder. A neighbor across the alley from the Jensen's had been questioned after the confirmed ricin analysis had put the Feds into full canvassing mode. The neighbor, a Mrs. Liggitt, had noticed a white luxury type car parked in the alley behind Jensen's backyard for a few hours on Thursday morning. Given Mary Simon drove a white Mercedes SL, the hope was her GPS would put her at the murder scene within the window of time Louise Jensen was murdered. That would provide a particularly helpful nail in the coffin of the late m'Lady Simon.

However, the GPS from Mary's car showed her to be at her office that morning until after three o'clock. Not so much as a quick trip out for lunch.

McClarey's third concern stemmed from a report dealing with connections between the victims and Mary Simon, and any common acquaintances they seemed to share. This was where the Feds truly shined a light into corners that the local police couldn't touch. Cross-correlating databases from legal, governmental agencies, public forums like Facebook or Twitter, and any financial records allowed them to check how and when individuals interacted. It was a bit disconcerting to McClarey to see first hand the reach these federal agencies had when the gloves were taken off. The mantel of "potential terrorist threat" provided wide discretion when it came to the Feds jurisdiction. Nevertheless, it was helpful for his current purposes.

The "Common Elements" report, as it was titled,

indicated several miscellaneous type connections. These included restaurants they all frequented, banking facilities they shared, on-line retailers used by all, and where they filled their cars with gas. The two items which caught his interest were from some of the connections that had not been brought up during his investigation and discussions with victim spouses, friends or other persons of interest in the case.

The first surprising connection was an interior design job for Tommy Hemmings. It had been completed the previous summer by Exciting Designs for Life, Kimberly Riggsby's design firm. Somehow m'Lady Riggsby had forgotten to mention this during his previous week's meeting with her. Then she'd indicated she didn't know the poker group individuals other than Louise Jensen. Of course, it could be a coincidence. Maybe Riggsby didn't know her client Hemmings was in the same poker group as the Jensens. But McClarey didn't much believe in coincidences. Especially when murder was involved.

The second connection made the hair on McClarey's neck stand up. He sat forward in his seat studying the report. It centered on a Limited Liability Company with Tommy Hemmings as the managing partner. The LLC was named Lion's Heart and indicated it was a venture capital investment in upstream medical research. The LLC partners included Hemmings, Louise Jensen, Mike Gentry, Charles Kohler, and Mary Simon. The financial manager who managed the LLC as a paid consultant and advisor was Greg Riggsby. The report flagged the fact that Greg Riggsby was the younger brother of Kimberly

Riggsby as a further point of intersecting elements. No further details of the LLC were captured.

"Ain't *dat* the leprechaun's pot o' gold!" McClarey said as he reread the last item to make sure he hadn't missed anything. "So I guess there's a bit more than yer unfortunate son's premature death linkin you and Louise Jensen now isn't there Kimberly?" he mused under his breath as he took a sip of tea.

McClarey sat back in his chair for several minutes. He looked through the ceiling as if he were studying the sky beyond the drop ceiling, concrete and I-beams of the police station. A slight smile curled from the edge of his mouth. He leaned forward reaching for his desk phone while fumbling in his tweed jacket's breast pocket with his free hand to retrieve his notepad. He flipped through a few pages of his notes to the page with Exciting Designs for Life as the header. Punching in the phone number he had used to set up his previous meeting with m'Lady Riggsby, he sat back in his seat as the phone connected.

"Exciting Designs for Life. Kimberly Riggsby speaking."

"Good day m'Lady Riggsby. This is Sergeant McClarey callin from the Santa Monica PD. You might recall we talked briefly last week for a minute or two."

"Yes, of course. Is this to let me know what is already in the papers?" she said, not bothering to disguise the sarcasm in her voice. "I've already seen the article about the crazy woman suspected of killing Louise Jensen and attempting to get her husband as well. If this call is to apologize for *wrongly* suspecting me, don't bother."

"Well m'Lady. You're right dat a lot transpired since our meetin, and it's fair t' say all fingers be pointin at Mary Simon as the culprit in the case. I'd promised t' get back in contact with you if we had any more questions. It turns out dere are a couple o' areas I think you might be able t' help clear up for me. I'm wonderin if I might be able t' come by and run a few things by you this afternoon, if dat's okay with you."

"Well, I suppose if you must," she said with a sigh.

McClarey heard the sound of pages turning in the background as she continued, "I'm working from home today. If you can come by sometime after two o'clock that could work. Do you have the address?"

"Not a problem m'Lady Riggsby. I'll be by a bit after two." McClarey heard the click of her phone disconnecting before he could say a proper goodbye. With a sniff, he placed his phone back in its cradle.

And I hope yer day is goin well Kimberly as my nose says somethin's about to turn wanky, as m'Lady Ford would say.

He tapped a few keys bringing up Kimberly Riggsby's Department of Motor Vehicles file, including her home address. Another few keys and Google Maps™ opened on his monitor. He put in Kimberly Riggsby's address, 6099 Long Canyon Road, Simi Valley. The satellite image of the property came into focus showing a large ranch style home set on a relatively large property by California standards, at least for the pricey Simi Valley area.

Her estate appeared to be about three acres or so with a dry creek bed running through the center of the property behind the house. Another smaller building structure was at the back of the property. A dirt or gravel path meandered from the west side of the house, through the creek bed and ended at the out-building at the back of the property. Beyond the back of the property, it appeared to be uninhabited hills of brush and trees. No neighboring houses. He zoomed in on the house and then the out-building to see if he could get any more detail on the Riggsby estate. Interestingly, the out-building appeared to be some kind of shed with its glass roof glinting from the California sun on the day the satellite took its Google Maps snap shot.

Looking at his watch, he noted it was closing in on lunchtime. With an hour drive to Simi Valley, he'd have just enough time to catch a proper lunch at one of his favorite pubs near the Los Encinos state park area, and still be able to keep his appointment with Kimberly Riggsby around two o'clock.

Grabbing his coat from the back of his chair, and retrieving his driving cap from his hat tree, McClarey whistled a bit of *O' Danny Boy*. He pushed through the swinging door stanchion leading out past the day sergeant's receiving station and the waiting room. His day was looking up. Lunch plus a nice drive through the hills north of LA to Simi Valley would give him a chance to think through his line of questioning for m'Lady Riggsby.

McClarey pressed the "unlock" icon on his key fob. The black Ford Taurus winked its lights at him as he climbed in and lowered his and the passenger's window to enjoy the warm day.

Pulling out of the police lot, he thought back on his

time as a detective and how cases that seemed too cut-and-dried usually were. The truth usually hid several layers down in the proverbial onion. His strength and his passion had always been persisting in peeling back those layers; meticulously and one at a time until the raw truth with all its unsuspected twists became undeniable.

This is what he lived for now.

His spirits were high as the mist on the mountain as his newfound clues seemed to be leading him to this stinky onion's core.

Chapter 27

With his stomach pleasantly full of fish n' chips and his mind relishing the thought of questioning Kimberly Riggsby, McClarey was northbound on the 405. About ten miles out, he turned onto the Ronald Reagan Freeway headed west towards Simi Valley.

Not knowing how deeply Kimberly might be involved in the Mary Simon case versus her brother, Greg, he would need to play his cards close to the vest as he questioned her. Key to him was to see what connections might pop out when specifically prodded on interactions she and her brother had with Tommy Hemmings.

The traffic was relatively light on the Ronald Reagan as the expansive countryside filled McClarey's view. The Santa Susana Mountains lay in the distance to his north. The rolling brown hills of Simi Hills were to his south as he passed from Los Angeles County into Ventura County. The typically dry spring and summer brought the valley and grasslands to a pale yellow with shades of brown. Dotted with coast live oak trees and chaparral evergreens, the scrubland's parched appearance begged for rain.

He missed the deep plush green of his Irish home-land the most when he traveled through the outer counties surrounding LA. It was hard for him to believe the many people who sought out this temperate, sunny place as their chosen nirvana. He couldn't imagine living here long term. To him it would be like living in a desert, always thirsty for the green hills he had called home for so many years.

The countryside once again turned into long sections of strip malls and retail outlets dotting the side roads as he entered Simi Valley proper. About four miles inside the city limits he saw the turn for Long Canyon Road. Exiting the freeway, he headed south to his destination. He was now in the valley the city was appropriately named after with the expanse of the Simi Hills stretching east as far as he could see. The amber hills trembled in fear of an errant cigarette or lightning strike that could set acres ablaze.

It was 2:05 as he pulled up to the gated entrance of Kimberly Riggsby's estate. At only three acres, it gave the impression of being much larger. The lack of major housing developments and the surrounding common space made her property seem to melt into the surrounding landscape with no lines of demarcation for where her property began or ended.

The entrance gate was rolled back onto its track. McClarey took this as a welcome to pull directly up to the front of the house where he parked in the circular driveway. Hearty shrubs of numerous varieties lined the wall on either side of the entrance gate. These provided some level of privacy from passing cars, although they weren't high enough to obscure the residence if one were walking by the front.

The property sported mature oak trees carefully positioned around the front entryway giving the house a majestic feel. The ranch-style home was very well maintained. Large windows and skylights had been designed to maximize the use of natural sunlight.

McClarey stepped from his car and approached the large front double oak doors and reached for the doorbell. Before he could engage the rectangular button announcing his arrival, an intercom speaker to the side of the door came to life. The voice of Kimberly Riggsby startled him, "I'm around back on the deck, Sergeant McClarey. Come around the outside of the house and you'll see me."

He hadn't announced himself. Video surveillance was probably embedded somewhere around the entrance so he could be observed discreetly. Nothing obvious gave any clandestine glass eyes away. It wouldn't be hard to believe the house was fully outfitted with a security system capable of detecting interlopers and informing the home's residents they had company. His experience in LA had been sophisticated security systems were expected for any high-end residence. Given the land and what he could see from the exterior of Riggsby's home, it certainly exceeded six figures.

He followed the pebble path around the east side of the house.

Skirting the three-car garage, he noticed a new model,

white Mercedes SL in one of the garage bays with the door open. *Now isn't dat an interestin coincidence, and I wonder what yer GPS might tell us.* He made a note of the model and license plate in his notepad.

He continued on towards the back of the house. As he rounded the corner, he was struck by the expanse of the backyard with coast live oaks, huge California sycamores and evergreen shrubs dotting the hillside, and fading into magnificent canyon views. The view presented an openness and beauty he hadn't seen in LA residences.

Kimberly Riggsby was sitting on an elevated deck with her laptop on a patio table. She looked quite casual in sky blue capris, a loose fitting, sleeveless blouse, and sandals. She waved for him to join her, motioning towards a set of steps leading up from a stamped concrete walk out area. The walk out area had a large sliding door built into the lower story of the house. The rear of the house seemed much larger than the front. The sloping terrain allowed for a large patio area below the elevated main floor of the house with its own outside patio. This gave it the appearance of a two-story residence from this view.

McClarey ascended the limestone stone stairs to join his host. "Good day m'Lady Riggsby," he said as he tipped his hat. "You 'ave a beautiful place here. I can see why you'd choose t' work wit a view like this every wee bit, yes ma'am."

Kimberly closed her laptop. She sat back in her padded patio chair, which squeaked slightly as the rocker part of the mechanism announced the weight shift of its occupant. "Hello Sergeant. Did you have any trouble finding your way here from LA?"

"No m'Lady. I rather enjoyed the scenic drive. Mountains and hills in their full glory as it were. But the view from 'ere puts it all t' shame. Quite nice with the canyon and hills surroundin you on all sides. Must be a glorious sunset in the evenin. Could be a bit greener t' suit me own tastes, but you don't look like ye've had rain in a donkey's age."

"Yes, this time of year is always dry. I've come to like the look so long as no one provides a spark. Wild fires are really quite the concern here in the valley. Now, how can I help you Sergeant? You said you had a few things I might be able to clear up."

"Yes, m'Lady. From our conversation earlier today, I take it ye've been keepin up on the Mary Simon case in the papers." He paused as she nodded and he continued, "As ye've been readin, Mary Simon has been implicated as the primary suspect in the murder o' Louise Jensen, and the attempt on Jim Jensen as well. Beyond this, we're lookin at other potential victims which we've not announced t' the press at this time. Dat's where I could use any help you might provide." McClarey looked at the empty glass and pitcher containing ice water sitting on the patio table and asked, "May I?"

"Please help yourself. I don't know anything beyond what I told you before, but go ahead. What is it you want to know?"

"One o' the suspected victims o' the late Mary Simon is Tommy Hemmings. Does dat name ring any bells for you?"

Kimberly shifted in her seat and looked away from McClarey. Appearing to ponder his question for a few seconds, she responded, "You know that name does sound familiar. I think he might have been a client of mine several months back.

"Let me check something," she said as she reopened her laptop and intently scanned through several folders on the screen. "Ah, here we go. Yes, I did some work for a Tommy Hemmings last October. A redo of his study. He had recently retired and was wanting to update his home workplace area. It wasn't a large job, mostly furnishings, window treatments, and a few wall hangings and desk appointments. Pretty basic. So how was Mr. Hemmings connected with Mary Simon?"

"It turns out Tommy Hemmings was one o' the poker group we talked about in our last meetin."

"Oh, I see. You're wondering why I didn't bring up the fact I'd done some interior design work for him given he was in the poker group with the Jensens?"

"Yes, dat did strike me as a potential oversight."

"Sergeant McClarey, I have no idea who the Jensens played poker with. Just because my son was around them *doesn't* mean he came home and gave me a blow-by-blow on who played in their little get togethers. He just shared there was a group of Jensens' friends who met to play regularly. That's *all* I knew."

"Very good, m'Lady; dat answers dat. I do have another interestin connection dat came up a bit unexpectedly." McClarey took a long moment to sip his ice water creating a look of impatience from Kimberly, and continued,

"Do you 'ave any family in the LA area m'Lady Riggsby?"

"Yes, I do. But what has that got to do with any of this?"

"If you'd humor me a bit, would you mind tellin me who yer family members might be?"

"My brother, Greg, lives in the San Fernando area. He's the only family I have left that I've kept track of."

"I see. And what does Master Riggsby do fer a livin?

"He's a financial advisor. An independent agent, but primarily works with John Hancock."

"Did yer brother ever know or do some work for Tommy Hemmings?"

Kimberly shifted again in her chair, and reached for her own glass of water at this question. After taking a sip she answered, "I don't know. My brother has as many clients as I do, maybe more. We don't sit around and discuss who each other knows when we're together."

"Guess dat makes sense," McClarey said as he locked eyes with Kimberly until she looked away. "I s'ppose I should have a chat with Master Riggsby t' clear up any fine points on his relationship with Tommy Hemmings."

"I suppose you should if it's all that critical to this Mary Simon case. Although I don't see what my brother knowing a victim of some psychopath has to do with anything. I'm sure a lot of people knew the victims of this Mary Simon. Probably much better than some casual acquaintance," Kimberly added as she leaned forward to set her glass on the table.

McClarey let her comment hang in the air for a few moments, "Yer probably right about dat m'Lady."

McClarey sat back in his chair and stretched. He let his gaze move across the full landscape of the Riggsby estate, and then commented, "Dat's an interestin place t' have a shed on the back part o' yer property." He pointed towards the building he'd previously checked out in his Google Maps reconnaissance. "Seems a bit far from the house t' be o' much use for storin what nots."

Kimberly seemed to be lost in thought for a second, before she responded. "It's a greenhouse. I like to grow a lot of my own fruits, vegetables and herbs. I built a shed and outfitted it with its own well water system and a partial glass roof. I'm quite proud of it actually. Would you like a tour?" she offered.

McClarey shrugged, "Why not? I think ye've answered all me questions for today. I'll be goin home from here so I've got time for the nickel tour, if you don't mind takin the time? I've always had an interest in gardenin and the like."

"Not a problem. I just need to make a quick call before we take a walk. Excuse me for just a moment," Kimberly said as she exited the patio. She stepped through the sliding screen door into a large family room with a vaulted ceiling.

McClarey hadn't intended to stay longer. But he couldn't pass up a chance to spend more time with Kimberly Riggsby. Who knew what might come out of casual conversation when her guard was down.

He had gotten pretty much what he thought he'd get from the trip, plus a few bonuses. Seeing her reaction to his questions about her brother had been obviously worrisome to m'Lady Riggsby. His soon to be scheduled interrogation of Master Riggsby should prove fruitful. Plus, the unexpected resemblance of Kimberly's car to the one seen behind the Jensen's residence the day of Louise's murder could be a real gold mine of information. He was already looking forward to the search warrant that would allow him to peruse through her GPS coordinates with time logs of the past few weeks.

Kimberly finished her call and slid the screen door to the patio open and smiled at McClarey, "So shall we go take a look at my pride and joy?"

McClarey and Kimberly made their way down the stone steps. Walking across the backyard to the pebbled path, they followed the snaking road from the side of the house to the greenhouse in the back. As they walked, Kimberly provided a bit of background on how she'd obtained the property after her interior design business had taken off five years ago.

She'd wanted to get out of the LA proper area. When she'd come across this property, it was love at the first walk through. She'd not regretted being a longer drive from work. The sunsets and views McClarey had commented on earlier more than made up for any inconvenience.

They reached the greenhouse a few minutes later, stopping frequently as she talked on their slow stroll across the property. McClarey couldn't help but think Kimberly had turned very congenial and talkative for their tour. This made his antennae go up.

Why the sudden change to Miss Hospitality?

She held the door open to the greenhouse for him and

with a slight smile said, "Come this way and I'll show you my grand project."

"Dat's all right, m'Lady. You should lead the way as it's yer turf," he said as he stepped forward and held the door for Kimberly to step through.

What is she up to?

The door slammed shut when he released it, pulled closed by a spring attached to the doorframe. Inside the greenhouse, McClarey was struck by how well it was laid out. Approximately thirty feet or so long and twenty feet wide. The open part of the building was laid out in well-manicured rows of vegetable and herb beds with miniature fruit trees lining the outer wall of the greenhouse on two sides. The glass roof was sectioned and cantilevered so it could be cracked open for ventilation with a rope and pulley mechanism if days became too hot. What appeared to be rolled up canvas shade covers were attached at the apex of the ceiling so the hottest of days could be attenuated with shade as needed. A sprinkler system was suspended a few feet above the planting beds and could be adjusted to different configurations with quick disconnect couplings installed every few feet along the flexible hose system.

McClarey let out a low whistle and commented, "M'Lady Riggsby, you weren't a kiddin when you said this was a set up t' be proud o'. A real first class operation ye've put together here."

"Why, thank you sergeant. I thought you might be impressed. It took me over a year to get it just right. I still find things to improve on when I get a few moments."

"M'Lady Riggsby, what's dat section in the far corner fer?" McClarey questioned as he pointed to a finished dry walled room in the southwest corner of the greenhouse. The room had a door with a keyed padlock inserted through sturdy clasps attached to the substantial door and doorjamb. The room took up about a fourth of the building with dimensions he guessed to be around ten by fifteen feet.

"Oh that's where we keep our specialty all natural chemicals and fertilizers. I don't use any herbicides or anything like that. We have to deal with insect pests using natural repellants. I thought it was better to keep those items locked up as a few could prove toxic if someone chose to enter uninvited."

"Speaking of toxic, you might be interested in a few of my more interesting plantings I cultivate as a side hobby to the edible part of my endeavors. Do you want to see?" she asked.

The hair on McClarey's neck started tingling. "Certainly, m'Lady Riggsby. What would you be meanin by *toxic* if you don't mind me askin?"

"Oh you'd be amazed at how many common plants or flowers can prove quite toxic to animals or even people," she said over her shoulder. She led him to the far end of the greenhouse where there were grow lights affixed over several beds of exotic looking flowers and plants that were mostly unfamiliar to McClarey.

"Take for example the white flowers in the corner of the bed. Lilies of the valley. A popular flower around Easter, and in a lot of people's homes. But if you were unfortunate enough to ingest one, it can make you quite sick or even cause death. Or take these purple beauties here," she said as she lovingly stroked the flower's petals. "You might remember this flower, Monkshood or aconite. I have one like it on my desk suspended in a crystal ball. Farmers used to use it to exterminate wolves. Quite effective, even if a bit inhumane."

McClarey watched her intently as she continued to share her depth of knowledge on one deadly bloomer after another. If he had any doubts to this point on Kimberly Riggsby's involvement in the deaths attributed to Mary Simon, he was rapidly losing them.

The question was why was she choosing to share this with him. Was she so crazy she just couldn't help herself? Or so confident that Mary Simon would take the blame that it just didn't matter anymore?

McClarey interrupted Kimberly after a few more minutes of her toxic plant lecture, "M'Lady Riggsby, I must say I've found this t' be highly interestin, but it's goin on three thirty. I'd best be gettin along before the traffic picks up for me drive back t' LA. I do apologize, but I should be takin me leave now."

Kimberly shrugged and looked at her watch, "You're right of course. Sorry. I do get carried away sometimes. It's my passion. What can I say?"

"Not a problem m'Lady. No need t' show me out. I can find me way back t' me car. Thank you again fer bein such a gracious host and I'm sure we'll be talkin again. Good day."

Kimberly extended her hand to McClarey which he

lightly grasped as he tipped his hat. "Until we meet again, Sergeant," she said and turned back to her precious toxic charges to tend to them with far too much loving care for McClarey's taste.

McClarey briskly walked to the door.

He watched Kimberly from the corner of his eye. He wanted to make sure the crazy wanker didn't pick up a set of pruning shears and come running at him, screaming all the way, like a scene from some American horror film.

Grasping the door latch and pushing it open against the attached spring, he stepped out into the full afternoon sun causing him to blink. And as he did, he saw a blur out of the corner of his right eye. It was coming at him from behind the door.

He tried to raise his arm to fend off the attacker. Reacting too late, he felt a crushing blow to the right side of his head. A fireworks display of shooting stars exploded inside his skull and he crumpled to the ground like a sack of potatoes.

McClarey landed on his back and tried to open his eyes. His right eye felt warm and was blurred with his blood causing a red haze in the sunlight. Willing his eyes to open, the shooting pain in his head increased with the intrusion of the sun's rays.

Trying to raise his head, he could see the outline of what he thought was a man standing over him with a shovel. The shovel made one more arc towards his forehead.

All went black.

McClarey woke to find himself in a chair.

His clothes had been replaced with a hospital gown. He could feel the cold metal surface of the chair on his naked legs and buttocks. The chair's seat felt as if it had a hole cut out under his bottom in what felt like the shape of a bedpan.

His arms were zip-tied to the chair's sturdy arms. His legs were similarly bound to the chairs legs and a heavy strap was around his chest. The strap restricted him from leaning forward more than an inch or so. He could tilt his head forward to see what looked like a metal handle on a pull out drawer between his knees.

His head was throbbing. It was as if a marching band had decided to attach a sousaphone directly to his brain playing a favorite fight song with gusto to the beat of his heart.

His vision was blurred. He couldn't make out much. As his consciousness returned, he realized he was likely in the chemical and fertilizer room crazy Kimberly had mentioned earlier. The door was open. He could hear two voices discussing his predicament.

"Okay, that should hold him for now. Glad I was able to get here before he'd left."

The first voice McClarey didn't recognize.

"We'll need to get his car taken care of so there's no trace. I checked his cellphone and it doesn't appear he made any calls today. I'll destroy the phone so it can't be traced. First I need to send a message to his supervisor letting him know the good sergeant has been called away for urgent family matters."

McClarey recognized the second voice as crazy Kimberly's.

"We can drive up to Lake Cachuma. Get rid of the car, and then you can drive me back," the first voice said. "I really think we should put him in the car. Cleaner if it's all taken care of at once."

"No. I need him to work out a few details of my plan. No one will come looking for him here as the Feds think Simon did it. They've got a nice neat little case with all the evidence lined up in a row, making their job open and shut. Why would they mess with that?"

Kimberly continued, "I'll get to use him as my guinea pig to get the mix just right. I want it painful, not deadly, until I've decided its over. And it only ends when that little prick Aiden begs me to end him, and *not* until Danny's birthday, June first."

"Besides, I need to see how my bidet chairs work out. If I'm going to spend any significant time in my lab, it needs to be neat and clean. Can't have my guests stinking it up with their bodily functions, now can we?" she chuckled.

McClarey heard footsteps of the man coming toward the door. He feigned an unconscious slump with his eyes closed.

"He's still out. Let's lock the room up and go. Should I gag him or anything?"

Kimberly replied, "No one could hear him so no need.

I'll padlock the door."

McClarey heard the door close and the padlock being inserted through the metal clasps of the door. The click of the lock followed. Footsteps receded to the greenhouse entrance. The bang of the outside door of the greenhouse slamming shut was the last sound he heard.

His captors had left to scrub the evidence of his visit away.

He tried pushing up with his bare feet on the concrete floor, but to no avail. His chair was bolted securely into the floor. He looked around the room in the twilight making its way to him through one small skylight.

Glassware lined a laboratory bench the full length of one wall. A cabinet containing multiple flasks, bottles and glassware supplies was in one corner with a refrigerator quietly humming away next to it. In another corner were what looked like IV bags, gauze pads, syringes, tubing and a few other miscellaneous medical items. Out of the corner of his eye he could make out the arm of a chair similar to the one he was in with its back to him and few feet away.

McClarey thought back on the conversation he'd just overheard crazy Kimberly have with her partner in crime.

Probably her brother, Greg.

What did they say?

Was it "work out the details of my plan?"…"Painful, not deadly"…maybe something about "not ending it until he begs me to end it."

McClarey exhaled deeply and lamented out loud, "I'm in the devil's nest, I am."

Chapter 28

As uncomfortable as his position was in his chair-prison, McClarey eventually nodded off. He startled upon hearing the bang of the door to the greenhouse as someone entered. Footsteps to the padlock. The sound of someone fumbling with the lock. The door to his torture chamber opened with Kimberly Riggsby stepping in.

"So how is my canary holding up?" she said as she stepped forward to examine McClarey's bindings, ensuring he hadn't been able to work anything loose.

McClarey couldn't control his anger from being waylaid and kidnapped, "Yer one crazy bitch. A real looney tune."

"Now, now, Sergeant. You haven't seen even a smidgeon of what I have planned for you," she chided, showing a toothy smile. She looked at McClarey like a feral creature about to tear the flesh from its cornered prey.

"You *know* they're lookin for me, don't you? And when they find yer little shop o' horrors, they'll be cartin you off t' the nearest padded room for the rest o' yer days."

"Sergeant, you may not have heard. Your dear late wife's father has fallen ill back in Scotland. You're on your way to see him now and won't be returning calls or emails while you attend to your extended family's needs."

"Very thoughtful of you. Exactly what your captain would expect of you, no less," she said with an almost gleeful lilt in her voice. As she watched the questioning look on his face, she continued, " Oh, didn't I mention that you emailed your captain an hour ago. You informed him your father-in-law had become seriously ill. You let him know you were taking the next plane to Scotland to help out. Told him it would take no more than a week. With the Mary Simon case pretty well wrapped up, you hoped it wouldn't be a problem for him. Plus you needed a few days vacation after all the extra hours you've been putting in."

McClarey glowered at her. The realization that no one was coming to his aid began to sink in. "Why are you doin this? You weren't even a suspect o' any wrongs. 'Til you pulled this boner o' an idea and tied up a policeman."

"Oh, I think you were more than a little suspicious of me, Sergeant. And my brother is even more paranoid than I am when it comes to tying up loose ends. He's the one who did the Google search on your background from your time over the pond. He said it wasn't difficult locating the info on your late wife's family in London."

"So dat was yer brother who showed me the backside o' a shovel on me way out?"

"Yes. It was very accommodating of you to take me up on my tour offer. I called my brother from the house. He was only a few minutes away and couldn't wait to come by to "greet" you. His handshake can be a bit over done when he uses a shovel, but effective I think you'd agree." She let out a short laugh as she turned from McClarey and moved to the medical supply table. Gathering several items from the table, she then went out of his line of sight.

McClarey could hear her working on something for the next several minutes. She seemed to be assembling something that was taking all of her attention.

"There," she said pleased with her work. "That should be just perfect." She then wheeled an IV tree with a hanging IV bag with hosing attached next to his chair.

Cutting the left sleeve of his gown back to his shoulder with a pair of surgeon's scissors, she wrapped a rubber tourniquet around his upper arm. A few veins popped to the surface after a few seconds. She inserted a Y-injection port into one of the protruding options. It simplified the procedure for drawing blood samples or administering of injection treatments through its second port. The configuration had become a popular IV choice for hospitals. This made it readily available to the general public through any major medical supply store.

"Now that was easy, wasn't it," she said as she patted his arm and released the tourniquet. "Unfortunately for you, the next part won't be easy at all." She pushed the IV apparatus up next to his chair and connected the drip line to the Y-injection port inserted in his vein. Carefully purging the IV line of air, she adjusted a thumbwheel device so a steady drip of clear liquid entered a visual monitoring tube. The monitoring tube was several times wider

DAN BLAIR

than the IV line itself and showed the drip of the fluid being delivered.

Once satisfied all was set up correctly, she returned to the work area out of McClarey's sight.

"So what the 'ell are you pumpin into me you looney bitch," McClarey said trying to get a rise out of his captor. He didn't think it could hurt his situation much at this point.

"Nothing to worry about yet. Saline fluid to keep you well hydrated and to provide an easy way to deliver a few little surprises." When she came back into his view, she was carrying a smaller IV bag filled with a yellowish green fluid. Attaching this to the IV tree, she looped the tubing from the new bag into the monitoring tube and began a slow drip of the colored solution into the saline fluid carrier.

McClarey watched the colored solution enter the previously clear tube leading to his arm. It slowly crawled through its length like a snake serpentining its way to deliver the lethal bite.

McClarey tensed and jerked at his bindings. His face contorted with fear as he watched the straw colored folly of his she-devil captor enter the Y-injection port on the way to his bloodstream.

"Careful, sergeant. I wouldn't struggle yet as the fun is just beginning," she chortled and watched him intently.

McClarey felt a warm, almost pleasant rush tracking the entry of Crazy Kimberly's potion into his bloodstream. This didn't last long. It rapidly turned to a burning sensation attacking every vein from the inside out. He writhed in pain against his bindings but to no avail.

"What the *'ell* have you *poisoned* me with?" he spat the words at her. The pain became unbearable. Shooting to every extremity of his body. The unknown toxin burned like nothing he'd experienced before.

"Do you know the damage poison ivy or oak can inflict on a person? If they happen to scratch their blistered skin to vigorously and end up introducing the noxious oils into their bloodstream it can be quite awful. Well, you're about to experience that one hundred fold," she said.

She moved to watch him from several angles like a scientist studying a mouse injected with some experimental drug.

McClarey screamed.

He felt the mixture making its way up his neck, setting his face and scalp on fire in a sensory blaze of excruciating pain. He felt as if someone had filled every one of his pores with lighter fluid and set them each on fire with tiny matches.

His thrashing did no good. His bindings were proving more than sufficient to hold him for his own personal tour of hell on earth.

Primal screams filled the small room and continued until he hyperventilated.

Passing out, his head rolled forward in unconscious relief and blackness overtook him.

McClarey became aware of tinkling noises around him. It sounded like glassware and metal.

He tried to open his eyes, but was only able to crack them a slit. They felt swollen to the point his lids might pop if he strained any further. He could see his arm where the IV protruded. His arm appeared red and irritated with large blisters covering the exposed skin all the way to his fingertips.

He raised his head to try to make out what the noises were with his limited vision. Crazy Kimberly came into his view. She was holding a glassware beaker in her hand with a tea bag suspended in the yellowish brew. She stirred the beaker with a metal stirring rod as she smiled at McClarey.

"So you're back among the living sergeant. Gave me a scare for a minute that I might have overdone it on my first try."

McClarey didn't respond. His lips felt as bloated as his eyelids and his tongue and inner mouth were swollen. He wasn't sure he could talk if he wanted to.

"I've got another little potion I can't wait to try out tomorrow. Thought I'd let you get your strength back first. Wouldn't want to over load the senses too quickly. Once the pain becomes intolerable, adding more really serves no purpose, now does it?"

McClarey grunted with a raspy voice, "Water."

Kimberly stared at him for a few seconds. She turned and went to the refrigerator, opened the door and extracted a bottled water. Removing the cap she returned to McClarey and held the bottle to his lips. He hungrily sucked at the bottle's opening. More water spilled down the sides of his mouth than went in, but it quenched his burning thirst. He became more aware of the swollen inner tissues of his mouth with the water's cool moistness. It provided some minimal relief from the burning sensation that still engulfed him.

Bending down to look more closely at McClarey, she sniffed, saying, "Well, by the smell of you, guess my little potions had the added benefit of a laxative. We should try out your bidet chair. Sorry I didn't have warm water installed, but it should still do the trick," Crazy Kimberly said as she disappeared behind McClarey's chair.

He jerked at the shock of cold water jets spraying his nether regions. "What the 'ell?" McClarey gasped in surprise. He could hear the water entering a drain beneath his chair as he clenched his buttocks against the cold intrusion. He heard the sound of a faucet shutting off, and she returned into his view.

"There. That's much better," she said as she offered him another drink from the water bottle.

He glared at her through bloodshot and swollen eyes as he accepted a few more sips of water. "You really are a sick bitch," McClarey whispered through clenched teeth.

She eyed him for a few moments and placed the bottle next to his chair. "There, that will be there for you later if you get thirsty," she laughed at her cruel little joke and exited the room.

McClarey could hear her placing the padlock through its clasps. Her footsteps receded and finally the bang of the greenhouse door announcing "Crazy Kimberly had left the building."

Left to the dark silence of his first night as a prisoner, his mind began racing. He found himself thinking, *so this is how a guinea pig feels, how many other nasty potions has this insane woman got in her bag o' tricks* and darker thoughts like *how much more will it take 'fore I beg her t' end me.*

Chapter 29

Aiden threw his backpack in the rear of his blue Toyota Prius. Slamming the hatchback top, he thumbed a text message to his dad.

He was leaving campus as soon as he picked up a few things at his room. It had been tough to stay on campus the last few days knowing his dad was recovering at the Santa Monica Hospital.

Aiden had called or FaceTimed™ him each day since they'd determined Jim had ricin poisoning. It had been clear from the calls his dad needed a few days under constant care to make sure he was out of the woods.

Aiden was near the end of the semester at USC's Keck School of Medicine. Finals were coming up the following week. He had figured it made the most sense to come home for a few days before finals started. He could move his dad from the hospital to home, get him settled in, and return early the next week for finals.

It was Wednesday afternoon. His dad had called him earlier to let him know that his doctor was okay with him

DAN BLAIR

returning home. The only caveat was he needed someone there to look after him for a few days, at least until he was feeling able to care for himself.

Aiden had finished up his last class before finals that same morning. Now free to head home and do his best Nurse Ratchet imitation for a couple of days. He pulled out of his parking spot at the Health Sciences Campus of USC. Driving the few blocks to Seaver Residence Hall, he parked in one of the "5 minute" loading spaces located in front of the dorm for quick student in-and-outs.

Dashing from his car to the front entrance, he inserted his key card releasing the electronic door lock. Jerking the door open, he took the stairs three at time up to the third floor to his private dorm room. He'd been fortunate to get this room as it was adjacent to the Health Sciences Campus buildings. Ninety per cent of his classes were held on the HSC, and it was only a few blocks from the hospital medical facilities. The room wasn't cheap at one thousand bucks a month, but nothing in downtown LA was cheap. He had to leave his car in Lot 70, a few blocks from the HSC campus given the shortage of parking around the dorms. Seaver Hall's close proximity to campus allowed him to walk everywhere he needed to go during the week. It was a fifteen minute walk to get his car when he needed it.

All in all, as good as you could hope for living in central LA.

He opened his dorm room with the same key card he'd used to enter Seaver Hall, shouldered through the door and grabbed his duffel bag from the open shelved closet. He stuffed it with the few essentials he'd need for a few days away: underwear, socks, gym shorts and a couple of favorite t-shirts should do it.

Stepping into the bathroom, he placed the miscellaneous items from around his sink into his hanging toiletry bag and zipped it shut. His eyes fell on his reflection in the mirror. His short dark curls framed his boyish face, eyes brown like his mother's had been, and sharp facial features like his dad's. He was definitely a Jensen.

He took one last look around his room for any basics he couldn't manage without for a couple of days. His eyes fell on his RED Beats™ wireless headphones hanging on a hook over his bed. He grabbed them and stuffed them in his bag as he headed for the door.

Reaching for the doorknob, his eyes were drawn to a few of the family photos he'd placed on the room's built in combination desk and shelf unit. The pictures broke up the rows of college textbooks and ready references. Great memories captured for posterity: his dad and mom with arms draped around him at age eighteen, palm trees and a Jamaican beach in the background, his folks looking very proud of him in his cap and gown from his college graduation, and a picture of him and Danny. His best friend from high school, Danny, floated in a blow-up raft next to him in an identical raft, just chilling out in his folks' pool.

It was always painful seeing his best friend in that photo. Danny's wispy blond hair set over sky blue eyes and a smile radiating some mischief yet to come. Aiden's need to keep their good times alive before the accident had over-powered his gut reaction to hide the picture of

Danny. He was tempted at times to tuck it somewhere he wouldn't have to look at it; and more importantly, wouldn't have to feel the crushing weight of accountability for his friend's death.

Strangely, the picture with Danny had become a motivating force behind his medical studies. Someday he'd be able to help people in emergency situations. He'd be able to make a difference for sixteen year olds cut and damaged from their metal chariots; those conveyances they'd wrongly placed their trust in to be indestructible shells. Someday he'd be able to do the things he hadn't been able to do for his best friend as he bled to death in his arms.

The slam of a door down the hall brought him back to the present. He closed his door, flew down the steps, and through the exit. Glad to see his car hadn't been ticketed for the few minutes he'd exceeded the "5 minute" loading zone maximum, he thumbed the key fob.

Opening his door, he threw the duffel bag into the passenger seat and backed out of the parking space onto Zonal Avenue. Slipping his headphones on with one hand and hitting a couple of buttons, the sounds of Death Cab for Cutie filled his auditory space. A couple of blocks later he turned onto North Soto Street. From there he caught the entrance ramp to the Santa Monica Freeway headed west to where his dad awaited at the hospital.

Thirty minutes later Aiden pulled into the Santa Monica Hospital and cruised the visitor parking lot for a space. Finding nothing, he exited to the staff lot where he pulled into his mom's reserved space. The hospital hadn't taken down the placard hanging from a small chain across the front of the space, "L.A. Jensen."

Soon some surgeon or hospital administrator would lay claim to such a prime parking place. But for now, why not use it?

Aiden entered his dad's room a few minutes later and discovered him sitting on the corner of his bed. Overnight bag packed and looking impatient to be somewhere, anywhere but here.

"Hey old man, you're looking like you've got someplace to be," Aiden said as he crossed the room in a couple of long strides to hug his dad.

"Good to see you, son," Jim said returning the hug as he stood up. "I'm chomping at the bit to get out of here and back to my own digs. *Especially* with my med school son making himself available to nursemaid me. Doc said you're to be fully at my beck and call for the next few days so I think this could work out well. I intend to get some first hand pay-back for all that Keck School of Medicine tuition I'm paying."

"So long as you need me to locate a bone or some anatomical part you've mislaid around the house, I should be good to go. But if you want me to actually treat some of your many ailments, I think that's a year or so away," Aiden said laughing as he grabbed his dad's bag.

"The nurse went to get an orderly to wheel me down to the loading ramp for old and discarded hospital refuse. If you want to get your car and meet me there, I'll be down in a few minutes," Jim said, mostly for the benefit of the nurse who had just peeked around the doorjamb at Jim. The nurse's face was cherubic in nature, with red cheeks and a pixie hair cut making her pleasant features appear a bit like a larger than life kewpie doll.

"So you're taking our favorite pain in the ass away from us," the nurse said to Aiden with a half-smile on her face. "What do we owe you if you promise not to bring him back?"

"Aiden, please meet Nurse Shithead, uh I mean Nurse Shead. Sorry that I still haven't gotten your name quite right," Jim said smirking at Aiden.

"I'll get the car while you two share some goodbye hugs and kisses," Aiden quipped as he exited, motioning for Nurse Shead to enter with a flourish. Looking back over his shoulder he saw his dad discreetly flip him the three-fingered "birdless" salute. *It was nice to see his dad was getting back to normal.*

Aiden pulled up to the patient discharge ramp and waited about ten minutes for his dad to appear. A rather burley African American orderly propelled his dad towards the wheelchair access curb a few feet from Aiden's car. He flipped up the foot rests on the wheelchair allowing Jim to step to the ground and attempted to support his dad as he stood up.

"I'm fine. No need to act like I'm some kind of *invalid* or something," Jim said gruffly to his would-be helper. The orderly rolled his eyes, and stepped back just enough to let Jim stand up on his own. He stayed close enough to be able to catch him if he suddenly collapsed.

Aiden closed the passenger car door once his dad was situated. Turning to the orderly, he shrugged, "Thanks.

What're you going to do when they're cranky old coots?"

The orderly chuffed a laugh and pushed the wheelchair back towards the door he'd just come through. He shook his head ever so slightly.

Thirty-five minutes later Aiden pulled into the driveway of the place he'd called home for all of his twenty-four years. He grabbed his duffel bag from the back seat where he'd moved it to make room for his dad. Snagging his dad's overnight bag, he rounded the rear of his car and opened his dad's car door.

"Oh so this is how it's going to be, huh?" Jim said in an annoyed tone. He looked up at Aiden with his duffel over one shoulder, carrying Jim's bag in his other hand, and his free hand extended to help Jim from the car.

"Come on Dad. You've been flat on your back for days. Is it so hard to accept a little help to at least get you in the house?"

Jim scowled but took Aiden's extended hand to help him step from the compact car. Jim walked ahead of Aiden to the front door. He reached in his pocket retrieving his house keys, unlocked the door, and pushed the door open motioning for Aiden to go in. Jim smiled and said dramatically, "Oh be it so humble, there's no place like home."

The next couple of days were mostly settling into a routine. He made sure his dad had adequate groceries, especially quick serve items: frozen pizzas, nacho fixings and his favorite microwave oven meals. While not the healthiest menu in the world, convenience was paramount. Once Jim regained his strength and ability to fend for himself,

Aiden would be headed back to school.

Aiden spent a lot of time studying for his finals. This left Jim to the most recent novels by Ken Follett, and re-reading his favorite oldie but goodie, *Pillars of the Earth.*

By Saturday afternoon, Aiden needed a break from studying and came downstairs, plopping on the couch next to his dad. "So I'm burnt out on "neck bones connected to the head bone" and how the circulatory system interacts with the lymphatic system. What have you got to entertain me? And it can't be anything about the human body or associated parts," Aiden said, cocking his head with a questioning look towards Jim.

Jim sat his book down, leaned forward on the plush couch and stroked his chin for a few seconds as if deep in thought. Leaning back with a self-satisfied look on his face, he said, "Maybe this is finally the time where I get to regale you with tales of my time in Vietnam."

Before Aiden could respond with any other ideas like *let's go for pizza* or *how about a sports bar,* Jim had launched into full storytelling mode.

"I call this first story, My Mad Minute," Jim said, looking at Aiden as if his story subject might mean something to him, or at least invoke some sense of baited curiosity.

Aiden looked back with a pained expression of placating his old man. Secretly he wished he could pull out his smart phone and start a sizzling game of Boom Beach, or Zombie Apocalypse, or even Words with Friends.

Jim reached forward for his cranberry juice over ice, took a long sip, and leaned back into the plush couch.

He looked at the ceiling fan as if it were a teleprompter

and began, "It was my first day in 'Nam, October twelfth, 1972. I was nineteen years old, two months short of my twentieth birthday, and one of the last draftees of the war."

"I was exhausted from traveling as we'd spent over three days getting there. Between staying overnight in different army bases in California and Hawaii on our way to Saigon, and the actual flights on MATS C-97s transport planes, it was unbearably long. The average air speed of the C-97s is only three hundred miles an hour."

"Our final leg of the trip had been in a Bell Huey transport helicopter to a large base camp in Tay Ninh, near the Cambodian border."

"I reported to my unit, unloaded my rucksack and went to sleep early, around 19:30 local time." Jim leaned forward raising his eyebrows at Aiden, "Now it's important for you to know that my habit back then was to sleep in the *nude*," Jim said and let the word "nude" hang there.

"Oh man Dad. Seriously?" Aiden objected.

"Yes, seriously. Well, it turned out it was the night of the Mad Minute. No one told me what that was or when it was supposed to happen as I was new."

"Around 22:00 hours I woke up to the sounds of a great battle…in an empty barracks. Scared shitless, I put on my helmet, flak vest, shower slippers, picked up my M16 and a bandolier of bullets, and headed to the perimeter of the camp to do battle."

Aiden sat forward, looking like he was starting to enjoy Jim's tale, much to Jim's delight.

"It turns out the Mad Minute is a drill where all weapons in a five-thousand person base camp are fired every two months or so toward the surrounding woods. It ensures no enemy troops have decided to get too close to the base perimeter. This includes artillery, machine guns, helicopter gun ships and anything with gunpowder and a firing pin."

"So here I am, naked from my slippers to my flak jacket, sloshing through mud up to my ankles from the monsoon season. No sidewalks or paths to be found. My shower slippers got stuck in the mud. I dropped my M16 and bandolier in the mud trying to get my slippers free, and now everything of use was caked in mud."

"Long story short, I never made it to the perimeter by the time the Mad Minute ended."

"But here's the worst part. At the end of the Mad Minute, the lights come on. Hundreds of soldiers discover me standing naked in the mud, and a good number of them decide to shine their flashlights on my dangling balls."

"My reputation is ruined on my first day in 'Nam. But I'm happy to be alive."

Jim sat back and let out a long breath, looking at Aiden who was smiling with his mouth hanging open in disbelief. As the image of his dad standing naked in the mud with hundreds of guys spotlighting his balls sinks in, Aiden's laugh began slowly but built quickly into howls of laughter; partly from the ridiculous visual of his dad, and partly as a nervous release from the stress that had built up over the last few weeks.

As Aiden got his breath back, he said, "Oh crap, Dad. That had to be like the worst thing ever." Continuing to chuckle Aiden looked questioningly at his dad, "So do you have any more stories from 'Nam?"

Jim looked thoughtful again and then nodded, "Yeah, one more comes to mind."

"It was after I'd been transferred to Saigon to join Military Assistance Command, Vietnam, or just MACV headquarters as we called it. The base was far from any fighting and totally safe, but we had to do guard duty once every month. No one cared about guard duty since we weren't in a hot zone. It was a very relaxed affair."

"I was assigned to a three-man machine gun squad post. I manned the grenade launcher. There was also the machine gunner and an ammo bearer."

"One night a full bird Colonel comes along to inspect our position. He tells us to "lock and load," which means get ready for battle. So I put a grenade down my tube and got ready as ordered. The ammo bearer was supposed to take out belts of ammo from his canister and insert them into the machine gun, but he didn't."

"The Colonel told the ammo bearer to get moving, but he still didn't. Finally, the Colonel who is now red-faced and two inches from the ammo bearer's face, orders him to open the fuckin' canister and take out the belts of ammo."

"The ammo bearer sheepishly opened the canister… revealing the only thing in it was one M16 bullet. It turns out he'd been too lazy to carry the heavy canister."

"At this point the Colonel was screaming in frustration at the ammo bearer saying, *this is the second time tonight this has happened.*"

"Fortunately, we weren't attacked," Jim added, finishing his story with a half-smirk as he looked from the ceiling fan back to Aiden.

Aiden laughed and shook his head, "Wow, that's not how any of the old movies talk about Vietnam. I thought it was all blood and buddies dying in your arms from shows like *Apocalypse Now,* or *Platoon,* or *Full Metal Jacket.*"

The smile on Jim's face faded and his jaw clenched as he looked at Aiden more soberly. "I only told you about a couple of the fun times. The other parts aren't much fun to talk about."

Jim sat forward and stared at his hands, clenched together, one hand squeezing the fist of the other, and continued, "I had never killed anyone or thought I ever would kill another human being before I went to Vietnam. Even in boot camp where the sergeants were screaming at us to "kill or be killed" and making us run into straw dummies with bayonets, it never really seemed like it might happen."

"I still have my M16 rifle in the gun locker in the garage. I take it out and oil it every couple of weeks. I even take it to a local firing range every month or so as it reminds me of the unbelievable destruction that something made by man can inflict on man. An M16 has a clip of thirty, 5.56 millimeter bullets. It's highly accurate up to five hundred and fifty meters for an average marksman. On semi-automatic it can shoot over forty-five rounds per minute, and on full auto it exceeds seven hundred rounds per minute. An M16 round makes a hole the size of a baseball coming out the backside of whoever is unlucky enough to get in front of one of these war machines."

Jim paused for a moment watching Aiden's eyes go a bit wider to hear his dad talking about something his young mind couldn't imagine. Continuing he said, "I didn't see as much action as a lot of guys. But between Tay Ninh and Saigon, I was a grunt sent out on night patrols and reconnaissance missions just like most of the jar heads over there. Those are the stories I don't tell and I've tried hard to forget. I guess I don't like waking up in wet bedsheets, sweating like I've run a marathon."

"I don't know how many Cong I took out, but it was more than a few. I never got into the body counting that all the brass was so interested in for the CBS News™ or for their next promotions. I do know that over six months in that jungle hell, I saw eleven men from my unit come back to the base in body bags. And it was just the way it was."

Aiden silently looked out the family room window as he took in what his dad had shared. In the quiet, he whispered, "I never knew Dad. I never knew."

Jim stood up taking a couple of steps towards Aiden, who stood as well. They hugged for a long moment and Jim patted Aiden on the back saying, "Well that was more than you probably bargained for from your old man, wasn't it?"

Aiden stayed in the embrace with his head resting lightly on Jim's shoulder, "You know Dad. I think about how you saw all the awful stuff you saw, and yet you're the most encouraging father. You were a great husband to mom and a real friend to everyone you know. It makes me think you've found a way to put all that bad stuff behind you."

"And that really gives me hope I can do the same," Aiden said as he pulled back from their embrace and met his dad's eyes.

"How do you mean?" Jim asked.

"You know, with the accident and all. I know how much worry I've caused you…and…used to cause mom, too. I guess I looked at it as my burden. Thinking it was heavier than what everyone else had to deal with. But when I hear you talk about what you saw … and had to do … I guess I realize I need to get past my problems too."

Jim broke off the hug, holding Aiden at arms length. He looked steadily into his eyes, "Son, I know you can… no…I know you *will*. And I'll be there to help you through it, whatever it takes."

They hugged again and sauntered towards the kitchen to make loaded nachos. Later they would check out which movie on demand they'd watch tonight as had been their habit for the week.

As they walked, Aiden looked at Jim out the corner of his eye and said, "So Dad, I don't suppose any of your army buddies got a picture of you standing naked in the mud? What I would give to have that…" Aiden stepped away from Jim as his dad delivered a fake punch glancing off Aiden's shoulder.

"*You couldn't handle it, son,*" Jim bellowed back in a bad and inaccurate Jack Nicholson impression from the movie *A Few Good Men.*

Both laughed until they hurt. And life seemed better for a moment.

Chapter 30

Sunday afternoon Aiden came down the stairs and dropped his duffel bag and backpack in the hallway near the front door.

Aiden and his dad had slept in late and gone to a breakfast place for brunch. Now they were back at the house enjoying a quiet afternoon.

Jim eyed Aiden's hallway items and asked, "Time for you to get back to the ole grind?"

"Yeah, I've got a couple of finals to finish studying for. Wednesday I'm done until summer school starts up," Aiden replied. He draped himself over both arms of one of the easy chairs next to the couch where Jim sat reading the Sunday paper.

"Do you want to watch the game? The Padres are playing the Red Sox." Jim offered with no real enthusiasm. Neither Jim nor Aiden had ever been avid baseball fans. A book was usually the preferred pastime for both. Jim leaned towards historical fiction novels. Aiden preferred a Koontz or Baldacci thriller.

"No thanks. I think I'll beat the traffic and head out if that's okay," Aiden said as he moved to join his dad on the couch.

Jim put his arm around Aiden, giving him a firm one-armed hug. "You know I really appreciate you coming to take care of your feeble old dad. You could be chasing some skirt at USC, or hanging with your buds on campus. Yet you chose to be here." Jim chuffed and added, "Doesn't say much for your party instincts, but I'm proud of you anyway, son."

"Never had much of a party passion. Besides none of my buds' lame sense of humor can hold a candle to your war stories," Aiden said as he returned the hug, and stood up.

"I'll give you a call when I'm on campus. Now take it easy and just live off the pizzas, nachos and cold cuts for a few days, okay?"

"Not a problem. They cover my three basic food groups; tasty, quick and easy," Jim said rising from the couch to walk Aiden to his car. "So what are you thinking about doing for your break after finals?" Jim asked as Aiden stowed his bags in his car.

"I don't know. Haven't really even thought about having time off, but guess I should go do something. Any ideas?" Aiden said questioningly to his dad.

"I'll think on it. If you want some time with your college buddies to hit some trails or wherever the young bucks tend to go these days, that's fine by me. I don't want to smother you with too much dad time, you know."

"Okay. Well I'll let you know if I get any offers from

the "young bucks." Or maybe I'll just come home and spend time with the *old stag*," Aiden smirked at his poke at his dad's vernacular from days gone by.

"All right, smart guy. Just drive careful and give me a call when you get there," Jim said as he closed Aiden's door.

Aiden lowered his window and waved as he pulled away from his dad.

It had been a great couple of days for them to spend time together. He couldn't remember ever feeling like he really knew his dad as a person before their Vietnam conversation the night before. Now he saw him differently. All his fears and regrets exposed from the war, but coming out the other side whole. That said a lot to Aiden about what kind of dad he had, what kind of man he had, for a father.

Aiden turned from San Fernando Road onto the I5 South, and drove the thirty miles to central LA, lost in thought.

Often when he drove alone, he'd think back to the night of the accident with Danny. These daytrips of his mind typically left him feeling like he was once again a helpless kid. Lying in the ditch unable to do anything but crawl to his friend and hold him in his arms as Danny's life drained out into the cold night air.

But this time, Aiden felt something different. He thought of his dad's sharing the awfulness of war, and losing multiple friends, but "that was just the way it was." Not resignation by his dad that war was inevitable or his dad's comrades were expendable. But rather the acceptance that there were things outside of his control. As much as Aiden felt the burden for Danny's senseless death those eight years ago, how much had really been in his control?

His thoughts had made the trip to campus pass quickly. He saw his exit to I10 East was a mile ahead. From there he took North Soto Street to Zonal Avenue and pulled into an open "5 minute" loading zone.

A quick trip to his dorm room to drop off his duffel bag kept him within the parking sign's rule. Pulling out from the loading zone, he was off to Lot 70 to park his car for the next few days. He hoped spots would be plentiful on an early Sunday afternoon.

Pulling into his assigned parking area with the big blue "Lot 70" rectangular sign, he pulled to the far end of the lot. There were still a dozen or more parking places unclaimed.

Grabbing his computer bag, Aiden exited his car and dialed his dad. "Hey Dad, I'm parked and on my way to the dorm."

"Okay Aiden. Give me a call in a couple of days, once you decide your summer break plans. I love you son."

"Love you too, Dad," Aiden said as he thumbed the disconnect button on his phone.

It was around three o'clock in the afternoon, and the lot was deserted except for him and what looked like a lady having some kind of car issue. Her hood was up. She was bent over the engine compartment of her car, a late model, gray Ford Taurus. She was parked along a line of cars leading back to Aiden's residence hall, so he stopped as he approached the back of her car.

"Having a problem?" he said, wincing at his words since it was too late to pull back such a lame observation.

A pretty blonde lady in her late thirties or early forties, dressed in skinny jeans and USC t-shirt, tilted her head to the side of the hood and peered at him, "Oh, you startled me. Yes, it doesn't seem to want to start. I've been away for a couple of weeks and the battery's probably dead. Or at least that's what it seems like."

"Do you want me to take a look at it? I'm not a mechanic or anything, but I might be able to see if anything obvious is wrong," Aiden said as he laid his backpack on the ground at the rear of her car.

"Sure, it can't hurt. See what you think," she shrugged as she stepped back from the engine compartment to let Aiden have a look.

As his eyes met hers. He was captivated by her heart shaped face and striking blue eyes. She seemed familiar causing him to stare for just a beat too long. "Okay, let me take a look," he stammered as he abruptly turned his attention to the engine compartment.

At this point, he was committed to look like he had half a brain when it came to cars. Unfortunately the truth was, if it was more than a loose cable, he was toast.

Leaning over the engine compartment, he stretched to reach each cable into and out of the battery, the alternator and any other thing-a-ma-jig he could wiggle. All seemed tight and no loose wires were dangling in space.

As he was about to let his lady in distress know that she had the wrong white knight, he felt a prick in the side of his neck. He jerked around to see her heart-shaped face smiling at him. She pulled back her hand with a small empty syringe between her thumb and fingers.

"What the heck?" Aiden questioned. He rubbed his neck where he'd felt the prick, not yet comprehending what had happened. "Who are you? And what did you stick me with...?" His words trailed off as his eyes rolled back in his head.

He slumped into the waiting arms of his blonde lady in distress.

Chapter 31

Greg sat in his Santa Monica beachfront office looking out towards the ocean. He looked as if he were contemplating the waves breaking on the Santa Monica pier on this fine Sunday afternoon.

He was actually enjoying some self-gratification, appreciating how well his planning had paid off when his cellphone buzzed. It was Kimberly.

"Hello Little Bear," she said using Greg's nickname he'd gotten as a toddler for carrying around a stuffed bear larger than he was.

"Hey sis. Where are you?" he asked, knowing she had been on her way to intercept the Jensen boy.

"I'm on my way home now. Everything came off as planned. Can you meet me at the greenhouse in an hour or so? I could use some help getting everything unloaded and secured."

"Sure, I'll be there," he replied. "Wait for me so nothing goes sideways trying to handle the package by yourself, okay?"

"Sure Little Bear. See you in a bit," she said as she ended the call.

As well as things had gone, he hoped his sister didn't screw it up in her revenge mode. She had shared her plan to kidnap the Jensen boy with him a couple of days earlier. He'd tried to persuade her to wait for some evening when the boy was alone. But Kimberly wasn't having it. She had felt the best time to strike was when he was distracted from his visit home, and would be off guard in the secluded parking lot where he left his car.

He'd insisted she at least use a rental car under an assumed name for her campus visit. Also, that she dress to blend in on campus. His final admonition had been for her to stay away from security cameras that might be positioned around the parking lot she was targeting for her mission.

Even with these precautions, a daytime abduction was risky. He was glad to hear all had gone as she'd planned.

He owed everything to his sister. She had raised him from adolescence, put him through college and remained the one person he could count on. She'd even helped him finance the start-up of his current John Hancock office.

His feelings of gratitude reminded him of those early days when Kimberly took care of their mother and him.

He had been only ten.

He remembered the tortured look on his sister's face. She was her mother's keeper through those days; the spiraling deterioration through the stages of needing some assistance to the point of being fully dependent on Kimberly for daily activities.

He had helped with chores around the house and tried to be as self-sufficient as possible. When it came to the harsher realities of taking care of an invalid mother, his sister had shouldered the burden and protected him. Kimberly handled the toileting, the bedpans, the sponge baths, treating the bedsores, and the general help needed by a body unable to control or repair its most basic functions.

One day when Kimberly was looking especially tired and at the end of her rope, he'd asked her why they couldn't get someone to help out.

Kimberly had looked at him and sighed, "Because we are poor, brother."

Seeing his questioning look, she'd continued, "Remember this time. Promise me you'll remember it well. Being poor limits your options. Someday you'll be tired and not want to keep going, but let this time drive you to be successful. Let this time be the spark to get through school, through college, and through whatever stands in your way. If you do that...if you keep your goals in front of you...you'll be successful with enough money you won't ever have to go it alone."

Greg had thought she sounded as if she was talking to herself as much as to him. The resolve he saw in his sister that day had inspired him. He knew he never wanted to feel that way again; or worse yet, to see someone he loved unable to extricate themself from a hopeless situation.

To be trapped by poverty was a life without options.

He vowed that day he would never let that happen to him or those he cared about. His vow had been a touchstone for him through his public school years, and even more so in his pursuit of a business degree and financial advisor credentials.

After graduating college and getting his financial advisor training, he'd moved through a few different firms. Over the next ten years he had gotten the experience he needed working under others. Then with the help of his sister, he'd branched out to manage his own office as the senior partner. He'd created a lucrative portfolio of clients and achieved a comfortable lifestyle.

And yet he always wondered if it was enough to keep him from poverty's trap. Deep down he knew the only way to be truly free of this fear was to be independently wealthy, which he wasn't.

Greg's fears had finally been assuaged when his relationship with Kimberly had taken a turn towards a dark sibling conspiracy they were now deeply ensconced in.

Two years ago Kimberly had approached him with her obsession of getting revenge for their mother. Her idea had been to use toxic or debilitating extracts from plants to bring justice to those she held responsible for her mother's horrific death.

The idea had intrigued him. In fact, to the point where he'd suggested they try her natural toxins out on one of his clients. The client had been wanting to remove Greg as the executor for his sizeable estate. This would have cost Greg a fat executor's fee.

Kimberly had been able to tailor a toxin to match the historical medical issue of the client. In this trial run, the client's weak heart and a history of non-lethal myocardial infarctions had made a lily of the valley extract just what the doctor ordered. Or in this case, just what the doctor would never suspect.

Given the success of their maiden journey into plant-assisted assassination, Greg had utilized Kimberly's skills on two subsequent clients. Each was disposed of in varied ways, matched up with their respective medical issues. No connections were made by the authorities to possible common denominators.

No one had suspected any wrong doing of Greg. The estates of the individuals had gone to their proper heirs. Greg was only the helpful advisor. He held the widows' hands. He helped them with all the difficult decisions of how to manage their late spouses' assets. And at the end of the day, where they might reinvest those assets; always making sure he assessed higher than average fees in the process.

Although these ventures into offing his clients had proven lucrative, Greg knew he couldn't continue down this path. Eventually, suspicions would be raised as to why his clients were suffering an abnormally high death rate. Plus the number of his clients with significant health issues at an advanced age were limited. Many of his remaining clients would have raised eyebrows if they met untimely ends.

About the time he realized his gig with Kimberly's deadly elixirs was coming to an unfortunate stopping point with his client base, he came across some insider information. An investor friend of his had received the information through a girlfriend, Karen. Karen was a lab technician working on a project for a drug in the early developmental phase. Karen's pillow talk leaked the fact that the drug was looking very promising in some early clinical data. Greg's investor friend had hoped Greg would help him strategize how they might make a killing with this information, setting themselves up for life.

Of course this information had made Greg's friend the next victim on Kimberly's growing list of plant-enhanced departures to the great beyond.

With his investor friend out of the way, Greg had gone to work developing his plan. He needed five "whale" investors, each willing to put in a quarter of a million dollar stake. This would allow him to arrange the purchase of the majority rights to the experimental drug. As the financial advisor to his "whales," he could construct the Limited Liability Corporation such that it fed into his plans.

While Greg was constructing his grand plan for his new drug's LLC, Kimberly had continued to pester him about getting on with her revenge. She had felt the trial runs were sufficient to show her methods were quite reliable, and given the lack of suspected foul play, ready for prime time.

The magical moment for Greg had been when Kimberly began talking about her intended victims from the Jensens' poker group. With a little research on his part, it became clear that several in the poker group were the kind of investors he was looking for. Better yet, the likelihood of bringing in multiple investors if one of their inner circle was investing increased the odds of success for such a complex plan.

With his "whales" now identified, Greg had moved to the most difficult part of his plan. He would need to keep himself clean as the LLC's advisor, and not a primary investor. Yet at the end of his yellow brick road, he would need to develop a pathway to the eventual pay-off via a third party. A third party of which he had control.

This last piece of the puzzle had taken him over a year to put in place. In his research, he'd found that Mary Simon had an estranged daughter, Averly. The daughter was an only child and living in Santa Monica. She worked at a high-end restaurant serving tables.

Greg had sought out the restaurant and Averly. He had casually tested the waters to see if she was married or had a serious boyfriend. Much to his delight, she had neither. Greg had then gone into full courting mode to win the unsuspecting Averly's affections.

This had truly been the long game.

The pieces to his complex plan meant he had to leverage his relationship with Averly, along with Kimberly's lethal skills, to take out the LLC's whale investors. And it had to be done in just the right order.

His cell phone rang bringing him out of his self-aggrandizing daydream.

"Hey babe," Greg answered looking at Averly's screen picture on his cell, "What's up?"

Averly Simon was twenty-two, young enough to be Greg's daughter. In the screen shot on his phone she was posed provocatively; her chin resting on her hands, blue eyes shining, and smiling a toothy smile. The sun was glinting off her shiny blonde hair, with bangs almost covering her eyes.

"What a crappy day I'm having," Averly complained into the phone. "I swear my mother made it her dying wish to torture me from her grave."

"Did she come by and shake her chains at you?" Greg chuckled in response.

"She might as well have. The funeral home is calling me to decide all these details I could care less about. Shit, I haven't seen her in the last ten years."

"I guess the police finally released her body to the funeral home. They have all the evidence they need from my murdering bitch mother, *the infamous Mary Simon*," she added dramatically.

"As next of kin, they want me to handle all the details as I'm the sole beneficiary in her will. I'd tell them to go to hell, but then my ex-step-dad, Michael, would probably step in. Who knows, he might get me cut out of the will altogether," she said with an exasperated sigh.

"Okay babe, just settle down. I'll be home later tonight and we can figure it out together," Greg said trying to soothe Averly's anxiety. "I'll be home late so wait up for me."

"Why can't you come home now?" Averly said with an exaggerated whine in her voice.

"Kimberly called and she needs some help with a business issue. It shouldn't take that long, so just wait up for me, okay?" Greg continued, "I'll bring some Bailey's. We can sip it in front of the fireplace and talk it all through."

"I suppose," Averly pouted. "Make it as fast as you can.

I do have tomorrow off, so we can make a late night of it if you know what I mean."

"I think I do," Greg crooned into his phone. "Love you babe. See you in a bit."

Greg slipped his phone into his pocket and headed for his car parked at the rear of his office building.

He slipped behind the wheel of his Lincoln MKZ.

He couldn't help but worry his sister was losing it. He got the revenge part. Hell, he even applauded her for it. It seemed almost righteous somehow to exact as much pain as possible on those responsible for their mother's downfall.

But her end game with the boy she blamed for Danny's death was unpredictable to him. Kimberly had not shared what she planned for Aiden. And he wasn't sure he wanted to know, or be sucked into her obsession.

Hope you don't screw the pooch, sis.

Or worse yet, get pulled over with an unconscious college boy in your backseat.

Chapter 32

Aiden tried to open his eyes as he felt someone lifting him by his shoulders. Blinking, he could see a man of average build with dark brown, clean cut hair had locked his arms under Aiden's armpits. He didn't recognize who Mr. Cleancut was but he was pulling Aiden from the back seat of a car.

He was too groggy to resist. His legs weren't responding as he tried to straighten them and stand.

His vision was blurred and out of focus.

He heard Mr. Cleancut saying something to another person.

"He's coming around. Be ready to hit him with another dose of sleepy time if he starts to struggle," Mr. Cleancut said looking down into Aiden's half-closed eyes.

"Okay. Get him inside. I'll unlock my lab's door. Once he's dressed and in his chair he won't be going anywhere," a female voice responded.

A blonde woman came into his view briefly, then moved away. He was unable to make out her facial features, but he knew her voice. It was the woman from the parking lot he'd tried to help. Her voice sparked his memory of trying to help her with her car in the USC parking lot, then feeling a prick in his neck as the last thing before he'd evidently passed out.

He blinked his eyes several times trying to clear his vision and reached up to rub them with his hands. His vision started to clear.

He appeared to be in some wooded area and no longer on the USC campus. Mr. Cleancut was dragging him through a doorway. Aiden could make out the smells of a garden and flowers as he entered the building. His legs were starting to work again, but only enough for him to give small weak kicks as his heals scraped across the cement floor.

Mr. Cleancut pulled him through an interior door to a smaller room. Aiden could see they weren't alone in the room. A man sat facing the door in a straight-backed chair with restraints around his legs, arms and chest. He was dressed in a hospital gown tied with a string at the neck. A couple of IV bags hung next to the man with tubing leading to his blotchy and blistered left arm. His facial features were distorted by the same swollen blotches and large blisters which seemed to cover all of his exposed skin. His skin color had a gray appearance between the inflamed areas, making it unclear if he was unconscious or dead. His fellow captive didn't stir as Aiden was dragged past him deeper into the room.

Mr. Cleancut propped Aiden into a chair with its back to his afflicted roommate. He saw the blonde woman approach him out the corner of his eye. Feeling a prick in his neck, his eyes drooped shut and he receded into unconscious darkness again.

Aiden woke to the sounds of someone drumming their fingers on metal.

He forced his eyes open as he raised his head to see where the noise was coming from. A man was leaning against a metal benchtop, looking bored. As Aiden's vision came into focus, he could see it was Mr. Cleancut providing the rhythmic tapping to some imagined tune playing in his head.

Aiden's legs and arms had been secured to his chair with zip ties. A notched belt encircled his chest completing his restraints. He was wearing a hospital gown, which sparked his memory of being dragged past his roommate dressed in identical garb earlier.

"Why?" Aiden said groggily. "What is...?" his voice trailed off.

"There you are. Back with the living again," Mr. Cleancut smiled as he looked down at Aiden's questioning face. "My sister will be here in a moment to fill you in on tonight's festivities."

Aiden heard footsteps approaching from outside the room. The blonde woman entered his field of view as Mr. Cleancut stepped off to the side. Mr. Cleancut seemed to be watching to ensure Aiden's bindings were secure. He stood resting his elbow on the stainless steel lab bench where he'd been practicing his finger percussion earlier. The bench stretched the length of the room's back wall.

"Thanks Little Bear. Everything is coming together

quite well," the woman said smiling and pacing in front of Aiden's chair, looking him over from head to foot.

"You looked like you might have known who I was for a second in the parking lot. Have you figured out who I am yet?" she looked down at Aiden, bending to place her face a few inches from his.

Aiden scrutinized her and knew he'd met her somewhere. It hadn't been recently, but someone he knew in his past. He shook his head, looking away.

"Well, it has been a few years. You used to come by my house pretty often when you were in high school. Mostly when I wasn't home, but we'd met a few times. I had you over for dinner more than once."

"Mrs. Riggsby?" Aiden questioned. "Danny's mom?"

"That's right Aiden. I knew you'd remember me, and please call me Kimberly," she said sounding pleased. "We're going to be spending a lot of time together reminiscing. Although I don't think you'll be enjoying it. In fact, I can guarantee you won't."

Mr. Cleancut Little Bear had been eyeing Kimberly a bit warily, seeming to be unsure of what might happen next. He said, "Well you're all set up for the evening. Do you need me to stay any longer? It's Sunday and after six so I should be heading home."

Kimberly laughed, "Yes of course. You should run along. I hope you're having fun with that little tart you're shacked up with. Just make sure she doesn't tire of you. Your plan all goes to shit if she doesn't eventually tie the knot."

"Don't worry about me. Your little brother has it all

under control," he said as he started for the door.

Aiden turned his head to watch Mr. Cleancut Little Bear's departure from the corner of his eye. He hesitated before exiting the room and appeared to be looking at Aiden's imprisoned roommate, "Are you sure the good sergeant is still with the living? If you need me to drop him off somewhere no one will find him…"

"No, he's still hanging in there, but just barely. He's my "canary in the cave." He's four days into what I have planned for young Aiden. Once he gives up the ghost, I'll have a good idea of how long my special regimen of goodies takes to prove fatal," she explained, smirking cruelly at Aiden to register her meaning.

Aiden had read about canaries used to warn miners. The unsuspecting birds were particularly sensitive to carbon monoxide, methane, or other potential toxic gases. If the miners saw the poor winged creatures keeled over in their cages, they knew it was time to exit their underground work place before it became a deathtrap.

"Drive careful brother. Aiden and I will be catching up on things."

"Okay, just be careful. All of this seems over the top. There are a lot cleaner and faster ways to take care of things, as you know," Mr. Cleancut Little Bear said with an edge of annoyance in his voice.

"You worry too much. And the fun is in the journey as they say," Kimberly said as she dismissed her brother with a flip of her hand.

Turning to Aiden, she met his eyes saying, "Now one thing I will be needing is the password to your laptop. You can give it to me now, or I'm sure you'll be *quite* compelled to tell me later if you choose."

"Your father will be worried about you in a couple of days if you don't check in. You know, when finals are done and all. I'll make sure he knows you've decided you need some time off. I think you've said on Facebook you like to backpack, so let's say you're headed to Colorado with a few friends for the next week or so. Sound about right?" She laughed as she saw the realization in Aiden's face that no one would come looking for him until it was too late.

"Why are you doing this? Danny was like a brother to me. I would give *anything* to have him back. There isn't a day that goes by that I don't wish for that," Aiden said imploring Kimberly towards reason.

"And *you* wishing he wasn't dead means *you* weren't responsible? *You* knew he didn't have a license. *You* let him behind the wheel of your car. *You* made that decision," she spat as she put her face inches from his. She held his eyes with her venomous stare for a few seconds.

"You probably egged him on that night," she added stepping away from Aiden and crossing the room to her lab bench.

Tears came to Aiden's eyes as he looked down in shame and said quietly, "You're right. I never should have let Danny behind the wheel. I know that. I've had to live with that."

Watching Kimberly's back as she busied herself at her benchtop, he continued, "I held Danny that night after the accident as he took his last breath. I didn't know what to do to help him. It's why I decided to go to med school.

I look at Danny's picture every day and remind myself why I need to pay it forward. Why I need to give back." His voice trailed off as he sighed deeply.

Kimberly turned and looked at Aiden, the tears now running down his cheeks. "Very touching, but you weren't his *mother*. You didn't center your life around him for sixteen years, sacrificing whatever it took to raise him alone without any help."

Kimberly crossed the room in two long strides, leaned down and shouted into Aiden's face, "*He was my everything!*"

"The pain of losing Danny was unbearable. I didn't think I could carry on. I woke up each day missing him and went to sleep more depressed than when I had gotten up. I found some solace in developing my green thumb for the toxic beauties growing outside this room," she said as she gestured towards the door leading to the greenhouse's growing area.

"And avenging my mother's death provided a focus for me. Especially when I stood over your mother dying in her garden," she said with cruel intent. She watched Aiden's jaw drop as the stark realization of what she had done swept over him.

Aiden sat in shocked disbelief.

He stared at his mother's killer, and now, his captor. His mind raced. He tried to process the insanity he was now part of along with the anger of being in the presence of his mother's murderer.

Kimberly returned to her lab bench and began explaining, "You might remember that I had Danny interred at a cemetery with mausoleum crypts rather than the typical burial plots. I couldn't bear the idea of putting my son under six feet of dirt."

"A couple of years ago it occurred to me I was not making the most of my time in my visits with Danny. The time was always too short, and with my work, I could only be there once or twice a week. I realized Danny needed to be closer to me so I could talk to him whenever the darkness became overwhelming."

"It turns out for a few hundred dollars, a member of the cemetery's maintenance crew can be bribed to look the other way. It was a cheap price to pay to have my precious Danny join me whenever I wanted," she said as she shrugged at Aiden.

She bent down and slowly pulled out a stainless steel drawer the length of her lab's benchtop, and continued, "So I guess it's about time you got to say hello to the best friend you claim you've missed so much."

Aiden was still reeling from Kimberly's confession of killing his mother. Her voice droned on about her grief and Danny's burial.

Watching her pull the drawer open, his mind nearly shut down. His teenage friend's body slowly materialized from the darkness of the drawer.

The drawer had interior LED lights which flicked on as it was fully opened. The intense light revealed the full macabre scene to Aiden. Kimberly had encased her son's corpse in what looked like a crystal clear resin. A life-size photo of Danny's face seemed to float a few inches above his head, fossilized in the resin. Danny appeared happy in the photo, which had a three-dimensional quality to it under the lights of his entombment. The photo appeared to be similar to the one Aiden kept of Danny in his college room.

Danny's body was dressed in a formal tuxedo. The bizarre outfit took on an eerie glow in the drawer's light. His hands and the side of his face were visible through the polymer casing, shriveled and in the early stages of bony decay. His hair was combed, but a few stray wisps seemed to float above his head; as if displaced by a gust of wind and now frozen for time eternal.

"My Danny never got to go to his high school prom, so I got him a tuxedo for his new resting place," Kimberly said in a self-satisfied tone. "I know he would have liked it."

Aiden felt the grief and anger of losing his mother compound with the grief of losing his best friend. An emotional storm washed over him. His mind flashed between being sixteen again and in that ditch holding Danny's lifeless body in his arms, and images of his mother lying lifeless in her casket as he looked on helplessly.

"You'll get to join Danny, you know. You'll be my birthday present to him," Kimberly said as she pulled out a full-length drawer beneath the one her son's body was displayed in. It was identical in length and depth. Its emptiness was illuminated by a light similar to the one showcasing Danny in all of his *Night of the Living Dead* splendor.

"The difference will be your face...captured in the final throws of the *agony* that you deserve." Kimberly seemed to be reveling in Aiden's unwavering stare at her handiwork.

Aiden felt numb. Coming face-to-face with his mother's killer. The horrific scene of his friend smiling from beneath his clear prison as if picking up a date for the spring fling. It combined to bury him in an avalanche of anger, grief, remorse...and hopelessness.

With his senses on overload, he barely noticed Kimberly as she wheeled her medical supply cart to the side of Aiden's chair. She began setting up an IV drip similar to the one he'd seen next to his roommate's chair.

He startled when he felt the prick of the needle entering his arm. Looking at his captor in compliant surrender, his mouth agape, he was too drained to struggle.

The initial warm flush of the IV fluids entered his body. The pleasant feeling washed over him returning him to a groggy, sleepwalking state.

His eyes went in and out of focus on his teenage friend of years gone by as the searing pain of Kimberly's liquid vengeance began its savage journey through his veins.

He remained transfixed on Danny's glowing countenance. His senses were assaulted by the screams and laughter echoing off the walls in Kimberly's room of horrors.

He realized it wasn't Danny screaming.

It was his own tortured cries mixed with Kimberly's maniacal laugh that filled this nightmare prison of pain and insanity with no way out; this corner of hell.

Chapter 33

Daly's cell buzzed. It was Jim Jensen calling.

Daly had been doing a final walk-through of a security system for a client's house in Burbank. It was approaching five o'clock in the afternoon on Tuesday.

"Hi Jim. How's my favorite mad scientist?"

"Hey Daly, I've been better. I'm probably all twitterpated about nothing, but I got an email from Aiden an hour ago. It left me a bit worried," Jim said, the concern obvious in his voice.

He continued, "The email said he's going backpacking with friends. That isn't a surprise since he said he was thinking about going on a hiking trip for his break when he was home a few days ago. What's strange is he said he's leaving his cellphone behind. No reception where he's going or something like that. What sense does that make? What if they have car trouble on the way? And even on some of the most remote trails in the San Gabriels, you can get cell reception if you search out a high point in the mountains."

"I tried to call him as soon as I pulled up the email,

but no answer. It went straight to his cell's answering service. He'd only sent the email to me an hour before I tried to call. I tried emailing him back and got one of those bounce back messages saying he'll be unreachable but will get back when he returns," Jim paused in his exasperation, obviously waiting for Daly to say something.

Daly sat thinking over what Jim had relayed to her for a couple of seconds, and responded, "Well, it doesn't sound all that irregular for a college guy to head out with his friends on the spur of the moment. A bit inconsiderate not to call you to confirm what he was planning, but…" Daly hesitated as she wondered if Jim's concern was based more on his recent loss of Louise. Aiden was everything to Jim now, so a heightened sense of paranoia for Aiden's safety wouldn't be surprising.

Before Jim could object, Daly forged on, "Why don't you try to reach him a few more times? It's almost five o'clock, maybe he'll pick up his messages after dinner and check in."

Jim hesitated for a few seconds as he seemed to be thinking over her proposal. "You're probably right. I'll do that. Hopefully he picks up my messages. That would give me a chance to discuss the wisdom of a wilderness hike without an exit plan if something goes wrong," Jim agreed with some relief in his voice.

"But if I can't reach Aiden, would you be willing to go with me to campus tomorrow morning? Just to check things out. You know, see if he talked with someone about his plans. Make sure his room isn't ransacked, and no toga parties in progress," Jim asked hopefully.

"Sure. I'll be glad to take a trip to USC. Haven't been there in a while so always good to see what the Trojans are up to. Plus I'd hate to miss a good toga party," Daly laughed. "Give me a call sometime before ten tonight and let me know what the plan is."

"Okay. Thanks Daly. I really appreciate it. I hate to sound like some old coot worrying about every noise in the dark. But I must say having an ex-cop on my speed dial is pretty comforting. I'll call you later. Bye."

"Talk to you later Jim," Daly said and hit the end button.

She had a couple more security checks to perform on her Burbank house and then she could head home.

Daly had thrown herself back into her and Mark's security business the last few days.

It had been nice to return to her everyday routines after the Mary Simon murders had completely rebooted her personal life over the past couple of months. The loss of dear friends along with being so involved in the resolution of the case had taken a toll on her emotional reserves.

She still didn't have a clear picture of what had driven Mary Simon's murderous spree. Nonetheless, she had decided to take a sabbatical from working the case. From her days in the LAPD Behavioral Analysis Unit, she'd learned on some of the more difficult cases to step away. If things weren't making sense and no clarifying clues were forthcoming, it was better to get away from the day-to-day details. Let the case percolate in her subconscious mind.

At ten thirty Tuesday evening, Jim called Daly's cell.

"Daly, no word from Aiden. I called a half dozen times, *and* sent urgent emails. I think we need to go to campus tomorrow." Jim sounded rattled.

"Okay, okay. I'll drop by your house in the morning and we'll go take a look see," Daly said trying to reassure her frantic friend. "How about I come by around nine o'clock? That will give Aiden tonight to contact you if he's just out late with the guys, okay?"

"Yeah, that sounds good. Okay, I'll see you at nine," Jim said distractedly as he hung up.

Daly turned to Mark who was engrossed in a DVR'd episode of the TV series *Blacklist™*. "Looks like Jim and I are taking a little trip tomorrow to check out why Aiden's gone off the grid," she said thoughtfully. Daly had filled Mark in earlier in the evening concerning Jim's worries about Aiden's deciding to backpack without electronic backup.

"You want me to join you?" Mark asked, pausing the DVR with James Spader in mid-sentence, and turning to look at Daly.

"No. I'm guessing we'll find a couple of Aiden's friends that can put Jim at ease, if not Aiden himself. It will probably be a visit for nothing. I don't mind being the adult moral support for Jim as he chews Aiden for cutting off communications and worrying his dad," she sighed and shrugged at Mark.

"You're a good woman, Daly Ford," Mark said leaning over to kiss her cheek. "Just don't pick up any young Trojan beefcakes while you're cougar'ing around campus."

He winced as Daly punched his shoulder, a little

harder than a love tap.

"And why would I be "cougar'ing" when my own personal beefcake is so easy," she cooed. She took the remote control from his hand, and pushed him back against the couch, locking eyes with him, projecting an intense, carnal gaze.

"Guess James will have to wait," Mark whispered resignedly. He wrapped his arms around Daly and gently rolled her onto her back on the couch. Returning her come hither look, he kissed her, and this time, longer and more urgently.

Mark raised his head, looking into Daly's eyes and whispered, "So I'm easy, huh?"

"Just shut up, beefcake," she said breathlessly as she closed her eyes and met his hungry lips with hers.

<hr />

Daly picked Jim up at his house shortly after nine o'clock. It was a bit cool for a southern California Wednesday in late May. Still, a pleasant morning with horsetail cirrus clouds breaking up the deep blue sky.

After their hellos, Jim let Daly know he hadn't heard anything from Aiden since they'd last talked. They traveled through the late morning traffic of LA on the I-5 headed south to downtown LA and the USC campus in silence. Daly didn't talk about Aiden being missing, and Jim was lost in his own thoughts as they drove through the morning sprawl of LA.

As they turned onto North Soto Street, Jim said, "Let's start with the parking lot and see if his car is there. Lot seventy."

"Sounds right, we can park there and walk back to his dorm so we cover all the bases of where he's likely been," Daly agreed.

Entering Lot 70, Daly slowly drove down several rows of cars as Jim expectantly scrutinized the lot looking for Aiden's car.

"There it is," Jim said excitedly, pointing towards a blue Prius parked in one of farthest slots from the lot's entrance. "I guess we know he didn't leave campus in his own car."

Looking through the windows of the compact car, nothing appeared out of order to Jim. The car was locked and belongings removed with the exception of a few empty Coke cans and fast food wrappers on the rear floor of the car.

Daly located an open space a few cars from Aiden and parked. Starting to get out of the car to join Jim, she hesitated, leaned back into her car, and rummaged in her glove compartment. After a few seconds, she pulled an official looking placard from the glove box. The placard was bright red with white lettering saying, "Official Police Business." She left it on the driver's side dashboard in plain sight through the windshield. Grabbing her shoulder bag, she joined Jim now standing behind her car waiting impatiently.

"There, that should keep campus security from ticketing us while we snoop around a while," Daly said nodding at Jim.

Daly and Jim walked the few blocks from Aiden's car to his dormitory with Jim leading the way. Daly was craning her neck at the surrounding buildings and anything that seemed to catch her interest along the pathway. She took notes in a small notepad produced from the back pocket of her jeans.

Arriving at Aiden's dorm, they loitered near the entrance for a student to exit the building. Within a few minutes, a mousy looking brunette with a backpack half her size shoved through the door, leaving it to slowly shut in her wake. Jim stepped towards the door as Miss Mousy hurried away, probably late for class.

Jim caught the door and held it open for Daly.

Daly stepped past him and said, "I don't suppose you have a key or anything for Aiden's room do you?"

Jim shook his head, "No, but there's usually a Resident Advisor on the floor. If I show them my ID, they should be okay with us looking around his room."

Daly nodded and followed Jim as they ascended the stairs to the third floor. Pushing through the fire door, they spotted the lounge halfway down the hall. Several students were sprawled around the room on couches or chairs watching Drew Carey on the TV. He was excitedly describing wonderful prizes as strangely dressed contestants screamed in delight.

"Excuse me," Jim interrupted as a couple of students looked towards the interlopers. "Is the RA for the floor around?"

"I'm the RA," a lanky sandy haired surfer dude in

cut-offs and a muscle shirt replied, not looking away from the TV. "What can I do you for?" he asked, still looking entranced by the game show host.

"Uh, hi. I'm Aiden Jensen's dad. I hadn't heard from him in a day or so and wondered if he'd said anything about going somewhere with his friends?" Jim approached the RA and stood over his chair looking at him expectantly.

"No man. I haven't seen Aiden around the last week. I wasn't really watching for him as the med school dweebs come and go at weird hours. No offense, man," the RA answered glancing up at Jim in half-hearted apology for his disparaging term for Aiden.

"Maybe you could open up his room so I can take a look around to see if anything might indicate where he's gone," Jim said as he firmly gripped the RA's right shoulder.

"Uh sure man," the RA said a bit startled by Jim's grip. He sat up now giving Jim his full attention, "You've got some ID to show me you're Aiden's dad, right?"

"No problem," Jim said pulling out his wallet and flipping his driver's license out for the RA.

Looking back and forth between the license and Jim, the RA seemed satisfied and stood up reluctantly. He led the way to Aiden's room and opened the door with his electronic key pass. "I'll need to stay here while you look around."

"Fine," Jim said curtly as he and Daly entered the room.

Aiden's duffel bag was in the center of the room. Jim turned to Daly with his eyebrow raised questioningly,

"It looks untouched since I saw it in my hallway Sunday afternoon."

Daly nodded, "I'll go and talk to a few of the other students and see if anyone's seen him since Sunday."

⸺⸺◈⸺⸺

Jim turned back to Aiden's duffel bag and zipped it open to look through the contents. He was hoping something might indicate where Aiden had gone with his friends…if he'd gone anywhere with his friends, which was looking dubious at best. Jim pulled out Aiden's course schedule binder and turned to the last couple of pages. He found Aiden's finals schedule, complete with course names, rooms and times for the finals, and the professors overseeing the tests.

Pulling out his smart phone, Jim searched the USC campus directory, locating the phone numbers for the two professors on Aiden's finals list. Having no luck in calling the first professor, he moved to the second.

"Hello, Doctor Witting?"

"Yes, this is Witting," the bored voice on the other end answered.

"I'm calling about Aiden Jensen, my son. I understand he is in your physiology class. I'm trying to track him down and wondered if he'd shown up for his final exam on Tuesday?"

"Well, unfortunately, he did not. Very unlike young Jensen. He's been one of my top students, but missing the final will certainly mean a repeat for the course if he doesn't make arrangements with me right away," Dr. Witting said with some indignation.

"So he didn't show up for his final, and didn't let you know he couldn't make it?" Jim asked with the concern level rising in his voice.

"No. And if it was to get an early start on summer break, that *won't* cut it with me," Dr. Witting added for emphasis.

Jim felt his insides turn cold, "Uh, I'm sure there's some explanation. I'll have Aiden contact you as soon as I can," Jim said hurriedly as he ended the call.

Daly returned to Aiden's room. Stepping around the RA looking bored outside the doorway, she announced, "No luck talking to any of Aiden's dormies. No one has seen him in the last week." She sat down on Aiden's bed eyeing Jim.

Jim was sitting in Aiden's desk chair with a binder in front of him on the desk. "I just got off the phone with one of Aiden's professors. He didn't show up for his final on Tuesday. The professor hasn't seen him this week," Jim's voice quavering as he shared his news with Daly.

Daly stood up. Walking to Jim's side and placing her hand on his shoulder, she said, "Okay, we've got enough to go to USC campus security. I'll call some of the folks I know in the LAPD to make sure they're aware and can be on the look out as well."

Jim's mind reeled with the thought of Aiden not just being unreachable by phone. Not just being with friends on some carefree backpacking trip. Not just being anywhere.

Missing.

Daly continued to busily make phone calls and talked to Jim as he sat numbly looking at Aiden's binder. His senses had shut down. Daly's voice sounded to him as if it were in a drum and unintelligible.

Daly gripped Jim by his left shoulder and with her other hand tipped his head back to look at her, "Jim, do you hear me? I've got campus security coming over right now. We'll tell them what we know and get their help in finding Aiden. Do you hear me?" she said anxiously a few inches from Jim's face.

"Once we get the missing persons request filled out, I'll get you home. Okay? You can wait there for them to call you with what they find."

Jim sat quietly at Aiden's desk. His eyes fell on the pictures of Aiden on his desk shelves. Happy at his graduation. Carefree on a Jamaican beach. Floating in their pool with his best friend. How could he be gone? Missing? It was too surreal for Jim to grasp.

Daly brought Jim a Coke from the hallway dispensing machine. She sat consoling him as they waited for campus security to arrive. Telling him that it would be ok. They just needed to expand the search and bring all the USC and LAPD resources into play.

It took about two hours to fill out the report with campus security. Daly and Jim provided what they knew. Jim shared the email from Aiden about the backpacking trip. Finally, they revisited the parking lot to identify Aiden's car.

Around two o'clock, campus security had all they

needed to begin the investigation. They got Jim's home phone number, cell number and email. Officer Gomez, the lead campus security officer, said he would contact Jim as soon as they had something on Aiden's whereabouts.

Daly turned to Jim after the final contact information was shared and said softly, " Okay. Nothing more we can do here. Let's get you home."

Jim stood up. He saw his drawn face in the mirror on the back of the door to Aiden's room. He looked tired, but not as catatonic as he'd probably looked earlier. Jim turned to Daly and agreed, "Okay, let's go."

Daly had pulled her car to the front of the dorm building on her way back from the parking lot, after showing Officer Gomez Aiden's car. She opened Jim's passenger door, and steadied him as he fell into the seat.

Slipping into the driver's seat, Daly said, "I'll get you home and call my LAPD contacts to bring them up to speed." She focused in silence on the road ahead for the thirty minute drive to Jim's house, glancing at Jim with a concerned look from time to time.

Pulling into Jim's driveway, Daly sat quietly for a moment then offered, "Jim, I know you're thinking the worst. I get that. But we don't know anything yet. He may not be missing. He may just be with friends as he said in his email. Let the resources at USC and LAPD go to work on this before you assume it's going to end badly. Okay?"

Jim looked intently at Daly and said in a serious tone, "It's been *three* days since anyone has seen Aiden. I'm not a cop, but I know if someone is taken, the first forty-eight hours is critical to finding them alive, right?"

DAN BLAIR

Daly sighed heavily, "Jim, that's only true in child abductions as a general rule. We don't even know if Aiden was abducted. There were no signs of struggle around his car or in his dorm room. It's not good for you to even go where you're going. Just try to get your mind off it for a while and wait by the phone. Let the system work for you."

Jim opened his car door and walked to his front door. Looking back at Daly as he reached to unlock the door, he could see her watching him.

She smiled at him as he caught her eye.

It was a sad and worried smile.

Chapter 34

As Daly pulled away from Jim's house, she could see him watching her leave from his entryway. The cold recollections of past kidnapping cases with the LAPD crept up her spine and caused her to shiver. Although she'd tried her best to calm Jim's fears, bad things did happen to good people.

It was the shits, but it was true.

Daly looked at her watch. 3:00 pm. She pressed the hands free call button on her Honda's steering wheel, and said, "Call Mark."

Mark picked up after the first ring, "Hey babe. Any luck tracking down our college boy gone wild?"

Daly filled Mark in on her and Jim's unsuccessful trip to USC. Plus the fact that USC campus security and the LAPD were now being brought into the search.

"Man, didn't see that coming. I sure hope he's not shacked up with some cute babe for summer break…or maybe I do hope that's where he is," Mark added as an afterthought.

"Yeah, that would be one of the better options," Daly agreed. "Well, I'm going to call McClarey and fill him in. Maybe he'll have some ideas, plus doesn't hurt to have all the police forces in the area aware Aiden is missing. I'm home now, so I'll see you later."

Daly pulled into her driveway and without getting out of her car, she dialed McClarey's cell. It went straight to voice mail. After trying a second time and leaving a message for him to call her, she thumbed through her contacts and located Captain McCollough, McClarey's supervisor at Santa Monica PD.

Hitting his private phone number, she waited for him to pick up.

"Hello, Captain McCollough, Santa Monica PD."

"Captain McCollough. This is Daly Ford. We met on the Mary Simon case briefly. I was helping Sergeant McClarey with some of the leg work," Daly explained.

"Of course I remember you. McClarey spoke very highly of you. He said we should hire you if you ever decided to get back in the catching bad guys business," the captain said pleasantly. "What can I do for you?"

"I'm trying to reach Sergeant McClarey and wondered if you knew where he was. He's not answering his cell."

"No, you won't be reaching him easily. He's out of the country. Had to leave very suddenly. Didn't even come by the station. He emailed me last Friday that his father-in-law was ill and he was needed back in London. Since the Mary Simon case had pretty much wrapped up, he felt he had some personal time coming and was going to use it."

"I don't know if you knew, but his wife had passed away a few years ago, so I guess he felt obligated to handle it for her. Not like him to rush off like that, but when family calls… He left in such a rush, several of the Mary Simon case files were still out on his desk," the captain added.

"Is there something I can help you with while he's gone?"

Daly filled the captain in on Aiden Jensen going missing. She said she was going to ask McClarey to keep his eyes open as he worked the loose ends on the Mary Simon case. McCollough offered that he would pass the word on Aiden being missing among his own officers.

"Captain, you said Sergeant McClarey left some files on his desk. Would those be some of the files he was going to go over with me? He'd okay'd me with the Feds to share whatever final reports they provided."

"Probably. I had one of my officers collect the reports and store them until the good sergeant returns. He did mention that he wanted to share the Feds' reports with you," the captain replied.

"While I'm waiting around to hear something back on Aiden, I could come down and take a look at the reports," Daly offered.

"And *why* would you be so interested in a case we've already put to bed," the captain asked curiously.

"I'd talked to Sergeant McClarey last week about helping him tie up some loose ends. It's the least I could do while he's out tending to family matters. Plus, it will give us a head start if I'm up to speed on the Feds' files when he gets back," she added.

"Well, far be it from me to turn down free help these days, especially with your background. Come on by whenever you want. I'll tell the desk sergeant to get you what you need."

"Thanks Captain McCollough. I'll swing by in a half hour or so. See you then," Daly said as she ended the call.

Daly dialed Mark. After a few rings, his recorded voice told her to leave a message.

She hurriedly talked into her phone as she pulled from her driveway, "Hey babe. I decided to head over to Santa Monica PD and check out some files McClarey got from the Feds. Weird, but his captain said he left suddenly to take care of family in London. Anyway, I may be late so get yourself something to eat on the way home. Love you."

Arriving at the Santa Monica PD station around three thirty, Daly had managed to skirt most of the rush hour traffic. Although there's never a good time to drive in LA and it's burbs, it's particularly painful to be out between four and seven o'clock in the afternoon.

Bounding up the stairs to the SMPD's main lobby, Daly crossed the dark gray tiled floor to the desk sergeant.

The desk sergeant looked up as he saw Daly approaching. Reaching under the marble top of his receiving area, he pulled out a box. "Captain said you'd be looking for this," he said matter of factly.

Surprised at this display of efficiency, Daly nodded with an impressed look on her face, "Thanks very much Sergeant. And relay my thanks to the captain when you see him."

"Would it be ok if I used one of your small conference rooms to look these over?"

"Captain said whatever you needed. That's good enough for me."

Daly wrestled the box from the shoulder high marble top. Smiling at the sergeant, she pushed through the swinging stanchion beside his desk, and made her way into an empty conference room.

Unloading the folders from the box, she spread them out on the table in front of her. The largest of the files was in an accordion folder several inches thick and marked "Common Elements." A smaller, but substantial folder was titled "Emails/Correspondence." The other files were the run of the mill classifications: forensics, phone records, witness accounts, and lab results. Several of the more basic files she had reviewed earlier with McClarey.

Turning her attention to the 'Common Elements" folder that was new to her, she began working her way through what looked like a few hours of reading material. About an hour into reading about every common gas station or restaurant visited by persons of interest to the investigation, she hit a name she recognized, Kimberly Riggsby.

She remembered McClarey mentioning her as the mother of the boy who died in an accident with Aiden when he was a teenager. McClarey had mentioned interrogating her after Louise's murder and feeling uneasy about her responses.

Daly pulled her laptop from her shoulder bag. Firing

up her MacBook Air™, she logged in to the LAPD website. She wasn't supposed to have access to the website since she had quit the LAPD and turned in her badge. However, she'd kept the website links active so she had a ready resource she could use in emergencies…or when she felt like it.

Pulling up the DMV records, she typed in Kimberly Riggsby. A relatively photogenic picture for a driver's license popped up on her screen. A heart shaped face with blonde hair over piercing blue eyes, almost fluorescent, looked back at her from the photo. She didn't recognize her as anyone she'd come across in the Mary Simon case.

The report indicated Riggsby had done some interior design work for Tommy Hemmings the previous fall.

Reading further, Daly noted a reference to Greg Riggsby, Kimberly's brother. He was the senior partner for a John Hancock office in Santa Monica.

Daly remembered meeting Greg Riggsby at a funeral, Tommy Hemmings funeral and maybe Chuck Kohler's as well. She was trying to picture him in her mind. Tapping his name into the DMV website still open on her laptop, Greg Riggsby's face appeared. Dark hair, short businessman's cut, well groomed, square jaw and brown eyes. Yes, that was who she remembered. He'd said he was a financial advisor of some kind.

Turning back to the Common Elements report, she read on. Her eyes widened as she reached the part about the Lion's Heart LLC. Greg Riggsby had been the financial advisor for a joint venture with Tommy Hemmings, Louise Jensen, Mike Gentry, Charles Kohler and Mary

Simon. Daly remembered Jim mentioning that Louise had been in some kind of venture with Mary Simon and Tommy Hemmings. She'd totally forgotten this little snipit of information from their session at the Saddle Peak Lodge a few weeks back.

"No *eff'n* way," Daly said out loud. As coincidences went, this was well beyond anything even close to a chance crossing of paths.

Daly was looking at the report in stunned disbelief when her phone buzzed. It vibrated loudly on the wooden table surface startling her from her intense reading.

It was Jim calling. She noted it was now after five o'clock according to her phone's home screen.

"Daly, Officer Gomez from campus security called me. They did a rush job to review the parking lot security tapes based on our missing persons request," Jim said excitedly.

"They were able to find the video of Aiden arriving in the parking lot Sunday afternoon based on the timing and car location. The video clearly shows him exiting his car and walking towards his dormitory." Jim paused for a breath and continued, "Then he appears to stop at a car with its hood raised. Gomez said the video is pretty sketchy as too far away to see all the details, but he appeared to be helping a blonde woman. They could see Aiden collapse and the blonde woman putting him in her car. They also have video of the car leaving the parking lot a few minutes later," Jim said taking a deep breath.

"Jim, that's great news. Well, I mean it's not great that Aiden was abducted, but it's great that they've got it on video," Daly replied as she sat forward in her chair.

"Gomez has shared the video with the LAPD and they have an All Points Bulletin out for the car seen leaving the USC parking lot, a gray Ford Taurus. What do you think we should do?" Jim bubbled with optimism in his question. His mood contrasted sharply with where he'd been when Daly had dropped him off at his house earlier.

"Okay, okay. Give me a second to think," Daly said. It had been three days since Aiden had been taken and it was unknown if his car was still in the LA area. Daly knew it wasn't good that they'd not received a ransom note. It likely meant the abduction wasn't for financial gain.

"You said the woman was blonde, right?" Daly said continuing to think as she pulled up the DMV photo of Kimberly Riggsby again. "I'm looking at a blonde woman of interest from McClarey's files on Mary Simon."

She shared what she'd learned in looking through the Feds' files provided by McClarey, emphasizing how the Riggsby siblings were crossing paths with their poker group. She felt all the intersections with their group had to be more than coincidence.

"It's a pretty big leap to assume Kimberly Riggsby is involved with Aiden's kidnapping because she's blonde. *But* if she's holding a grudge over losing her son, maybe she's the *real* killer, and not Mary. It would mean she had been after you and Louise. Maybe Aiden too. Or Aiden could be a pawn in her twisted end game," Daly mused out loud as she realized the logic of the scenario she was laying out wasn't so far fetched.

"We've got to do something!" Jim's voice had taken on a panicked pitch.

Daly felt a measured calm sweep over her. She'd faced several crisis situations on the LAPD and learned to quiet her mind when all hell was breaking loose. The best response to chaos was to detach from her emotions and apply logic and analysis.

Her voice level and commanding, she answered, "Jim, I need to call Mark and ask him to swing by Kimberly Riggsby's office. I'll ask him to see what he can come up with that might allow us to go to the police credibly. I'll let him know to look for anything that might be linked to the poker group, especially you, Louise and Aiden."

"I'm going to do the same at Greg Riggsby's office in Santa Monica. Do some snooping on my own. I'm guessing they're in this together. Hopefully we get something we can go to the police with so we're not just pointing fingers at a blonde with history with Aiden." Daly paused as she finished sharing her plan of action with Jim.

Jim sputtered, "What can I do? I've *got* to do something to help."

"Let Mark and I handle this for the moment. We'll keep you in the loop on whatever we find. If you don't hear from us in a couple of hours, give us a call."

Daly continued, "If we find anything pointing to Aiden's abduction, we'll get the police involved. Hell, even if we don't find anything, we'll get the police involved. It would just be easier if we had something concrete. Calling the police now would mean they'd potentially tip the Riggsbys off that they're suspects as part of the questioning. That might give them time to cover their tracks," Daly explained.

"Okay, I'll hang here by the phone while you two do your sleuthing," Jim agreed begrudgingly. "But call the minute you learn anything."

"Will do. I'm calling Mark right now."

Daly hit Mark's speed dial button and brought him up to speed from when they'd talked a mere two hours earlier.

"We need to cover all the bases and quickly to get something we can take to the police. Based on the files I've been going over, I'll take Greg Riggsby's office and see what I can dig up on this LLC and anything connected to Aiden. If you take Kimberly Riggsby's office, we'll cover the most ground in the shortest time," Daly suggested.

"Sounds right. It's after hours so I'll take along my "special tools" for uninvited guests. Have you got your lockpick set with you?" Mark asked.

"Always just a glove box away," Daly quipped.

"Ok, let's check in with each other once we're on site. If we're dealing with a couple of looney tunes here, we can't be too careful," Mark said with concern.

"So now you're the one warning me about looney tunes?" Daly laughed nervously. "This is just another walk in the park for your badass of a wife."

"I hear you, Miss Badass. I'd like to see you keep your badass in one piece. Just be careful," Mark admonished.

"You got it beefcake. I'll send you Kimberly's office address when I hang up."

"Okay. Time for Ford and Ford to kick some ass," Mark replied. Slipping his phone in his pocket, he bolted from his office to his car.

Daly brought up both of the Riggsbys' offices and home addresses on her computer. She transcribed these along with screenshot photo attachments from their drivers' licenses into an email to Mark, copied Jim, and hit send. She noted Greg Riggsby's office was in Santa Monica, only a few minutes from the police station. Mark would have to head towards their home in San Fernando as Kimberly's office was a few minutes from where they lived.

She scooped the Feds' folders into the box by the desk and exited the conference room.

It crossed her mind that she didn't have her Walther PK 380 with her for this reconnaissance mission. She'd just have to make sure it stayed purely a sneak and peak operation. If anything looked more than that, time to call in the boys in blue.

"Okay, badass. Let's get back in the saddle and ride," she said under her breath pushing through the police station's exit door into the late afternoon California sunshine.

Chapter 35

Mark arrived at Kimberly Riggsby's address on Hubbard Street at seven thirty p.m.

The traffic from his Santa Monica office had been worse than the usual snarl. Too many cars all leaving in the same direction. It had taken him over two hours, mostly due to the traffic, but he'd also stopped at his house along the way to change clothes. He now wore dark slacks, a black turtleneck and black loafers. More appropriate attire for his evening plans.

Daly had texted him around six thirty, while he'd been in transit. She'd let him know she was at Greg Riggsby's office and beginning her search.

Mark circled the parking lot. He located the large block numbers for the address positioned over the entrance to Kimberly's building. A freestanding business directory was positioned near the parking lot along the front entrance walkway to the building. It listed Exciting Designs for Life as one of the ten or so businesses housed within the modern concrete design, room 66 on the first floor. The directory even included a layout of where the businesses were located by floor as an added help to client's seeking their tenants' services.

Parking in a spot farthest away from the building's entrance, Mark doused his headlights. He sat surveying the parking lot and area around the office complex. Most everybody had gone home so he was one of only two or three cars parked in the lot. It was a relatively dark night with little moonlight, so only the perimeter lamppost lights lit the parking lot. Floodlights were positioned around the building lighting up its concrete fascade. Sealed windows embedded in the walls marked where the office areas were located.

Mark texted Daly, *Arrived at site. Getting ready to go in.* He didn't want to call her as she would be in the middle of her own operation at Greg Riggsby's by now. Nothing like a cell phone ring to alert the authorities to your presence.

Mark placed his own phone in silent mode.

By the floor layout he'd seen on the directory, Mark knew Kimberly's office was at the end of the building. It was part of a first floor protruding from the west end of the building. The building design was a stair-stepped configuration with each progressive floor inset thirty feet or so to the east from the preceding one. It gave it the look of a giant concrete Lego™ stairway. The design allowed Kimberly's office the benefit of open space above its roof. He could see angled skylight structures jutting from the first floor roof's flat surface over what was likely Kimberly's office space.

Exiting his car, Mark walked away from his targeted

office and into the shadows of other buildings in the complex. He skirted the buildings, staying in the shadows as he circled back towards his destination.

Looking through the windows of Kimberly's office, he could see the interior dimly lit by a red glow. The source of the light was an exit sign floating above what appeared to be a private exit from the rear of her office space. Not typical for office buildings, but certainly a perk for the tenant snagging it.

Mark crept around the back of the building and crouched near the private exit.

He set his "special tools" kit on the paved entrance outside the door. The kit was a leather satchel, a little smaller than a briefcase, with a shoulder strap and zippered opening. He extracted a couple of thin metal strips, some adhesive putty and an electronic device the size of a pack of cigarettes from the kit. He turned on the electronic device and passed it around the outside edge of the door. A soft high-pitched beep sounded as it passed over the alarm contacts. He inserted thin metal strips into the edge of the door at the contact locations, affixing the strips to the doorframe with putty.

Reaching into his kit again, he removed a slim black case a little larger than a wallet. Holding his LED flashlight in his mouth, he flipped the case open and selected a couple of precision picks. Holding a pick in each hand, he inserted them carefully into the narrow key opening in the door's lock. Feeling the inner workings of the lock through his metal extensions, he deftly steered them through the lock's interstices. With a couple of tries, he heard the desired click.

Pushing the door open, he listened for any sounds announcing him as an intruder. Hearing nothing, he slung the leather satchel over his shoulder and entered the office.

After securing the metal strips on the door's alarm contacts with more putty, he left the door ajar. It would make for a quick exit if needed.

Mark said a silent thank you to Uncle Sam and his Special Forces trainers. He had been trained by the Army for forced entry of buildings as part of his explosives specialty. In a war zone, that meant shooting a lock off or using small detonation devices. Given his high value as an IED expert, he had also trained with Special Forces on the more clandestine skills: picking locks, disabling or bypassing electronic locks, cracking safes, and generally getting into about anything he wanted; quietly and without detection. He hadn't been asked to use his US funded breaking and entering skills in Iraq, but it sure was coming in handy now.

He padded silently across the plush carpet keeping his flashlight pointed at the floor. His free hand shielded his LED helper from being seen through the windows. He didn't want passing security guards or a curious jogger spotting a light bouncing around Kimberly's office after hours.

He sat behind the desk and began going through file drawers recessed beneath the desk's glass top. After perusing the files for thirty minutes or so, he hadn't found anything suspicious or related to Aiden. There was a file for "Hemmings," but it was the details of an interior redesign of Tommy Hemmings' study. Business invoices, blueprints, drawings and miscellaneous approvals from municipal and county agencies filled the file drawers.

Standing up, he moved to the windowless west wall of the office and a six-panel door leading to another room. Opening the door, he stepped into a narrow kitchenette space. Closing the door behind him to a crack, he used his flashlight to scan the room.

He could see the space provided the ability to heat up food and drink via either a stove top or microwave, a sink for clean up, and a small refrigerator under the cabinet counter. Shelves above the counter held several jars and tins. Labels on the containers indicated different kinds of teas, coffee beans, spices and a range of beverage and soup mixes. A small coffee grinder and French press were at the back of the counter top.

Mark opened a few of the cabinets. Typical cleaning supplies were beneath the sink along with paper towels. A narrow floor-to-counter cabinet pull-out held a trash bin.

Opening two large opposing doors below the counter top and to the right of the sink, he saw the doors were a false front. Behind them were metal doors sealed with a combination lock.

Noting the brand of the lock, Mark extracted the appropriate tool from his kit. Placing a stethoscope type sensor near the lock, he inserted an attached earpiece. Turning the combination lock's dial slowly he listened for the tell tale clicks. With his second try, he heard the clack of the lock welcoming him to take a look-see.

Swinging the metal doors wide, he was able to see

multiple shelves on glider pull-outs. The shelves contained varied sizes of bottles, tins and canisters. Pointing his flashlight at the containers, he could see labels telling him this wasn't the backup tea and coffee pantry.

He recognized a few of the labels from the police reports for the Mary Simon murders: lily of the valley, castor beans/ricin extract, and hemlock. Other labels were foreign to him but sounded equally as toxic: snakeroot, strychnine tree fruit seeds, narcissists, choke cherry leaves, and nightshade. Several dozen bottles and canisters filled the hidden space.

Pulling out a bottom drawer below Kimberly's toxic potpourri of plant extracts, Mark said under his breath, "Now what the hell is this?"

When the glider pull-out was fully extended, he could see a set of individually labeled spoons set in notches in a felt-lined case. Each spoon's label consisted of three block letters glued beneath it.

Mark stared questioningly at this strange display of eating utensils. No two spoons were identical, appearing to be from different table setting designs.

The labels were: DRB, RSB, WMM, TJH, CLK, MRG, LAJ and MSS. Mark puzzled over the meaning of these letter trios.

Then it hit him.

"*Holy shit*," he exclaimed out loud realizing the labels were people's initials.

The initials of his deceased friends shone back at him illuminated by the brilliant light of his LED torch; TJH for Tommy, CLK for Chuck, MRG for Mike, LAJ for

Louise and MSS for Mary Simon.

Captivated by the bizarre contents of the secret cabinet, Mark didn't hear the footsteps behind him until it was too late.

He rose and turned his flashlight towards the sound.

Seeing only a glimpse of blonde hair, his vision erupted in an explosion of stars. The blow to his head, which had ignited his starry fireworks show, drove him to the floor.

As his head throbbed and vision blurred, he saw two blonde attackers over him. They were staring menacingly at him. Their arms pulled back in tandem and dealt a second blow delivering him to darkness.

———◦《◉》◦———

The pain of his throbbing head caused Mark to stir.

He opened his eyes, squinting from the light of the room and the pain shooting through his temples. His hands were bound behind him around the back of a chair. His ankles were bound to the legs of the chair.

It took him a minute to place his surroundings. He was in Kimberly's office. The track lights on the ceiling seemed to be piercing his retinas with their spotlights focused on him. The black out blinds on the windows had been pulled shut to foil any curious passers by.

A woman matching the photo Daly had sent of Kimberly Riggsby paced in front of her desk, obviously agitated. She wore faded jeans, a light gray sweatshirt and running shoes. Her hair was pulled back as if she hadn't had time to fix it before hurrying to her office.

Seeing that Mark was awake, she picked up his wallet from the desk. Flipping it open to the ID window, she said, "So, Mr. Ford I presume."

Mark's eyes began to focus, adjusting to the light as he stared at her. He didn't reply.

"I assume you have a good reason for breaking into my place of business. Would you care to tell me to what you're doing here?" she asked calmly.

Mark could see it was approaching nine by the clock on her wall. He noted a motion detector in the upper corner of the room he'd missed during his earlier breech of the room.

Kimberly must like to keep tabs on her office when she's away.

A cell on Kimberly's desk began to vibrate. Mark could see it was his phone, taken along with his wallet while he'd been unconscious. Daly's face was smiling at him from his phone with her name emblazoned across the screen. She'd be worried by now that he hadn't contacted her. He needed to stall for time and hope she would decide to come check on him.

"Looks like someone's trying to reach you," Kimberly said with a curious lilt to her voice. "Guess you'll just have to call back later."

Mark launched into explaining his presence. "I'm trying to help a friend find his missing son. I had reason to believe you might know something so I came by to talk. You didn't answer my knock, but the door was open so

I came in to look around. I know I shouldn't have and I'm sorry. I know this looks bad. I *really* don't want any trouble," Mark rambled, not sounding convincing even to himself.

Kimberly scoffed and resumed her pacing while she talked, "My door was *obviously* locked and your little bag of tricks is proof enough of your larcenous entry."

"The curious part…is why you'd think I know anything about your friend's missing son," she mused rhetorically. "It's also bothersome you decided to break into my kitchen cabinets. What were you hoping to find, Mr. Ford?"

"I don't know. I was snooping and got carried away," Mark sniveled trying to keep the conversation going. "At this point, why don't you call the police. We can straighten this out with them. I'm willing to face the music for making some bad calls and overstepping my bounds."

"No, Mr. Ford. I think you know a lot more than you've been willing to share."

"The police idea will *definitely* not be happening. Besides I think your caller, Daly was it, will likely be paying us a visit. We need to make sure we're ready when she comes by."

Mark glared at her as she moved towards him.

She had a large wad of paper towels in her hand. Pressing them into his mouth as a gag, she said, "There now. Since you don't want to talk about your little intrusion tonight, we'll make sure you don't alarm anyone that might be joining us."

Kimberly retreated to her kitchenette, AKA her toxic

pantry.

Mark could hear her close and open some cabinets. She reappeared a few minutes later with a small syringe in her hand.

Walking to Mark's side and looking down at him, she said, "I think my little friend here will solve any unwanted visitor problems, don't you? A prick for the pricks as it were," she said with a laugh watching his eyes widen with fear.

Mark jerked against his bindings. They were tight, not giving him any hope of escape.

He knew her syringe contained something far worse than oolong tea, and was meant for him or Daly, or both.

He desperately hoped Daly had hit the panic button and was bringing the Calvary.

Chapter 36

Daly pulled into a beach parking lot along Pacific Coast Highway 1 in Santa Monica. She parked so she had a view of Greg Riggsby's John Hancock office entrance from across the busy highway.

It was five thirty in the afternoon. People were busily coming and going. Joggers were running along the beachfront after a day at work or school.

Going to the trunk of her car, she grabbed a gym bag with some spare running gear. She kept a change of clothes with her in case she decided to go for an impromptu run at a work site. Walking a hundred yards down the beach she found a public restroom to change in. She emerged five minutes later wearing dark jogging pants, a USC sweatshirt, Nike cross trainer shoes and a slim style waist pouch for holding her what nots.

Returning to her car she dropped the gym bag with her street clothes into the back seat. Opening the glove box she retrieved her lock pick set and zipped it into her waist pouch. Settling into her seat she decided it was best to wait. Let the activity on the beachfront street settle into a post workday lull.

Spotting a small snack kiosk down the beach, she realized she was starving. She'd skipped lunch as she'd spent her day with USC campus security, shuttling Jim around and then poring over files at the police station. She decided to get a sandwich and coffee and return to her stake out.

At six p.m., Greg exited through the three-quarter glass door with John Hancock scripted on it, pulling it shut behind him. Strolling down the sidewalk, he seemed to be enjoying the sun and sounds of the surf. He crossed the highway to a parking lot, adjacent to the one Daly was watching from. A few minutes later, she saw him pull onto the Pacific Coast Highway. He turned at the first eastbound connector road towards the 405. From Greg's DMV records, he lived in Encino, a half hour drive away.

Munching on her ham and cheese sandwich, she continued to surveil the streetfront. Sipping her mocha latte and listening to her favorite Sirius station, Alt Nation, she passed the next half hour. She wanted to be sure Greg hadn't forgotten something at the office and decided to make a quick return.

At six thirty Daly stepped from her car and began casually jogging down the paved path along the beachfront of Santa Monica. She jogged north to the intersection of a traffic light for Highway 1. Crossing the famous road, she jogged south down the storefront side of the street.

She stopped in front of Riggsby's John Hancock office. With hands on her knees, she looked like she was catching her breath after a long run. Actually, she'd not even worked up a sweat.

Ensuring no one was within observing range on the storefront sidewalk, Daly slipped the lock pick set out of her waist pouch. Stepping to the beveled glass door, she inserted a couple of the metal implements. Within a few seconds, she felt the lock's gears submit to her probing with a noticeable click. She stepped through the door and moved behind the reception counter to the office area. She quickly closed the shades on the street-facing windows.

The sun was setting over the Pacific across the street. The receding orb provided more than enough light to easily maneuver around the space, even though filtered through the closed shades.

Daly located Greg's desk and sat in the executive style chair behind it. Pulling her phone from her waist pouch, she texted Mark, *Arrived. Beginning search.*

After about an hour, she had been through the desk files and skimmed through most of the contents of a standing four-drawer file cabinet. She'd found nothing pertinent to either Aiden or any of the poker klatch.

Her phone vibrated to signal an incoming text. It was Mark letting her know he'd arrived at Kimberly's office and was beginning his own sneak and peak.

Slipping her phone into her waist pouch, she looked around Greg's office for any likely places he might keep files of a sensitive nature. Noting a door at the back corner of the office, she rose to check it out. The door wasn't locked. Opening it, she located a light switch and turned it on. The space appeared to be a combined storage and coat closet. In the corner was a two-drawer file cabinet.

Kneeling in front of the cabinet, she could see it was locked. Accessing her tools from her waist pouch, she picked the lock. It hadn't taken much given it was one of those spring-loaded button types using a simple key that came with the unit.

Sliding the top drawer open, she saw the cabinet held Riggsby's Lion's Heart LLC files. She had wondered why she hadn't found the LLC files in her search of his main office. Greg had apparently wanted to keep these folders away from the prying eyes of the one or two people that worked with him.

Sitting cross-legged on the floor in front of the Lion's Heart cabinet, she began to peruse the files. As she came across what looked like particularly important documents, she snapped pictures with her phone. It took her thirty minutes or so to skim through the files, and then return them to the cabinet as she'd found them.

Although nothing in the files related to Aiden, she hoped the LLC documents might come in handy later; maybe helping convict the Riggsbys of her friends' murders. She didn't understand how the mechanics of the LLC worked given all the legal jargon. Since the partnership consisted of five of her friends who were all departed, there had to be a motive in there somewhere.

She pushed the cabinet's lock button to resecure the stored files as she'd found them. Standing up, she stretched her muscles, stiff from sitting in one position for too long, and exited the closet.

It was a little after eight o'clock. The sun's filtered light

DAN BLAIR

had vanished, so the office was lit only by the dim glow of the digital faces of a copier in the corner and a coffee maker on a beverage cart. Navigating by the light available, she reopened the window blinds and returned to the front entrance. Pausing to ensure no passer-byes ran into her leaving the office after hours, she exited, pulling the self-locking front door shut behind her.

Jogging north on the streetfront sidewalk, she retraced her path to the traffic intersection and then south along the jogging trail to her car. The path and street were well lit by lamps. A couple of folks shared the jogging path with her, although several hundred feet away, as she returned to her car.

It was a moonless night with the ocean appearing black in the distance. The subtle roar of the waves breaking on the beach came to her over the sounds of intermittent cars passing by on the highway. She unlocked her car and sat behind the steering wheel thinking through her next moves.

Mark would be less than an hour into his search of Kimberly's office. She hoped he found something of use there. Her little sneak and peak hadn't gotten them any closer to finding Aiden. Nor had it produced any evidence pointing to the Riggsbys as suspects in his abduction.

She decided to wait on calling or texting Mark. She didn't want to distract him, or worse yet cause him to be discovered by a security guard intrigued by what that buzzing sound might be.

Starting her car, she pulled from the beach lot, joining the sparse but steady stream of cars on the Pacific

Coast Highway. Alt Nation played *Come a Little Closer* by Cage the Elephant as she turned onto Santa Monica Boulevard towards the 405 freeway. "How appropriate," she muttered as her thoughts turned to Jim and the hell he was going through waiting for something...anything to help him find Aiden.

Reaching home around quarter to nine, Daly dropped her gym bag in her mudroom. Pulling up a bar stool to her kitchen island, she sat, one foot on the ground, and texted Mark.

Any progress to report?

She then dialed Jim to update him on what little she had to share.

"Daly, what did you find?" Jim said answering after one ring.

"I just got back from checking out Greg Riggsby's office. Nothing of much help there. I found the LLC files Louise was a partner in, but nothing to indicate any interest or plans concerning Aiden," she shared, knowing Jim wouldn't take this well.

"Well what did Mark find at his sister's place," Jim asked undaunted by Daly's disappointing report.

"Mark's look around Kimberly's is in progress. I texted him just a minute ago so hopefully he comes back with something as soon as he's able," Daly said, hoping this would calm Jim's understandable anxiousness.

"I'll give you a call as soon as I hear back from Mark, or ask him to call you directly. If we don't get something concrete from Mark's visit to Kimberly's place, we'll put our heads together to decide how to get the police involved," Daly offered, knowing Jim was looking for actions they should take.

"Okay, that sounds good. I haven't heard anything further from campus security or the LAPD. Right now, Mark's search at Kimberly's is all we have going for us," Jim shared, talking to himself more than Daly. "Call me the second that Mark finishes at Kimberly's, okay?"

"Will do. Jim, I know you're worried, but we're going to drive this to ground and find Aiden. Just hang in there a little while longer," Daly begged. She ended the call.

When Daly received no return text from Mark by nine o'clock, she began to worry something had gone wrong.

She didn't want to call the police if she wasn't sure he was in trouble. Mark would be none too happy with her if the cops showed up at Kimberly's and arrested Mark for breaking and entering. Not the most credible allegation if you're pointing your finger at a potential kidnapper from the inside of a jail cell.

Better to check things out herself. She could call the police if she found things were out of hand.

Walking to her and Mark's bedroom, Daly retrieved her Walther PK 380 from the bedside gun safe, along with two ammunition clips. She slapped one of the eight-round clips into the butt of the gun and pocketed the other clip. Slipping the gun into its belt-clip holster, she tucked her deadly insurance policy into the band of her jogging pants.

She texted Jim as she headed to her car, *Going to check on Mark at Kimberly's office. If u don't hear from me in an hour, call the cops.*

Pulling up Kimberly's office address from the email she'd sent out earlier, she headed for Hubbard Street, about ten minutes away.

———◄(●)►———

Daly circled the parking lot at Kimberly's office. She studied the directory sign to locate Kimberly's office, and then parked her car a few spaces away from Mark's car.

Creeping around the west end of the office building, Daly saw the lights were on and the shades drawn in the end office on the first floor. The directory had indicated this was Kimberly's Exciting Designs for Life space.

Staying in the shadows, out of the floodlights illuminating the buildings outer walls, Daly made her way to the rear of the building. She could see there was a private entrance into the office. Its door appeared to be slightly ajar. Taking a wide circle around the door's entrance, she stayed in the shadows, approaching the windows lining the office's back wall. Crouching under the middle window of three, she carefully peeked through a sliver of space between the drawn window blind and the casement.

Daly could see Mark sitting in a chair, his arms awkwardly behind his back. Probably tied. His legs were tied to the legs of the chair. He was conscious. A bright red line of blood extended from his hairline down one cheek. He was gagged. The blonde Kimberly Riggsby, looking like her DMV photo, sat in a chair behind him with a hand on his shoulder.

Daly reached into her waist band and drew her Walther from its holster, flipping the safety off.

Taking a deep breath she crouch-walked under the windows to the side of the private entrance. With her gun in a two-handed shooter's grip, she steadied herself to enter the room.

Daly kicked the side of the door, already ajar.

It flew open, loudly crashing into the interior wall.

Daly took a quick step into the room and screamed, "Get on the floor bitch." She knew the element of surprise needed to be combined with a "shock and awe" type entrance as the best way to throw a perp off guard. Hopefully, scaring them into an easy surrender.

Kimberly didn't flinch at Daly's "shock and awe" entrance. She ducked calmly behind Mark, using him as a shield.

Daly didn't have more than an inch or two of Kimberly as a target around Mark's head and shoulders.

"I wouldn't do that. One prick from this would mean *instant death* for your boyfriend," Kimberly threatened. Her voice conveyed her resolute intent.

Daly watched Kimberly's right hand appear with a small syringe at the side of Mark's neck. She had been holding it out of sight behind Mark's shoulder. Her thumb was on the plunger, ready to inject whatever liquid death it contained.

Daly's training took over and her mind went crisis calm as she kept steady eye contact with Mark. She rolled the options over in her head; take a shot at Kimberly… high risk she might hit Mark; shoot Mark through his shoulder or side…Kimberly would probably use the syringe as it wouldn't be a kill shot; bolt and call the cops… Kimberly might kill Mark when she ran or hold him as a hostage leading to an out of control situation.

No good options.

Daly lowered her gun, staring daggers at Kimberly's eye, visible around Mark's right ear.

"Put the gun on the floor and kick it to me," Kimberly demanded in a low, steady voice.

Daly was silently wishing she'd hit 911 on her phone before entering the room. She hadn't foreseen this blonde bitch getting the drop on her with a lethal injection posed at Mark's neck.

Kicking the gun across the carpet towards Mark's captor, Daly asked, "So what's next? You tie me up and make your get-away?"

"And *why* would I want to get away?" Kimberly scoffed as she stood up and retrieved Daly's gun. Holding the gun on Daly, Kimberly pushed the chair she'd been sitting in to the side of Mark's chair.

Staying several feet from Daly, Kimberly motioned toward the empty chair with her gun.

Daly obeyed the implied command, walking begrudgingly to the chair and sitting next to Mark.

Kimberly stepped behind Daly's chair. Daly could see Mark turning his head to keep his eyes locked on her. Mark struggled against his bindings. His muffled voice urgently tried to warn her of something.

Daly felt a sharp blow to the back of her head. A wave of pain exploded behind her eyes, radiating from the point of impact and rattling her teeth.

She felt herself collapsing from the chair to the floor. Free-falling into an abyss.

The image of Mark's frantic face faded into blackness.

Chapter 37

Jim paced in front of his fireplace.

He paused when his phone buzzed to read Daly's text, *Going to check on Mark at Kimberly's office. If u don't hear from me in an hour, call the cops.*

It was a few minutes past nine p.m.

Although Daly and Mark were doing everything in their power to locate Aiden, things did not appear to be going well. Mark had been at Kimberly's for over an hour with no word. Daly appeared to be in search of Mark to make sure he hadn't fallen into some kind of trouble.

And still no indication of where Aiden might be.

Jim knew Daly was experienced in dealing with abductions from her past LAPD experiences. He also knew he couldn't have a better set of friends than the Fords at a time like this. But he still felt something more needed to be done. He needed to do something other than wait for news from the front lines.

Time was passing at a snail's pace as he continued to wear a path in the carpet.

A picture on his mantel caught his eye. It was a family

photo of Louise, Jim and Aiden. They looked happy on a beach with the Jamaican sun setting behind them in a burst of orange, purple and all colors in between. The photo felt like it was some memory from a previous lifetime, yet it captured their happiness a mere year ago.

Taking a few steps to the couch, Jim fell back into the plush cushions and threw his head back against the headrest. Closing his eyes, he realized how tired he was. He knew he couldn't sleep, but the graininess and burning of his eyes seemed to recede as he rested them.

His thoughts returned to a few days earlier on the same couch. He had been telling Aiden stories from his Vietnam days. He couldn't remember a time more precious to him. He and Aiden had bonded more deeply that day than ever before.

Whether this bonding was due to shared things from the war he thought he'd never talk about again, or their shared loss of Louise, or his brush with death from ricin poisoning, he didn't know. But he knew Aiden had felt it too.

He knew he was wallowing in life's unfairness. Just when they'd moved to another level of relationship, Aiden had been taken. He couldn't escape the despair he felt.

He so wanted Aiden back.

Time passed slowly.

Jim cycled between frantic thoughts of what might be happening to Aiden at the hands of his abductors, and happier times with Louise and Aiden vacationing, or biking, or camping. The roller coaster of anticipation of harm to Aiden interspersed with joyful family memories was excruciating. It felt as if his mind would split, half going to the dark and half going to the light, if he didn't do something.

The image of Aiden being abducted, now transposed with Kimberly Riggsby's DMV photo as the abductor, kept flashing into his mind. He imagined the scene of Aiden being lured to Riggsby's car. Being subdued. The car leaving the parking lot. He played it over and over in his mind, even though he'd not seen the actual video from USC campus security.

At a quarter to ten p.m., Jim felt he could wait no longer. He tried to reach Daly. Getting her voice mail, he then tried Mark. Voice mail again.

Standing from the couch, he returned to his agitated pacing in front of the fireplace.

Raising his fists in the air, he let out a primal scream of frustration. The echo of his scream reverberating off the walls of his empty house did nothing to appease him.

"I need to do something!" he said out loud in frustration.

He considered calling the police as Daly had instructed, but she'd said to wait an hour. It had only been a little over a half hour since she'd left her message.

"To hell with it!" Jim exclaimed. "I used to be a soldier. When did I turn into such a wuss?"

Turning on his heels, he crossed the room with long strides and descended his basement stairs with purpose. In their finished game room, he reached under the ping-pong table, retrieving a key from a recessed ledge. He then proceded to their general storage room, and the gun locker residing there. Unlocking the five-foot-tall metal cabinet, Jim stood staring at his personal arsenal.

Louise had hated having guns in the house. Probably due to the Hippocratic Oath she'd taken and her general love of all things living. At this moment, he was glad he'd not given in to her desire to go sans firearms.

Considering which gun would best suit his mission, he selected a Remington twenty gauge shot gun. Thinking back on Aiden's recent trip home, he returned the shot gun to the locker and grabbed his M16 rifle. For good measure, he holsterd his Colt M1911 pistol, the standard issue side arm for the Army during the Vietnam War. Strapping the belt with the holstered .45 around his waist, he then stowed the M16 magazines into large pouches on the utility style belt.

Jim's face took on a hardness as he held the M16 in his hands.

He hadn't thought he'd ever kill again.

But Aiden's life was at stake.

He needed to do whatever was necessary.

It was just the way it was.

Jim bounded up the basement stairs with his contraband rifle slung over his shoulder. His holstered .45 and the ammunition pouches bounced against his hips.

Thumbing his phone's home screen to life, he pulled up the email from Daly with the Riggsbys' home and office addresses. Exiting the house, he flipped the garage light on and grabbed his car keys from their wall hook. Opening the hatchback of his car, he placed the M16 killing machine under a blanket, which somehow made it seem a bit more legal. He slammed the hatch shut, jumped behind the wheel of his Prius sedan and backed from his garage into the street.

Slamming the gear selector into drive, he tromped the accelerator and stared coldly ahead.

He hoped his jungle instincts were still there and would serve him well on Hubbard Street.

As he sped off into the night, he promised under his breath, "Louise, I'm *not* going to let them hurt our boy."

Chapter 38

Mark's startled elation at Daly's kick-ass entry and bloodcurdling scream at Kimberly turned to trepidation.

He saw no SWAT detail on her heels. No flash bangs detonating around their feet. No tear gas canisters filling the room with choking vapors.

Kimberly's ruse was playing out as the sick bitch had planned.

She'd known Daly would be unable to patiently wait for the police to arrive if she displayed him like a trussed up turkey in a butcher's shop window. Mark's hope was Daly had thought to call the police before her entrance.

The Quicker Picker Upper gag kept him from uttering any more than muffled grunts as he watched the nightmare scenario play out. Daly had joined him as a fellow prisoner, with escape looking dubious at best.

His heart sank seeing Daly subdued next to him. Her brave assault had turned impotent. Her love for him had surrendered her to Kimberly's whims.

Kimberly stepped behind Daly, pointing the gun at her head. She smiled as Mark's eyes went wide with fear. She appeared to be toying with the idea of ending Daly as he watched helplessly. His shaking head and unintelligible pleading for Daly's life only made Kimberly's smile grow, contorting into an evil grin.

She suddenly tired of her sick game. She drew Daly's Walther up over her shoulder and brought it down in a vicious chop to the back of Daly's head. Daly collapsed to the floor and laid there motionless.

Mark's immediate relief from Daly being spared a bullet, was replaced by a slow burning anger.

He watched Kimberly retrieve bindings from her back room and secure Daly's hands and feet. She disappeared through the private exit and returned a moment later with a blue plastic tarp, about six feet square. Placing it on the carpet, she rolled the unconscious Daly onto the tarp.

She tucked one end of the tarp around Daly's feet and legs. Holding onto what looked like handles sewn into the end of the tarp near Daly's head, she was able to easily slide Daly across the room. Propping the door open, she dragged Daly over the entrance steps and into the dark beyond Mark's view.

Returning to face Mark, she stared down at him. "Now I'm going to untie your legs so you can walk to the car. *Don't* get frisky. I guarantee if you try to run, I'll shoot you. And if I miss you, I'll go straight to little Miss Daly and shoot her. *Understood?*" she asked, placing the gun in the center of Mark's forehead and pushing his head back a few inches to make her point.

Mark nodded.

Stepping to the side of Mark's chair and kneeling, Kimberly untied his legs. Lifting up on his arms bound behind the chair, she helped him stand. Kimberly pushed the Walther into the middle of Mark's back, ordering, "Let's go."

Mark exited the private door and saw a car with its headlights on. It was parked about twenty-five yards away, the only car in the parking lot. Located at the rear of the building, the lot appeared to be a service area for a couple of large garbage dumpsters at the edge of the blacktopped area.

Kimberly gave Mark a rough nudge in the back towards the glaring headlights of the car. The bright lights caused him to squint. The throbbing in his head from Kimberly's earlier assault intensified as the LED lights' radiant spikes penetrated his skull.

Opening the car's driver door, she reached up and pulled the paper towel gag from his mouth saying, "Remember, no noise or your girlfriend gets a bullet."

She untied his hands. Stepping back with the gun trained at his chest, she handed him a zip tie saying, "Put this around both wrists and pull it tight with your teeth."

Mark did as instructed.

"Get behind the wheel. You're driving," she commanded.

He slid behind the wheel of her car, a Mercedes. Looking up at her, he reasoned, "You know this is not going to end well. If you leave now, you'll have time to get away. We won't be able to stop you."

"Shut up and put your hands on the steering wheel," she barked, retrieving a long zip tie from her jeans pocket. Keeping the gun pressed against his left ear, she handed him the long zip tie and said, "Put this through the steering wheel and then through your wrist cuffs." She then tightened the shorter zip tie around his wrists to ensure he couldn't wriggle from his flex cuffs.

Mark had significant slack in the longer zip tie snaked through his wrist cuffs and around the rim of the steering wheel. The slack provided him the freedom of movement needed to turn the steering wheel, but not enough to reach any of the car's other controls. Kimberly then opened the rear door and sat behind Mark with the gun resting on the back of his seat. The business end was pointed at his right ear.

Mark looked at Daly, lying helplessly in the passenger seat. The makeshift tarp sled had been wadded up and thrown in the back seat. Her head had lolled to the side against the window; the back of it matted with blood from Kimberly's rude gun salute. Mark jerked against his bindings in anger, but was immediately met by a gun muzzle pressed against his right cheek. It gouged at him like death's reminder that he wasn't in control.

"She'll be fine. Just a Tylenol away from a great day when she wakes up. That is, if you don't get cute and make me put a hole in her," Kimberly threatened. "Just drive where I tell you to go. You never know, you and your lovely wife might just live to see another day."

Kimberly reached over Mark's shoulder and slipped the car's gearshift into drive, "Now head towards the edge of town. Take a right out of the parking lot to the 405 freeway and I'll tell you where to turn after that."

Mark eased the Mercedes S Class out of the service lot and accelerated as he turned onto the road leading to the 405. The 405, or officially the San Diego Freeway, led south from the San Fernando Valley, past Santa Monica, and ended up in southeast LA's Irvine area, sixty miles away. The 405 was a main artery for the LA area, providing multiple options to go west towards the mountains and national forest areas surrounding the northwest edge of Los Angeles, or east into the city.

He saw it was 9:30 pm from the car's digital display. Kimberly directed him to turn west on 118, the Ronald Reagan Freeway. Mark recognized she was taking him towards the Simi Valley area, west of San Fernando. He remembered one of the Riggsbys' addresses Daly had shared in her email was in Simi Valley.

He drove into darkness. The only lights beyond his captor's headlamps were the sparsely placed light poles along the freeway.

A blood-red crescent moon appeared in the western night sky ahead of him. The moon looked as if it might drip poison from its lower lip; onto Mark and all he held precious in life.

The miles passed slowly as Mark drove towards the undisclosed place he and Daly would likely exit this life. His mind churned over the events leading him to this point, hoping for something that might prove useful.

Daly wasn't moving. She had let out a low moan a few minutes into the trip indicating she was alive, but had remained unconscious.

Hoping to get Kimberly talking while he desperately tried to think of a way out of the impossible situation, he chided her, "So you've got quite a project as a hobby. You know, killing innocent people and keeping a curio case of your sick exploits. That's what the little spoon display was all about back at your Pandora's pantry, right? Some kind of demented trophy case for the sanity challenged?"

She chuckled softly in the back. "You have no idea. People like you and your friends think they can pollute the world with their *toxic garbage*, in the name of making a living. Guess your friends found out it doesn't come for free. Each one contributed a memento to represent the gluttonous filth they promoted. Their spoons made it into my collection when their scum-sucking, polluting lives *ended*."

"So anyone who doesn't meet your twisted sense of good nutrition gets on your kill list? I bet it's quite a burden being the Whole Foods police for the world," Mark needled as he watched her in his rearview mirror for a reaction.

Kimberly continued, ignoring his barb, "And what a *pleasure* it was sending each of their worthless souls to the next world. I hope they spend an *eternity* rotting in the same garbage they spewed during their time on earth," she hissed through clenched teeth.

Seeing he'd successfully agitated her, Mark forged on, "At least my friends weren't sick psychos. Maybe something you ate brought out your bad side. Did you ever think of that?"

Glancing again in the rear view mirror, he saw her blue eyes flash.

"Plus, I guess you can add kidnapping to your resume. You know we have you on video taking Aiden from a USC parking lot, right?" Mark said matter of factly hoping to confirm Kimberly had abducted Aiden. "I'm sure it won't be long before the police show up at your doorstep and shut down your twisted funhouse. You'd better hope they find Aiden is ok. Kidnapping and murder will definitely get you the needle in this great state of ours."

"If they had me on video, they would have done something already," Kimberly scoffed and continued, "That little prick and I are getting to know each other. In fact your illegal entry at my office interrupted one of my heart-to-hearts with young Aiden. I had to rush off when I saw you bumbling around, thinking you were so sneaky."

From her comment, Mark assumed the motion detector he had seen at her office had a video feed. Information too late to help avoiding capture in her office, but good to know if he ever got out of this. It could provide footage of her assault on Daly and him.

"Sorry to inconvenience your fun," Mark said with disgust. "I guess Aiden is alive then?" He locked eyes with Kimberly in the rearview mirror waiting for her answer.

Hesitating and then smiling, she said, "For now. He needs to suffer. Suffer like the *garbage* he is. He took away the love of my life and now he's *paying* for it." The loathing in Kimberly's voice was palpable.

Her face contorted into a half snarl. "Now shut up and drive. Cretins like you will never understand. And it won't matter much longer whether you do or not."

She instructed him through a few turns off the Ronald Reagan Freeway, and into a Simi Valley neighborhood. High-end houses sitting on spacious lots lined the road. "That's it on the right. Pull through the driveway gates and around the garage. Follow the gravel path to the building at the end."

Mark pulled in as instructed. After rounding the garage, he veered onto a narrow gravel path winding down a hill and then up towards a stand of willow and Fremont cottonwood trees. The trees lined the path and obscured the outline of a building until they were within a few feet of the structure.

He pulled the car to the front of the building and stopped.

The headlights bathed the faded brown siding of the structure in their LED radiance. Large cantilevered windows set below the roofline were visible on the long sides of the rectangular building. More large cantilevered skylights completed a roof of primarily glass. Supporting ribs and cross pieces for structural integrity were visible through the roof's glass shell.

Chaparral evergreens arching ten feet above a floor of sage scrub bushes hugged the building on either side. The woody shrubs framed the building in the dark so the edges appeared to melt into the surrounding vegetation.

Kimberly reached over Mark's seat. She shoved the gearshift into park, and removed the car keys from the ignition in one motion. She stepped out of the car and walked to the passenger's side door, opening it.

Daly fell halfway out of the car, still unconscious.

"Ok, wake up little princess," Kimberly said as she pulled Daly upright and patted her cheek lightly. Getting no response, she slapped her harder.

"You soulless bitch," Mark spat at her as he jerked violently at his plastic cuffs.

"Now don't get upset Mark. I could have used the butt of my gun," she chortled.

Daly's eyes rolled open. She moaned softly, "What... where are we?"

"Don't worry your little head, Daly. Just get up and walk through the door right ahead of you. You can rest in there."

Daly braced her zip-tied wrists against the dash and straightened up in the seat enough to look at Kimberly. She squinted, trying to focus on her face, "Where are we?"

"Shut up and move your ass," Kimberly said as she pointed the pistol at Daly's right eye, now focused on the black hole that led to a bullet. "I'm not a patient person, so up and out of there."

Daly swung her right leg clumsily out of the car and grasped the car frame with her bound hands, pulling herself up. Kimberly shoved her with the gun barrel in the direction of the building's door, and walked behind her the twenty steps or so to the entrance. Kimberly reached around Daly and grasped the door latch, pulling it open for Daly to step through and into the darkness beyond.

A few seconds later, fluorescent lights illuminated the window of the door they'd just stepped through. Light flooded from the side windows and the roof of the green house. With the bright lights piercing the night sky, the building had the eerie sense of a space ship about to take off.

When Kimberly had entered the buildiing, the door had slammed behind her, pulled shut by a spring mechanism. Mark took the opportunity of her exit to begin jerking desperately at his bindings. He could feel a little give. The issue was it would take too long to work them loose using nothing but brute force.

He looked around the car for anything that could prove useful to his predicament. His eyes locked on his reflection in the vanity mirror in the visor over his head. He saw his bedraggled face and five-o'clock shadow making his cheeks look hollow.

What the hell had he gotten them into?

It was bad enough to be in the clutches of some bitch with a psycho food jones, but bringing Daly into this mess with no way out was unthinkable. He peered at the mirror as his hazel eyes peered back in disgust.

In anger, he headbutted the mirror.

It cracked.

Seeing the break in the mirror, his eyes glimmered with hope. He butted the mirror again, but harder. A few good blows and the glass broke from its frame in the visor. Mark bent down with his mouth and picked up the biggest of the shards, about three inches long. Holding it with his lips and teeth, he transferred the sharp fragment to his right hand.

Awkwardly sawing with his right hand, Mark finally felt the cuff on his left hand fall away. He continued freeing himself with the shard. With his hands free, he slipped the broken glass into his front pant's pocket. He could taste the blood from his tongue and the corners of his mouth where he had cut himself on the glass piece's sharp edges. He quietly opened the car door stepping into the shadows away from the lights of Daly's prison.

He felt blood dripping from a cut on his head as it serpentined down his cheek.

He made his way into the woods; his eyes adjusting to the darkness as he stumbled through the underbrush and between the large trees. He was able to see the outline of huge California sycamores, coast live oaks and chaparral evergreens as he moved through the shadows. He stopped to pick up a tree branch about three feet long and two inches in diameter, murmuring to himself, "This should come in handy."

Working his way back to the southern side of the greenhouse, he squeezed between the thick chaparral shrubs and the edge of the building. Along the edge of the building he tripped, losing his balance and fell forward into a freshly dug hole. The hole was about six foot long and three feet wide. It was a shallow two feet deep, but he had no doubt what its intended purpose was. The only question was if the grave would now be for him and Daly, rather than whoever Kimberly had originally planned.

Picking himself up, he continued along the edge of the greenhouse to the southeast corner. His eyes fully adjusted to the darkness as he waited there.

Kimberly had finished securing Daly inside the building. Mark could hear her footsteps approaching the door as she returned to collect him from the car. She stepped through the door; the straining of a spring creaked as the door swung open, then slammed shut with a bang.

She stepped into the night, striding towards the car. Within a few feet of the car, she stopped suddenly, seeing Mark was no longer bound to the steering wheel. She pulled the Walther from the back of her jeans' waistband. Holding it in front of her with one hand, like someone less than sure of how to properly hold a handgun, she did a quick three-sixty check of her surroundings.

"*Shit.*" She spat the word into the night. "Mark. You're not playing by the rules I gave you. Now I'm going to have to bring your little *whore* out here. Blow her brains out while you watch. Is that what you want? *Is it?*"

No sound from her quarry. Only the sound of crickets discussing the warm California evening came back to her.

"Ok. We'll do it your way, but I know you're out there. You can't leave your princess behind and run while she's left to die, can you?"

Through the branches at the corner of the greenhouse

Mark could see Kimberly reach into her jeans pocket and extract her phone. As she continued to scan the area for any sign of Mark, she made a call. Mark could only make out a few words of her animated conversation from his hiding place.

"He's loose…now…yeah, bring that too." The call lasted a few seconds. She pocketed the phone.

Kimberly backed her way towards the greenhouse. She scanned the area with the Walther held in front of her, sweeping the automatic left to right and back. Steadily retracing her steps to the building's door. She reached behind her with her left hand to pull the door open.

As her hand grasped the door's handle, Mark exploded from his shadowy cover. He caught Kimberly with a half baseball swing across her right cheek with the tree limb. Kimberly let out a sharp grunt as she fell into the door, slamming it shut. The Walther discharged into the night, splintering a branch next to Mark's head.

He was on her, reaching and finding her hand desperately gripping death's tool. Mark's left hand clutched the gun barrel, pointing it away.

She was a formidable opponent. Surprisingly strong, she fought to bring the gun back to any part of Mark's torso where it could wreak its havoc. The diminished strength in Mark's right arm from his war wound was clearly handicapping his struggle against a fit adversary.

"You're going to *regret* not staying in the car," she said straining as she fought for control of the gun.

"The only thing I regret is ever meeting your kind of crazy."

Mark shifted his weight into Kimberly. Using his hip to leverage her away from the door, he slammed her into the side of the building. The jarring hit against the structure caused her to exhale sharply.

Mark felt the gun loosen in her grip.

Desperate to disable the stunned Kimberly while he had the upper hand, he shifted his weight away from the building. He created enough room between them to rear his head back, and then slammed his forehead into her face with all the force he could muster. The punishing headbutt created the sound of crackling cartilage giving way to his cranial battering ram.

"How's that feel, sweet pea," he growled through clenched teeth.

Her nose erupted in blood that streamed into her mouth. Her face contorted in a half-smile as the taste of blood seemed to give her some twisted pleasure. Her bloodstained teeth took on the look of a wild animal's fangs fresh from tearing at its prey.

Mark lowered his shoulder and shifted his weight into Kimberly using her as a shield to receive the full impact as they crashed into the building's siding. The thud of her collision was accompanied by the sharp wheeze of her lungs expelling any air left in them, followed by a deep gasp. Her hands loosened on the gun with the impact.

Mark was able to twist the gun in her grip.

Just as the gun seemed to be his, the deafening sound of the Walther firing shattered the night.

They both froze for what seemed a lifetime, but was measured in a split second.

DAN BLAIR

Their eyes met, locked and then her look changed. The animal rage that had consumed her turned to sudden realization. She slumped against the wall as Mark stepped away with the Walther in his hand.

As she slid down the wall in slow motion, the blood-stain on the front of her sweatshirt bloomed full red. The darkest red he could imagine. The kind of red that means nothing is left to say.

Mark looked down at her. He felt a combination of relief and triumph. Yet a sad sort of pity for the deranged Kimberly came over him. She had finally been freed from her unholy quest.

His silent reflection shattered as he was jerked back into the present by Daly's cries. Dropping the gun, he bolted inside towards Daly's voice.

"Mark. Mark. Oh please don't kill…" Daly shouted from her chair before she could see who was opening the door.

Mark rushed into the greenhouse.

She gasped and let out a deep breath as he came to her side to work her ropes loose. "I thought she'd killed you. I thought that *she-monster* had killed you," she sobbed as her freed hands wrapped around his neck. She kissed him like he was life itself.

"It's ok babe. It's ok. She's dead," Mark whispered as Daly shivered in his arms. "Let me get her phone and we'll get some help."

Helping Daly to her feet, they exited the greenhouse from hell's back acre. Daly had her arm around Mark's shoulder, leaning heavily on him.

Mark leaned down over Kimberly's motionless body. Reaching into her designer jeans pocket, he pulled out her phone.

Just as Mark finished dialing 911, a car came barreling up the gravel path with its headlights blinding them and skidded to a stop in the loose gravel. The driver's door flew open. Mark could see a man's silhouette step out with his arms held straight in front of him and pointed at Mark and Daly. He stepped around the front of the car into the headlights. The bright lights glinted off the Glock automatic in his grip.

"What have you done? What have you done?" Greg Riggsby said.

His hands shook with rage. The Glock moved back and forth between Mark and Daly. His eyes then focused beyond Mark and Daly and came to rest on the crumpled figure of Kimberly against the greenhouse wall. The car's headlights created a macabre scene of scarlet death lit up against a backdrop of faded brown siding.

Greg's gaze came back to Mark's bloodstained shirt and then traveled up to meet Mark's eyes squinting into the blinding headlights.

Sputtering, he bellowed, "You've killed the *only* one who understood."

Returning his gaze to Kimberly, Greg let out a mournful sob, "Kimberly. Why? Why?"

After a long pause Greg seemed to compose himself. His voice shook with anger, "For that, you're going to watch your wife *die*…helplessly in *front* of your eyes… *then* you're going to join her."

Chapter 39

Jim pulled his car to the curb a block past the Simi Valley address Daly had sent in her earlier email. It was around quarter to eleven p.m.

He had come from Kimberly Riggsby's office in San Fernando. Finding nothing there but the Fords' cars in the office parking lot, he'd crept up and looked through the crack in the shade to Kimberly's office. He had seen some furniture out of place, but nothing indicating anyone was there. He'd surmised something had gone wrong given no call from Daly or Mark, and their abandoned cars.

Not knowing whether they would be at Kimberly's home address, Greg Riggsby's home, or some other unknown address, he'd decided to check Kimberly's home first. If they weren't there, he'd head to Greg Riggsby's home in Encino as the next stop.

On his drive to Simi Valley, he'd toyed with calling the police as Daly had instructed when she'd went to look for Mark. Since the Fords weren't at Kimberly's office, sending the cops there would just create further delay in finding them, and potentially Aiden.

Also, he didn't want to tip the Riggsbys off. He could imagine some clumsy cops showing up at the wrong place, giving them time to cover their tracks. No, he needed to confirm where the Fords were with his own eyes before calling 911 if possible. If he could confirm the Riggsbys had the Fords, and hopefully Aiden too, he could call the police.

Quietly closing his car door, he retrieved the M16 from his hatchback. Unsnapping a utility pouch on his belt, he removed an ammunition magazine and clicked it into the rifle's underbelly. Ensuring the safety was on, he headed for the entrance gates of Kimberly's house.

Approaching the front gates, he could see the house wasn't lit up as if anyone was home. Crouching, he followed the hedge along the circular driveway leading to the front door, staying in the shadows and away from the footlights around the driveway's perimeter. Looking through the windows along the front of the house, he could see no movement.

Continuing around the house to the garage, he saw the door was up and no car was in the bay. Rounding the back of the garage he could make out the back of the house by the light of landscaping lights, likely on a timer.

As he was about to approach the back patio area of the house, he saw the headlights of a car approaching from the front entrance. He flattened himself against the back outside wall of the garage, out of the line of sight. The car didn't turn into the garage, but veered onto what sounded like a gravel path. It accelerated towards the back of the property.

Just as the car started down the path, a loud bang echoed across the property. A few seconds later, another bang. The second bang was clearly a gun discharging. Jim didn't think the gunshots were from the car which had just passed him. They seemed to be coming from a few hundred yards away.

Moving to the brush and trees along the gravel path, Jim began jogging towards the illuminated headlamps in the distance. Out of breath and still a hundred yards away, he was close enough to make out the car's silhouette. He could see there was a building beyond it in the car's head-lights. A soft light also glowed through the windows and roof of the building from some interior source.

Jim could make out voices as he slowed. Continuing to stay several yards into the wooded area off the gravel path, he moved from tree to tree in the darkness. Inching closer to the voices, he heard the end of an angry tirade.

"...*then* you're going to join her."

Jim could see the man talking held a gun outstretched in a shooter's stance. The gun was pointed at Daly and Mark's squinting faces in the car's bright lights.

The shooter continued angrily, "My sister didn't deserve to *die*. She was the only one doing something about the filthy and unnatural poisons being proliferated...the *avalanche* of junk food smothering us. I was *proud* to help her rid society of unclean pigs. The unrighteous garbage mongers who *spewed* their toxic wastes into peoples' lives while getting rich from selling their crap to the naïve. She was too *good* for this world."

Jim's eyes adjusted to the contrast of the darkness and the bright car lights. He could see the shooter's face as he began pacing back and forth in the car lights, continuing to berate the Fords. It was Greg Riggsby. Although Jim had only met him briefly at one of his friend's funerals, the DMV photo Daly had sent in her email matched the face in the headlights.

"If you're thinking the police will come to your rescue, well let them. When the cops arrive, you'll both be *dead*. A home invasion gone wrong. I'll tell them you forced my sister to her greenhouse for unknown reasons and shot her. When I arrived, I had no choice but to shoot you both in self defense."

Riggsby approached Mark and Daly, motioning for them to move back near Kimberly's body.

As Riggsby moved near Mark, Jim saw Mark slash out at Riggsby with what looked like a piece of glass as it glinted in the lights. The makeshift knife cut a deep gash in Riggsby's left cheek as he stumbled back, discharging his gun. The bullet caught Daly in her left shoulder and knocked her to the ground.

Mark lunged at Riggsby and fought for control of his gun. As they rolled side to side, struggling for the Glock, Jim burst from the woods, running to join the battle. He clicked his M16's safety to the off position.

Riggsby punched Mark with his left fist, and jerked his pistol free. Pointing it at Mark, he scrambled to his feet and yelled, "Get back, I'll kill you right now. Before your little bitch if I have to."

Jim raised the M16 to his shoulder. Taking aim

at Riggsby's legs, he unleashed the fury of the automatic weapon. Multiple 5.56 millimeter rounds riddled Riggsby's legs as he dropped to the ground screaming.

Out of his mind with anger and the adrenaline rush of his assault on Riggsby, Jim stood over him. His smoking weapon pointed at Riggsby as he writhed on the ground screaming.

"You *son-of-a-bitch*. You and your crazy sister killed Louise, and kidnapped my son. Now tell me why I shouldn't just *blow your head* into a thousand pieces," Jim snarled over his screams.

Kicking Riggsby's foot, Jim demanded, "Where's my son you bastard? Where have you got him?"

Riggsby's screams subsided into gasping moans. He looked up at Jim's face, flushed with rage, and whimpered in pain.

Jim drew his handgun and leaned down into Riggsby's face. He pressed the muzzle between his eyes saying, "Tell me now, or I pull the trigger."

He cocked the hammer on the gun.

Riggsby's panicked voice was high pitched as he pointed to the building, "*No. Don't.* He's in the greenhouse. In the back room."

Jim continued to look at Riggsby for a long moment, debating whether to pull the trigger or not. Holstering his handgun, he stood up, kicking Riggsby's gun away from him.

Mark had scrambled to Daly and was cradling her in his arms. Her head was on his chest. He had torn a sleeve from his shirt and was pressing it against Daly's left shoulder to staunch the bleeding.

Jim held his M16 in his hands as he stooped down at Mark's side. "Is she going to be ok?" he asked.

"It looks like it went clean through. I think she'll be ok once it gets patched up," Mark said looking up at Jim thankfully. "Never happier to see you old friend. You got your phone with you? I need to call 911 for an ambulance."

Jim slipped his phone from his pocket and handed it to Mark. "I'm going to find Aiden," he said as he stood up and walked towards the greenhouse. His mind spun as he walked towards the building hoping Aiden was still alive; scared to death of what he might find inside.

As Jim approached the building's entrance, he saw movement from the corner of his eye. Lit up by the headlights, he could see Kimberly slowly pulling herself up from the ground like she was starring in some zombie apocalypse movie. She had a gun in her hand and was pointing it in his direction.

Jim dropped to one knee and emptied the magazine of the M16, turning her chest into a spray of blood and one big gaping wound. The impact propelled her backwards a few steps as her gun flew into the shadows. Kimberly's mouth sagged open and her eyes stared vacantly into the night as she crumpled backwards.

Splayed out on the ground and illuminated by the headlight beams from the car, she was an effigy to madness. Posed as if the puppeteer had cut her strings, her part in his psychotic play finished.

Dropping the empty M16, Jim drew his sidearm. Rising to his feet, he slowly approached Kimberly's corpse. He heard a voice coming from near her and raised his gun, prepared to unleash another burst of death if she was somehow refusing to die. He saw the source of the voice was a cell phone laying a few feet from Kimberly. Picking it up, he said, "Hello."

"Sir, this is the Simi Valley Police. You called 911. We've dispatched a patrol unit to your location. What is your emergency?" the 911 operator asked.

"There's been a shooting. Send an ambulance," Jim said as he pocketed the phone, leaving it connected so the life squad could locate them.

Jim glared down at Kimberly. She wasn't breathing. No active bleeding, only the oozing gore of flesh torn apart by the metal-jacketed invaders he'd unleashed on her.

"*That* was for Louise," he spat. Her glazed eyes looked back vacantly.

"Jim, are you ok?" Mark shouted urgently.

"I'm good. Going inside to look for Aiden. The cops and an ambulance are on the way."

Entering the building, Jim kept his gun in front of him in a two-handed grip. It was unlikely anyone waited for him. The Riggsbys were lying on the ground outside, one dead and the other hopefully bleeding to death. However, given the craziness of this night, he wasn't taking any chances.

Stealthily crossing the main area of what appeared to be a greenhouse, Jim stopped at the padlocked door of a room at the rear of the space. Listening at the door, he heard a low moan. Sounding as if it could be Aiden, his pulse quickened.

Hitting the padlock with the butt of his gun, he could tell it wouldn't be easily jarred open. Stepping to the side of the door, he shot the padlock. The .45-caliber slug shattered the lock and reverberated through the greenhouse, causing the glass windows and ceiling to shake.

Grasping the doorknob, he opened the door with his left hand, peering into the dark room. His right hand held his gun at the ready should some unknown partner of the Riggsbys await him.

Squinting into the darkness, a sliver of moonlight cast shadows across the space. He could make out the forms of two people sitting in chairs, back to back.

"Aiden. Is that you? Who's with you?" Jim asked as he took small steps towards the dark silhouettes.

"Dad, it's me," Aiden rasped hearing his father's voice.

Jim's heart jumped in his chest at Aiden's voice. "Aiden, you're alive."

He holstered his gun and located the light switch to the room, flicking it on.

He could see the other person in the room with his back to Aiden appeared to be Sergeant McClarey. McClarey was dressed in a hospital gown. He didn't move. His face was barely recognizable. Oozing fluid dripped from the blisters and scabs covering his face. His lips were cracked and swollen. The skin visible from his arms and legs was gray and mottled. Jim couldn't tell if he was breathing or not.

Jim gasped, " My god, what did they do to you?"

Striding past McClarey to Aiden's side, Jim used a

knife from the lab bench to cut through Aiden's bindings. Aiden was also wearing a hospital gown. He carefully extracted the IV needle from Aiden's arm. Aiden's face was blistered and swollen similarly to McClarey's, but he managed a weak smile.

"Dad! Thank God you found me," Aiden rasped in a dry whisper.

"Nobody's going to hurt my boy. Not now, not ever." Jim choked out the words as tears of joy streamed down his face. He put his arms around Aiden in a long, but gentle hug.

Jim helped Aiden to his feet, placing Aiden's arm around his shoulder for support as he helped him from the back room. When he exited the greenhouse, a stream of police cruisers and an ambulance were snaking their way up the gravel path to them. The police cruisers braked to a halt on either side of the Riggsbys' cars, officers exiting their vehicles with guns drawn. The sound of the sirens came to an abrupt halt.

"It's ok, it's ok," Mark was yelling, a bit too loudly with the siren noise doused.

Several officers crouched by their car doors with guns trained on Jim as he exited the greenhouse. "Drop your weapon, and get on the ground," the lead officer barked at Jim.

"It's ok, he's one of the victims," Mark explained desperately.

Jim used two fingers to slowly draw his .45 from its holster and dropped it to the ground. Then raising his free hand over his head, he said, "My son needs medical attention."

Officers slowly stood up keeping their guns trained on Jim as they walked to him. Once they had taken Aiden from Jim, Jim fell to his knees and put his hands behind his head. Jim explained, "There's another man, Sergeant McClarey, in the back room tied up. I don't know if he's alive or not."

EMT's appeared at Daly's side. Daly let out a cry of pain when they moved her to the stretcher. Mark walked beside the EMT's escorting her to the ambulance. He explained she'd been shot and what her blood type was so they could call ahead to the hospital.

Daly smiled up at Mark, "Always the mother hen."

Mark returned her smile, and squeezed her right hand saying, "You just hang in there Miss Badass. We'll get you fixed up in no time."

A few moments later McClarey was escorted out of the greenhouse on a wheeled stretcher by two EMT's and whisked to another waiting ambulance. "I've got a pulse," one of the EMT's said. "Call the ER and tell them we're coming in hot with four victims. Two with gunshot wounds and two with undetermined poisoning of some kind."

Greg Riggsby was being attended to by an EMT where he lay on the ground. They were trying to stabilize the bleeding from the gaping wounds in his legs. They moved Riggsby to a stretcher, and brought him to the ambulance where they'd loaded Daly.

When Jim saw Greg was about to be loaded into Daly's ambulance, he yelled out to get one of the policemen's attention, "*Hey*. He's the guy who shot her and he was trying to kill us all before you guys showed up. Make sure you cuff him for the ride."

"I think we're going to cuff you all until we can straighten this shit storm out," the officer replied. "Now get in the cruiser." The officer roughly pulled Jim to his feet and escorted him to the back of one of the black and whites.

Jim sat in the back seat of the cruiser with its blue and red lights flashing. Through his side window, he saw them cuff Mark and lead him reluctantly away from Daly's ambulance. He was placed in the cruiser next to Jim's.

Jim sat back in his seat, his cuffed hands digging uncomfortably into the small of his back. Closing his eyes, he blew out a deep sigh. Relief flooded over him like a warm shower.

Aiden was alive.

All the confusion of his arrest...who did what to whom...all that could be dealt with in due time.

Thank God, Aiden was alive!

As Jim's cruiser pulled away from the greenhouse, he opened his eyes to see Kimberly's body lying in the headlights of her brother's car. Officers were collecting shell casings, while a forensics team busily bagged anything they came across that was more than the detritus of the woods.

Jim's relief turned to a dark sort of satisfaction as he stared at Kimberly's lifeless body bathed in light. Nothing would bring Louise back to him. But knowing her killer had paid the ultimate price seemed like justice. And the fact that he'd delivered that justice seemed...righteous.

Chapter 40

Mark was draped over the counter at Dr. Girdwood's office talking with Ilene, Dr. Girdwood's multi-tasking receptionist, RN and wife. It was Friday afternoon around two p.m. He had brought Daly in for a check up to ensure no infection or other complications from her gunshot wound.

Dr. Girdwood was a GP who saw patients in the after-noons at his private office in San Fernando, while spend-ing mornings doing rounds at Valley General Hospital in Simi Valley. He'd been on call when the multiple gun-shot victims interrupted his quiet Wednesday evening. As one of the attending doctors, he had cleaned and stitched Daly's bullet wound.

Ilene was more than a little bit interested in the Wednesday happenings. The chilling account of abduc-tions and mayhem had made the area news on Thursday. The newspaper had indicated Kimberly and Greg Riggsby had been responsible for kidnapping and assault on multiple victims. Kimberly Riggsby was dead at the scene from multiple gunshot wounds, and Greg had been arrested by the Simi Valley PD. Greg was currently under room arrest at Valley General Hospital, recovering from multiple gunshot wounds. The newspaper had indicated no motive for the Riggsbys and sparse details on how the messy affair had unfolded.

"So you knew the Riggsbys?" Ilene questioned with a white toothy smile, leaning forward on her elbows.

"I wouldn't say we were friends, but I'd met Greg Riggsby a couple of times. I didn't know anything about Kimberly before Wednesday's craziness," Mark answered.

"My husband said Greg Riggsby had two armed guards stationed outside his room at Valley General. They'd handcuffed him to the bed rail, too."

"I'd say they couldn't watch that whacko closely enough based on our run-in," Mark scoffed. "He and his nut job sister were serial killers who took out several close friends of Daly and mine. Once they get him patched up, I hope he's offered a lifetime of free housing at some Super Max. Or better yet a life-eliminating cocktail delivered direct to his veins."

As Ilene was about to unleash a barrage of questions on Mark, Daly appeared through the door connecting the waiting room to the patient examination rooms. She was wearing a navy blue sling around her left arm to immobilize it. Seeing Mark hanging over the counter, she asked, "Are you telling tales, hubby dearest?"

"Just getting to the part where I swing in on a rope and whisk my wife out of harm's way, hon," Mark smiled and winked at Ilene.

"Was that before or after you allowed her to take a bullet?" Daly said with a smirk.

"Well, uh, guess it's time to be moving on. Wouldn't want to be fact checked by the story police. It's been good talking with you, Ilene. I'll have to stop by and fill in the gaps another time," Mark shrugged as he followed Daly, shaking her head as they exited the office.

"You know you probably ought to keep the Riggsbys' details to yourself until after the trial, right?" Daly chided Mark as she opened the passenger door with her free hand, easing herself gingerly into her seat.

"You're right my dear. Blame it on waiting room boredom," Mark said sheepishly.

"Let's take a ride to Valley General and check in on Aiden and the good sergeant," Daly suggested. We can catch dinner in Simi Valley on the way home.

Mark lowered the top on his 428 convertible, slipped his sunglasses on and pulled from the parking lot. Daly reached into the passenger door's storage compartment and extracted a tennis visor and her sunglasses.

She leaned back and sighed contentedly, "Nice day for a drive." The afternoon sun was still high in the sky. It was a cloudless blue sky and in the low eighties making it a perfect afternoon to be anywhere.

Turning onto a side street from San Fernando's main boulevard, Mark drove a few blocks to the on ramp of the Ronald Reagan Freeway towards Simi Valley. A half hour later, they entered the Valley General Hospital's visitor lot. Windblown, Daly stored her visor and pulled a brush from the glove compartment, running it through her hair a few times.

"Okay, let's go see how our young med student is doing," Daly chirped, swinging her legs out the door. She used her right arm to push up from the seat and pushed her door shut, joining Mark. Holding his hand, they walked around the circular drive of the hospital's entrance portico. Separating at the revolving entrance door, they rejoined hands and crossed the lobby area to the bank of elevators serving the five-story Valley General hospital.

Punching the button for the fourth floor, Mark leaned casually against the side railing as the doors closed. Noting no one else in the elevator, he gave Daly a lascivious grin and pivoted to give her an amorous kiss. His hands started to slip from her waist to her rear end.

Daly grasped his left wrist in her free right hand, and giving it a light twist said, "You know they have cameras on these elevators, right? Evidence of you groping an injured woman wouldn't help your reputation with the community. Especially after Wednesday night's "meet and greet" with the Simi Valley PD."

"Oh well, I've been in the back of their cruiser before. At least *this* would be for something worth while," Mark replied as he nuzzled her neck.

The elevator audibly announced the fourth floor, and the door opened. Daly pushed Mark away as a doctor and a couple of orderlies grinned at them. Daly stepped through them with her head down, while Mark sauntered behind and shrugged at his male audience. One of the orderlies said quietly to Mark, "Get a room…but they're not cheap here." He grinned at his co-workers as he joined them in the elevator.

Mark followed Daly down the hall to room number 405. The door was open and Jim was fully laid back in his recliner beside Aiden's bed. A book was laying face down and open across his chest. He was dozing. Daly approached the edge of Aiden's bed, while Mark stood beside her.

Aiden was sleeping.

Aiden's face and hands were covered in some kind of white lotion, probably to help the itch and promote healing. Under the lotion, Mark could see large blisters, interspersed with healing scabs where blisters had been. He had been in to see Aiden the day before, but hadn't been allowed into the Intensive Care Unit. Only immediate family were allowed to visit ICU. He'd sent a nurse in to let Jim know he was there. When Jim had come out, he'd talked with Mark a few minutes. Jim had indicated the doctors were trying to flush the toxins from Aiden's bloodstream with a saline IV, while keeping him comfortable with pain meds. Aiden was responding well, but pretty dopey given the heavy-duty meds he was on.

Jim had told Mark that McClarey was in intensive care receiving a similar treatment to Aiden's. Given he couldn't visit Aiden or McClarey, Mark had returned home Thursday afternoon to sit with Daly. She had been sleeping off the pain meds given her by Dr. Girdwood the night before in ER.

Mark had called Valley General around noon Friday to check on Aiden and McClarey's status before leaving for Daly's appointment with Dr. Girdwood. He'd been told both had been downgraded from "critical" to "serious." They had been moved to rooms down the hall from one another on the fourth floor earlier that morning.

Daly softly touched Aiden's hand as Mark looked on. Aiden didn't stir. He appeared to be resting comfortably. He had tubes coming out of his nose, an IV drip attached to his arm, and a catheter bag hanging from the lower rail of his bed. His breathing was deep and even. His vitals for blood pressure and heart rate also looked normal as the monitor beeped softly in the background.

Jim stirred after a few minutes and sat up in his recliner abruptly when he saw Mark and Daly at Aiden's bedside.

"Well hello you two. Caught me napping," Jim said as he closed his book and laid it aside. "He's been sleeping most of the day since they moved him out of ICU earlier. They told me he's out of the woods, but will need several days to flush Riggsby's crap out of his system. Very fortunate we got to him when we did they're saying. Another couple of days and he'd have had permanent damage."

"That's a relief," Daly replied, releasing Aiden's hand and moving to the small couch beside Jim's recliner.

Mark sat beside Daly and asked, " Does that mean Sergeant McClarey won't fully recover since Riggsby had him several days more than Aiden?"

"I'm not sure. His captain, McCollough I think he said his name was, came by to see me Thursday morning. He wanted a detailed statement of Wednesday night's events. He said McClarey appeared to have significant kidney damage and some liver issues as well. They won't know if he'll fully recover for several days. Scary to think what that Riggsby bitch had in mind for Aiden, or worse," Jim said as he shuddered, then added, "May she rest in the hottest hell."

"I think McCollough is with Sergeant McClarey now. He stuck his head in the room a little while ago to say hi. We can meander down the hall and see how McClarey is doing. Maybe his captain can shed more light on the Riggsby psychos and how all the pieces are fitting together," Jim offered as he stood up. "I don't think Aiden will be waking up soon, let's go."

The three friends exited Aiden's room and traveled four rooms down the hall to 409. McClarey's door was ajar. Jim entered first after a light knock on the door, with Daly and Mark following close behind.

McClarey was sitting up in bed, awake and talking with Captain McCollough who was sitting on a couch next to the bed. McClarey's face and visible skin were covered in the same white lotion Mark had seen on Aiden. He was covered with blotches of what appeared to be healing scabs on most of his face and arms. His lips were cracked and swollen, but coated in Vaseline ointment.

McClarey's voice was raspy and forced as he greeted Jim and the Fords, "Well a good afternoon t' me partners in crime."

"Hello Sergeant, thought we should come by and see how our favorite Irish copper was doing," Jim said as he stepped to McClarey's bedside and lightly touched his arm.

"Never better. Luck o' the Irish, you know. Buggered

and wrecked but still kickin," McClarey rattled through raw vocal chords, forcing a smile with his cracked lips.

"Sorry my spidey senses didn't kick in a little sooner," Daly lamented joining Jim by McClarey's bedside, then continued, "I wasn't on to the Riggsbys prior to looking at the Feds' files you left for me."

McCollough interjected, "Yeah he'd been worked over for a week by the time you all showed up at the Simi Valley scene. The Riggsbys were thorough, sending the email to me saying Sean would be helping with family in England. Plus the email they sent to Mr. Jensen saying Aiden was going hiking with friends. Both sent from their own devices so they looked legit," McCollough said shaking his head.

"How's the young Master Aiden faring?" McClarey croaked.

"He's resting, but it looks like he'll make a full recovery," Jim answered.

McClarey nodded and whispered, "He's a tough lad."

Mark joined McCollough on the couch and asked, "So anything shaking loose on the Riggsbys?"

McCollough took a deep breath, "Well, given your help on this one, I guess we can share where we are. Just keep it to yourselves. The Feds wouldn't appreciate me reading you in on this until they've got it all buttoned up, okay?"

Daly, Jim and Mark nodded their agreement.

"The evidence gathered at Kimberly Riggsby's greenhouse plus the pantry area of her office paint a pretty clear picture. Fortunately, Mr. Ford's late night entry into the office won't render the evidence inadmissible given he didn't do it in any official capacity," McCollough said giving Mark a disapproving look. "For future reference, breaking and entering is a felony if you had any doubt."

Mark shrugged and protested, "The door might have been open. My memory is a little cloudy from getting my head bashed by Miss Riggsby."

"Anyway, the pantry was full of toxic extracts from plants found in her greenhouse. The specific ones she used on Kohler and Mr. Jensen's wife were ID'd. They're still working to get the autopsies completed on Hemmings and Gentry. We found the e-Coli used in Mary Simon's milk in her greenhouse refrigerator. The Feds took over the analysis and clean up at the greenhouse lab given the ricin samples moved it into bioterrorism jurisdiction."

"The spoon trophies Mark found in her locked pantry drawer will take some legwork to run down. We're guessing they'll match each of the victims' flatware. That should connect Kimberly Riggsby to each of the victims. Along with the initials identifying each trophy, it isn't much of a stretch to connect her with the murders," McCollough shared.

"You mean that sick bitch was in my house stealing a *spoon*?" Jim said incredulously shaking his head.

"Pretty sure of it. We'll need to take a look in your kitchen to confirm, if that's okay?" McCollough asked.

Jim nodded his approval.

"We've already confronted Greg Riggsby with the evidence against his sister, the assault and attempted murder on Sergeant McClarey, and a second attempted murder charge for shooting Ms. Ford. He's agreed to plead accessory to the murders to take the death penalty off the table. He's being interrogated by the FBI now given the bioterrorism connection," McCollough said as he sat back in the couch awaiting their questions.

"So what's the motive for Greg Riggsby to help his serial-killing sister? I assume Kimberly was driven by her son's death in Aiden's case," Daly asserted, leaning on the edge of McClarey's bed. "I saw the Feds' Files indicating an LLC agreement. It linked Greg Riggsby with Tommy, Mike, Chuck, Louise and Mary. But how is *that* a motive? Seems something is missing to me."

"That's not clear. We're continuing to question Greg, but he's not indicating the LLC has anything to do with the murders, just a coincidence," McCollough answered shaking his head.

Continuing, McCollough added, "Kimberly's motives are clearer. As you said, her son, Danny, died in an accident for which she blamed Aiden. She also had a twisted logic for ridding the world of people she connected to her mother's death. Apparently, Kimberly and Greg's mother was morbidly obese and eventually died from complications of gastric bypass surgery. Hemmings, Kohler, and Gentry were each associated with parts of the food industry Kimberly had focused her anger on, according to her brother. Ms. Jensen was a target given she was a gastroenterologist who did gastric bypasses, again according to Greg Riggsby."

"Mary Simon was set up to take the fall for the murders according to Riggsby; potentially after Sergeant

McClarey questioned Kimberly as best we can piece it together. Sean here, shared the fact that Mary Simon was a suspect in Ms. Jensen's murder with Kimberly Riggsby. He had questioned her earlier in the same day the ricin-tainted chocolates showed up in Mr. Jensen's gift basket. It appears she took the information Sean provided and created her patsy, using Pat Hemmings as her delivery service," McCollough said returning his gaze to McClarey.

"And dat was my mistake. I was tryin t' flush Kimberly out o' the weeds for what she might know 'bout Ms. Jensen's case. I shared some facts I should o' kept t' meself. Never occurred t' me she'd use it t' set up an alibi," McClarey said remorsefully. "Poor m'Lady Simon. I might as well o' done her in meself."

McCollough reached over and touched McClarey's arm, saying, "Nothing says Riggsby wouldn't have pinned it on her at a later time in some other fashion. Mary Simon was a likely suspect given the nature of the poisonings. Mr. Jensen even said he'd suspected her at one point in his statement."

"I suppose," McClarey reluctantly agreed.

McCollough continued, "We're also looking into three of the trophies we found with unidentified victims. Greg is staying vague about who they might be. He did offer that Kimberly might have tried her poisonous extracts out on some unlucky guinea pig clients of his."

"Apparently Kimberly Riggsby was big on trying things out. Sean was her test case for the nasty IV concoction she had intended for Aiden. She tried a few different combinations. The doctors said the main damage was done by the poison ivy and poison oak mix. It causes something equating to whole body shingles, and the blistering typically associated with poison ivy. The combination of a few of her nasty home-grown toxins can also cause damage to internal organs," McCollough said as he looked at McClarey, who was looking at his hands with a pensive stare.

"With Riggsby taking the plea deal of accessory to murder, the hearing should be quick. Assuming no surprises, we won't need any of you to testify as we have your statements. We still need to get Aiden's detailed statement when he's feeling up to it," McCollough finished.

"He's doing much better today. I'm guessing Aiden will be able to provide the statement by tomorrow," Jim confirmed.

"There is one area of creepiness we haven't released to the press," McCollough paused uncomfortably, then continued, "Kimberly Riggsby had encased her son, Danny, in a block of some kind of plastic. We found him in a display drawer of sorts in the greenhouse backroom. Weird beyond words. The drawer had lights in it like she pulled it out to look at it. Greg claims he knew nothing about it, so I guess it's been Kimberly's little secret the past several years." McCollough continued as he locked eyes with Jim, "I'm thinking Aiden may be able to shed some light on this. He spent time with her in that room. Kimberly never mentioned her son to Sergeant McClarey while he was captive, but she may have discussed things with Aiden when Sean was unconscious."

"I understand, Captain," Jim said solemnly. "Let's get

all this over with so we can move on."

"We'll be as brief as possible. I've asked the Feds to join us when we question Aiden so he only has to deal with it once," McCollough assured Jim.

The group sat in silence a few moments, letting Captain McCollough's account soak in.

McClarey cleared his throat and croaked a question at Daly, "Does it hold water for you m'Lady Ford? Or do you think there's more layers t' the onion?"

Daly nodded and said, "Yeah, it feels like we're finally there. No doubt about the Riggsbys being behind it all. It's unfortunate in a way that we're unable to test Kimberly's story against her brother's," she said thoughtfully. Then shrugging, "All in all, it feels consistent with what we know to be true. I think we can put the nut job Riggsbys behind us and move on."

A nurse poked her head in the door and caught Jim's attention. She had a pleasant smile, shoulder length brown hair, and her nametag said "Karen Kruse, RN." "Aiden is awake Jim. He's asking for you."

"Thanks Karen, I'll be right down. Oh Karen, please meet Mark and Daly Ford, Captain McCollough, and I assume you've met Sergeant McClarey," Jim said cheerily.

"Nice to meet you all," Karen said motioning with the "queen's wave."

"Karen is an old friend of Louise's from some past medical conference boondoggles. I had forgotten she worked here at Valley General. Louise and I enjoyed some fun times with Karen and her husband, James, at a few of Louise's events. Hanging out at the molecular bar was a real favorite," Jim smiled and winked at Karen.

"Now *those* are some memories," Karen chortled. "Don't be long. Aiden's expecting you," she said exiting the room.

Jim nodded at McClarey and McCollough as he rose to leave.

"Daly and I can join you if that's okay," Mark offered with a half-question in his voice.

"Give me a few minutes, and then come on down, okay? I want to bring Aiden up to speed on what's been happening while he's been sleeping his life away," Jim said as he walked to the door. Looking back over his shoulder, he added, "I can never thank you all enough for helping me get my boy back. I owe you all; anything you ever need, just let me know."

"Go see yer lad, Master Jensen," McClarey said in a loud whisper, motioning for Jim to leave. "And thank you as well for savin me skin…dat is what's left o' it."

After Jim had disappeared down the hallway, Mark turned to McCollough and asked, "So I'm assuming all is copasetic between the Simi Valley PD and Jim, right? I mean using his M16 was a little over the top, but hard to argue with given the circumstances."

McCollough sighed, "Yeah, I've smoothed that over with the Simi Valley PD. Clearly cases of self defense given both Riggsbys were armed, and you're the witnesses to that. They're insisting on modifying the M16 so it's not full automatic capable before returning it. Jim will get it back once he applies for licenses for it and his .45."

"That's great. Well, we want to have you and Sergeant

McClarey over for dinner when he's up to it," Daly said cheerily. "If it wasn't for the sergeant's due diligence in going over the Feds' files, I don't know how this might have ended up. You've got a fine detective there, Captain McCollough, but I guess you know that."

"Yes, and I wish I could convince him to stay on with the Santa Monica PD," McCollough said looking at McClarey. "Sean has decided to end his sabbatical in sunny California and return to London when he's fully recovered."

"I'd be less than honest if I said I wasn't missin the green hills o' England. I've got family there through me late wife and I'd be a stone's throw from Ireland. Dependin on what type o' ailments turn out t' be more permanent, it would be good t' be near me family," McClarey explained in a raspy whisper.

"Well, we'll miss you Sergeant McClarey...Sean," Daly said as she stood up and squeezed his hand. "And my dinner invitation is still good. We'll make it a proper send off since you're leaving us."

"Done and done," McClarey rasped smiling at Daly and nodding at Mark.

There was a soft knock on the door. A pleasant looking woman, no more than five foot tall and dressed in green scrubs, peeked around the door at McClarey. "Sergeant McClarey, are you ready for your therapy session?"

"Well if it isn't me own Florence Nightingale. M'Lady Flora, please meet the finest mates t' get a bloke out o' a tight spot. This is Master Mark and m'Lady Daly Ford, and me boss, Captain McCoullough," McClarey croaked, smiling through painfully cracked lips.

"Pleased to meet you. I'm Cheryl Flora, the sergeant's physical therapist. He won't be so happy to know me when he sees my plan for today's session."

"Oh she's a peach. Strong for a wee maid, and helpin me get back in the swing o' things," McClarey gushed hoarsely.

"We're going to stop in on Aiden, so we'll let you get to your therapy, Sergeant," Mark said as he rose to leave.

"I need to be getting back to Santa Monica to catch up on some paperwork myself," McCollough said, standing and shaking McClarey's hand.

Walking down the hall together, McCollough turned to Daly and said, "You know with Sergeant McClarey leaving, I'll be short-handed. Could always use a good detective. You know, someone proven in the field and all. Just let me know if you're interested."

"I think I've already turned that page, Captain. The quiet life of selling security systems with my husband is looking pretty good after the last few months. Thanks for the offer though. I'll let you know if I get the itch to get back in the game," Daly offered as she shook Captain McCollough's hand.

McCollough nodded at Mark, and strided down the hallway towards the elevator.

Mark and Daly returned past the four rooms separating Aiden and McClarey and knocked lightly on Aiden's door. "Anyone home?" Mark said in a high-pitched voice.

"Come on in Daly, and bring your girlfriend with you," Jim chuckled. "Aiden's been brought up to speed and wants to thank you two for all you did."

"Mr. and Mrs. Ford, my dad said you helped him save me. Thank you for everything," Aiden said weakly. He tried to lean forward, so Jim inclined Aiden's bed with the remote hanging from a chord.

"Your dad is the real hero, Aiden. He didn't let anything get between him and saving you. He even rescued Daly and me in the process. I'll never be able to live *that* down," Mark laughed as he moved to Aiden's bedside.

"I guess one of the Riggsbys got you as well," Aiden said motioning towards Daly's sling.

"Yeah, a lucky shot. My husband forgot to step in and take the bullet," Daly chuffed, giving Mark a light shove with her good arm.

"And *there's* another thing I'll never live down," Mark said rolling his eyes.

As they were catching up with Aiden, the nurse who had summoned Jim from McClarey's room earlier, Karen Kruse, joined them. "Well, seems we've got a party goin' on," she said cheerily with twinkling eyes.

"It's summer break and we're all in the hospital. That can't be right," Aiden laughed.

Karen stepped up to Aiden's bedside and checked the monitor, looked his IV tube over, and began taking his blood pressure. As she busied herself with Aiden's vital signs, she asked, "So have you all got plans for summer break?"

"I was going to spend some time with my Dad doing something, but it got psycho interrupted," Aiden replied.

"Yes, I got the whole low-down from your dad while

we were waiting for you to return to the land of the talking." Karen added seriously, "I can't imagine what you went through. I'm just glad to see you back on the mend."

"What are you doing for summer break?" Aiden asked.

"Heading to Grenada with my husband, James. He's a Certified RN Anesthetist here. We're taking off in two weeks for a Sandals resort, all inclusive and ocean breezes to keep you cool. You and your dad should come along…" she prompted, looking at Jim.

"You know, that sounds like a great idea," Jim chimed in. "A week in the Caribbean with my son and a private nurse to bring me my drinks…what could be better?"

"Sorry to burst your bubble, but *this* nurse doesn't double as a pool girl when she's on vacation. You'll be getting someone *else* to handle that," Karen laughed as she winked at Aiden.

"So do we get to come along on this beach excursion? My wife might forgive me for letting her take a bullet if I follow-up with a Grenada get away," Mark added as he eyed Daly.

"I'll get you all the info tomorrow. I know they have openings as I just checked on moving my room closer to the beach and it wasn't a problem," Karen said excitedly as she removed Aiden's blood pressure cuff.

"Summer break here we come," Daly shrugged as she smiled at Aiden. "What better crowd do we know for a good time. No guns allowed though," she said raising an eyebrow at Jim.

"The Simi Valley cops disarmed me, so I'm in," Jim smiled putting a hand on Aiden's leg.

"It's a plan. I'll play travel agent once Karen gets me the details," Mark offered.

"Just put it on my tab," Jim added. "*Plus* we can celebrate my retirement from ConGrowth Foods after thirty-three years. I've decided to teach at USC to be closer to Aiden. I'll be talking to a friend of mine who runs the Food Science Department after I take a few weeks off."

"Dad, you don't have to do that," Aiden protested. "You love your job."

"I want to. I really do. It will allow us to match up our time off. Maybe we can do lunch once in a while on campus. I'll promise not to hang around too much and embarrass you."

"No worries, Dad. It sounds great if you're good with it," Aiden agreed.

"Grenada here we come, on three," Mark said placing his right hand over Aiden's bed. The others added their hands, one on top of the other, to Mark's.

"One, two, three. *Grenada here we come!*" they shouted, causing a passing orderly to stop and look at them questioningly as they laughed uproariously.

Chapter 41

Mark nursed a Carib beer from a chilled mug. The waves crashed rhythmically into the sand beach causing a feeling of zen to come over him. The Caribbean breeze blew steadily making the plus eighty degree day feel like a perfect seventy-five.

It had been two weeks since he and Daly had decided to join Jim and Aiden Jensen for a vacation in Grenada. Mark had made the arrangements to match Karen Kruse's itinerary, the RN at Simi Valley General who had suggested the trip. Karen had become fast friends with Jim and Aiden while Aiden was her patient.

Flags for multiple Caribbean islands flapped in the wind atop thirty-foot poles on the central pier for the beach. The Sandals resort they were staying at had operations in multiple countries including Jamaica, Antigua, St. Lucia, the Bahamas, Barbados and Grenada; each with it's own flag whipping in the ocean breeze. A large almond tree's branches stretched out ten feet above Mark's beach lounge chair providing a shady oasis. Palm trees over twenty feet tall with green coconuts hanging in clusters under their lower palm fronds were plentiful on either side of the almond tree. Smaller palm plantings, no more than five feet tall, broke up the landscape between Mark and the beach. They'd been spaced carefully to provide future shady spots for sun burnt vacationers.

Daly was playing solitaire on her iPad, sipping a strawberry daiquiri. Daly's sling was gone. A purple, puckered stitch line the length of a quarter was visible above her swimsuit top, just below her left collarbone, providing a remnant of the Riggsbys night from hell.

Mark read a Baldacci novel from his Kindle Fire when he wasn't entranced by waves borne out of the turquoise water.

Aiden splashed in the ocean with Jim. They would throw a Frisbee until they became bored with that, then dive into the waves attempting to body surf. When tired they would swim to one of the six-foot diameter ring floats bobbing fifty feet from the beach. The floats were tethered to cement block anchors on the shallow seafloor to keep them in place. Lying across the mesh centers of the floats they would rest in the sun until ready to resume the beach game of choice.

Daly looked up from her iPad's screen watching Jim and Aiden frolic, and said wistfully, "Maybe having kids isn't the *worst* idea in the world."

Mark looked at her, "You're not just teasing me, right?"

"We'll talk," Daly said, smiling as she sat up in her lounger to kiss Mark on the cheek.

Karen and James Kruse strolled up to Mark and Daly's

lounge chairs around noon. They had been walking the beach and were ready for lunch.

"Let's do the Spices restaurant today," Karen suggested. Both Karen and James had Island Girl drinks in their hands, the resort's grapefruit based drink of the day. "Grenada is called the Island of Spice, you know. They've got wall hangings in the restaurant telling which plants the spices come from: Nutmeg, mace, cinnamon, bay leaf, and ginger. You name it and its story's on the wall."

"Sounds good to me," Daly agreed, slipping her iPad into her beach bag.

Mark stood up and waved his arms at Jim and Aiden to come join him. Seeing him, Jim and Aiden dived from their floating rings and began a mad race to the beach. Aiden easily won.

"What's up fellow beach bums?" Jim asked as he toweled off.

"Lunch at Spices today. Let's go, I'm starving. We haven't eaten in at least…an hour," Karen said as she mugged a frowny face.

The group sauntered off to lunch laughing. Aiden and Jim playfully pushing each other off the path leading to the resort's central area like ten year olds, Mark and Daly hand-in-hand, and Karen and James leading the way. They passed large Medjool Date Palms on either side of the walkway, and entered the Spices restaurant through a trellis covered with bougainvillea vines: bright red, pink, orange, and yellow flowering vines overflowed the arched entryway's apex and hung down the sides. Young oleander trees lined the outside of the restaurant's open balcony where they sat down to eat. The balcony overlooked an infinity pool in the center of the resort, and the beach fifty yards beyond it.

Karen went to the railing of the open area and waved to Denise Gregg, an avid antique collector from Napa Valley. She'd met her at the pool bar the day before. Denise was by the infinity pool with her husband Travis. Mark was amazed at Karen's ability to befriend total strangers and know their lifestory within a few hours. Her schmoozing skills were truly impressive.

Bob Greene, the Grenada Sandals' head sommelier, approached their table. Karen and James had known Bob from previous visits to the resort. They'd introduced him as "Bobby G" to their group at a wine tasting the previous evening.

Bobby G had been a golf pro in Ohio, then turned successful financial advisor for the years he and his wife Lori raised their three kids. Once they were empty nested, they had decided to chuck it all and moved to St Bart's as an adventure. Bobby G had refined his wine pallet and sommelier skills to the point he was hired by one of the top French restaurants on St. Bart's. A visiting Sandals executive had been impressed by Bobby G during a scouting trip for potential new resort locations. He offered him a job as head sommelier for Sandals' St Lucia operations on the spot. Bobby G had later moved to Grenada when they opened a new Sandals a few minutes outside St. George's, the capital of Grenada.

"So how are my Californian beach worshippers today? I have a very nice Brunello from the Montepulciano area. A Tenuta de Siesta 2010 vintage. It would go well with the Italian buffet today. Would you like to give it a try?" Bobby G offered to heads nodding approval.

"Bring it on Bobby G," Karen encouraged as she rose to visit the buffet.

Bobby G returned when they completed their buffet run, plates overflowing with antipasta appetizers, mouth-watering pasta dishes, and salads. He poured the aromatic red wine for the group.

Mark tapped his water glass with his fork to get the group's attention. Smiling he raised his glass and toasted, "The poet Edward Young said, "Friendship is the wine of life." Here's to life and spending it with the ones you love and depend on."

They clinked their glasses together, and drank deeply; like they were drinking from chalices filled at the well of tried and true friendships.

Old friends and new friends, enjoying life...and life was good!

Epilogue

Averly Simon pulled her car into the visitor parking lot of the California State Prison in Lancaster, California. The prison was located on the edge of the Mojave dessert, about seventy miles north of L.A.

Averly sat looking at the foreboding ten-foot high fences surrounding the block building facility. Strands of razor barbed wire topped the fence like a giant slinky toy with fangs. Three strands of electrified wire ran through glass insulators attached to posts spaced a few feet apart along the top of the fence. Elevated guard shacks were placed inside the fence corners with large spotlights visible. A guard manned each of the shacks. Part of the open space near the building was blacktopped with basketball hoops, barbell weight sets, and metal bleachers placed around the exterior of the recreational area. The remainder of the space inside the fence appeared to be bare dirt and created a buffer between the recreational area and the outer fence.

Four weeks had passed since her fiancé Greg Riggsby had been arrested and pled guilty as an accessory to his sister's killing spree. There had been no trial given his plea deal of twenty to thirty years in a Max prison facility. His sentencing hearing had taken place a week earlier sending him to this southern California prison with a mix of short-timers and more serious criminals.

She half-smiled, contemplating how all had worked out in a plan she couldn't have hoped to conceive in its entirety. Fate had smiled kindly on her, beautifully dropping the missing pieces into her lap.

She had learned about Greg's manipulation of his sister's penchant for poison posies. He'd used Kimberly's killing spree to consolidate sole ownership of a start-up venture investment. From the different correspondence she'd found in a hidden laptop in Greg's study six months previously, she had pieced together his plan. Greg was the financial advisor helping to form a five person Limited Liability Corporation invested in a venture capital drug company called Lion's Heart.

The initial opportunity had started with Tommy Hemmings. He had approached a few of his close friends from a poker group about the Lion's Heart opportunity. Of those friends, four had decided to invest with Hemmings: Charles Kohler, Mike Gentry, Louise Jensen and Mary Simon, her mother. The LLC was structured such that the original owners could sell their shares at any time to the remaining members. The sale was at a pre-determined price or current market cost of the shares once the company went public. If any partner passed away, their shares would be offered to the remaining partners and be redistributed equally. If any partner chose not to purchase the shares available, then the right passed to the remaining partners.

Her first reaction had been to turn Greg and his crazy-tunes sister into the authorities for planning to murder five innocent people. But Greg's plan was quite precise in the order of who Kimberly was to eliminate. The last person to be eliminated was her bitch of a mother. Being the last LLC partner to die, Mary Simon's estate would have the right to purchase all the shares and be the controlling investor in the Lion's Heart venture.

It became clear to her there was a better way.

If she played her cards correctly, and with a little luck, she would finally get what was due her: revenge on her sniveling mother, a bountiful inheritance, and be free and clear of any suspicion. Her hands would never have any blood on them from the prerequisite demise of all the partners in Lion's Heart.

All she had had to do was let Greg and Kimberly go about the eradication of the five shareholders of the LLC, including her mother. She could then claim her inheritance. As an added bonus, her psychopathic fiancé was out of the way thanks to his stupidity in coming to the aid of his more deranged sister. Greg's incarceration seemed only fair based on the timeline she'd pieced together from his hidden laptop documents and emails.

Greg had first taken a romantic interest in her after he received some insider information on the preliminary results of the Lion's Heart clinical study. His emails to his sister revealed his intent. Averly was his way to weasel into joint ownership of the LLC once they were married.

As the heir to Mary Simon's estate, Averly could purchase the Lion's Heart partners' shares using the proceeds of her Mother's estate. This would make her the sole investor of the LLC. Of course the dust would have to clear from the multiple estate settlements of the previous four diseased partners before this would be apparent.

Averly was about to be worth hundreds of millions if not billions. Lion's Heart would announce their early stage success with an Alzheimer drug within the next year. Those clinical trials would show the drug halted further deterioration of memory function and in some patients delivered a significant reversal of the devastating effects of the disease.

In a way, she'd committed the perfect crime. No one would ever know she had knowledge of Greg and Kimberly's demented plans prior to the murderous spree. Her inheritance from her mother was substantial for someone like her, but her mother's mortgaged house off-set a large portion of the cash proceeds. She wouldn't be an obvious co-conspirator in it for the money.

Most importantly, Greg's plan shared in the emails to his sister had been to use Averly as a pawn. He had planned to eliminate her after they were married and the multiple estate closings had settled down. Being the clear beneficiary to his wife's estate, Greg's motives would be obvious to the authorities. Especially with a little help from her.

She entered the prison through the visitor clearing area and registered for her visit. After requesting to see Greg she took a seat and waited until she was called. In about twenty minutes a guard entered the waiting room and called out, "Averly Simon. You're up."

She followed the guard into a room with a row of glass windowed visitor booths separated by partitions. She sat down in the booth indicated by the guard and waited for Greg to be brought in from his cell.

Greg appeared through a door on the other side of the glass about five minutes after she sat down. He moved slowly on his crutches, grimacing with each move towards his chair, and sat down across from her. Although he'd not lost either of his legs from Jim Jensen's assault, the damage had been significant. Picking up the phone, he indicated for her to do the same. Greg began to talk to her about planning his appeal.

Averly listened distractedly for several minutes, not saying anything.

"...so I'm thinking if we get married it will help my chances on appeal, what do you think? Are you even listening to me?" he asked in an annoyed tone seeing she wasn't paying attention to what he was saying.

"Greg, I'm afraid an appeal would be useless at this point. I've turned over your laptop with all the email correspondence with your sister. It will clearly show you were behind the murders and complicit to the nth degree. There's even a few emails indicating I was likely to be next on your hit list. After we were married, of course, just to tidy up loose ends. You were a naughty boy," Averly said finishing her revelations by clucking her tongue and waggling her finger back and forth in a "naughty boy" motion.

Greg's mouth gaped open. An incredulous blankness

spread across his face as the color drained from his cheeks.

She continued, "This will be the last time we talk. I really want to thank you for all you've done. I won't spend a dollar of my inheritance without thinking how much I owe you."

As she stood up to leave, the reality hit Greg like a pile driver. He stood up, dropping the phone, and leaned forward on the glass separating them. He began to beat his fists on the glass as he yelled at the disappearing click of her shoes on the tile floor, "*No! No! No!*"

She smiled as she exited the prison's visitor waiting room and walked to her car.

Poor Greg. He always did have a blind spot when it came to overestimating his sister and underestimating me. Guess he'll have a few days to think that over. At least until I can arrange an "unfortunate accident" with a small advance from my mother's estate…just to tidy up loose ends.